CW00548811

A Soul to Heal

Duskwalker Brides

Book Two

Opal Reyne

Cover art: Sam Griffin
Internal Illustrations: Opal Reyne

Trigger Warning
Major spoiler below

Please only read further if you have triggers, otherwise you will seriously spoil the book for yourself.

Firstly, I will list what triggers **AREN'T** in the book so you can stop reading in order not to spoil it: No rape, non-con, purposeful harm done to the FMC by the MMC, torture, suicide/self-harm, ow/om drama, mental/emotion abuse, incest, abortion, drug/alcohol abuse, breeding, or animal abuse.

There is fat-phobia ONLY in the first chapter. The rest of the book is embracing our beautiful, voluptuous selves.

There are vivid reflections of being cheated on (not by the MMC). Delora suffers from PTSD and depression.

This book has the pregnancy trope.
If that isn't something you are interested in reading, I do ask that you take into consideration that this is a book about monsters. You'd be missing out on something quite funny, cute, interesting, as well as minorly vital to the series. You will experience everything, the pregnancy, the birth, and afterwards. If that isn't something you can handle reading due to trauma, I am so sorry you have faced hardship.

The child is put in a situation of danger. No harm comes to the child, but villains are cruel and will try to destroy everything you love without care for morality. My villains always try to be as horrible as possible, but never fear! My characters are strong and will _always_ save the day.

As always, my books have minor gore.

Author's note on language

I'm from AUSTRALIA.

My English is not the same as American English.
I love my American English spoken readers to bits. You're cute,
you all make me giggle, and I just wanna give you a big 'ol hug.
However, there are many of you who don't seem to realise that your
English was born from British English, which is what I use (although
a bastardised version since Australians like to take all language and
strangle it until it's a ruined carcass of slang, missing letters, and
randomly added o's).

We don't seem to like the letter z.

We write colour instead of color. Recognise instead of recognize.
Travelling instead of traveling. Skilful instead of skillfull. Mum
instead of mom. Smelt is a past participle of smell. We omit the full-
stop in Mr. Name, so it's Mr Name. Aussies cradle the word cunt like
it's a sweet little puppy, rather than an insult to be launched at your
face.

Anyway, happy reading!

To all the *depressed* MonsterFuckers out there,

This book is for you.

Sometimes we just need a big, bad monster to come along and remind us that life is worth living. It helps when they are scary enough to chase away our nightmares and naughty enough to tease us with their cock.

This book is also for my fellow plus-sized babes.

We deserve love too, and my Duskwalkers don't discriminate. They love us all, even the soft and squishy

ONE

Delora wiggled her shoulders side to side while splaying and stretching her fingers, both done in an attempt to free herself from the rope bindings around her wrists.

As she was ushered through the dense forest, her heavy breaths came out like snorted muffles against the cloth that had been tied around her head. As it absorbed the saliva within her drying mouth, her throat grew sticky.

The ground was muddied from the rain that had drizzled recently, and her dress, which had been dull, grey, and plain, was now dirty from walking. Though the top of her was only dirty due to light sweating, the bottom of her dress was caked in mud from falling to her knees multiple times.

She knew her long black hair was matted terribly by what she had seen fall across her brow, obscuring her vision more times than she could count. It was also tangled with twigs and stray leaves.

The forest canopy above glittered with soft sunlight on the early morning of this autumn day. Down here, it was mostly shaded, which caused the breeze that rustled the leaves to feel chillier than it was. Snow hadn't begun to fall yet, but she was sure in two or so weeks, the pretty powder would start to blanket the ground.

That only left them with the sounds of dead leaves and sticks to loudly crunch under their footsteps. There were around twenty-two people making this walk, and most of them were armoured soldiers.

She'd fought against her captors, despite knowing it was futile. They thought she deserved this, and, in some way, so did she.

The longer they walked, the more her struggles eased.

Not once had they come across any Demons. She was sure they would have shoved her in front of it and ran for their lives if they had.

It's why they were here, after all.

On the first night they had set out with her bound, about a day's walk from their relatively large town, they'd set up a campfire for the night. Almost everyone had been on watch for their surroundings since the darkness brought hissing and wailing terrors.

Only one person had stayed in the camp to watch over her with a horribly twisted sneer of disgust.

The middle-aged man who'd remained as her guard had wrinkles of laughter around his eyes and frown marks across his forehead from years of stress. His brown stubble beard hid most of his age, but his green eyes said he had little charm behind his dark expressions.

Every time he stared at her, Delora narrowed her eyes with contempt, just as she did now when the man turned to glance over his shoulder.

When he saw her expression, he lifted his eyes to the man behind her with a certain look. The soldier behind her shoved his elbow into her back to force her to stumble.

This had been done many times during their *pleasant* little stroll.

"You should learn to drop that look." The man shook his head as he brought his eyes forward to watch his footing. Then he lifted an arm to give her a waved shrug. "It's your own fault you're in this mess."

Delora tried to speak around the cloth that was shoved so deep in her mouth it was pressing over her back molars. Her words only came out garbled.

"Listen to her snort like a little piggie!" One of the guards walking with them laughed.

Delora's sight flicked to him with a menacing glare from the corner of her eye. At first, his expression of cheer was cut short. Then he remembered her predicament and turned away from her with a crooked smirk.

She began to shout against her cloth and stopped walking. Even when she was shoved again, she refused to fall or move.

"*Ugh.* What is it now?" Jetson, the leader of this excursion, bellowed while turning around. He waved his hand for someone to untie her mouth. "What do you–"

"I need to fucking piss!" Delora's voice broke an octave from disuse, and it was far more hoarse than normal.

After starting from her shout, his upper lip twisted into disgust about her normal bodily function – like she was nothing but a mindless creature and should just pee herself.

Jetson stepped forward to grab her face in one hand, squishing her cheeks in against the side of her teeth. He yanked her closer. Thankfully, it helped to massage her aching jaw. "Another one of your tricks, no doubt?"

"It wasn't the last five times I asked!"

He bared his teeth at her. "It was the first two, though."

Ah, yes. The first two times Delora had asked to use nature as her own personal bathroom, she'd attempted to flee. The first time, she'd run when they had their backs turned. The second, as she was being watched, she tried to silently strangle the man.

It hadn't worked. Jacob, the guard assigned to her, had screamed before she managed to get her hands around his throat.

He hadn't managed to fight her off. Unfortunately for Delora, his big friends had.

When her bladder gave an uncomfortable throb, as though it was moments from bursting, Delora's brows twitched with a cringing frown.

"Just..." She gritted her molars before turning her eyes away from Jetson. "Just let me pee. I really need to go. Please."

He threw her head back, but at least the word, "Fine," left his thin, cracked lips.

Delora was ushered around a tree, but she wasn't given the privacy she would've preferred. It didn't matter. Not much did at this point. She'd had to do this multiple times over the two days since they'd left their first campsite.

No Demons had come the first night, nor the second, and the men were impatient to return to their families. They were also braver than she'd ever imagined since they were taking her closer with every step to what most believed was Hell on Earth.

Her eyes scanned over the twenty armed men Jetson had with them as she came around the tree, and it was no wonder they were willing to brave such a dangerous walk.

With her as an offering, they were free to toss her body and run home to save their own arses.

"Tie her face."

"Afraid I'll say something to upset you again?" Delora said with a humourless snort.

A silent signal was given.

"She cried for you!" Delora laughed as hands grabbed her aching biceps, pinning them behind her to shove that cloth in again. "Oh, Daddy! Please help me, Daddy!"

Everything she just said was a lie.

"Don't mock me!" He interrupted his men from binding her wrists again when he backhanded her across the face. The hit was so hard that her head twisted to the side and spittle sprayed from her lips. "My little girl was a beautiful innocent that you destroyed!"

"Innocent?" Delora let the shock of his words show in her widened eyes. "She had my husband's cock inside her!"

"Maybe if you looked like less of a fattened pig, then he may have been faithful to you."

A nerve was struck within Delora, one that sent both seething rage and burning insecurity running through her at the same time. Her clothes that were perfectly tailored to her rounded size suddenly felt too tight. Constricting even.

Her words were spoken quietly, but they rang with the last bit of venom she had inside her and the defeat that she felt.

"Your daughter was nothing more than a ripe whore, and my husband was nothing but an arrogant bastard. They deserved their ends."

"Our commander was a hero," a guard yowled. He grabbed the shirt collar of her dress and yanked her to the tips of her toes.

Her body arched into his. "He killed three Demons in the short time he was our leader."

Delora let her lips curl into a dead smirk.

"And yet, he talked shit about all of you behind your backs." After her eyes left his inch-long blond hair, brown eyes, and strong chin, they wandered over his leather uniform. A family crest had been beautifully carved into the metal breastplate situated over his torso. "Lester is your name, right? Apparently, you have the smallest dick he'd ever seen."

His cheeks instantly heated before his eyes darted among the men he'd taken command of after she killed Hadith, her husband.

Bingo. And he knew it, too. They all averted their gazes, shame resting upon their features. *They'd also said the same thing.* She almost wanted to laugh.

She didn't understand how men could be so *cruel* to each other, especially those they called friends or comrades.

"Regardless," Jetson murmured, "murder is still punishable."

"Yeah, by imprisonment," Delora bit back. "But, because you're our *wonderful* Major, I'm being tossed into the wild. I didn't realise our town was full of sadistic assholes. Everything would be different if it wasn't your daughter I'd killed."

"Becoming Demon shit is the most you deserve." Lester chuckled as he let her dress collar go. "Are we done talking with her? I'm afraid she'll start oinking, and we might eat her instead."

Delora knew they were being openly and unnecessarily cruel because they were angry. They were trying everything to ruffle her but were too stupid to realise their comments on her weight meant almost nothing.

"You can say that again." Another guard chuckled. "I'm so fucking hungry, and my wife promised me a good meal when I get home."

"Yes," Jetson sighed. "Let us continue. I have a wife to console when I return home."

The cloth was shoved inside Delora's mouth, and she was forced to walk again. At least the small break had given her a moment to rest her aching knees and feet.

As she had done over the past few days, she reflected on her actions while they travelled. It was hard not to.

Lampshire Village was a relatively large town with high stone walls to protect it from Demons. The Demons weren't always there. They hadn't been around when they'd left for their journey or she would have been fed to them there, but her people had made sure they were protected.

They lived a five-day walk from the Veil and were situated up near the mountains. They were too far away for the supposed Duskwalker that visited the smaller towns below in the valley. They often believed the other towns lied about the creature's existence. Either that, or it was smart enough not to come near them, since they were fortified and would likely attack it from the walls before sending out a small army to defend against it.

Her village was a military one.

They believed in their strength to such a high degree that they were one of the rare villages to have trees inside their walls this close to the Veil. They were also big enough to have large farms and two-level houses.

Throughout the day, dozens of guards walked on every level of the village, separated by rings that created walled platforms of stone bricks. Those rings eventually came to the middle of the massive hill the town resided on to the building at the very centre. The guard stronghold.

At night, they doubled the number of guards patrolling and stood on the walls as lookouts.

The Major, Jetson, oversaw the village as he was once the commander of soldiers. He was a hard, strict man, but it had always been told he'd loved his wife and children without question.

So, in killing his only daughter, Delora had signed herself the foulest of death warrants.

Jetson was also doing this as a political move. People had begun to think he'd gone soft. It was why he was leading this expedition in the first place, rather than just killing her.

He was trying to prove that he was still a fearless and ruthless leader. Delora just got caught in the crossfire of his schemes, laying herself on a silver platter for punishment.

I really fucked up. She didn't know if she'd do it again.

Delora gritted the cloth in her mouth as though she was trying to grind it into dust between her teeth.

She held regret for her actions, but she'd been pushed and pushed and *pushed* into a desolate corner. She had let her emotions run high and out of control the day she'd found Jetson's daughter beneath her husband.

Her large village was filled with lovely people who were friendly and welcoming, but they could also be cruel in their own way. Gossip was a constant source of entertainment, and as the years passed after she'd been brought there from her smaller village to wed Hadith in an arranged marriage, she had become someone to ridicule.

She wouldn't have known about their hurtful words if it wasn't for Hadith telling her about them. *Prick.*

Delora had once been what some would call beautiful. She didn't really think she wasn't anymore, but others had a tendency to look at beauty with their own skewed perception.

When she had married Hadith, she'd fallen in love with the strong, burly man almost instantly. It seemed he'd been just as fond of her.

However, as a guard, he was often out on patrol, and he started coming home later and later.

For Delora, this meant she found herself alone for longer hours of the day in a village that was closely knit with those who had been raised there. It had been difficult to assimilate herself within the groups of women that had grown up with each other.

There were those that welcomed her, but they had their own lives and couldn't attend to Delora's lonely heart when she was forced to suffer in her empty home.

She learned to comfort herself, which left her body stagnant. Her appearance started to become plump as she aged in the five years she'd lived there.

Her beauty was the cost of Hadith's neglect. And, of course, he didn't like that. He'd only agreed to marry her upon seeing her beauty. That was her only value to him.

The warm and loving husband she'd married had turned into someone spiteful.

If only I could have divorced him... That had never been an option. She'd brought it up once, and she'd regretted it ever since. Things had taken a turn for the worse.

She clenched her fists, causing an ache to shoot up her tired arms bound behind her back.

At least he never hit me. He was a gentleman in this way, but his actions around her were harsh – and just as frightful.

Delora never complained. She continued to play the role of the doting wife despite the fact that he was mean, called her vulgar names, and touched her like she was an unruly bear.

I should have seen it coming...

She thought the day he'd been unusually merry with her, asking her to cook a grand meal that evening for his guard friends, that things were changing.

He was getting older, and they'd both needed to work on their marriage – it was a one-way street at that point.

After everything I put up with... I'm so damn stupid.

After two years of terrible depression, where she felt like a dreary cloud over the village, it was the first time she'd felt light within her when Hadith had ushered her out of the house with a kiss and a playful arse grab. She'd rushed to town in the hopes of returning quickly.

A part of her wished she had never left. A different part of her wished she hadn't left her shopping list behind. Then, another part told her it wouldn't have mattered, as she doubted this was the first time Hadith had cheated on her. It was just the first she'd learned of it.

She'd returned home and quietly opened the door in case he was napping since he'd been working the night shift that week.

What she'd heard was two people in the middle of sex. *Good* sex. The kind where the woman was moaning like she was in heat and the man was just as deep in passion. Hadith was giving compliments, something Delora hadn't received in years, while a woman called his name.

Delora clenched her eyes shut, wishing she could erase that memory forever. Especially when it struck a burning heat across her torso. Not of anger, but a horrible, emotional pain that felt almost physical.

Jealousy had torn through her. That was *her* husband doling out the appreciation she'd been begging for... to someone else. That was her husband on top of another woman.

Darkness had been growing within her for years. A darkness that gave her sleepless nights from the horrible dreams that riddled her. Darkness that ate at her conscious like a disease when she was awake and alone in that dimly lit house because she no longer had the *energy* to light it properly.

He'd never hit her, but he still abused her, still called her feral names she didn't deserve. And now he had the audacity to be balls deep in another woman after everything she'd been put through?

No. *Fuck* no.

Still, Delora didn't know if grabbing her sharpest cooking knife and shoving it repeatedly into his back was a good idea. The girl, Cindy, had screamed for help beneath him, but Delora couldn't get past the fact she had come to her home to sleep with her husband. They were in *her* bed. They soiled it with their love making after she'd washed and changed the sheets that morning after another sleepless night by her-fucking-self.

Cindy knew they were married. She was a buxom redhead, and young – only just nineteen. Something Hadith seemed to prefer, even though Delora was only twenty-six.

Cindy had even passed her in the street that very day with a smile and a friendly wave, making her way up the hill as Delora was walking down it. A planned affair. Cindy had looked her right in the eyes with every intention of crawling on top of her husband's cock.

Did they laugh behind my back? How long had they been doing it?

Cindy was just as guilty as Hadith.

It was Hadith's fault, as he should have kept his mediocre dick in his pants and remained faithful, but Cindy knew full well that what they were doing was wrong.

The only thought that ran through her head as she rammed her knife between Cindy's perky breasts was, *Fuck you too!*

Perhaps another mistake... because since then, Delora had felt undeniably *empty.* She'd thought it would make her feel better, but as she sat on the floor gripping her face with blood-soaked hands and digging nails, it had been horrifying.

It was hard to keep sane in a world filled with monsters – not just beyond the walls that made the town feel like a prison, but also in your home, your heart, and your mind.

Regret had instantly sailed through her once she sobered from her bloodlust. Then, not even moments later, guards rushed inside to see the carnage she'd produced.

Cindy's screams for help had been heard.

Delora was languid when they grabbed her. She no longer cared what happened to her.

She had done something almost every person secretly wished they could do when they'd been cheated on, been betrayed. But that's what it should have remained: nothing but an intrusive, wishful thought.

She wanted to rot in prison – it would be no different to the empty life she'd been living. *Prison would have been just as cold and lonely and boring.*

She never envisioned that she would be forced to walk through the forest for her actions, but she should have known that Jetson would want a more morbid justice for his daughter. His wife, with tear-stained cheeks, had been the one to spit on her face when she was forced to walk through the village gates.

Deserved.

This walk? She also deserved it.

At least I'll get to disappear, she thought as she saw the world open up past the trees and knew they had finally reached their destination.

It wasn't that Delora wanted to die – she very much didn't – she just couldn't see the point in trying to live anymore. She was merely existing, and there wasn't much happiness in just moving through the motions of life.

"We're here," Jetson said. Then his face twisted into a cringing frown before he covered his nose and mouth with a handkerchief he pulled from his coat pocket. "When they said the Veil smelled awful, they weren't exaggerating."

Delora's stomach churned as she was forced to breathe in the stench that was wafting from the Veil canyon. A black mist covered the trees as far as the eye could see.

It appeared as though a giant had clawed at the earth to create the scene.

She eyed the span of trees before she was shoved closer to the edge, allowing her to look at the fall that was at least a kilometre drop. The smell of rotting decay was even more pungent and rancid at the edge.

Tears welled in her eyes – not from sadness, but from the sting of it. She tried to back away while shaking her head.

That smells disgusting. And plummeting to her death was the last thing she wanted to experience. *How long will I fall for?* A few seconds? Minutes? She didn't want to spend her final moments knowing she was going to splatter against the ground.

"Look at her!" Lester chuckled. "She's scared now that we're here. Did you think we were joking this entire time?"

Scared? Funnily enough, she wasn't afraid. She wanted to disappear, and death was a way to disappear; she just didn't want to *know* when it was coming. She also didn't want it to be painful.

Her eyes found the sun and wondered if this would be the last time she'd feel its gentle warmth.

Will falling hurt? She'd occasionally had a nauseating sensation in her stomach when she'd jumped off ledges playfully as a child. She worried that feeling would be intensified the longer she dropped.

"Let's just get this over with," a guard mumbled, his stark gaze darting around the area. "Who knows how long it'll be before a Demon comes this way. It's the Veil. We're just asking for trouble the longer we remain here, even in the daylight."

She was surprised none had already come, with the fact that there were so many of them. Was it luck? Falling to her death at least seemed more pleasant than being eaten alive.

"He's right, we need to go," another demanded. His metal armour clanked together when he moved at a sudden sound in the distance.

The group began shuffling their feet nervously. These were not Demonslayers, and soon enough their growing fear would bring monsters upon them.

"Alright then," Jetson sighed, waving his hand like he did often.

Lester pushed her right to the cliff edge, the tips of her boots almost toeing it, as he said, "I hope you're still alive after you hit the ground."

Delora gave a cruel smirk when she turned around to face them.

She may have regretted what she'd done, but it had still felt amazing to have done it. She'd freed herself, no matter her end. *Better than living with that limp-dick moron.*

"You can't even look remorseful, you fucking bitch!" Jetson shouted when she met his gaze. He was so annoyingly loud.

Just to piss him off, Delora turned her eyes downwards and pretended to weep before throwing her head back and laughing against the cloth.

Do it! she thought as her shoulders shook from her crazed laugh. *Hurry up and do it before I scream!* Panic was bubbling inside her like a froth. She could feel it, the want to tear up in fear of what was about to happen.

DO IT!

Lester shoved her chest hard, and she fell backwards with her dress waving through the air around her. Delora plummeted. She clenched her eyes shut tight and held in her scream.

Oh, fuck. Oh, fuck! Holy f

TWO

I am no good at this, Nameless thought. Fumbling with his black shirt, the third button he was trying to shove through the hole slipped under the pads of his large fingers.

My hands are too big.

They shook with the struggle of doing this simple task, as well as the uncomfortable feeling of having his razor-sharp claws sheathed.

Why can I not do this? He tried once more. Clamping his tongue with his back teeth in concentration, he held the little round button and tried to poke it through the slitted hole.

It didn't help that his bony snout was long and in the way. He had to twist his head so he could see out of one eye while darkening the other.

It slipped. His claws unsheathed by accident, one of them stabbing through the delicate material.

He gave a terrible distressed whine when he realised he ripped the shirt and dropped into a crouching position while gripping his antlers.

No matter how many times I try… it is hard.

After a few moments of fretting, he slid to his knees, hoping that trying to concentrate on standing might have been hindering him. He'd only recently gotten the hang of standing on his back legs properly, and walking for a long period on them still wasn't truly comfortable. It distorted the muscles in his legs and lower back.

He managed to slip the button through and then his glowing

eyes, which hovered inside his empty eye sockets like swirling vortexes, turned to a deep blue at the other two he needed to do. The higher he went, the harder it became, as he couldn't see.

Yet, he practised, learning. And every day, he felt just as useless as the one before.

He sighed in relief when he managed to get the last one done before lowering his arms and letting them fall to rest on his trouser-covered thighs.

But I am better than I was in spring.

Autumn was his least favourite season, as even in the Veil's forest, some of the leaves wilted and turned orange and red. Those leaves then fell from their branches and scattered all around the entrance of his cave, daring to enter it.

Every morning he cleaned outside, and he was always dismayed that the following day he would find a leaf on top of him when he woke mid-afternoon.

However, it was also his favourite season.

I have eaten two other humans since spring. They had changed him. They made him a little smarter, gave him a little more dexterity.

It wasn't enough. Nameless knew it.

I am not like Orpheus. Orpheus, the Mavka who always walked on his back legs, always strung together intelligent sentences. The Mavka who knew how to do everything with little effort and rarely struggled with his tasks.

Nameless raised a hand to his fox-shaped snout and tapped the side of it with a sharp claw in thought. *I want to be better.*

That required hunting more humans and Nameless was... losing his interest in hunting them. He wanted the humanity it brought, but he no longer wanted to see them torn to shreds and bloodied by his own claws and fangs.

Instead, he wanted to know what they felt like... warm and with life.

He looked at the darkness of his cave. It was only brightened at the entrance because the sun was still setting but never truly lighted the Veil. It was always dark here, always cold, and he was always alone.

Orpheus never visited him, but Nameless tried to find any

excuse to meet him at his home. *He does not like me near there.*

He didn't understand why.

I mean no harm to Reia – his female.

Opening his bone jaw to part his upper and lower fangs, he let out a louder sigh than normal. *She is nice. I want a human like her.* Perhaps one that didn't smell like sticks and thorns, but a human nonetheless.

He wanted a human to touch. He didn't quite understand the difference between a male or a female. He just wanted a friend. *A friend.*

Someone he wouldn't eat.

After he stood, he brushed off his dirtied trousers as best as he could. *First, I have to find one that does not smell of fear.* Otherwise, he would eat it.

He wasn't good at controlling his urges to consume. Fear and blood, no matter the creature it came from, would instil an insatiable need to feed and destroy in a crazed, frenzied haze.

He was *always* hungry. Never satisfied, no matter how much he ate. *So,* he wondered, *how can I stop myself from eating the human I want to befriend?*

He could handle a tiny bit of fear, a tiny bit of blood, but if it was more than a drop in their scent, he'd claw and bite until they were wholly in his stomach.

This was all pointless to ponder if he refused to go hunting for them. He needed to go above the surface of the Veil, to climb the cliff wall and go to the human world above, to find one.

Releasing another sigh, he began to walk on two feet and a hand to exit his cave, since it was more comfortable. He knew he had a long walk ahead of him – a walk in which he would try to use only his back legs.

He had much to do today. He was building something, and it was quite a distance to walk to it.

He would have to avoid the Serpent Demon that owned the forest territory just outside his cave. He didn't like Nameless walking through his forest, but he needed to venture through it to get where he was going.

Nameless walked into the small patch of dirt outside. There was a magic salt circle he'd carved around his home that protected it from Demons. After Mavka, or Duskwalkers as humans called them, consumed at least one Priest or Priestess – a rare human with an affinity for magic – they could start producing magic themselves. He didn't remember when he had consumed one, only that he must have, considering he could use magic.

Nameless checked to make sure the protective circle was still intact so he could plan for his day without worrying his home might be entered while he was gone.

I must cut down another tree and remove its bark. Then I must shape it. Which tree should I remove?

He could think about the humans as much as he wanted, could ponder and wish, but it wasn't like one would fall from the sky.

A whistling sound caught his attention, and he twisted his head in thought. *What is that?*

While crouched on one hand and both feet, he started to turn towards the sound that was coming, oddly, from above.

He only got a chance to glimpse something blurry before it crashed into him, landing directly on top of his body. The impact of it sent him hurtling violently towards the ground and into unconsciousness.

THREE

Nameless woke with a start.

When he noticed something weighty resting on his back, he twisted his neck to look over his shoulder. Then he tilted his head at what he saw. *A human?*

The sound of bones rattling and groaning noises caught his attention, and he looked around the outside of his cave where he lay. Attracted by the human's scent, three small Demons had come to loiter just beyond his protective salt circle, teetering on the edge of it.

They didn't say anything – they appeared too little to have the ability to speak – but their animalistic noises were bothersome.

Many autumn leaves were scattered, telling him much time had passed from when he was last awake. With his lack of pain, he knew he must have been unconscious for an entire sun cycle.

Mavka healed within a day. They remained injured, unable to heal until a day had passed, and then whatever ailed them would heal within the span of a minute. A small cut, a missing arm, even their entire body. As long as their fleshless skull was intact, they would come back to life.

The human must have snapped his neck when it landed on top of him and his jaw hit the ground. He was lucky the bone of his skull was the strongest part of him and was nearly indestructible – which was likely the only reason he was still alive.

Since he wasn't in pain when he woke, he wasn't sent into a rage from agony. He was able to register what had happened with a clear head.

Nameless began to stand, letting the human slide off him carelessly as he looked up at the cliff wall that housed his home.

It fell? A human had literally fallen from the sky.

He walked along the wide span of the salt circle to make sure it was still intact and safe before returning to the human.

He twisted his head once more, seeing it had those lumps on its chest that signalled it was a female. They always smelt sweeter than the males, and he crouched down to sniff her hair. The smell of crisp red apples and frosty snow coming from her made his body shudder at its pleasantness.

Then he placed his ear hole against those mounds. He expected it to be dead, considering its massive fall, but it was surprisingly still breathing – although weakly.

Did I soften her fall?

That didn't mean he didn't notice her multiple broken limbs. She wasn't bleeding, but parts of her flesh were red like there was blood collecting beneath her skin. Much of her looked swollen.

Using the backs of his claws, he carefully tilted her head so he could look upon her face. One side of it was bruised terribly, and when he sniffed closer, he noticed there was dried blood tracking from her nose and temple. There was also a piece of cloth tied around her head and shoved between her teeth – not that he knew what it meant, though he used his claw to free her of it.

He looked at the Demons. Now that the blood was dry, it wouldn't send any of them into a frenzy, but he could see their claw marks gouging the rocky dirt. He could only imagine how much they must have been frothing to get to her when it was fresh.

It was still unpleasant and caused his green orbs to redden in hunger. He shoved his fingers into the wet nose hole of his bony snout to hide from it, then proceeded to sit next to her in his crouched position in hopeless thought.

She is broken. Very broken.

Her back was twisted in a way that was obviously unnatural, and her ankle, bared since she wasn't wearing any shoes, sat the wrong way. Her arm was loose from its shoulder socket even though her hands were tightly bound behind her back.

He imagined there were more injuries beneath her long clothing.

She hadn't woken since her fall, and he grabbed her not loose shoulder and shook her. She didn't wake, didn't make a sound. Her eyelids didn't even flicker.

Nameless knew she wasn't dead, but it didn't seem like she was going to wake anytime soon.

She will be in pain if she wakes. It seems humans falling from the sky is not a good thing.

Am I the cause of this? Did his wishful thinking cause this woman pain? His orbs turned a reddish pink from embarrassment. Shame grabbed his stomach and twisted it.

The right thing to do would be to fix her because of his mistake of getting a human to fall from the sky, but he didn't know how to do that.

He raised his free hand and held his snout so he could tap a claw to the side of it. Thinking was hard for him, and he generally required the action to help him focus.

I could eat her. That would stop her pain and ease his guilt since she became food. There was no harm if the human didn't know it was his fault.

He moved his hands and leaned forward to sniff her again, shuddering at her scent. *But I like the way she smells.* He slipped his purple tongue between his teeth to lick them, the want to lick her skin nagging at him.

He wondered how many other humans would have given him the same reaction had they not been filled with fear.

As the wind gently blew a light flurry of air and leaf litter around him, he sat with her for a long while, thinking about what he should do. He blatantly ignored the Demons.

Do I eat or help her? How do I help?

He tapped a knuckle against the brow of his skull, trying to force thoughts into his mind by sheer will alone.

The only reason he picked up her broken body by one arm and dragged her inside was because she smelt of red apples and frost. He wanted that aroma to fill his home for however long it took to fix her.

Apparently, Mavka could heal wounds, but he didn't know how, and he didn't think Orpheus did either. They'd only come to learn this recently. The idea of being able to do something the other Mavka couldn't do excited him. He always felt inadequate compared to Orpheus.

Nameless could practice with this human who was sleeping. If he couldn't do it, then he would eat her and tell no one of his failure.

The Witch Owl said I just needed to have a reason to learn spells. The Witch Owl was strange. She had once been human, but no longer was, since she had strong, icky-smelling magic. He wasn't completely sure if he trusted her, even though she always seemed to go out of her way to help Mavka, to help Nameless.

She was dark-skinned with long, curly brown hair. Her eyes were charcoal black, perhaps because the shadows of the Veil wouldn't reveal their true colour, but she had this lovely, deep voice that he had always found... soothing.

She could also turn into a human-sized white owl using her feathered cloak and hood.

She flew over his home often, and he'd always wondered why. She'd never told him the few times she'd spoken to him.

He laid the broken human down in his nest that shielded the cold and dirt from crawling over him while he slept.

This human wasn't currently making him hungry, and he did *want* to help her.

I do not know what needs to be sacrificed. In order to do most protection spells, blood must be sacrificed – whether it be animal or human. He didn't think that would be the requirement since he was trying to remove her wounds, not add to them.

Perhaps my own blood?

Kneeling next to his nest, he presented his foreclaw and the wrist of his other hand. If this didn't work, at least he would hide some of her scent with his own.

I will need to ask Orpheus how to hide a human's scent. That Mavka knew how, and Nameless would get his cleansing oils when he had made his final decision about this woman's life.

There was a high likelihood that she would be afraid of him when she woke, and he would go into a craze at the scent of her fear. If that happened, it meant this had worked, and he could show off his newfound, glorious power! It would also grant him a little more humanity in her death.

They can no longer call me stupid! More excitement thrummed as he drew his claw over his wrist and let it drip onto her ankle.

He grabbed it tight in both hands and demanded, "Now heal."

Nothing happened.

"Hmm." He took his hands away and tapped at his snout a few times. He heard the clinking of it within his skull. "Wrong words?"

He gripped it again, closed his sight, and concentrated.

"I heal you of your wound."

Nothing.

Nameless tried multiple things during the course of the day and night. He placed leaves and dirt on her ankle and then poured water over it. He spoke nothing, then proceeded to shout at different intervals. He even tried to straighten it in frustration and then winced when he heard a bad sound, like wet bones moving.

His growls, huffs, and whines echoed off the rocky walls of his home.

When day broke the following morning, he sat next to her feeling dispirited. He couldn't do this.

Orpheus had showed him how to cast a protection circle, and he'd produced one after his third attempt. He had been at this for *hours*. Gruelling, long hours that dragged on forever and birthed frustration within him.

Holding her ankle and wishing for it to heal, he bent his head forward to rest the top of it against his outstretched arms, his snout nestled through the middle of them.

Nameless wanted to heal this broken human woman's ankle more than anything.

If I heal her, would she stay with me?

That thought had grown throughout the night.

Perhaps this human was supposed to fall from the sky so he could fix her and then she could become his. He wanted a companion; he wanted someone to hold. Already she filled his mind with thoughts of her rather than the echoing loneliness he always felt. Her presence was already a comfort for him.

She was... beautiful.

Her hair was that of a raven. Black with flecks of highlights, due to its glossiness, shining against any light. Her small and pointy nose, her round cheeks, her thin upper lip that sat above a plump bottom one... Her features were strange to him as he didn't have lips or flesh on his face like her, but that didn't make her any less bewitching.

Her body was soft, so unbelievably *soft*. It was thick, large, and so curvy it dipped and filled part of his nest with its malleable warmth. It was tan and covered in these little dark spots here and there, like on the back of her calf and the side of her jaw.

He wanted to know what those spots meant.

Nameless had been given a lot of time to become obsessed with the way she looked, the way she smelled. The way her heart beat in her chest and filled his mind with a rhythm rather than quietness.

I do not want to eat her anymore. Every second in her presence filled some of the void within. The idea of eating her because of his own failure was like a sickening pool of acid in his gut.

He also worried if he did save her, she'd be frightened, and he'd lose her wonderful presence to hunger. He worried about that outcome, and part of him considered not healing her and allowing her to remain a comforting, but sleeping, presence in his life.

But Nameless wanted her to open her eyes and show him what colour they were. He wanted her to speak and let him know the sound of her voice in hopes he would find it soothing. He wanted her to greet him in the way Reia greeted Orpheus: with open arms and a lip pressed to the side of his snout right behind his nose hole.

Nameless wanted her to stay.

"I would bear your pain for you if I could, soft human."

The coolness of magic radiated between them.

Agony shot through his leg, and he let out a harrowing yelp when the bone in his ankle snapped with a distinct *crunch*. He clawed at his own leg in confusion, unsure what was happening.

White filled his vision from fright while terrible whines escaped. His shaking hands lifted his trouser leg.

It was broken. His leg was broken!

How did this happen? Anger should have filled him as a result of the pain, but there was no enemy to attack. No one had given him this wound.

"Wait." His head turned so he could face the woman and found her own leg was straight and no longer bruised.

Another yelp tore through him as he disturbed his injured leg to move closer and hold her limb.

"I-I took her wound?" He stared at his own broken ankle. It radiated a piercing feeling up his entire leg, like his bone was on fire. "That is the sacrifice? I must bear her wounds instead?"

Nameless didn't know what to do then. All Mavka hated pain.

I did it. He figured out the spell. *I discovered what must be done, but I do not like this.*

The only thing that pushed him forward, to force his body to grow broken in sacrifice for hers, was knowing she would wake.

He would fix this human, and he would make it his. He would shove mud in his nose to stem the worst of the smell of fear if he needed to.

Sliding his hands up her legs, he touched her everywhere over her body while he continuously thought about taking her wounds for himself. Two of his ribs broke and elicited sharp whines from him. His stomach ached like some of his organs were bruised and swollen. He even began to bloat in some areas.

He was forced to stop when he could no longer use any of his limbs as though his spine had broken. He waited for a day, watching her the entire time, thankful that his severed spine stopped him from feeling any pain.

Her chest rose and fell the same rate. He could hear her lungs and heartbeat like a lulling rhythm that eased him. *Tha-thump. Tha-thump.* His mind grew lax from that sound and her pleasant aroma that he took in with each draw of breath.

As soon as he was able to move, he fixed her shoulder and discovered her fingers on one hand were broken. Then finally, he worked up to her head, revealing just how... pretty her face truly was.

The moment he took the wounds around the side of her skull, his head pounded. He was undeniably dizzy. His own skull was under immense pressure, like it was fractured, but when he touched it, it thankfully wasn't.

That didn't mean hers hadn't been.

Perhaps I cannot break my own skull like this.

He didn't allow the dizziness to make him collapse.

Humans required food and water, and he didn't know how long this one had been without. Even though it was dangerous, he stumbled out of his cave with one direction in mind.

Orpheus' home has vegetables and fruits suitable for human consumption. Nameless would sneak his way into his territory to steal some.

That might just be as dangerous, if not more so, than the journey there in his disorientated state with the Demons lurking about in the Veil.

Delora woke with a dry mouth, like it was coated in thick sand. She was so dehydrated she didn't even have saliva to help her swallow, and trying to caused her to choke when her throat stuck together.

Water. She tried to beg for it, like anyone might be there to hear her, but all that came out of her mouth was a wheeze. *Water.* Lifting her hand to grasp for something, anything, that might quench her thirst, it barely moved under the power of her lethargy.

Her eyes lightly flickered open when something round, like a shallow bowl, was pressed to her lips. Her vision was murky since her eyes felt just as dehydrated as the rest of her. It was also dark, as there was no light from the sun or a candle.

The bowl tipped up and fresh, cool water began to enter her mouth. She swallowed it in desperate, greedy gulps. She didn't care that it was filling her mouth too quickly and dripping from her lips and down her chin to soak the front of her dress.

The bowl was taken away.

"Please, more," she begged in a broken, hoarse voice.

The bowl came once more. Delora gulped heavily and nearly cried when it was empty and taken away.

Instead of answering her plea with more, something else was pressed to her lips. It was hard, pointy, and vaguely tasted of a dirt-covered carrot. She was too weak to take a bite.

"T-too hard," she told the darkness.

Actually, it wasn't just darkness. There was a light, but it didn't illuminate anything other than itself.

Two floating green orbs danced in her blurred vision, highlighting a whiteness around them, but nothing more. She couldn't make out what the rest of it was, but that floating green was oddly... comforting.

It chased away her apprehension at being in the dark.

There was light with her. She wasn't alone. That was all that mattered.

Where am I? Did I die? The afterlife seemed a little too real. Her thirst and hunger were too prevalent, but she hoped this was the void regardless.

Something much softer was placed against her lips. It was round, and when she took a bite, she knew it was a blueberry by its taste as it burst inside her mouth. More were fed to her before a lumpier fruit was given – a raspberry.

By the time she was able to take a singular bite of a strawberry, Delora had used all the energy she had and collapsed. Whoever it was helping her kept pressing food to her mouth, but she couldn't part her jaws anymore. Couldn't lift an arm. She couldn't even keep her eyes open.

A mixture of smells came to her. The most prevalent one was human waste. Once her mind found that pungent smell, it latched on to it, and she was undeniably embarrassed.

She couldn't voice this, couldn't even physically react. No tears fell, even when the person began to wash her with a light, careful touch and a cloth.

If this is the afterlife, I wish there was a way to die even further.

Delora had to allow this person, who she still hadn't seen a single piece of, to clean her. The food and water were enough to stop her hunger and thirst, but it only gave her enough energy to keep on breathing, for her heart to keep beating.

She succumbed to sleep halfway through being cleaned.

FOUR

Delora woke to dimness. There was barely any light except for a large, ring-shaped entrance, but it was muted against the shadows that remained present despite it obviously being daytime. It did, at least, allow her to see the imprint of shapes around the area she was in.

There was no longer a terrible smell. Instead, she was surrounded by something more delectable. *It smells like vanilla bean and cream.*

Her large village had been lucky enough to source seeds to grow some in the greenhouses they had, but only those who lived lavishly were able to consume it. That didn't mean Delora had never enviously smelt that sweet, tantalising aroma when she passed their houses.

Laying on her side, Delora curled into that *rich* smell and something that tickled the tip of her nose, lips, and cheek as she inhaled and exhaled. She ran her hand against what she was resting upon.

Is that fur?

Her brows knotted when she also felt something else, something loose. Her eyes were adjusting to the darkness, and she squinted them as if that would allow her to see better.

A feather? A black one.

She didn't know why she was compelled to sniff it, but her eyelids flickered in contentment when she found the creamy, vanilla bean scent captured on it. Actually, she noticed everything smelled of it – the fur, even her own wrist.

A piece of material lightly slapped against her cheek. It was black and hard to see, only visible because of the contrast against her tan skin. She realised it was the long sleeve of a shirt.

She hadn't been wearing anything sleeved when she'd been tossed from the cliff. Looking down, she found her dress had been replaced by a long black shirt. It was so big on her it covered her all the way to her knees.

The buttons had been done up terribly, one missed and another through its hole instead, creating a loop that nearly caused her breast to slip out.

Delora clutched it to her body as her eyes began to dart around. *This is a man's shirt.* She was in a man's home.

She couldn't be dead.

She was relieved since she had never truly wanted to die, but also disappointed because she had mentally prepared herself for it. She felt the loss of not being able to blissfully disappear from her own bleak life. Now that she was feeling a little more coherent, she knew the afterlife wouldn't have been filled with thirst and hunger, or the mortification of being so dirty that she'd needed cleaning and to be changed.

A sob broke from her, and tears began to drip over her nose and cheek as they fell to whatever she lay upon. *I survived?*

She'd been tossed into the fucking Veil! *I should be dead.*

And yet, somehow, she had survived. She wasn't even in pain. She should be broken, should at least be in the process of dying. Something should have come along and eaten her by now. *How is this even possible?*

She had no idea where she was, but she wondered how a human had taken her from the Veil and healed her.

Priests and Priestesses couldn't heal extensive wounds, so how had this man?

Her cheeks warmed. *An angel?* But she didn't think they were real.

Yet the rich smell that invaded her senses was heavenly. She almost wanted to start licking at the shirt that was saturated in it.

Her tears eventually dried. Even if an angel had saved her... What did that mean for her? She had nowhere she could safely go unless this person decided to help her by taking her to a new village.

I'm too tired to walk anymore. After walking for five days, she wanted nothing more than to rest. Although her dreams had been plagued with nightmares, making her even more tired, sleeping felt... safe.

It was a worldly escape.

She was too cowardly to kill herself, but she also knew she was no longer brave enough to live.

I don't know what I want anymore.

Love was a burden. Friendship was a burden. Family was a burden. She was a murderer; she didn't deserve freedom.

Her head was a jungle of confusing and conflicting thoughts, and she already knew she didn't have the will to not be lost in it.

She thought more tears would fall, but none came.

Delora felt empty of emotions. Hollow to the point that there was not even the tickle of tears in her sinuses. She just laid there and looked at the shadowy ceiling with bleak eyes.

After a little while, someone ducked through the opening of the room she was in, taller than the entrance and blocking out the light almost completely. They froze when they realised she was awake.

She frowned slightly when she saw nothing but two floating green orbs. They were each about the size of a small child's fist and appeared to swirl like a fire vortex, slowly moving in a rotation.

That's a very strange light. But like before, she noticed they didn't actually illuminate anything.

"You are awake." The voice was such a deep baritone, so heavy and laden with velvet smoothness that it sang through her body like a quiet drum.

It was so pleasant she almost wanted to close her eyes in satisfaction at being allowed to hear such a beautiful voice.

Definitely an angel.

No human man could have produced a sound that decadent, nor could they smell that good either. She was hoping his voice might bounce off the walls and tantalise her ears again.

"I have obtained more water for you," he stated, and she finally made her eyes shut just so she could listen to him. She couldn't remember the last time someone spoke so quietly to her, with such a gentle trickle of emotion. "I used the rest washing you before."

That made her fling her eyes open as mortification stung. There had been no accusation in his tone, no mock or sneer, but Delora felt embarrassment all the same.

He started moving around the room, letting the dim light from outside fill the space, but it did little to show him. He looked tall, *too* tall, as he placed the bucket he'd been holding down on the ground. His back shadowed the front of him against the light, making it impossible to see, other than a single green orb floating where she thought his face should have been.

Is that some kind of headlight? Humans often used flame headlights to see in the dark.

"How long have I been here?" she asked weakly.

She found a way to lean against something to keep her upright position. It was hard when she had been expecting a pillow to soften her slightly raised position in the bed.

"A few days." She couldn't help noticing that he continued to face away from her. Most people would have lit a candle by now to allow them to talk in light, but he remained where he was, crouching next to the bucket. "You were very broken. It took me a while to heal you."

"How did I even survive?" she whispered, more to herself than him. "When I hit the ground, I should have... splattered."

Is that what she wanted?

"You landed on top of me. I think I cushioned your fall and took the impact myself."

Delora's face paled.

"Oh my, I'm so sorry." Her horror fled quickly, and she knit her brows together. "How did you survive then?"

"I healed. Then I brought you into my home."

Healed? she thought. *Humans can't heal.*

She wished he would turn around so she could see him, if only a little. She wanted to look at her saviour, to know if he was as beautiful as his voice and scent.

"Are you an angel?"

Her heart didn't race as it might have if she were anyone else.

To meet something as fantastical as an angel should have filled her with awe. Instead, she felt the cold emptiness she had experienced walking here.

She wanted to feel awe, to feel alive, to feel anything at all rather than the hollowness she felt now that she could no longer torment Jetson for all the pain she couldn't dish out on Hadith. She never knew she had a spiteful side like that. She'd always done what she was told without complaint.

"I do not know what that is, but I am no *angel.*"

Not an angel. He said she'd fallen on top of him, which meant he had been inside the Veil.

"Are you a Demon, then?" No fear entered her. Being eaten meant she would disappear, but she wasn't really fond of the idea of the pain that would come first. "Did you fix me so that you could eat me when I'm better?"

Perhaps I would taste better that way.

"No." The word was said softly, but it held a darkness to it. It gave his voice an even deeper bass that made her skin prickle.

"You aren't a Demon, no? Or you aren't going to eat me, no?"

He reached up and covered the green glowing ball with his hand, as if he was hiding it. "Both."

"What are you then?"

"Something that does not plan to hurt you," he answered. "You do not need to be afraid. I will help you feel better."

"What are you?" Delora pressed more firmly, not liking that he was evading her.

The ray of light coming in allowed her to see him sigh heavily, his shoulders lifting on a large breath before it sounded out of him.

"I am Mavka."

"Mavka?" Her brows knitted further together, and her lips puckered along with them. "I've never heard of a Mavka."

"It means forest creature. It is what the Demons call us."

"And humans?"

He reached out to grab something shallow from the ground and dipped it into the bucket, then he offered it to her. She thought she saw the *glint* of something black and smooth – but more importantly, sharp – on the ends of his fingers cupping the rim of the bowl.

His hand was so big it almost swallowed the underside of it completely.

"You should drink more water. I still have the food you would not eat from earlier."

Delora didn't know what she was lying in, but it had slight walls, as if she was in a recess of some kind, with furs to cushion it. It wasn't a bed, she realised. She didn't know what it was, but he was at the foot of it.

"I'm too tired to reach that far." A complete lie.

Well, she thought it might have been a lie since she didn't even attempt it. She just wanted this so-called *Mavka* to come closer so she could see him.

He leaned to the side more and only closed the distance by a few inches while tilting away. She didn't take what he was offering.

When he realised she wasn't going to, he pulled his arm back and held it in front of him. She thought he might be looking down at the bowl of water.

"Are you still too weak to drink it by yourself?" He sounded disappointed, perhaps even a little dismayed.

Delora lifted her chin defiantly. "Yes."

He stayed quiet and unmoving, staring down at the bowl that reflected the green lights.

Then he let out another big sigh. "I guess there is no other way then."

He began to slowly move closer, appearing as if he was crawling on a single hand and both his feet. Something lightly clipped against the ground along with his movements instead of the tapping of feet or shoes. He moved in front of the light, obstructing her view, as he came to her.

There was a moment when she thought she might have seen *antlers* on top of his head. Her lips parted on a gasp when she realised those green lights weren't lights at all but were floating on his face like eyes.

Glowing orbs that highlighted the fleshless face of a fox skull.

"You're a–"

Before she could even finish her sentence, he'd already

placed his large hand to the back of her skull and forced her head backwards so he could place the bowl against her parted lips. He poured the contents into her mouth. She gulped it down so she wouldn't drown as her eyes widened, staring up at him.

She gripped the sleeve of his shirt. Those green orbs seemed to look directly into her soul as if they were peering into all of her sins.

"You're a Duskwalker," Delora managed to gasp out when he pulled the bowl away to allow her to breathe.

He pressed it back after a few huffs.

"Yes. That is what you humans call us."

Delora clenched her eyes shut when the water came a little too fast this time, slipping from her mouth to drip down against her chest. She yanked on his sleeve, and he backed away.

Delora began to cough, letting go to press the back of her wrist against her mouth.

"Was that too fast?" He seemed genuinely concerned.

I should have just done it myself.

"N-no, it's fine."

She was too freaked out to give any other response.

"I will be more careful," he offered, bringing the bowl back to her lips.

She turned her head away as best as she could with his warm hand still holding it. "I don't want any more."

No, instead she wanted to gawk at the creature in front of her. He couldn't allow her to figure out what he was and not let her absorb it. No wonder he had been hesitant about her seeing him!

Sure, he wasn't a Demon, but this wasn't technically any better. He was still a monster, just one that didn't have a freaking face!

Before her very eyes, his glowing orbs floating in front of his hollow eye sockets turned a reddish pink.

"I did not mean to hurt you."

He placed the bowl in her lap, and she realised he'd come to the conclusion that she didn't trust him to feed her water anymore. She stared down at it, seeing her bare legs just below the black button-up shirt she was in.

Something similar was covering his chest, as well as a pair of black trousers wrapped around obviously unguligrade legs. She couldn't see his feet, but the backs of his hands were visible and, even with the dim light, she could see they had protruding white bones from his knuckles all the way to his wrists. Dark-grey flesh covered the rest of them, and they were *huge*.

No wonder she'd felt warmth radiating all around the back of her head and neck. She bet that if he placed his hand against her face, he'd cover it completely.

Her eyes travelled along them, from his arms to the wide span of shoulders that were haloed by the dim light. Then he leaned back, heading into that light to highlight the antlers she realised she *hadn't* mistaken seeing.

Even crouching, he towered over her. She could only imagine how large he would be in comparison to her if they both stood.

She lifted her hand to brush over her hair in shock, while darting her eyes around the area she was in. She was able to better define the walls, floors, and ceiling. She had thought it was just so dark she couldn't see timber, but she'd been looking at rock the entire time. *Cave* walls.

The room wasn't as dark or as big as she thought it was. She looked over what she was sitting in.

"Is this a nest?" she squeaked out.

The walls were covered in furs, with an occasional large branch sticking out.

"Yes. This is my bed." He reached forward and lifted a bowl of food into the nest next to her. "I had nowhere else to put you that would be soft."

I'm in a nest... In a Duskwalker's cave. Home? One that washed me, saw me naked, and changed me into his own clothing. She eyed him carefully. *One that is feeding me and giving me water.*

"What are you intending if you aren't going to eat me?" Delora narrowed her eyes. "I'm not going to be a pet."

His head tilted, making a rattling sound that she only ever heard from the Demons outside her village walls. It was like the sound of dry bones clicking against each other.

Well, that's gross.

"Pet? I do not know what that is. I just wanted to make you

better after you fell from the sky." He twisted his head the other way, leaning closer, which made her lean away. "You are not afraid of me."

No, Delora wasn't afraid. He might eat her, might hurt her, but she didn't care if it meant her death. What was a little bit of pain before it all blissfully ended?

She wasn't afraid to die, therefore she could not fear her possible grim reaper. That didn't stop her from being concerned by how much she enjoyed the smell and voice of a Duskwalker, a monster.

Her lips twisted into a cringe.

He wasn't ugly, but when faced with the skull of a fox that was much too large for any animal to have – like it was bigger on him – she found it hard to look at. But perhaps that was because she didn't find him truly unpleasant.

Those glowing orbs were rather pretty, especially when they faded back to green and seemed to swirl with so much life.

The antlers on his head branched and forked three times and looked like an auburn colour from what she could tell.

He had fangs, noticeable ones at the front because of the two long ones at the top and the short ones at the bottom. The rest were sharp, pointed, triangular teeth.

It was obvious he had a bite that could kill within a second.

She'd also seen that long, slightly curled claws tipped all of his dark-grey fingers, black and shining against the dim light.

"Why did you save me? Your kind eat humans."

Why hadn't he just put me out of my damn misery before I woke up?

"No eat," he bit in a dark tone, the bass of it sending a wave of goosebumps over her flesh again. Then he nudged the bowl of food closer to her. "*You* must eat."

Her stomach grumbled loudly with anger that she hadn't immediately dove for it. Heeding to both the demand of her stomach and the Duskwalker, Delora finished her water so she could place the wooden bowl of food on top of it.

She took the last strawberry available, seeing the one she'd taken a bite out of earlier was decaying now that she'd exposed its insides to the air.

"Are you the Duskwalker that visits the villages for a human offering in exchange for a protection ward?"

She sincerely hoped not; she wasn't interested in that.

"No, that is another." He slowly reached into the nest she was in and grabbed the hand that she wasn't using to eat.

The only reason she let him take it was because she was curious about what he would do. He examined it, spreading warmth into her cold fingertips, as he brushed his clawed thumb over it.

"Your hands are so little," he commented with a note of wonderment in his voice. She noticed then that he never opened his bony jaws to speak, as if he was talking from his mind. "Your skin is also very smooth."

Delora ripped her hand away.

"You've obviously never spoken to a human before, but I don't really want to be examined."

She shrunk when his glowing orbs turned red, and a light growl came from him. "This is not true. I have spoken to another human, but I am not allowed to touch."

He reached for her again, and she dodged his grabbing hands.

"Hey, no," she snapped, before pointing her finger at him. "I don't care that you saved me. Don't touch me."

She expected him to be angrier, but instead his orbs turned green. He raised his hand so he could tap at the side of his snout.

"No? Don't touch? I do not understand why I cannot. I have said I mean no harm, and I already touched when I removed your soiled clothing."

Delora lowered the carrot she hadn't had the strength to eat earlier.

"Why do you keep bringing that up?" She was pretty sure it was obvious she was uncomfortable with it! "I'm not yours to touch, and you shouldn't keep reminding a person that they peed themselves!"

She was pretty sure it was more than just pee, but she didn't *dare* utter it.

"Why not? Is this not a normal human function?"

Her lips parted with shock. "Are you stupid or something?"

"Yes." He grabbed the side of his snout and rubbed it, before looking off to the side. "I have been told I am stupid."

Delora brought her lips into her mouth to bite them shut. *Someone told him that?* She didn't know why she found that both pitiful and funny at the same time.

"Look, it's because I didn't *mean* to do it. Just... stop bringing it up. I'd much rather forget."

"Okay, I will not then."

She went back to eating her carrot and grumpily chomped on it. When she was done with everything she could eat in the bowl, she placed it down beside her.

The Duskwalker nudged it back at her.

"You should eat more."

"I can't eat that. Why would you even give me an uncooked onion or potato?"

At her rejection, he lowered his hands inside the nest to pick up the bowl. He grabbed the onion and lifted it to the hole in his snout where his nose must be, sniffing it before sneezing like it irritated his senses.

"There are certain foods that must be cooked for humans to eat them?"

Delora grew terribly dismayed. She didn't have the will for life, why would she have any strength left in her heart to teach a creature the ABCs of her kind?

"Yes," she muttered before laying down since she was still weak. Eating had used up all her energy, but she at least felt better. She rolled over to give him her back. "I'm tired. I'd like to sleep more."

Just my shitty luck. I come across one of the only Duskwalkers that would rather save a human than kill it. Of course, it would be that way. Why would life be so easy for her?

It had never been merciful before.

Nameless stared at the back of the human with his head tilted.

I thought she would be thankful. He had been *hoping* she would be. Whenever Orpheus did things for Reia, she would reach to him with an affectionate touch to his snout or give him a smile.

Those smiles were hypnotic even to Nameless. He'd been hoping this woman would give him one so he could see what it was like to receive a smile. Instead, she looked miserable, and the dark circles under her eyes that he'd originally thought were bruises had not faded.

Maybe when she is feeling better she will smile for me. Did humans require energy to feel positive emotions? *I know so little about them.*

His sight drifted to her laying in his nest, curled up in his furs, on top of his feathers, and wearing one of his shirts. Her thick, shapely thighs caught his attention simply because they had been smooth and soft under his touch when he'd washed and changed her.

There was much of her that was different from him, which was basically everything from head to toe. Little toes that he was curious about touching since he'd seen them wiggle. Wiggle!

He looked down to his own hoofed feet. They were similar to that of a deer, except three-toed – they had only recently gone from two to three after the last human he ate. He tried to wiggle them, but alas, they barely moved as he still lacked complete dexterity with them.

The yellow of joy faded into his vision. *Her eyes were like bark.* They were so rich and held a certain strength to them. Nameless had found many treasures in the dirt, and he wondered just how many he'd see in her cinnamon-coloured eyes.

His orbs brightened in their yellow colour to signify his joy.

She wasn't afraid of me! Not once had he scented her fear and a thrill coursed through him. *A female of my own.* One that wasn't afraid, was able to look upon him, and wasn't fretting about leaving his nest or cave.

Nameless waited until she was truly asleep, her breaths shallow and even like they had been over the last few days. Then he slowly placed his hand inside his nest and leaned in to sniff the back of her hair and take in her aroma.

He closed his sight as he let it fill his senses.

He carefully lifted his other hand and used the very tip of his claw to brush her hair behind her ear so he could see her face. He didn't care that she hadn't smiled, that she had dark circles under her eyes and messy hair.

She was beautiful with her black hair similar to his fur – he liked that they shared a common trait between them. Her brown eyes were molten, and her lightly tanned skin looked delicious in a way he'd never experienced before. He thought she would be remarkably comfortable against his hard body.

Does no touching mean I cannot hold either? He wanted to know what it was like to feel the body of another against his own. He wanted to shelter her in his warmth, in his scent, his body, and protect her completely from everything beyond him.

I am strong, he thought with confidence, backing up so he could start collecting the loose feathers in the nest and place them on top of her. *I can protect.*

The feathers had come from his very body and were saturated in his scent. They would do for now to hide her own.

I must make her safe.

As best he could with his clipping hooves, he moved quietly around his small cave as he took a large bowl from the ground and scooped it inside a bag of salt.

He checked the salt circle, eyeing the four Demons that continued to teeter around his home who sought the female inside it. They avoided him, moving to the other side of the circle, but refused to leave as they rattled, snarled, and wailed.

I must get rid of them. Nameless knew he couldn't have them lurking here.

She may not be afraid of him, but he was sure she would become distressed to see these vermin. He gave them a growl, and they scattered momentarily before coming right back.

If they were the cause of her fear and he ate her by accident in a frenzy, he would be furious.

But how do I get rid of them? He stared down at the remaining salt in his bowl. Sure, he could kill these Demons, but more would eventually come.

He hadn't gone to see Orpheus to obtain an oil that allowed a spell to hide the human part of a human's scent. He was hesitant to do so. He didn't want Orpheus to know he had one.

Nameless was worried he would take her for himself or eat her just so Nameless couldn't have her. It made little sense, but he was already feeling rather possessive of her.

I must trick the Demons by hiding her scent underneath many other distracting ones.

An idea came to mind, one Orpheus would surely scold him for.

"What a waste of salt," he mocked to himself, pretending to be that know-it-all Mavka as he stepped out of the protection to carve a full circle outside of it with his claws. The sound of scraping dirt filled his ears. "It is used for protecting, not for hunting. Mur-mur-mur." He sprinkled salt inside half the carving he'd made, leaving one half unsalted. "Look at me, I am a smart Mavka who makes the antler one feel useless. Who tells him all his ideas are stupid even though he thinks they are fantastic."

Orpheus would surely mock Nameless for what he was about to do, but he didn't have any other ideas, and he thought this one might be suitable.

He gently coaxed the Demons in the direction of the half-filled salt circle by walking towards them and side-stepping them when they went the wrong way. They backed up slowly, growling and snarling, but they didn't attack him.

They knew he would kill them if they tried, not that they were aware of their oncoming demise.

Once they were inside the circle, the salt he'd already laid down stopped them from going any further back. Their heads darted around uncertainly when they were unable to escape.

They didn't get the chance to run out of it before he sprinkled more into the carving lines he hadn't filled yet. They were trapped completely inside it.

"What a waste of salt, Mavka," he continued. "Now you will have to acquire more sooner than you needed to."

Regardless, he had achieved what he wanted, no matter how he did it. He had a human to keep safe; he would waste any resource necessary.

He casually grabbed one of the small Demons by the head

before it could bite him. While it yelped, he walked with it into the forest and searched for a large broken branch on the ground.

When he found one, he picked it up and walked with both until he was a safe distance away from his home. Then he tore open the Demon's throat with his claws and purposefully spilled his blood along the ground in a wide arch.

He shoved the sharpest edge of the branch through its body and staked it to the ground, giving any Demons in the area something to hunt. The smell of it and its blood spilt across the dirt should help to hide that he had a human beyond it.

He was thankful that the smell of Demon blood wasn't enticing to Mavka since it was foul – although he'd eaten many in the past.

He repeated this action with the three others he had, creating a semi-circle of dead Demon bodies in the forest to shelter his home. He didn't know how long this would last, but he would check if he could smell her after his other idea.

Using his own claws, after washing them of the putrid smell of rotting decay that came from spilling Demon blood, he cut down his wrists. He spread his blood over the entrance of his cave and along the rock walls outside.

Her scent was light and gentle. Once his blood dried, it shouldn't attract the Demons as there wouldn't be a fresh body, but it would shelter her scent.

He checked the area by sniffing the air before giving a nod of approval. It wasn't perfect. If a Demon came closer just by wandering, they would notice her scent despite all this, but it should do for the time being.

He entered his cave to find her still lying where she was before. He crouched as to not tower over her in case she woke.

I am tired... and she is in my bed. Nameless hadn't slept since he brought her here.

FIVE

There was something encasing Delora in complete and utter warmth.

It was difficult to determine where it started and ended, as the heat came from her feet, up her backside, and all the way over the top of her head.

It also came from the front of her as two large, long limbs held her tightly. One wrapped around from underneath her head, as if supporting it like the pillow she lacked, then crossed down her chest and wrapped around her arm. The other limb came from above, running over her stomach to clasp the outside of the thigh she was laying on.

A big and strong chest pushed against her as large lungs filled with oxygen before quietly shrinking under an exhale.

The smell of vanilla bean and cream invaded her senses so wholly it dazed her groggy mind.

Delora couldn't remember the last time she'd been held like this. It was tender and so protective that it made her feel small and in need of protecting.

Darkness penetrated her vision when she flipped open her eyelids. She felt disorientated. She patted the unusually thick arm covering her. Her brows knitted, finding it unfamiliar. Then she finally touched their face – to find that it wasn't a face at all, but rather a skull.

Her mind sobered instantly and woke from the haze she was in. Delora scrambled, feeling lost in the dark. She clawed out of the arms of the creature that had been laying with her *intimately!*

Darkness gave way to show two glowing green orbs that suddenly came to life.

"What is the matter?" the Duskwalker asked.

Asked! Like what she was doing was strange in comparison to him holding her while she slept.

She didn't like that she found the grogginess of sleep present in his voice so light and gentle and... and nice that she was almost upset with herself for waking him.

That's right. I'm in the Veil, and a Duskwalker saved me.

"Why were you lying with me?"

She didn't see the arm wrap around her midsection before it pulled her back in. Claw tips dug into her side as she was yanked, struggling to stay where she was to no avail. Within moments, she found herself back in the position she'd just woken up in.

"Hiding your scent," he stated, before he curled around her tighter, as if what he said was just a cover up. "I have made sure the Demons will not discover a human is within my home. This will also help."

Yeah, no shit. All she could smell was his scent, and she knew it was all over her.

One of his arms moved to sprinkle something on top of her while she was holding the sides of her head.

"What's that?" she squeaked, wondering what terrible thing he had placed over her.

She hoped it wasn't something as barbaric as leaves or dirt.

"Feathers. They will cover what I cannot."

Feathers, she repeated in her mind. *Not much better.*

"Can... can you please let me go?"

"No," he bit. "I have not slept properly since I brought you here. Healing you and watching over you has been draining, and I must sleep in order to protect you. This way is best."

Her only solace was that she couldn't feel any male genitalia, which was easy to determine since he had her pressed up against him so tightly she could feel the lack of it with her backside.

He's going to sleep. Delora lay motionless, not daring to move in hopes he would pass out quicker. She refused to allow even a finger to twitch. As if he was truly exhausted, the Duskwalker's breaths evened out, and his hold loosened just enough to tell her he was asleep.

After a long period of time, she gingerly shuffled her position until she was lying on her back to stare up at the ceiling.

She didn't know how long she'd been asleep, but she'd been awakened by twisted dreams. It was dark now, and that envelope of nothingness was somehow comforting. His heavy weight kept her trapped next to him just as much as her lack of will to move, but it was soothing in its own way.

Her eyes drifted to where she thought his face must be.

I'm just lying here next to him. She was waiting for the drive to move away to grow in her, but it never did. *Why am I here?*

Was being a captive of a Duskwalker her punishment for what she had done? *Am I a captive, though?* He hadn't told her she couldn't leave, but there was no point in doing so.

He said he wouldn't eat me, so what does he want with me? She drew her lips tighter together. *Do I even care?* As long as he didn't plan to hurt her, she really couldn't think of anywhere to go that wouldn't end in her death.

There would also be no happiness. Delora no longer had faith in living with her fellow humans.

Do I really want to live in a place like the Veil, though?

Her thoughts grew silent when no answer came to her.

SIX

Nameless anxiously paced next to his nest while the human continued to sleep inside it.

Something is wrong with it. It had been two days since he'd rested beside her and had woken again to find the female creature still lying there... and then she continued to do so.

From what he knew of humans and had seen of Reia, they were generally active and chatty creatures. Reia would often speak with Nameless, and when he came across humans, they were usually talking with each other in pairs before he attacked them.

He was unsure of when this female was awake, as she only ever moved to turn or when he forced her to eat and drink by his own hands. He'd been reluctant to at first, but when he realised she wouldn't feed herself, Nameless had taken on the duty of doing it for her.

He'd tried to take away her invisible wounds, but he felt no change within himself, as if she was fine.

But she wasn't.

She continued to have dark circles under her eyes whenever she opened them, and her stare seemed... bleak? Dead even.

If she was sick, his magic should have healed her and transferred it to him.

What is wrong with her? Nameless felt like he was failing, and no matter how hard he attempted to speak with her again, it seemed as though she'd lost her voice.

Her pretty voice which was soft and medium pitched.

He wanted her to share it with him again.

He was beginning to feel agitated as he didn't know how to help the human who seemed... broken.

Restless, he went outside. His sight fell onto a patch of dirt that held rotted dill herb seeds. Orpheus had told him to plant them in a place where they would receive adequate water and sunlight. That was the only spot that received any light, but only for an hour each day, maybe less. It was just outside of the shadows on the other side of a small path next to the cliff wall where the tree line dipped in just slightly.

Is she like a plant? Does she need sunlight to be well?

He reached back to scratch at the fur next to his shoulder blades with uncertainty. He knew so little about how to care for a human, but he had often seen Reia sitting in the sun in their garden.

In a short while, that dirt patch – that he'd made sure was within his salt circle – would receive the only sunlight near his cave.

He turned his sight up to the sky to note the arc of the ball's rotation, then scratched just below his skull where feathers grew from him. One came loose and swayed back and forth as it drifted towards the ground.

What if it is a bad idea to move her? A small whine rattled his chest before he made his decision. *If she requires more sleep, she can just do so on the ground.*

Then he turned around and paused with a thought. *I do not need to plant her into the ground, do I?* He shook his head. He'd never seen Reia do that.

As quietly as he could manage with his clipping hooves, he approached the woman and tentatively slipped his large hands under her. She stirred only for a moment before relaxing within his large palms.

The moment he picked her up to cradle her within his arms, she shot awake and pushed at his chest.

"What are you doing?" she asked with wide, panic-filled eyes.

A slight tangle of fear danced from her skin. It was a delicious, gut-clenching scent within the air, and his eyes immediately turned crimson.

"Control your fear," he warned, halting with her in his arms. "I do not want to eat you, but I will not be able to control myself if you do not."

"Why are you picking me up?" Her heart rate seemed unusually fast from what he could hear, and her eyes continued to dart around. "I-I don't like being picked up."

"You are too weak to move, but I am going to take you outside."

That seemed to settle her, and her fear scent softened – but it hadn't been strong to begin with.

"I'm too heavy, you'll drop me." She was in a lax position, as if she worried about him dropping her, but he could feel the tension within her body. "Put me down."

"Heavy?" His head tilted sharply. "You are not heavy. I have lifted much weightier things than you."

Ignoring her request to be put down, Nameless walked from his cave to where the sun was already filling that spot.

He watched her dark brows knit together at his words as her lips puckered and almost hid the top one completely. They appeared exceptionally malleable, and he was growing more curious about them each time she made any expression with them.

"I don't want to go outside," she muttered as her eyes fell away from him to look upon the ground.

He didn't know why she averted her gaze, but his heart sank at the idea of it being because she didn't like to look upon him.

"I liked the darkness of your cave."

"You are not well." He placed her on the ground with her back against the wall. "I am putting you in the sun."

"I'm not a plant, you know."

Her eyes fell upon the forest, and something seemed to shadow her expression while he moved to sit a few feet away from her.

"No, not a plant," he mumbled, hoping she didn't come to the conclusion that he'd thought he needed to take care of her like she was one. "Human," he added.

"I guess it does kind of feel nice." She brought her knees up and laid her forearms across the top of them before resting her chin against them. "It's warm."

Her eyes flickered to him momentarily before going back to the forest.

"You kind of sit like a dog."

He twisted his head until it was almost upside down so he could see the way he was sitting. His arse was against the ground while his feet were pressed flatly against it.

"It is hard to get back up with hooves. This is the easiest way." He rose his hand to his snout so he could tap the side of it. "Would you prefer I did not sit like this?"

It wasn't much different to how she was sitting, except she had a wall supporting her back.

"No. I don't care."

She turned her head away to stare at nothing.

This is helping. This was the most he'd spoken to her since the first time she'd woken. *Humans require sunlight.* He was keeping a mental note of all the things he needed to remember to care for her wellbeing.

His tail, which was fox-like and fluffy, tapped against the ground twice. "Do you have a name?"

"Of course, I have a name," she grumbled. "What kind of person doesn't have a name?"

"I do not."

Sliding her face against her knees, she brought it to him with a tight frown. "You don't have a name?"

"No." Then he shuffled slightly closer. "What is yours?"

"Delora. My maiden name was Delora Theralia." Her eyes lowered before she added, "I guess I don't need to add the maiden part anymore."

His sight changed from its normal green hue into a dark yellow as curiosity ran rampant through him. "You have two names?"

"Well, yeah. Most humans do."

"What is the purpose of this?"

"I guess it's so that if there was another human named Delora, you'd be able to separate us because our last names would most likely be different."

Nameless tapped at the long length of his snout.

Humans have such complex things for identifying themselves. Is a face and a single name not enough?

"Will... you give me a name?"

He wouldn't be selfish and ask for two. One name would make him happy.

Delora lifted her head a little as her eyelids fluttered. He noticed that the colour of her brown eyes grew lighter in the sun and almost appeared to have flecks of honey and gold. He tried to control his tail from tapping against the dirt in joy at seeing this mesmerising difference.

"You want me to name you?"

He placed his hand against the ground in order to lean closer in anticipation. He nodded.

"Yes, this would please me greatly."

"I don't know." She rubbed at the side of her neck with her palm before she looked away. "It's kind of weird for me to name you. That's something a parent usually does for someone."

His tail stilled as a coldness rushed through his heart. His shoulders slumped. *Why does no one wish to give me something special to be called?*

When Reia had first told him what a name was, he asked this of her. She'd also rejected him. *Am I not deserving of a name?* It appeared to be something important, and yet it was something he severely lacked.

He'd also asked Orpheus, but he hadn't liked any of the names he'd given him. Fox-face. Annoyance. Antler-head.

The silence that was ever present in his life was heavy between them as he reflected on this, his orbs glowing with a deep well of blue.

SEVEN

Delora brought her eyes back to the Duskwalker after a short while of avoiding gazing upon him. *What kind of person asks for a name?*

She should know someone better before giving them something as important as a name. She didn't want the responsibility or the shame she'd feel if she tried to give him one he didn't like.

I've never even given someone a nickname.

Despite her rejection, many names came to her. Robert, Klaus, Andreas, but none of those seemed right for him. They were... they were too human.

However, she lowered her hand from her neck when she saw he was looking off to the side with a defeated slump in his posture. She was starting to become curious about the changes in his 'eye' colours, as they happened quite often.

What does blue mean? It didn't take her long to realise it showed his sadness, her own chest echoing the same deep well of it.

Her heart panged terribly, causing the corner of her eyes to bow and her teeth to sink into her bottom lip from the inside.

What kind of monster do you have to be to make a Duskwalker sad?

He was such a strange-looking creature.

It was the first time she'd seen him in any form of light, and now that she could see him properly, all his details were visible to her. The auburn-coloured antlers on top of his head were large and branched, with the bottom forks curling above his forehead. His fox skull was completely white rather than cream coloured, and the shadows on it were a cold blue because of the contrast.

His body was massive; she thought he had to be at least seven feet and six inches, and even taller with those antlers. The way he sat made it obvious that his long legs matched his long and mostly slender body. His shoulders were wide, while his waist was unusually narrow.

Muscles pressed into his shirt from his chest, arms, and legs, but she thought it may also be something else making him appear beefier – like maybe he had *fur* beneath his clothing.

She could see his hoofed feet. They were odd as they were separated into three toes, but they weren't as strange as the protruding white bones that ran over the tops of his dark-grey hands that rested limply against the ground.

He looked strong, wide, and yet, somehow lanky because of his narrowed waist and hips... and his limbs! They were slightly longer than what a human would have. He had long arms that almost reached the lower part of his muscular thighs rather than midway.

He wore black clothing that looked new but was slightly dusty. Black fur poked out from the cuffs of his pant legs and the shirtsleeves around his wrist. Whereas black feathers haloed the back of his skull like the Victorian collars many women wore in the sketches she'd seen in library books in her village.

The floating orbs that hovered in his eye sockets were ethereal, almost beautiful in their own way, and it shot guilt through her to see them such a deep blue.

The light she was sitting in suddenly became too bright, like she didn't deserve to sit in something so pleasant.

Delora weakly got to her feet.

His head shot to her. "What are you doing?"

"I don't want to sit in the sun anymore. I'll get a sunburn if I do." Though, she didn't think that was true since she could barely feel the sun through the mist of the Veil.

"Humans can burn from the sun?" Delora noted the hint of curiosity in his tone, but his eyes remained that saddened colour.

"Yes." She walked towards him since he was sitting in front

of his cave entrance, but paused momentarily when she was next to him. She quietly said, "You don't want me to name you."

Finally, his eyes changed to something else. Dark yellow shifted into his orbs as he gave a questioning head tilt.

"Why?" he asked.

Delora heard the dirt being disturbed when he moved to follow her inside the cave.

"Because I'm a terrible person," was her answer as she crawled into his mostly hard nest. She laid on her side with her back facing any sort of light so she couldn't see it.

"How are you a terrible person?" The tone of his voice seemed genuinely confused, and slightly higher pitched, but still in his deep, dark baritone.

Delora clenched her eyes shut.

"How many humans have you killed?" Silence followed her question, and she eventually twisted her back just enough so she could see him crouching next to the nest. "How many have you eaten? You're a Duskwalker. It's no secret that your kind are just like the Demons, so don't bother hiding it."

He shuffled nervously on his feet. "But you will hate me or be afraid if I tell you."

"I won't," she answered without hesitation.

Hatred was too intense of an emotion for her to have the will for. The emptiness she felt was consuming, and only the slightest of emotions were able to slip through.

He scratched at the side of his neck while turning his head away to look around the cave walls before slowly bringing it back to her, finding her still staring at him and bravely holding his gaze. He paused when he realised this.

His answer was quiet, like he didn't truly want her to hear it. "Twenty-nine, I think."

Only Twenty-seven more, and I'll catch up to him. She stiffened and rolled over, bringing herself into a ball.

"You–"

"I don't hate you," she interjected, in case he took her movement as that. "I'm not even afraid."

How could she be? He had only done what was natural to his kind, whereas what she had done was *wrong*. He killed for food, a normal part of being a creature in the food chain. It was no different to a human killing a chicken for their meat.

What Delora had done was act against normal morality because she'd been spiteful, jealous, and enraged. She was disgusted with herself that she was still glad she'd killed Hadith and Cindy. She didn't want them to be alive and happy when they were the reason she felt so miserable.

I'm the monster, not him.

Delora flinched when something hard, like the backs of curved claws, touched her hair to move part of it behind her ear.

"What is wrong with you?"

"What do you mean?" Her lips tightened together as she clenched her eyes shut.

"You are not what I have seen from other humans. Did... did I not heal you completely?"

Delora's chest rose and fell with bigger breaths as liquid began to bubble against her closed eyelashes. It was the first time she felt like crying since she'd first woken up here.

"This is not your fault."

Was she really trying to console a Duskwalker? Yet, the idea of laying her sins bare to him didn't feel like a terrible idea. He wasn't a human who would judge her. She also doubted he'd truly understand.

That was the only reason why she opened her mouth to reveal part of the truth.

"I don't want to be alive anymore," she whispered. "But I also don't want to die."

Delora wished there was a different plane of existence she could go to where all her pain and longing and sadness would vanish so she could feel something nice. A place that existed beyond Heaven and Hell, Earth and the Veil.

"I do not understand."

At least he's honest. She thought she might have been upset if he pretended to understand what she was going through.

"I'm in so much pain." She opened her eyes to let the tears that had been collecting fling and splatter against her cheeks. She reached up to grab at the shirt he'd dressed her in, clutching at the chest of it while crossing her ankles and desperately trying to bring herself further into a ball, as if that was the answer to disappearing. "It hurts so much inside."

It was a numb kind of hurt, which seemed far worse than any cut from a blade or any burn of fire.

"How do I heal you of this kind of wound?"

She leaned into the nest behind her.

Delora shook her head, her voice breaking an octave as she cried, "You can't."

It seemed the moment she started crying, she was unable to stop. Her bottled emotions were spilling over, and she didn't know how to let them out and feel better. She felt both numb *and* had a lingering, painful burn, like it was on her flesh.

"It's not a wound that can be healed. It's deep inside in a place that can only be touched by me, and I hate it so much."

She is broken, Nameless thought as he leaned closer to Delora while she lay crying and helpless in his bed. Crimson lifted into his sight as anger and a hunger like he'd never experienced before filled his entire being.

The intricate muscles in his biceps and around his shoulder blades tightened in aggression, causing his claws to dig into the animal furs covering the nest floor.

I will fix her. He would fight whatever this invisible foe was until he vanquished it. He would protect her from it until she was no longer in pain.

But first, he *needed* something from her.

"If you do not want your life, then give it to me," he commanded with a husky voice.

Just the idea of it sent a pleasant thrill through him.

"P-pardon?" she asked in surprise, her voice cracking due to her tears. She rolled over slightly to greet him.

"If you do not want to be responsible for your life, then give me your *soul*."

He would protect it, nurture it, and keep it safe for her if she did not want to. He would make it his, then he would make *her* his.

Mine. He growled the word darkly inside his mind.

Nameless had chosen this human for himself, and he would make her his bride. Her smell was mind-tingling, and her voice body-quivering. Her beauty, on the other hand, was a completely different matter, and he didn't have the intelligence to formulate the words of appreciation he had for it.

He was desperate to touch her, but she said she was not his to touch. Nameless would *rectify* that.

A gentle hint of fear rose in her scent, but it wasn't enough to distract him from the mouth-watering smell of red apples and frosty snow. His tongue itched to lick across her skin.

"My... my soul?"

She rolled over to her back, her long, straight black hair pooling in his nest like a glossy puddle. He wanted to rake his claws through each individual strand, knowing there were thousands of them – not that he knew how to count that high. He wanted to touch each one individually, to know its feel, its length against the others.

Her *pain* had called to him in a way he'd never felt, and he would erase it, even if it took him eternity.

When he didn't answer her, instead just inching closer as his orbs grew redder, he smelt a hint of heat in her scent. Her hands flew to her chest when he saw a spark of light coming from it.

"Will it hurt?" she whispered.

"No." At least, he didn't think it would. "And I will protect it, always, so that you are never hurt again."

Her long and pretty eyelashes flickered from his words, and he thought he saw the sharp edges of her eyelids soften. The dark bruises underneath her eyes were still apparent, but just the minor change made her seem more relaxed.

Does she want someone to protect her?

"Okay," she said, as the smell of her fear dissipated. "It's not like I really need it. And I don't... I don't really want my life anymore."

Nameless was surprised it was so easy, considering how long

it had taken for Orpheus to obtain Reia's soul. But Delora just pulled her cupped hands away from her chest, and he saw it.

He tilted his head in confusion when it wasn't what he envisioned at all.

Whereas Reia's soul was in the shape of a human woman with floating hair made of fire hovering between Orpheus' Impala antelope horns, Delora's was... *black,* like charcoal. It also didn't seem to be floating since she was holding it by one of its arms as it dangled limply between her pinched thumb and middle finger.

"Here." She basically tossed it into his palm when he reached towards her with his hand facing upwards. "I don't care what you do with it as long as it doesn't hurt."

He stared at the tiny thing laying lifeless in the crease of his palm. He would have thought it was dead if it weren't for the fact that it was lukewarm and the tips of its hair flickered with some flame.

It was the last bit of light on it, and he wondered what would have happened had it been snuffed out completely.

Nameless didn't care. When the urge to eat it became far too difficult to resist, he placed it in his mouth and swallowed. A shudder of immense pleasure shook him afterwards.

There was a warmth in his gut, lukewarm, but remarkable. Instantly, his insatiable hunger faded. It was as if all this time he'd been doing nothing but waiting for this woman to give him her soul.

EIGHT

Delora felt like a baby bird as she sat in the middle of the Duskwalker's nest and let him feed her by hand.

He seemed set on doing it this way, like he thought she couldn't do it herself since he muttered, "You are feeling weak. I will help you."

She'd woken not long ago from a nap after giving him her soul, and she didn't know what he'd done with it to begin with, but she could clearly see it floating between the branching forks of his antlers. Goopy black string was knitted around it by its outstretched arms and tied its legs together. They also supported its chest and neck with wrappings. The head was hanging forward limply, while the hair on it was swept to both sides of its chest, barely giving any flickers of life.

In some ways, she thought giving him her soul would make her fade away, but she was kind of thankful she hadn't died. She worried all that was on the other side was lonely darkness, or worse, eternal damnation.

She also didn't mind this.

The way his sharp claws gently scraped underneath her chin in a light tickle so he could place a strawberry to her lips... was tender.

The only reason she was allowing this was because she was still tired, which was ridiculous with how much she'd been trying to sleep over the past few days. It was like her mind and body no longer had energy against her crumbled will.

When she was done with the strawberry, he lifted a shallow

bowl to her lips and carefully tilted it so that water slowly entered her mouth and didn't drown her. His claw tips brushed against the column of her throat as she gulped, and she couldn't help looking into his glowing green orbs.

She liked them.

They had been off-putting at first, but she'd grown to find them comforting to look upon within the shadows of the cave and the darkness of his form.

It was currently nighttime, and they were the only things that allowed her to know where he was. That she wasn't alone in the dark.

Once she'd finished drinking, she slipped her hand over the nest to find the edge to know where she was on it. She gasped when his much larger hand grabbed hers.

She yanked her hand free.

"What is the matter?"

"You surprised me. I didn't know you were going to grab my hand."

The only reason she saw something wave in front of her face was because it momentarily obstructed her vision of his glowing orbs.

"Can you not see in the dark?"

His voice was laced with curiosity – it always was when he asked a question. Its depth always lightened into something more boyish.

"No. Humans can't see very well in the dark."

Delora heard him moving by his clipping feet before a match was struck, giving a small flame. He lit a thin candle, one that appeared as though it had never been lit before. He tried to place it on the ground, and it immediately fell over.

When he realised it couldn't stand on its own, he placed rocks around it until it was supported, yelping when hot wax landed over his fingers – more in surprise rather than in pain from being burned.

"Is this light better? I did not know you could not see before."

For the first time, the cave and all its details were shown to her since it was brightened from the inside. It was relatively clean and organised.

There were crates filled with housing items such as bowls, cups, candlesticks, and cutlery. There were piles of rope and tools for carving all stacked up on one side.

She also saw his nest as a whole.

"Are you no longer hungry or thirsty?"

It seemed her needs were his first priority, as he'd pushed for both when she'd woken.

I wonder if he would have forced me into the sun again if it was daytime.

"I'm fine now," she muttered. "Thank you."

Although he'd held her while he slept one other time, the Duskwalker had never crept inside the nest with her while they were both awake before – until now.

Delora leaned away, but she didn't get far with the wall of branches behind her as he towered over her much smaller form. He sat in front of her.

When he reached over to her, she stayed still. She was curious about what he would do. As he'd promised, he had never hurt her, and she'd come to trust him enough in that.

He lifted her hand and brought it closer to his orbs before grabbing the other, seeming to examine them in close detail.

His hands swallowed hers in darkness, and she could feel his claws lightly stabbing into her wrists. He turned her hands over, dropping the first so that he could run the pad of a finger over the creases in her palm, before turning her hand back over to look upon her nails.

"You have nothing to protect yourself with." He pressed the pad of his finger against one of her long, rounded nails until her finger tilted back at the first knuckle. "Is this why humans wield those sharp, pointy silver sticks?"

A slight frown marred her features. "Do you mean a sword?"

"Sword?" His orbs turned a reddish pink before he said, "Yes, I knew that was what they were called. I was just testing you."

No, you weren't.

His thumb ran over the back of her wrist before he dropped his hand. Before she could stop him, he grabbed her ankle. Delora yelped when he lifted it, incidentally dragging her across the nest and almost upside down so he could examine her foot!

"H-hey! Put me down. I told you not to touch me."

The fact she'd allowed him to hold her hands escaped her in that moment with the precarious position she found herself in.

"You said you were not mine to touch. Now you are, and I want to discover you."

The leg he was holding onto was straight and partially in the air, while the other was bent from her struggling.

Delora's face paled when she saw that her pubic mound was bare, uncovered, and the lips of her labia were parted due to her position. Heat flared in her cheeks at the same time she shoved the shirt she was in down to cover herself. But he hadn't been looking at her there, as if it wasn't much interest to him.

Oh, hell no! Delora squirmed, fearing his hands would start sliding up her body.

She let out a squealing peal of laughter when he tickled her foot. His hands hadn't gone up her body, they had moved to her feet, and his fingers were now wiggling her toes in fascination.

"So strange. Humans have little toes that are fragile." When he glided his claws underneath the arch of it, she started laughing again, now trying to get away from the torture that sent tingles of strange agony up her limb. "Why are you laughing?"

"Because it tickles!"

He stopped, and she was finally able to take a breath. She turned to face him, seeing that he had cupped his snout in thought.

"Tickles? It makes you laugh?"

She had the vague impression he didn't know what any of this meant. He drew two claws underneath her foot, and she squirmed again, laughing, when she didn't find this the least bit funny.

"Please stop!" she squealed while desperately trying to yank her foot away. Delora was almost on the verge of tears, but not from joy or happiness, from frustration. "It's not a pleasant feeling. It's like torture."

He stopped again, and his orbs turned to dark yellow. He moved her foot one way and then the other, inspecting it like it was the most fascinating thing he'd ever seen.

"Why do you have a function on your body that is torture?"

As if he truly didn't care for her answer, he did something that she should have found horrifying and yet found remarkably... adorable. The Duskwalker placed his own foot against the bottom of hers to compare them.

Now she understood why just her own foot was fascinating to him because, for a moment, she was curious about the oddity of his. She hadn't truly looked at them, since there was so much to look at on him that was strange to her.

Then, despite what she'd said to him, he tickled her fucking foot again! An involuntary movement pulled her ankle from his hold, and she accidentally kicked him in the face.

A curt growl was the only warning she received before she was shoved against the bottom of the nest and pinned there. She felt remarkably small and helpless beneath him. Delora wasn't short for a human, not with her height of five feet and seven inches, but that didn't matter against the sheer size of a Duskwalker.

"You kicked me!" he roared, his jaws parting to show her his deadly fangs.

The angry red of his orbs screamed *danger*.

"You were tickling me! I didn't mean to kick you."

He gave her a snorting huff. "You are mine, so I will not hurt you, but that does not mean you can hurt me!"

The smell of him invaded her senses, and she averted her eyes when she felt a little warmer this close to him. Heat rose in her cheeks as she squeezed her thighs together.

"W-what do you mean, I'm yours?"

Her question seemed to distract him enough from his anger because he eased back a little. "You are my bride."

Her eyes widened just slightly as her lips parted.

"No, I'm not."

"You gave me your soul. You gave me permission to eat it and hold it for you, tying yourself to me for eternity."

"Is that what I did? That's why you wanted it?" Her eyes flicked to where it hung, tied between his antlers. She gaped at it. "Why would you want me as your bride? I told you, I'm a terrible person."

"I have yet to discover this from you." He leaned around her on his elbows and brought his claw tips to her cheek to brush her hair away from her face. "I want to protect you. That is why I asked you for it. You are in pain, and I want to ease you of it because I understand."

Delora scoffed. "How would you understand what I am feeling?"

Delora was curious about why she wasn't fretting underneath him. Did she truly trust him, or did she just have no regard for herself anymore? As long as she wasn't in physical agony, the startling realisation that she didn't care what happened to her was the only reason it made this bearable to discover.

Perhaps this is my eternal punishment. Her carelessness had tied her to a Duskwalker. She had no one else to blame but herself for her decisions. *I'm so stupid. I should have asked more about it.*

He reached up to place his hand over his heart.

"Because I have felt pain here too. I have lived over a hundred years, and when I was shown just how alone I was by seeing the happiness of others, I found it difficult." Then he placed his warm hand against the side of her face to hold it. "Your presence in my home has already eased this for me, and I wish to ease your hurt in return."

His words were so sweet that it made her stomach sick. She didn't feel as though she deserved them, even from a creature such as him.

"You can't fix it," she said before she bit her bottom lip so tightly she feared she'd make it bleed.

"Why not?"

Delora didn't respond because if she had the answer, she would have tried to fix herself. She didn't know if it was the regret she'd felt for murdering two people or if it was the fact that she'd left her original village, a place she could have been happy, to marry someone who had turned out to be cruel. Was it the treatment she'd received for *years* that made her feel the numb pain she was in? She felt like the only way to fix herself was to remove the last five years of her life from her memory, but she also didn't want to forget it. It was what made her who she was today, not that she particularly liked herself.

"You will come to regret your decision," she finally said,

turning her head to the side to look away. "You will regret asking me for my soul. You have only cursed yourself."

You will come to hate me, just like Hadith.

NINE

The following day, Delora sat up in the nest to watch the Duskwalker leave after they both realised she had little food.

"Now that you have taken my hunger away, I will try to hunt for meat to make you strong." He scratched at the side of his snout, not in thought, but in another emotion she couldn't distinguish with his lack of facial expression. "I have seen another human eat meat, and now I know I can procure some for you since I will be less likely to consume what I catch for you."

"What about the fruit and vegetables you have been bringing me?"

She knew she was being selfish in asking for more, but the idea of eating a staple diet of just meat didn't sound appealing to her. It was often greasy, and he didn't have a cooking hearth.

He rubbed at the feathers around his neck. "I... cannot get you anymore for now."

Delora cast her gaze downwards and said nothing. *I should just be thankful he is going out of his way to feed me.*

This was the first time she'd been awake when he left, and he hesitated at the entrance of the cave. The backdrop of the ring of muted light, since it was shadows despite it being the middle of the day, made him seem gigantic next to it.

"You will stay?" He cocked his head in a strange way, but his tone held the *tiniest* threat in it.

She threw her hands up to gesture to her surroundings with a huff of annoyance. "Where else would I go? If I go outside by myself, Demons will eat me."

He pointed to his nest. "Here is safest. The Veil is dangerous. Do not go into it."

Delora brought her hands up to cross them and rub the sides of her arms. She didn't need the reminder.

"Okay," she answered quietly.

He nodded, before ducking at least two feet to clear his antlers as he left the shallow cave.

Is this my life now? To live in some small cave on the outskirts of the forest belonging to the Veil?

She turned her head up to stare at the rocky ceiling, straining her neck and feeling the stretch all the way up her throat. Her hair fell to dangle behind her back as she closed her eyes. *But I don't want to live in a cave.*

There was very little for her to do. She may not want to do much, but she at least wanted the *option*.

But she also didn't want to ask for more from the Duskwalker. She felt strangely at ease around him.

There was already an unspoken level of trust, and Delora appreciated everything he was doing for her. She'd be dead if it wasn't for him healing her broken body. She probably would have been eaten if he didn't lay the salt circle he'd told her of that kept the Demons away. She would have died of starvation and dehydration if he didn't actively make her fill both needs, and she was unsure if she truly would have tried to consume as much as he was making her.

Knowing he was gone made the area seem colder, almost lonelier.

I don't know why he is caring for me so much. She hadn't done anything to warrant such... kindness, not from what most would call a monster or a nightmare. But she'd seen enough of both over her life in many forms, and she didn't see him as either.

To Delora, he was a person. An odd-looking person who had a very strange face.

But with her eyes closed, she couldn't tell the difference between him and a human except for the clipping of his weird hooves or the massive warmth he wrapped around her whenever he cupped her face to make her drink or eat.

He wasn't very smart, but he understood enough to know

what she needed without her asking for it. Yes, she needed food, water, and something soft to lay in, but every human did also need sunlight, and to be spoken to softly.

I guess... I kind of like him. What a strange thought.

Delora noted the sound of rustling coming towards the cave before she heard the familiar scraping of claws against the entrance. The Duskwalker often supported himself with his hands while wielding his massive weight and height.

He came right to her within a flash before she could even open her eyes. *Did he forget something?* Maybe he'd been testing her to make sure she truly wouldn't leave before he *actually* left.

However, the form in front of her didn't smell like him. Bile rose in her throat when the odour of something rotting stung her nostrils.

She flung her eyes open just as the branches around the nest she was in *crunched* beneath heavy hands.

Sharp red eyes bore into her own. Delora was face-to-face with a snarling, flat-faced but human-looking Demon.

She didn't get the chance to look at the rest of him before he grabbed her around the jaw, cutting off the scream that was now locked in her throat. He gave her an evil smirk with a mouth that was far too wide.

"I wasss wondering when he would leave," he said, his voice a grungy tone that hissed out on his 's'.

Delora was pulled into shadowy light when something coiled around her with strong, flexing muscles and then he yanked her from the cave.

Her feet dragged along the ground before she was lifted by something that had encompassed her entire body. The Demon used it to turn her, so she was facing him.

Eyes drawn wide, she stared at the humanoid face of the Demon whose nostrils were slitted over a pressed nose. His lips were thin but puffy, and they highlighted how far his wide mouth reached, since the sides of it nearly came to his rounded ears. His pupils, encased by the red irises of a Demon, were slitted.

His skin was black like a void. So dark, in fact, that it appeared like the night sky, and she wondered if stars ever glittered in his flesh. Surprisingly, he had short black hair that was patchy, leaving parts of his scalp bald.

He removed his hand so he could wrap something around the bottom half of her face to stop her from talking or screaming, and her eyes drifted down his muscular body to see that he had no legs. They were replaced with what appeared to be a snake tail covered in iridescent black scales.

Delora shook her head at the horrifying creature in front of her, desperately trying to free her arms that were captured within the coil of his tail and stuck to her sides. The only thing free was her legs from the knee down, and when she kicked them, his dangerous smirk grew wider.

"Your ssscent is ripe with fear," he *chuckled*, before he brought her closer to sniff her by sliding his disgusting, slitted nostrils against her exposed neck. "But it isss not human, like when I first caught your ssscent in my territory."

Put me down! she mentally screamed while squirming.

She could feel the plumper parts of her body moulding between the coils of his tail, and it proved to her just how hard he was squeezing her. She could barely breathe. Any harder, and she feared she'd *pop*.

"Why are you afraid, creature that looksss human?" He leaned his head to the side, and his hair flipped that way to reveal more of the bald parts of his scalp. "I do not plan to kill you."

Delora stopped moving, her chest rising and falling rapidly, to stare at him intensely. She was afraid. She was very afraid of the monster that had her in its clutches, regardless of how it looked partly human. She'd never heard of Demons looking like this – so close to human, but still obviously not.

It made him seem even more dangerous.

She tried to calm herself, but it was hard to look upon him without being terrified or grossed out. *H-he's not going to kill me?*

"Yet," he snickered, causing her stomach to knot. "Firssst, I will find out why that Mavka hasss been keeping you. It'sss odd that he hasss been keeping hisss meat alive for ssso long."

Her struggles renewed at the idea of the Duskwalker being in danger when the Demon started dragging her into the forest.

Don't hurt him! He'd been her saviour. She may not truly care for him, but she didn't want to see him hurt because of her.

"Control your fear!" he hissed as he slithered on the base of his tail. Despite holding her in the rest of it, he was swift as he moved through the forest. "You will attract more Demonsss if you don't. You are lucky it doesss not bother me."

When Delora could do nothing but feel more fear, terrified of what was going to happen, the tail coiled tighter until she couldn't breathe. Her lungs were in excruciating pain from being squished. Before she knew it, her head slumped forward, and her vision darkened with white dots.

She couldn't breathe in, and the more she breathed out, the tighter it became.

Someone... help me...

Nameless held up the dead rabbit he had by the ears as he made his way down the Veil's cliff wall by jumping from one large, jutting rock to another. He knew of another safer path, but that was much too far away, and he wanted to be quick.

He'd left Delora only a few short hours ago, and he worried for his human every minute she wasn't within his sight.

He didn't even pause when he assessed the dead creature in his hand, unsure if it was even something she could eat, but it was all he could manage to catch. He hadn't even targeted it in his hunt.

He'd tried hunting for a deer, but every time he had to chase one down, his instincts and thrill for the hunt would grip his mind tightly, and he mauled it to pieces. He wasn't even hungry when he devoured it, since her soul had satisfied that part of him, but it was like he had a violent nature he couldn't control.

His orbs turned reddish pink when he thought perhaps Orpheus might be able to control such a terrible instinct inside himself.

The only reason he had the rabbit was because it had been

laying on the ground near the last deer he'd eaten. It looked as though either he or the deer must have knocked it against the tree in their struggle and killed it.

"As long as I do not tell her, she will not know," he muttered, bringing his mind eagerly back to the female he had in his keeping.

The pretty human he was trying his hardest to resist touching for worry he'd scare her away.

When his feet found the dirt of the Veil's canyon, he paused to turn his head in the direction of Orpheus' home.

Why can he touch his female, and I cannot? Then he remembered what he and Reia had told him to do when it came time for him to find his own human. *They said I must be... slow.* That he had to ease their fear, even if he could not see or smell it. That, when he found his own human, they would likely be wary of him and he couldn't touch until they were ready.

He scratched at the feathers sticking out just below the back of his skull.

But how do I know when she is ready? He brought his hand forward so he could stare at it. *I want to hold her when she is not sleeping. I want her to reach her hands up and stroke my snout.* He bet it would feel phenomenal.

He'd asked himself many questions about her state of wellbeing, but the one he pondered most was really a calling of his own. *Is she lonely?*

Nameless wondered if she felt the lack of his continuous presence. If... she missed him.

His stomach twisted from the selfish thought of hoping she felt lonely without him there. Yet, he couldn't stop himself from wishing for it, hoping she would one day desperately cling to him.

It was that thought that drove him closer to her location as his sight glowed bright yellow in joy. It hadn't happened yet, but one day he *would* claw her walls down.

However, the moment he approached his home, he knew something was terribly wrong. Someone had purposely brushed dirt into his protective salt circle from the outside to disturb it, but there was also a familiar foul scent in the air.

He didn't need to enter his cave to know that her smell of red apples and frost was light and old, but he did so anyway. Dread crept through his stomach, and he backed out of the entrance with a pounding heart.

The only thing that brought him relief was how he couldn't smell blood and hoped she may not have experienced pain, but he thought he perhaps would have preferred that than to know she'd been taken by *him.*

Nameless let out a deafening roar to the blue sky. *No!*

He didn't hesitate when he turned around, and on all fours, leapt into the forest to chase after them.

What is he doing to her?

If anything, Nameless would prefer a quick death for her, but if the Serpent Demon had taken Delora, he feared he was slowly eating her while she screamed.

She will return to me if she dies. Nameless was the keeper of her soul.

But the Serpent Demon liked to swallow his food in one go – while they were still *alive.* He knew that would be horrifying for her.

His vision turned white, and his body began to morph at just the image of her face filled with agony and fear.

His legs became even more deer-like in shape to support his four-legged position so he could run harder, faster, towards his destination. His arms grew in thickness, supporting his need for added strength to hold up his heavy torso now that he was completely leaning on it. His clothing sunk beneath his flesh as it puffed out, revealing long fur while more feathers protruded from his back, shoulder blades, and thighs.

Although he was following their scent, he knew the only place the Serpent Demon would've taken her was his nest.

His feet clipped against the ground while his hands thudded in quick double strikes. The longer he ran, the more prominent his snorting, exhaling huffs became through his nose hole until he had to part his jaws to let them ease out of his lungs.

He didn't need to go far to get to his destination.

He skidded to a halt when he came to a small clearing backed by thick forest. Human bones lay carelessly upon the ground, with more creating a partial mound.

The opening revealed the Serpent Demon in the middle of the area, holding Delora hostage in his tail.

Her position was limp, with her head slumped back. An arm was loose, as if the Demon wasn't holding her very tightly.

Nameless feared the worst.

He wanted to charge. He wanted to attack. But with how he was holding her, Nameless instead shuffled his feet. He kept his distance so the Serpent Demon wouldn't crush her; he also did not want to accidentally hurt her while trying to fight Delora's captor.

"Is she..." he started, his voice distorted, grainy, and booming due to the shift of his form and the strain that put on his body.

"I didn't give her any of my venom," he answered, cocking his head before squinting his eyes at Nameless as if he was assessing him. "I thought ssshe would wake after I stopped crushing the breath from her. I wanted to talk with her when we returned to my nessst, but ssshe hasss not woken." Then he grinned, uncoiling her chest just enough that there was a gap so he could press his ear between her breasts. "But do not worry, I can hear her breathing."

Nameless eyed the two living humans behind them, one lying limp on top of the other. He knew the Serpent Demon must have given them his sleeping venom by the fact their chests were still rising and falling.

He was saving his meals for later.

"Why did you take Delora?" He bounced the tip of his snout towards the two unconscious humans. *"I can see you have other humans."*

"You are in my territory, and all thingsss in my territory belong to me," he answered coldly, pulling Delora away so he could hold her slightly to the side.

Her head rolled and her glossy black hair dangled that way.

"I was here first!" Nameless roared. *"I found my home long before you arrived here."*

The Serpent Demon let out a horrible hiss, revealing sharp rows of fangs – not one of them flat in shape like a human's – as he opened his wide maw with agitation.

"I fight for it! I allow my kind to roam through it, but you are the only one who insssissstsss on ssstaying. No matter how much I warn you or attack you, you won't leave!"

And no matter how many times they fought, neither had truly won the battle. Nameless had been infected with sleep venom and eaten by the Serpent Demon. Only to emerge once more where his intact skull remained resting on the Veil's cold, hard ground. His head had been too big to swallow with his antlers.

Nameless knew to keep his distance from those lethal fangs. Especially the longest two on his upper mouth that gave the dose of sleeping venom.

Only Demons who had eaten a large quantity of venomous animals and had also eaten a human with the ability to utilise magic could produce something such as magical sleep venom. He'd also heard from Orpheus about an Arachnid Demon who had eaten so many Priests and Priestesses that she had been able to access one's memories and show her victims the faces of their loved ones. She created sorrow in her victims because she liked the taste of their sadness.

Demons like this, nasty but strong, had eaten many humans throughout their lives and were difficult to kill. They were also cruel.

Many bordered the territory he was in, as well as Orpheus' home. Mavka avoided them, as the fight was often bloody and dangerous.

A Mavka's only solace was that if their skull remained intact, no matter where they were or what had happened to them, whether that be partially eaten or wholly, they would return within the span of a day. They would rise from their skull in a gooey form until they settled and their claws, fur, or other features, such as his feathers, grew back.

The growth happened within seconds, and the one time the Serpent Demon had killed him had taught him to always keep his distance. They'd had many claw fights, and there had been a few close calls when Nameless had almost been caught in his tail, but most of the time... he fled.

He never engaged this Demon as he was a formidable foe, but with Delora in his clutches, he *wouldn't* back away now. Even if it cost him pain, even if it meant he'd be forced to sleep, Nameless would try to save her at all costs.

TEN

Restless, Nameless continued to shuffle his weight between his hands, his desire to charge ever growing, and the inability to do so hammered at him.

"Give me Delora," Nameless demanded.

Since Nameless had refused to acknowledge the command and complaint about him remaining in the territory, the Serpent Demon's flat nose crinkled in anger.

He'd already been planning to vacate his cave, but Nameless just needed to wait a little longer before he could. Unfortunately, it didn't look like he'd worked fast enough, and now Delora was in danger due to his lack of efforts.

With a snarl that quietened quickly, the Demon turned Delora until she was facing him, partially blocking Nameless' view of the right side of his body and face.

"What isss your interest in this food?"

"Delora is not food!" Nameless roared, his crimson-filled vision flashing brighter.

She would *never* be food. Not for him, and definitely not for any Demon that laid their filthy eyes upon her!

He took a hesitant step forward in aversion when the Demon brought her closer to sniff at her face.

"Ssshe doesss not sssmell human." Then his red eyes peeked around her to glance at Nameless. "But ssshe once did."

Nameless gave an answering snarl as he realised the Serpent Demon must have been observing them from afar.

"Why isss her sssscent different?" He tilted her slightly with the use of his tail. "What did ssshe become? I sssee sssomething is now glowing between your antlersss."

There was no point in Nameless hiding her soul from his view, despite the urge to. He'd seen it, and he was right. Although he would continue to call her his human because that's what she was to him, Delora had changed when he had eaten her soul.

Nameless refused to tell this creature anything about her. That was until he brought her forward with his fangs near her neck.

"Tell me, or I will envenom her now."

"Phantom," Nameless quickly snapped, darting closer before halting when the Serpent squinted his eyes at him.

Delora was a Phantom, a creature that lived on the cusp of life and death. She could never die; her soul was eternally tied to a living anchor, him.

"I do not know what that–" the Serpent Demon started, before Delora slowly lifted her head.

Nameless couldn't see when she opened her eyes, but he knew she did when she let out a blood-curdling, ear-piercing scream. The smell of her fear burst into the clearing like a wave, calling to his desperate need to protect her. His feathers and fur rose in apprehension.

The Demon reared his head back in surprise before his face marred into a terrible cringe at the sound.

Nameless charged recklessly. He had already leapt less than a few feet away from them before the Demon could dart his head forward to sink his fangs into her neck.

The Serpent Demon yanked her sideways so he could put space between Nameless' maw and his own body. Pushing against Nameless' chest when they went tumbling back, Delora flailed in the air as they twisted and then screamed harder.

Using the thick base of his snake tail to support himself and give him strength, the Demon managed to spin them around to slam Nameless against the ground. He hissed with drool-covered fangs open wide from above.

Nameless snapped his jaws multiple times with clipping sounds when his mouth shut around air. He was pinned against the ground at the rounded ball joints of his shoulders by the

Serpent Demon's hands, while the base of the Demon's long tail kept his hips down. It gave him little room to do anything else but dig his claws into the Demon's chest, sides, and back.

The horrible wailing that came from Delora irritated the Demon enough that he slapped the tip of his tail around her face to quiet her, but it only intensified her fear.

It was thickening in the air, and it made his heart grow tight in sympathy for her.

I have to comfort her before she brings more Demons here. But he couldn't do that.

Instead, he was forced to grab the Serpent Demon around the throat to stop him from darting his head forward to sink his fangs into the arch of his shoulder. He would have gone for the throat, but Nameless' bony snout was blocking a clear path to his neck.

He spared Delora a glance, seeing the whites of her eyes were red and heavy with tears, and her brows were waved into a frown. She wouldn't know it because of his orbs, but he held her stare simply because she refused to look away from him.

Was she pleading for his help? Was the look she was giving him undoubtable trust? Did she know that Nameless would do anything to save her?

He wanted her to have faith in him.

He was the keeper of her soul. He would protect it and her until the end of time.

When it was obvious the Serpent Demon was unable to envenom him, he released one shoulder. With a quick strike, he slashed across Nameless' chest and the end of his snout.

The bone was spared any permanent marring, but his body instantly welled with dark-purple blood. Nameless yelped at the pain, and his efforts doubled.

He squeezed the Demon's thick neck tighter to squish his oesophagus, but the Demon raked his claws over the back of Nameless' hand, ruining the tendons in his fingers before he could squeeze any harder. All he could do now was push his throat to keep him at bay while his other hand cut and gouged into flesh.

The stink of rotten meat leaked from the Demon's wounds, as if his blood was infected with decay.

The Serpent kept them close together as Nameless kicked his feet to get out from under him, to no avail. Under the sheer heavy weight, his tail forced his hips to the ground. Nameless also wanted to stay within striking distance.

He worried that the moment they separated, the Serpent would target Delora.

They each had one hand to strike with until they interlocked their fingers by accident. Nameless curled his fingers through the gaps to dig his claws in between the Demon's hand bones. With another hiss, he released a spray of thick saliva – it was sweet, like it was mixed with his venom – and tried to free his injured hand from Nameless.

He held strong. But there was nothing Nameless could do until he got above him.

The thumping of footsteps in the distance and crushing forest debris was the only warning they received before a small Demon on all fours slid into the clearing. With a harrowing giggle, like a small child with a wheezing cough, it turned its red eyes on Delora with glee.

His orbs flashed white with dread at the newcomer while the Serpent Demon snickered from deep within his nostrils.

"Yessssss! Help me kill the Mavka," he commanded, gaining the attention of the Demon.

Its body appeared to be like a human walking upside down with disjointed elbows and knees.

However, when it opened its mouth, it split its face down the middle from its nose down to its chin. A flailing tongue came out to swipe across its cheek.

It continued to giggle, its red eyes bowing with humour, but neither were prepared when it jumped onto the Serpent's tail and began clawing at it to get to Delora.

A shrill cry came from the Serpent Demon when the smaller one tore at the meaty flesh of his tail with both its hands and feet.

"What are you doing?!" He tried to look over his shoulder at the Demon but was forced to give his attention back to Nameless when he tried to use the Serpent's loss of focus to snap his head forward suddenly. "Do not go after the human. Help me kill the Mavka, and you can have her!"

Delora's feet wiggled like she was kicking as she leaned her head back and away from it. When the smaller Demon started climbing closer to her face, the Serpent Demon whipped his tail and flung it away – only to have it crawling over him again moments later.

Before long, another Demon came. It was even smaller than the first, with wings for arms. It tried to flap up, using its bird-like legs to climb his tail. It was desperately trying to get to the food that was releasing intense pheromones of fear – despite there being other humans in the clearing.

The Serpent Demon slammed his tail down on top of it with Delora still in its hold.

There was no dying scream; it was crushed to death instantly.

The way the Serpent Demon slightly twisted his body gave Nameless enough room so he could roll them over with a claw swipe from his right hand across his face. He squirmed underneath Nameless while clutching at his shredded face, hissing and wailing at the depth of his agony.

He managed to buck Nameless off.

His flailing caused Delora to slide from side to side across the dirt. Bones scattered while the small Demon that originally came into the clearing was forced to dodge the tail as it tried to get closer.

It kept missing when it leapt.

On his way to Delora, Nameless sprinted the few feet separating them and clawed into the small Demon. He swiped at it and sent it flying. Nameless then straddled the Serpent Demon's tail and swiped his claws into it with slashing strikes, knowing that trying to uncoil her would do nothing.

He needed the Serpent Demon to release her of his own volition.

"Please stop crying, Delora," Nameless pleaded while he caught her horrified gaze. She looked so afraid, so helpless, so little and fragile, and his heart clenched tightly at her dirt-covered and tear-stained appearance. *"The smell of your fear is bringing more Demons upon us."*

The inner edge of her brows turned upwards into a pained expression, her eyes bowing. Nameless knew it was an apology even as her tears fell faster. Her scent didn't soften. Now that he was closer, staring directly at her with their faces only a few inches apart, he could see she was visibly trembling.

"Trust that I will save you."

She clenched her eyes shut like she was trying to gain the will and nodded. Her trembling eased ever so slightly, and she took a strong breath through her nose before her eyelids opened once more.

Her vision seemed clearer and less frightened.

Her ease disappeared when her eyes opened wide. It appeared as though she was trying to talk against the tail tip covering her mouth. Nameless tried to rip it from her, but she shook her head and looked past him.

A muffled scream came from her right as Delora's back arched as if she was being crushed, her face wincing horribly.

She had been trying to tell him that the Serpent Demon had risen behind him. He grabbed one of Nameless' antlers and tried to snap his neck.

Unfortunately for the Serpent Demon, who didn't know that Mavka could rotate their necks comfortably almost three hundred and sixty degrees, it only twisted his head around. It allowed Nameless the freedom to tackle him to the ground with a snarling growl.

The small Demon he thought he'd killed tried to claw its way to Delora.

With a hiss, the Serpent Demon got out from underneath him and used his arms to walk around the clearing as Nameless gave chase. When he turned to flee in an opposite direction, his extensive wounds caused him to abandon his grip on Delora to save himself.

He flicked her across the clearing.

Nameless didn't get the chance to assess the horrible *crack* he heard, not when the Serpent Demon suddenly twisted and rose to tower a metre above Nameless. With his fangs bared and his hands raised with clenched fingers to present his lethal claws, the Demon was covered in claw marks and blood from head-to-tail. One of his eyeballs was lost from its socket when Nameless had clawed his face earlier.

With his tail freed from its duty, his agility and mobility would be heightened, and Nameless knew that this fight was going to be even more difficult than before.

But Delora was free from him, giving Nameless the opportunity to be more ruthless. ***I will destroy him!***

He gave a high-pitched war cry before he dove for Nameless, who answered with a rolling, vengeful snarl.

Delora gasped when her body was tossed against a thick, low-hanging branch that snapped under the pressure of her flailing legs. She fell to the ground with a *thwap* that resonated through her. Her head ached like she'd hit it, but she knew the vertigo she felt meant she had whiplash.

Dizziness blurred her vision just enough to make it murky.

Agony shot up and down her right leg because of her knee, but she still weakly tried to get to her hands, one foot, and the opposing knee. Her arms were shaking, and she didn't know if that was from pain, fear, or stress. Her torso strained from being crushed, and her arms and legs ached from being in an uncomfortable position for so long.

She was sure she had a red mark around her face from the Demon's tail. *Everything... hurts.*

Her head shot up when she heard that *creepy* giggle like a five-year-old little girl, and then she let out a shriek when it came straight for her.

Holy fuck! Ohfuckohfuckohfuck! Delora scrambled backwards on her arse after she fell to it, pushing herself with her heels to get away faster.

Just before it could reach her, the Duskwalker's giant body was behind it. He grabbed the Demon by the head with one large hand and both its shoulders with the other, then lifted it off the ground and *tore* it apart right before her very eyes. So close, in fact, that most of its maroon blood splattered over her body.

Delora had been surrounded by red eyes, but it was only his that made her pale from the viciousness with which he'd killed it.

Yet she didn't pale in fear of him, but rather *for* him.

The Duskwalker was covered in claw marks, and seconds later, he was grabbed around one of his hooves and yanked across the ground on his front. He'd risked turning his back on the snake monster again for *her*. To save her.

"You want to sssave her ssso badly?" The Snake Demon crawled over his body with his sharp claws moving in her direction. "I'll make sssure you can't!"

The Duskwalker grabbed him around the middle of his exceptionally long tail and held him back right in front of her. She brought her feet up when the tip of a claw nicked the underside of her left foot, and it gouged at the ground instead.

They both shot forward when the Demon suddenly used his strong, muscled arms to drag himself closer. The Duskwalker lost his footing but was quick to steady himself with one hoof forward.

There was nothing he could do but hold the Demon back. It was obvious the moment he tried anything but holding on, Delora would be rent to pieces within seconds.

"Run, Delora!" the Duskwalker roared, turning his head to her.

He was staring at her rather than his opponent, and that made it all the more frightening.

Without a second thought, she heeded his command, knowing he'd only tell her to flee into the Veil if he thought it was safer. She knew it wasn't. Her limp from her injured knee meant she was a sitting duck.

She pushed forward regardless.

Shrub branches swiped against her face and body, but she didn't care if they cut her. The horrible sounds behind her, that didn't soften no matter how far she ran, were bloodcurdling. She could hear the thumping of bodies hitting the ground, the trees when they rustled under heavy blows, and the hissing and snarls that made her hair stand on end. The Duskwalker gave a horrible, crying *yelp* that echoed over the distance, and Delora clenched her eyes with a sob.

The air felt cold with how fast she was running, chilling her body and adding an extra bite to her shivers. With her eyes closed, her feet stumbled, but not because they'd gotten caught on something. Delora realised just how much her head was throbbing and how dizzy she was.

She was sure the only thing that kept her moving was the adrenaline pumping frantically through her.

Delora wasn't given a chance to breathe as a small Demon began to give chase. She refused to look over her shoulder to see it. She just focused on what was in front of her, which was nothing but darkness and trees.

Within moments, it grabbed her ankle.

She knocked her head again when she hit the ground before she was dragged backwards across the forest floor, its claws slicing down her leg. *Oh Gods! Oh no!* With panicked hands, she managed to grab a broken branch from the ground.

When she was turned over, she screamed and stabbed it forward.

"Yuk!" was its response as she felt resistance when she sunk it into its body.

The only reason she opened her eyes was because nothing was happening. She expected to be bitten.

Bile rose, and she instantly regretted looking when she saw she'd stabbed it right through the eye and straight into its brain. It was lightly thrashing, but she knew she'd managed to kill it as blood ran down her barbaric weapon and coated her arms.

The smell was awful, but she barely registered it. She just heaved its body to the side and found her feet again.

Delora swayed, her knees buckling. Her vision was so murky she couldn't see the tree root directly in front of her and ended up tripping over it. Her body was unbearably numb, and she tried to blink through winking lights so she could see.

I can't run anymore.

She just walked, supporting herself with the occasional tree trunk, unsure of where she was going.

All she knew was she had to flee, that everything was *scary*, so scary, and that she was terrifyingly *alone* in the Veil.

Where... where am I? Where could she go to hide?

It was like her ears were filled with cotton, muting most of the sounds around her. She didn't hear nor see the next Demon she'd brought upon herself. She only knew she was in the clutches of it by the red of its eyes and the fact that it was above her.

Delora didn't fight it.

There was simply no point.

She didn't know where it started or ended. She wanted to fight, to live. She was desperate to take her next breath, but instead, she just lay there.

Something bigger took a hold of it – she could only tell by the silhouette of its body. The deafening, rage-filled roar above her sounded so familiar that it eased her, and the two glowing red orbs that floated in front of a white blurred skull brought her all the comfort she needed.

The Duskwalker was her light in the dark.

Knowing he was there, Delora allowed the dizziness to overcome her.

ELEVEN

Delora felt the gentle sway of her legs as they bounced whenever the Duskwalker cradling her in his arms took a step. Comforting warmth enveloped her, and the smell of vanilla bean and cream hid the smell of rotten blood covering her. She buried her head into rough cloth that was torn enough that she could feel fur tickling her cheek.

Her fear was gone now that she could tell all was quiet, except for the Duskwalker's deep but rhythmic breathing and the sound of his mismatching footsteps.

Being cradled by him, she felt undeniably safe.

Where are we? She didn't know how long she'd been asleep. It must have been days, considering she was no longer in pain.

She knew that wasn't the truth when she opened her eyes to look around. They were deep within the forest with barely any light present, but it was enough that she could tell he was still covered in wounds from his fighting.

Four slashing marks gaped his chest as did the one across his shoulder. His shirt was so torn to pieces that Delora could see white bones. She had thought his entire body would be covered in black fur and feathers.

It took her a while to notice he was limping, and she turned her eyes up to look at the underside of his long bony jaw. His orbs gave off a bright red hue.

"Thank you," she whispered, curling into him while keeping her eyes on his face. He tilted it just enough that he could see her past his snout. "Thank you so much."

He resumed watching where he was going.

"I will always protect you." Delora bit her lips together in reaction to his words. She'd never had someone say something like this to her with such a strong sense of resolve. "I am sorry I could not do more. You were hurt because I failed you."

She shook her head against the bottom of his firm chest.

"Y-you still came for me. You didn't have to save me. I've done nothing to warrant your help."

"You have done more than you know."

Her eyes flittered up to her soul that hung limply between his antlers. *Is it because of that?*

Deciding she didn't want to know, she asked, "Why am I not in any pain?"

From what she could tell, not a single place upon her body was sore or aching. She couldn't feel the slash on her ankle, the bruising in her sprained knee, or even the crushing ache she'd felt in her ribs, hips, and face from the snake Demon's constricting tail. Her head also didn't throb so terribly, and she was able to see clearly.

"I have removed your wounds from your body." His voice sounded strained, and the ends of certain breaths whistled with a quiet whine.

Pity for him assaulted her.

"How did you do that? Not even Priests and Priestesses can heal another so quickly. It takes time to heal a person, and they generally need herbs and symbols."

At least, that's what she'd heard about the way they used their magic. She'd never met one other than to officiate her marriage. There had been two living permanently within her village, but they often distanced themselves from others and always covered their faces and bodies as not to allow any part of them to be seen.

Most didn't like them, as they were believed to be of a strange cult.

"I do not know how to heal wounds. I can only take them for myself and heal them with my own body."

With her eyes widening, she tried to twist so that she could see his leg, but he held her firm so she wouldn't fall.

"Are you limping because of my wounds?"

"You were hurt rather badly. I could not allow you to stay within the Serpent Demon's nest because he was trying to attack you, but perhaps I should not have told you to run. I did not know you had broken something in your knee."

Delora bit her lips together as tears began to well in her eyes. "I'm sorry."

His head turned down to her.

"Why are you crying?" White flashed in his orbs momentarily before returning to red. "Did I not take all of your wounds? Are you still in pain?"

She shook her head. "You're in pain because of me. I couldn't do anything to help and only ran away."

I'm a fucking coward. She clenched her eyes shut in disgrace.

"I do not mind," he reassured, his deep and rich voice holding every bit of sincerity. "This is my sacrifice for you, and I chose it. Your body is too delicate and small to ever be in lasting pain."

Delicate and small? Those words hadn't been used to describe her appearance in such a long time that she could barely believe they'd been uttered.

She opened her mouth to refute him, but then realised she was being held by a gigantic Duskwalker who was towering, strong, and completely different to a human.

He'd survived against that frightful Demon, whereas any human would have been torn to pieces. She knew the only reason she'd survived was because she had been used to taunt him.

A rustling sound in the distance made her jump in his arms, and her eyes darted with panic around the thick brush.

"Did you kill it? That Demon."

"Yes. Thanks to you being there and bringing more Demons, I was able to kill him when I have never been able to before."

It'd been so strong that Delora had thought they were both going to die. She didn't care enough to know how he'd killed it. They were alive, and it, thankfully, wasn't.

She was sure she was going to have nightmares because of it.

Perhaps nightmares of it would be better than the ones I've been having. Delora didn't mind being spooked, but her current dreams left her mind feeling frayed and clogged with terrible thoughts.

"A-and what happened to the other humans I saw?"

Did... he eat them? She realised she didn't actually want to know if he did.

"I do not know. I came to find you, but I am sure other Demons came."

Silence fell upon them, and she took in the mismatched thud of his feet, the way the debris of the forest floor crunched beneath him, and his pain-filled breaths. She closed her eyes and secretly leaned her head against his chest so she could try to find his heartbeat.

Tha-thump. Tha-thump. Tha-thump...

Once she found that strong pounding, any tension in her body eased. It didn't matter that he was different, a monster, a strange creature. A Duskwalker. He'd been kind to her, and she'd *never* be able to forget what he'd done for her.

"Magnar," she quietly mumbled as she opened her eyes.

His head cocked before tilting upwards slightly, like he was trying to think. His floating orbs turned reddish pink for a moment – something she was beginning to discern was a sign of embarrassment.

"I do not know what that word means."

Fidgeting with her fingers in front of her chest, a small flare of heat assaulted her cheeks.

"It's a name that means strong and fierce warrior, a protector." When he suddenly halted from walking and pointed his head downwards to look upon her, Delora's cheeks burned hotter. She averted her gaze. "I'm sorry. I'm not really good with stuff like this, naming things, but if you don't like it, I can think of something else."

But he was her protector, which is why that name had come to her. She liked it for him, but she would think of something better if he hated it.

"Magnar is your name for me?" he asked, his tone laced with curiosity.

"Yeah, but if you don't–"

"I have a name!" he yelled with joy, his eyes turning bright yellow as he leapt, making Delora squeal in surprise when they both went into the air.

He almost fell when he landed back onto his injured leg, stumbling to right his footing so he didn't drop her. Then he spun in a circle while lowering his skull so he could press the side of his jawbone against the entire side of her face.

"I like it. I like my name. I like that you chose it for me."

He began to nuzzle her, and tenderness bloomed within her chest. Her lips quirked like they wanted to curl upwards.

"Magnar," she whispered as she brought her hands up to cup the end of his snout to return his little embrace.

She watched his floating orbs turn a bright flamingo pink at the same time his body seemed to shudder in pleasure. He nuzzled even deeper against her.

Her heart warmed at how he was reacting to something as simple as a name, and she watched her blackened soul *crack* in her periphery. A fissure emerged across the stomach with an orange glow, like when a burning coal was struck with a poker to reveal the hot ore beneath its charcoal state.

Delora blinked at it.

Something just happened to my soul.

TWELVE

Delora sat in the nest within Magnar's cave, watching as he collected random items he had lying around. They'd both woken not long ago after their stressful evening the day before, and he'd disturbed her when he'd begun loudly digging through his things.

He'd lit the used candle that was on the floor in the middle of his cave to allow her to see what he was doing.

The flickering flame brought to light that he was still terribly injured, and despite the fact that they were no longer bleeding, his wounds didn't appear to be healing.

She'd offered to wash them, but there were too many of them for her to bandage. When he told her not to worry about either, since any infection he got would disappear with his wounds, she'd grown dismayed.

He didn't seem to understand that she just wanted to help him in some way.

Even though he said they'd heal, it worried her that they appeared to be in the same state as they were before they'd gone to sleep.

She was clean since she'd kicked him out of his own cave so she could wash herself with a bucket and cloth. She was also wearing a different shirt he owned.

Magnar hadn't bothered to change, considering he'd ruin his new clothing with blood.

He eventually stood facing the wall where everything he'd collected rested, tapping at the side of his snout with a claw. When it appeared as though he was satisfied, he began placing all the items into the square cloth he'd placed on the ground next to them.

Just as she was about to ask him what he was doing, something miraculous happened before her very eyes.

While he was crouching down, black sand appeared out of thin air and began wrapping around his body. Her eyes widened in surprise, but it was like he didn't seem to notice what was happening or didn't care. When it started filling his wounds, it bubbled like black goop and attached itself to the seams before lacing to the other side.

She watched as his wounds mended shut and then instantly vanished.

"Holy shit," she whispered when his entire body was healed within a matter of seconds.

He shook his body to disturb the remaining black sand that circled him as if it was checking his body for more wounds, before fading into nothingness. Magnar scratched at himself in a few places he had once been injured and then grabbed his clothes to go outside.

"Why are you leaving?" she asked, unsure as to why he felt the need for privacy.

She knew he didn't have anything to hide. He was covered in fur, and she had never felt any genitalia on him after all.

He paused at the entranceway.

"I do not wish to frighten you."

Before she could respond, he left, giving her no opportunity to ease his anxiety about her seeing his body.

Is what is under his clothing that bad? His body mostly appeared humanoid but with fur and feathers. She didn't think it was that bad.

When he returned moments later, he grabbed a dumped piece of cloth that, when spread apart, was obviously a cloak. He slung it across the back of his shoulders before tying it together around his neck. There was a hood on the back of it that had two unbuttoned sections that appeared as though they would button around his antlers to cover his head.

"I would prefer to carry you for your own safety," he said while, almost shyly, scratching at the side of the nose hole of his snout. "But I am wondering if you would prefer to walk by yourself. It will take us most of the night if you do."

Delora shot her eyes to the entrance to peer outside with a frown.

"Are we going somewhere?"

He approached and held his hand out to her, his fingers long, but thick and welcoming.

"I am realising that it is not safe to keep you here. I thought the salt circle would be enough to protect you, but I did not think the smarter Demons would understand that all they needed to do was throw dirt onto the circle to disturb it."

Her trust in him was the only reason she reached up to slip her hand into his, allowing it to swallow her own as he lifted her to her feet with care. Then he guided her out of the nest.

"Where are you taking me then?"

When she released his hand, she nervously gripped at the shirt that was far too big for her, even though she mostly filled it out around the chest and stomach area. Although it was long enough to come above her knees, this wasn't something she could just walk around in willy-nilly.

Imagine if another human saw me. Or, rather, them together.

He walked back to the cloth and folded it over the bits of rope, the candles, the bowls, and everything else he'd put in it before he lifted it and wrapped it around his back like a satchel. He tied two sides of it across his chest by going under one arm and over the shoulder of the opposing one.

He can't take me above the surface. Humans will probably attack him, especially Demonslayers.

As much as she hated the cave, if it was safer for *both* of them, then she would help to make it as secure as possible so they could stay here.

"Do not be afraid," he said as he turned to her. "But I will be taking you deeper into the Veil. Almost half a day's walk for me, in fact."

Her face paled. "Deeper? How will that be any safer?"

He was talking about taking her deeper into where Demons lived. That was suicidal.

"Trust me, Delora," he beckoned. "I can carry you to ensure

your safety while we walk. It will also mean we can move faster than your small legs will allow, and the quicker we get there, the better." Delora felt like he was making as many excuses as he could when he added, "I will also keep you warm."

Although it was autumn, she hadn't found the temperature too unbearable in the Veil yet, considering its constant shadows.

With a sigh and a bashful glance at his face, she stepped closer and nodded.

He was slow as he crouched down with his arms moving around her body. He gently pulled her from her feet to cradle her within his arms like he'd done when he'd brought them back to his cave.

"Cover yourself as much as you can with my cloak to hide your body."

Delora did as she was told until all that was poking out from it was part of her face.

"Are we going to come back here?" she asked as he ducked through the low entranceway.

"No, we will not need to. I have taken everything I care to carry. Our new home will be much better."

His strides were fast, but not uncomfortable, as he took them into the forest. Delora clenched her eyes shut once they broke through the tree line and were surrounded by darkness. The sun was setting, making the Veil all the more eerie.

He stopped but held her tighter, as if he was attempting to give her a comforting embrace.

"Control your fear. Anything moving in the Veil can be targeted, but the fact that you no longer smell human and that most Demons do not attack Mavka means this will not be too dangerous. However, the smell of your fear, even if it is a little, will cause us to be attacked." He turned his sight down to her, and she held his green orbs. "Trust that I will protect you."

With a deep breath, she tried to calm her heart that had begun to race and felt herself easing on her exhale. He nodded and started walking.

Like before, she bounced in his arms, and Delora spent the long walk quietly contemplating everything.

The terrible events with the Demons had stolen some of her

darker thoughts from before she'd been tossed into the Veil, and it allowed her a brief time to let her mind not fixate on them.

"Magnar..."

He immediately turned his head to her.

"I like this," he stated before she could speak. "I understand why a name is so important now. I know you are speaking to me directly, and I understand that I will always respond to it."

She wondered who he'd been having conversations with to know what a name was and how it made everyone an individual.

She didn't comment on it.

"What is a Phantom? How come my scent has changed, and what does that really mean for me?"

"You will never die and will always be by my side. I believe a part of you is dead, and I think if I was to die, you would perish also. But for now, you have a beating heart, and that is all that matters."

"Is there anything more you can explain to me about it?"

"Hmm." His head cocked a little as it turned to the canopy of trees above. "If you are to die, in body but not in spirit, you will come back to me after a short period of time."

"Oh," she gasped. "So that's what you meant when you said I'd be by your side for eternity. What if I was to run away though?"

An *immediate* growl rumbled from his chest and vibrated against her side, causing her eyes to open wide. His orbs turned a bright crimson red.

"You will always return to me," he said with that growl present in his tone, making it seem more threatening. "And I will hunt for you until you do."

She didn't like that she could feel his claws digging into her skin.

"I didn't mean I was going to," she quickly interjected. "I just didn't understand how I would always be by your side if I was to leave."

"Whether you leave, or I leave, you will return to me – no matter where I am in the world. I am your anchor, and your body cannot be without the presence of your soul."

"So, I'm like a Ghost?"

As far as she knew, Ghosts were attached to an anchor like a house, a doll, or a specific tree – a place where they may have died or something they were attached to when they were alive.

"Yes, and you can also turn transparent." His eyes eventually faded back to their normal green, and he gave a thoughtful hum. "You are suddenly curious about this when you were not before."

"That's because I hadn't cared about anything," she mumbled, but even she was surprised she was feeling a little livelier than she did before. She still felt rather numb, but it didn't seem as overwhelming. "What do you mean, I can turn transparent? Like... can I turn into a Ghost or something at will?"

"Yes." Her eyes widened at his admission, and she wondered how she was supposed to do that. It sounded so freaky! "But do not try to do so now. You will be out of my arms when you turn solid, and that is not safe."

Delora nodded but continued to contemplate this.

If I had known about this earlier, I could have escaped that awful Demon. She wished he'd told her. Or rather, she wished she hadn't been so careless about this sudden change in her that could have prevented them both from getting hurt.

After a while of Delora dozing off into a half-awake state, unable to fall asleep due to the dangers around them, she noticed the area just in front of them seemed brighter. It was the only change she'd seen in the environment in their many hours of walking.

They were heading in that direction, and a small gasp left her parted lips.

She thought her eyes might have shined with the reflection of the luminescence that radiated against the ground in a barely noticeable glare. It was a spike of an iridescent green magic symbol connected to a massive circle that ran around a partially cleared area.

Trees still heavily dotted within the circle, and when they got closer to the middle, there appeared to be an eleven-pointed star. Its points almost appeared like swords with nautical points in between them. It was bordered by two circles, the inner one much thinner than the outer one.

Like his glowing orbs, it wasn't a light. When she looked

down to his hoofed feet, barely any of it illuminated except for what directly touched the ground.

"What is it?" she asked, but her growing state of shock intensified when she saw the shadowy silhouette of a *building* at the centre point of that strange, dim glow. "There's a house?"

Delora couldn't believe there was something like a house in the middle of the Veil!

"It's a protection ward," Magnar answered, placing her on the ground when it was obvious her squirming meant she wanted to be put down. "I cast it in order to protect the surrounding area from Demons."

"So, it's safe? How did a house come to be here anyway?"

Her eyes drifted over the shadow of the building, but she couldn't see it well because of the lack of light. She couldn't wait until the sun was shining so she could take in its details properly.

"It should be far safer than the salt circle. And as for your question of how it came to be, I have been building it."

Delora swiftly turned to him with her jaw ajar. "*You?*"

He turned his gaze away from her to sweep it over the area himself.

"I started a few months ago." He scratched at the feathers around the back of his neck. "I know humans do not like living in caves, and that when I found a human who wanted to give me their soul, I needed to build it for them so they would be comfortable."

Something stirred in her chest, perhaps warmth and tenderness mixed into one, as her face softened with these fuzzy emotions.

"So, you built this... for me?"

That's all she could think. He may not have known she would be the one to give her soul to him, but she was the one who had, which meant he'd been doing all this for *her*. She'd never had anyone go to such extreme extents just for her sake.

He seemed to like that her mind came to this conclusion because his glowing orbs changed into a bright yellow in her direction.

"Yes. I have been doing this all for you so that you would be happy here with me."

Delora turned back to look at the house as he came to stand next to her.

"How come you didn't bring me here earlier? I would have preferred to come here than stay in the cave."

"Ah," he muttered, his orbs turning a reddish pink. "Because it is not ready. I still have a lot of work to do, but the inside is at least secure."

Magnar allowed his sight to drift from the house he could see clearly in the dark to Delora, who was staring upon all the work he'd done so far. For the first time since she'd fallen on top of him all those days ago, her expression didn't appear saddened or cold. It radiated with awe, and although her lips didn't curl into any form of smile, the sparkle in her eyes was wonderous to him.

He'd planned to start coming here and work on building this place further for her in secret – he would have run the distance in his more monstrous form to save time. However, the moment he'd realised that the salt circle wasn't enough to leave her there without his presence, Magnar knew he couldn't wait.

Even if she was a little uncomfortable, or having her around made him insecure about how much he thought this place was lacking, her safety was his priority.

He was sure her look of awe would fade once she saw it in the light.

Despite his doubts, he stepped forward to lead the way with hope that perhaps she would like it, even if it was barren and unprepared. Delora had come into his life too soon, but he would try to make the best of it as he could.

Perhaps she would like to help me. The idea of that elated him.

He wouldn't allow her to do any hard work since he was content with doing it, but he wondered if they could shape this place together.

Magnar wanted her to see this as her home.

"W-wait," she said, grasping his wrist with her hand. When he turned to look at her with a twist of puzzlement, Delora glanced around the area before bringing her eyes back to him. "I can't see properly."

Delora had never reached for him before, and he was unsure of what to do. Magnar allowed her to hold his wrist to guide her as he slowed his pace to keep within her strides.

His sight spanned over the entire log-cabin house he'd been building. Although the outside was secure and weatherproof, it still required much work.

The windows were boarded up as he didn't have the glass required for them, but he wanted to keep dirt, dust, and leaf debris from blowing inside. The door was something he was working on and was only a couple of logs attached to each other by rope that were then attached to one of the logs that acted as a doorframe. There was no latch or lock, and he eventually wanted to obtain a proper door, similar to what Orpheus had for his own home.

There was a walkway to a porch, but he hadn't finished the fencing for it yet, nor the roof and its supports.

He slowed even more when she nearly tripped on the first step of the porch. Magnar waited for her to make her way up all four of them until her feet found the flat, even surface.

Just as he went to push the door open, he paused.

While he was nervous, he also wanted Delora to see the inside in its entirety.

"Wait here."

He abandoned Delora so he could open the creaking door and then closed it behind him.

Removing the makeshift cloth bag from around his torso and gently placing it on the ground, he pulled some candles and matches from it. He was thankful he'd obtained these items before Delora came.

He grabbed the candles with thicker bases, having learned the thin ones didn't stand on their own, and placed them on the ground sporadically before lighting them.

He shuffled his weight on his hooves as he looked around.

There was no furniture, no interior walls, no cooking hearth. There was nothing but the temporary nest he'd made so he could sleep here when he didn't need to go back to his cave. It was sitting in the corner against the wall on the side opposite the door.

"Magnar?" Delora asked from behind the door before he heard her hands pushing against it.

It was obvious he'd been taking too long and she was impatient to see. Rushing forward, he opened the door, and her body shone in the dim light he'd created.

When he stepped out of the way so she could come inside, he watched her lips part as she took in the fairly large interior of the house. It was wide and quite a few metres long.

Her eyes scanned the area. "There are no rooms?"

He shook his head, incidentally causing the sound of rattling bones to clack from him.

"No. I have not made them yet."

As soon as she was in the middle, she spun in a lazy circle. The house was tall to accommodate his height with his antlers, but she seemed dwarfed in comparison to its size.

Did I make it too big? He thought it was about the same size as Orpheus' home, which he'd only entered once so he could understand what the inside was to, at some point, look like. But he wondered if perhaps he'd made a mistake.

"And you made this?" She turned her brown eyes to him.

Magnar thought he saw a flicker of *something* when the firelight reflected in them.

Was it appreciation? Disappointment? He didn't know humans well enough to know what her expression was.

Is her ability to smile broken? If she had smiled, he may have understood better.

"This is really awesome, Magnar." Her voice was light and uplifted, making his body sigh out with relief when she spun in a circle again. "I can't wait to see what it looks like when you're done. You're really talented."

Yellow brightened his orbs, and he scratched at his snout with bashfulness. "Really? You like it?"

"Well, yeah. I could never build a house." She gave a small shrug. "It's pretty barren, but I'm sure it will look great once you're done."

She likes it! Magnar almost bounced on his feet with glee, but instead, he rushed into action. He came up beside her and pointed to the back of the house.

"I was intending to make three rooms. Apparently, you humans need a washing area and prefer to have your own space. I was going to put where I should sleep at the back so that the washing area and your room would be facing each other." He then made his way to the left and lifted his hands in front of a large area. "I was going to put what is called a *kitchen* here, with something that you could use to cook. And over here" – he walked past her to where his nest currently was – "I was going to put a seating area with a fireplace so you do not get cold. Apparently, you humans get cold in winter, as you do not have fur or feathers. And then here–"

When he turned around to point where she was standing, he paused, noticing her look had softened into something lovely. Her eyes that had always appeared bleak seemed gentled to the point even the dark circles under them didn't appear so prominent. Her mouth had tightened, but the ends were no longer pointing downwards. They were curled upwards just ever so slightly.

Even her posture had drooped, like she was relaxed, while her head had tilted slightly.

Magnar wanted to ask what her expression meant, but he didn't want to seem ignorant.

Why is she staring at me like that? He didn't know why his heart began to thump wildly in his chest. *And why does she look so... pretty right now?*

THIRTEEN

Delora had never seen anything more adorable than watching this massive, scary-looking Duskwalker dashing around to show her his plans in obvious excitement.

When he stopped to stare at her, Delora thought she may have been standing in the way since his finger had come up to point where her feet were.

She gestured to the ground while stepping to the side.

"And here?"

Something about his delight had touched her. She didn't want him to stop on her account.

Instead of explaining, he came forward and reached out. He glided the back of his claw tips against her jaw and over her ear so he could brush them into her long hair.

"If you do not like the design, you can change it."

Delora had almost backed away from him, but his words kept her feet where they were as she accepted his touch. She even turned her eyes upwards so she could stare at him with them only a few inches apart.

I never realised he was so tall. Delora only came to the bottom of his chest, and she had to crane her head up to meet his gaze.

"It's fine," she answered. "I don't mind what you do with it."

Even though she responded, it seemed as though their conversation was forgotten. He leaned his head to the side while coming closer to inspect his fingers tangling in her hair. Magnar pulled them away, only to comb them in again playfully, as though he was tantalised by the simple strands. A delicious shiver rushed over her body when his claws scraped against her skin.

Then, the very sharp tips of them raked over her nape. A breathy gasp fell from her as shivers danced all the way to her legs. Delora's knees almost gave in when he leaned even closer and sniffed just behind her ear, as if he couldn't stop himself from taking in her scent directly from her.

Thankfully, he'd been there to support her when she accidentally leaned into him, but she let out a squeal when he swiftly picked her up a moment later.

She was beginning to get used to being held, which was something she never thought she'd ever be comfortable with, but it was hard to feel wary of being dropped when he was so strong.

He always made sure she was secure in the cradle of his arms.

"Why are you putting me in here?" Delora asked when he carefully placed her on the furs in the middle of the nest with her feet under her so she was sitting on her knees.

"You almost fell," he answered, causing her cheeks to heat in embarrassment.

She couldn't believe the simple touch of a Duskwalker made her knees go weak. *I think I even moaned!* The urge to cover her face in embarrassment assaulted her.

However, Magnar entered the nest as well and sat directly in front of her with his legs crossed. Before she could stop him, he reached forward to grab a few strands of her hair and pulled them over her shoulder so he could examine them.

"Your hair is lovely." He leaned forward to sniff the ends of it. "I like that it is black. That your colouring is like mine."

His comment made her look at the darkness of both her hair and his hand. The fur covering the back of it went down his wrist before it disappeared under the sleeve of his shirt. He still seemed darker, with almost a blueish tint, but she stopped comparing them and just observed his hand.

It was large and belonged to what anyone would call a monster. But Magnar had used that same hand to protect her, had used those deadly claws to touch her so gently that she'd shivered from the touch.

That's why when he pressed it against the side of her neck and face, covering her in such welcoming warmth, Delora didn't pull away from him.

She did wince when he stroked his thumb over her cheek and his claw almost stabbed into her eye.

"Your skin is silky."

There was a part of her that had always known he wanted to touch, but she'd rejected him up until this point because she'd found the idea of it abhorrent. Not anymore.

"C-could you be more careful of your claws?" she begged when he touched over her cheek a second time and she quickly had to shut her eye, otherwise he would have poked her in it.

"Am I allowed to touch more if I do this?"

He brought his hand back and his claws *retracted*. She didn't know he could do that.

"Yes. As long as you don't hurt me, I don't mind if you touch."

What could be so bad anyway? As she said, if he didn't hurt her, she couldn't see the harm in it. She was a human woman, and he was a male Duskwalker – from what she could tell – but she doubted he'd understand what some of her body was meant to do. Sex or intimate play with him didn't seem likely, or rather, at least instigated by him.

His floating orbs turned yellow with what she gathered was joy. "I would never hurt you, Delora."

He started caressing parts of her face. He started with her cheek, then his thumb ran over her eyebrows with the direction of the hair and then strangely, the opposite way. His touch was gentle as he almost tickled her lips, and he grew fascinated by this place.

He brushed the fuller lower one over and over again. It was almost how a lover did when they wanted to kiss but were resisting the urge and instead trying to entice the other to make that leap.

While he was doing this, she couldn't break away from looking up at him. Her eyes were unfocused as she thought, *I just realised I probably won't have sex again.* Delora hadn't been too fond of her past experiences with Hadith, but there had been a handful of times, mostly in the beginning, that she'd enjoyed herself.

Once Hadith had discovered that she couldn't just come because of a few lame dick prods, he grew lazy and only thought of himself. She'd made herself come when he wasn't around to satisfy her urges.

That only pushed her to feel more alone.

She couldn't decide if she was relieved she wouldn't have to go through that anymore or disappointed. It may not have been great sex, but it was sex with someone, connection with another, with enjoyment being the goal.

Her vision refocused back to the Duskwalker in front of her, who had just run his thumb up the curve of her nose before tickling across her eyelashes on one side. Then her eyes followed his hand, or rather, his fingers.

They're so long... and thick. Now that she knew his claws could retract, they could go into places she hadn't thought possible. *Just two would be bigger than most men's dicks.*

Her face heated, especially when her inner walls clenched, and she had to squeeze her thighs together. She couldn't believe she had been toying with the idea of him, a Duskwalker, fingering her!

Oh my gods. What's wrong with me?

Lost to her own shocking thoughts, she hadn't realised his hand had been travelling downwards until he grasped one of her breasts.

Delora flinched. Then she held his wrist to stop him, her face so hot and flustered she feared her head would explode. Her mind, that hadn't been thinking innocently, couldn't handle him touching an intimate place right then! She knew he'd eventually go there, but she hadn't thought she would be thinking about him in that way when he did.

Her nipples were even hard and more sensitive than before.

"C-could you touch somewhere else for now?"

He gave a puzzled head tilt.

"Why?" Then he had the *audacity* to bring his other hand up and hold the other, lifting its weight completely in his palm. "I like this place. It is squishy."

To demonstrate this, he squeezed both, and they moulded into the spaces between his fingers.

"Ah, because..."

How was Delora supposed to explain that her breasts were an intimate place on her body without having to further explain what that meant?

"You can touch me here too," he offered, grabbing her hand to place it against his chest.

His chest was strong and firm, filled with hard muscle. Her mind blanked on why his own hand placement wasn't wise when she gave his pectoral muscle a squeeze – an appreciative one.

Hadith had been muscular since he'd worked most of his life as a guard for the town, but Magnar's body was *dense,* like his lean frame was hiding his strength until it was touched.

Mesmerised by the feeling of it under her palm, and the fact she got the impression of fur moving underneath his shirt, she continued to knead his pectoral muscle. She also thought she could feel something... hard sitting over the top of his flesh where his rib bones would be.

"Although we mostly have the same form," Magnar said when one of his thumbs curiously brushed over a hardened nipple, "this place is different to mine. Do all females have such mounds on their chests?"

Delora looked down to see her breast filled only half his big hand. But it still *filled* it whereas a smaller woman wouldn't have.

"I guess some don't have such big ones," she mumbled. Her core spasmed when he *flicked* a nipple with his thumb. "We call them breasts."

He nodded, and she was thankful he didn't ask what their function was. Instead, both his hands lowered. He grabbed the fat of her stomach, squishing it in his hands.

Delora jumped back in surprise.

When he leaned forward to do it again, she grabbed both his hands to stop him.

"Please don't touch me there. I don't like my stomach being grabbed."

Magnar had just gone ahead and squeezed the rolls of her

belly without care.

"But I like this place on you," he grumbled disappointedly, his orbs turning blue. "It is soft. I like that you are soft all over. You are bigger than the other human I know."

Delora's lips parted in shock as her eyes widened.

"Did you just call me fat?"

Did a Duskwalker really just call me fucking fat? She couldn't believe it!

He tilted his head with obvious lack of understanding.

"Is that why you are bigger? Because you are fat?" He then proceeded to poke the side of her stomach. "It makes you fit in my arms better."

Delora sighed when she registered that he truly didn't mean anything bad by it. She didn't realise she'd been anxious about this until now. She'd never seen anything wrong with her size except for how Hadith had treated her, but now that he was gone and this Duskwalker seemed to prefer her this way, a burden was lifted off her shoulders.

How can such a creature be more accepting than most humans I know? She almost wanted to cuddle into him in appreciation.

Then her brows drew together from something he said earlier.

"Wait... You said you know another human?"

Magnar nodded as he, what he probably thought was slyly, eased closer so he could grasp her thigh below her shirt and touch her skin directly. Green lifted back into his orbs.

"Yes. Reia." He kneaded her flesh, his big hand barely wrapping over the top of her plump thigh. "She is bonded to a different Mavka named Orpheus."

When his palm started sliding upwards, Delora shoved her hand against her pubic mound so he couldn't go curiously exploring in places he shouldn't.

"There is another Duskwalker who has a human?" His hand slipped under her shirt, and he grasped the meaty handles of her hips. She chose to ignore it in the interest of their conversation. "Are they the ones that taught you everything?"

"Yes," he answered once more. "They told me to build you this house so that you will be happier with me. The cave is bad.

Too dark and dirty, they said."

A puzzle piece clicked into place.

I'm not the only human who has given their soul to a Duskwalker. She was surprised, but also relieved. She thought she would be stuck with Magnar by herself, never to see another human again, but this Reia person could be someone she could speak to.

Then again... people had been cruel to her in the recent past. She was uncertain if she would really want to be under the scrutiny of another human being.

Could... this Reia make him realise that I'm actually a terrible person? The idea of losing this sweet and gentle creature, that was being delicate with her body and kind to her with his words and actions, left a hollow feeling in her chest.

When Magnar delved down to grab her backside, his gliding hand caused her skin to prickle with goosebumps. Delora held his wrist to stop him. His hands were starting to go to places she wasn't quite sure she wanted them to, and yet her body was starting to... tingle in anticipation of him doing so.

"I-I think that's enough touching for today," she mumbled as she brought his hand forward. "I'm a little tired after our walk, and I'm sure it's late."

Not that she could really tell since the Veil was mostly dark.

FOURTEEN

The snake-like Demon coiled its slithery tail around Delora's entire body tighter and tighter until she was unable to breathe. It was like they were floating under deep, endless water as she tried to scream into the void that surrounded them. She couldn't see the ground, couldn't see the sky.

Her eyes searched the empty horizons, desperately seeking a saviour.

When she saw Magnar, his Duskwalker form highlighted in dim light that came from nowhere, she managed to wrangle an arm between the coils and reach for him.

His green floating orbs offered her the only comfort she could find. Their lights were like a beacon to shine over her fear and brighten her out of darkness.

"H-help me," she begged, her voice straining under her collapsing lungs. "Please."

"**No,**" he answered coldly, and the comforting green faded away to the flaring red of rage. "He has told me what you have done."

Just when she was about to ask who, Hadith materialised beside him in the void as a tall, muscled brute with short hair and a beard. Her face paled at seeing him alive.

"Murderer!" Hadith yelled, stepping forward and suddenly turning into the corpse she'd left behind.

His clean brown hair turned sloppy with blood. It covered the sides of him as though blood seeped from his wounds in his back and over the sides of his body.

"You murdered people," Magnar stated with a growl.

"So have you!" she rebuffed, still reaching forward for his help. Her arm was suddenly swallowed up by the snake's limb that refused to relent.

He turned his back to her and stepped away. "But I do not know any better."

He suddenly vanished into thin air in a puff of black glittering sand.

"Please!" Tears welled in her eyes before they fell in heavy drops. "Don't leave me here like this!"

"It's what you deserve," Hadith gritted through his blood-covered teeth, more of it dripping from his mouth to dribble down his chin. "You will always be abandoned. Will always be alone. Nothing *will want you."*

"Come here, tasssty human," the Snake Demon hissed as he turned her away from Hadith. She was forced to stare directly into the wide maw of his mouth as he opened it. "I'll rid the world of your terrible presssence."

With the white glow of the afterlife present in the back of his throat, his fangs spread further around her head.

It was as if he intended to swallow it whole.

Delora woke with a start, sitting up in the nest with her breaths sawing in and out of her rapidly. Her gasp awake was a reflection of her scream in her dream, and she swiftly looked around with darting, panicked eyes.

Within seconds, Magnar was next to her, crouching on the other side of the nest. She didn't mean to jump away from him in fright, but she flinched regardless.

He retracted the hand he was using to reach for her, perhaps to pet her hair comfortingly, and placed it on the nest wall to steady himself in his crouched position.

"What is the matter?" The green she *needed* to see in his floating orbs was instead a colourless white. "You reek of fear, Delora."

It was just a dream. She placed one of her shaking hands against her forehead to rub it, sweat dotting her brow. Then she used her palms to rub into her closed eyes to rid herself of her sleep. *I wish the nightmares would stop.*

They were mostly of Hadith, always of what she'd done. Of blood, screams, and tears. Sometimes he was the one to push her off the edge of the Veil's cliff walls. Other times, he'd manage to wrangle the blade from her and stab her with it instead.

Occasionally, Cindy appeared just to scream, and she hated how scared the girl sounded.

She'd have perverted dreams of Cindy and Hadith together, fucking as they made fun of her. It was as if Delora was a fly on the wall, unable to do anything but bear witness.

After being taken by that terrifying Demon, Delora had begun dreaming of it. Sometimes Hadith wouldn't appear, but sometimes he'd come to watch her being eaten with a revengeful grin. She hated it the most when the Demon's face turned into Hadith's. It had been two nights since then, but she kept waking only to go back into a new chaos.

However, that was the first time Delora had dreamed of Magnar.

"I'm sorry," she said behind her hands until she lowered them. "I just had a bad dream, is all."

She would probably count that as the worst one she'd had yet.

Sitting there for a few moments staring at her feet blankly, she wondered when she'd started caring for Magnar to this degree.

"Is... there a way I can fight your dreams for you?" he asked, his tone laden with so much concern it made her eyes bow. "I do not like that you are afraid of them."

"No," she answered, her voice breaking.

His head tilted before he grabbed a small wooden bowl that had been on the ground and offered it to her. Inside was a small handful of blueberries, raspberries, a strawberry, a carrot that appeared to have been washed, and even a random lemon she wouldn't be able to eat.

"Will food help?"

He grabbed a blueberry and tried to feed it to her like he often did.

Tears collected to the point she couldn't stem them, and they fell as she parted her lips to take the berry. He fed her silently as she cried, her body heaving.

Magnar didn't seem to mind her pathetic tears, content with caring for her until there was nothing remaining in the bowl except for the lemon. Delora was so thankful he didn't back away like most men would at the awkwardness of this and didn't pressure her to talk about her problems when she didn't want to.

She just wanted to cry. At least she was able to now, whereas before, she'd felt so empty.

"It is bright outside. Would you like to see the rest of our home?" he asked as he brought a shallow bowl of water to her lips and made her drink. "I am excited to show you."

No. Delora wanted to lie on her side in the nest and weep.

The only reason she nodded was because he had said he was excited. *I don't want to disappoint him.*

After helping her to her feet, Magnar led her to the door and opened it, revealing patches of sunlight that managed to touch the earth. They were small as there were too many trees to allow wider gaps, but she never expected the sun to be able to reach the ground at all.

She noted the porch didn't have fencing or a roof but could tell there were plans to eventually add them.

She could still see the green magic symbol that was only lost in the small areas of bright sunshine. The grass around the yard was patchy, as it was evident that many trees had been dug up. Someone had covered a few holes with dirt to make those spots flat.

The sun was mostly around the porch and house since inside the protective ward there was still much of the forest present.

"I thought you said the protective circle only kept those out from walking across it," Delora commented. "Couldn't Demons just climb the trees and pass through?"

Magnar shook his head. "That is only for the salt circle. This ward creates a dome."

As if to demonstrate this, he pointed upwards. It took a moment, but she eventually spotted the glittering of green above them in the sky.

When her feet found the dirt at the bottom of the porch, she took a few steps and turned around to look at the house. It was made of logs from walls to roof but appeared structurally sound, and it seemed even bigger from the outside.

Magnar walked to the left, and Delora followed.

Eventually, they made their way to the very back of the house. Once there, she discovered a large fenced-off area where a few small shrubs and plants appeared to be growing. The trees backing it had been pulled out of the ground more here, and she could see the sun washing over it completely to the fence line.

"This is the garden," he told her, scratching at the side of his neck feathers. "But it is not ready. Much of it died at first, but I am learning how to better take care of it. I did not know some plants required more water than others."

"There looks like there is so much here."

Delora walked around the fence line until she made it to the gap that allowed her to go inside and properly examine what was growing. She could see the stems of different vegetables, many fruits, and a vast number of herbs – some even looked ready to be picked.

Magnar didn't join her. He made his way over to a spot that was diagonal from the side of the house where a young tree was growing. It was no bigger than her hip and appeared as though it would take years to mature.

"You smell like apples, like this tree. I am glad I chose this one to grow rather than the other fruit trees."

Delora perked her head up in his direction and blinked her eyelids rapidly in surprise. *I smell like apples?* She lifted her arm to sniff it, but all she smelt was the faded aroma of his vanilla scent on his shirt.

"How come it's so big?" she asked, eyeing the size of the tree.

If he had planted it from a seedling at the same time as the rest of the garden, it should be no bigger than a stem.

"I traded for it at this size and carried it home on my back."

"Traded for it?" Delora's brows drew together in a thoughtful frown. "Like you bought it?"

That didn't make sense. *Where could Magnar buy an apple tree from?* She couldn't see his big Duskwalker ass walking through a human village in search of one.

Instead of answering, his head turned sharply to the left and focused on something down the side of the house. He then backed up a step with his arms coming up as though to block.

"Oh shit," he said, right before Delora heard the thumping of quick footsteps coming their way.

Magnar was then barrelled to the ground by a gigantic, fur-covered monster.

Delora gasped in shock when he smashed against the ground before he rolled, his head going in awkward angles due to his antlers. His eyes morphed to crimson, while his body began to turn more monstrous.

Before he could orientate himself and get to his feet and hands, his antler was grabbed. He was yanked forward across the ground, slipping to his belly, before the creature crawled above to stand on top of his back on all fours. It held Magnar's snout against the ground with a large hand.

I thought he said Demons couldn't get through his ward!

She stepped back in fright, worried it would come for her, and she tripped over onto her backside in the garden. There was a crunch of something snapping under her, but her mind was too busy being rivetted to the monster in front of her attacking Magnar.

Delora was torn. Part of her wanted to go to Magnar and help him, while the other part wanted to flee. Instead, she remained petrified where she sat with her eyes wide.

Then they widened further when she realised it wasn't a Demon at all, but another Duskwalker.

He was standing on top of Magnar's legs and an arm to keep him down, and he lifted his snout only so he could smack it against the ground.

"How dare you, Mavka!" the other Duskwalker snarled, a deep, dark rumble present in his voice. ***"How dare you come to my territory and steal from our garden!"***

Magnar reached his free arm back so he could claw into the side of the Duskwalker's neck.

"You do not understand," Magnar stated, his voice distorted alongside his physical changes.

They both looked similar to each other, but also completely different.

Whereas Magnar had black feathers poking out from his

short, deer-like fur and a fox skull, this Duskwalker had long, wolfish fur and his head was that of a wolf. He also had Impala antelope horns instead of deer antlers.

Magnar had more bones protruding through his fur than the other Duskwalker, and his feet were hoofed, whereas the other had human-looking feet that were more like paws at the toes.

They shared the same black colouring, and their body shapes were mostly similar – except the new Duskwalker seemed bigger in terms of muscles and width.

"Did you think I would not smell your fresh scent this morning?" The Duskwalker lowered his head and pushed more of his weight forward when Magnar was trying to push up off the ground. **"I wouldn't have helped you had I known that you would be a thief!"**

Magnar, who had been caught unaware because he'd been showing Delora around the garden, was now stuck in a position where he could do nothing else but claw with his free hand. His eyes turned a pale red, and Delora's heart squeezed when she thought he looked fretful and frightened.

"But I needed it. I need it for–Ahh!" Magnar let out a horrible squealing yelp, like an injured fox, and shook his head side to side to free it from the Duskwalker's grip.

"I told you I would break your skull." He lifted Magnar's snout and smacked it against the ground again. **"I told you I would–"**

"Orpheus, stop!" a female yelled from the side of the house before she came into view.

Her long blonde hair streamed behind her as she ran straight for both Duskwalkers. Then she started bravely shoving her shoulder into the one named Orpheus.

She was dressed in a pale-grey dress that was knee length and had a brown girdle around her torso. Her dainty slipper shoes were black, and she lost one when she continued to try and push him off.

"Get off him, Orpheus!" When her pushing did nothing to help, she grabbed one of his twisty horns and tugged with both hands while digging her heels into the ground. "I don't mind that he took from the garden. Talk to him first. He might have a good reason."

Orpheus roared in her direction, refusing to get off Magnar, but he never turned his rageful actions on the human woman.

"That is your garden! Your food!"

"Just let him talk," she pleaded. "I'll be really mad with you if you hurt him."

"I did not know where else to get food, and I needed it for Delora!" Magnar yelled as he continued to thrash.

Oh shit. This is my fault? Her heart stammered. She couldn't stop the guilt that twisted her insides.

"Look at his antlers, Orpheus," the woman commanded. "He has a soul! He found a human."

Another growl emitted from Orpheus, but he moved his hand from Magnar's snout so he could grab one of his antlers and tug his head to the side. He inspected Delora's soul up close.

"Why does it look dead?" He sniffed at it. *"What did you do to it?"*

My-my soul looks dead?

That's when she noticed a bright flame between Orpheus' horns in the shape of a human woman. It looked strong and healthy as it floated there with goopy strings attaching it to his horns. When she observed her own, it appeared limp and charcoal.

In comparison, hers really did look like a dying coal. *Is there something wrong with it? Or me?*

The woman, realising that Magnar had obtained a human soul, looked around as she tugged on Orpheus' horns. Her gaze eventually fell on Delora.

"You big bonehead!" she yelled, pointing in her very direction. "Look over there! You're probably scaring the shit out of her."

Orpheus turned his head in her direction, and it was as though his red orbs saw into her entire being. The hairs on her arms stood on end.

With Delora under his stare, Magnar seemed to grow frantic.

His orbs turned completely white, and he thrashed until he managed to buck Orpheus off. He immediately sprinted to Delora and stood above her protectively on all fours, keeping low as if he wanted to hide her with his own body.

"Mine," Magnar warned, his body puffing menacingly at the simple, yet possessive, declaration.

Orpheus, on all fours as well, made his way to the other woman and tucked her protectively into his side with his arm in front of her. Even though he was on his hands, their faces were almost side-by-side, with her only slightly lower.

Both Duskwalkers mirrored each other's sounds by snarling and growling, but both had taken a stance with each woman – like their priorities were them rather than to fight.

"Is that Reia? The human you were telling me about?" Delora whispered, tucking her head down so she could come out from underneath Magnar.

Delora tried to stand. Magnar wrapped his arm around her torso and held her to his chest before she could get to her feet, keeping her on her knees in front of him.

"Stay," he demanded, his voice sounding calmer than it had moments ago.

Her being in his hold was soothing him.

Delora kept her eyes on the woman who she knew *must* be Reia by the fact she was with this other Duskwalker. She was pretty. Even with the small distance between them, Delora could determine this. Her blonde hair fluttered in the light wind that blew around them all, pushing the long strands to the side.

"So, you have found your own human to claim," Orpheus stated. His orbs remained red, as though he refused to calm his aggression, but his voice didn't sound as distorted as before.

Magnar answered with a deeper growl.

"However, you didn't have one a week ago. What have you done to trick this human into giving you her soul?" Reia patted the side of his neck and her lips moved as if she spoke to him. He shook his head. *"It is far too soon. Does she understand what she has done?"*

"Yes," Magnar responded, squeezing Delora tighter against him until he was starting to hurt her ribcage. *"She understands that she is mine."*

"Do you?" Orpheus' head never moved to indicate it, but she knew he was looking upon her.

Delora curled into Magnar, unwilling to respond as she gripped the fur on his bowing, more animalistic chest for comfort. She didn't know Orpheus, didn't trust him, and his earlier display of aggression had freaked her the fuck out. She was sure she still smelled of fear, and she worried he would suddenly charge them both while Magnar was holding her.

He'd managed to pin him against the ground.

That was enough to show her he was strong, and the speed in which he'd bombarded Magnar when he first arrived had been startling. Could Delora become accidentally injured if the two Duskwalkers were to begin fighting above her or near her?

Reia rolled her eyes and tried to step forward, but Orpheus proceeded to pull her back so she couldn't leave his side.

"It's fine. He won't hurt me."

"He stole your food, Reia. We no longer know what he will do now that he has his own female," Orpheus stated.

"But I trust him." Reia turned her face to them. "You won't hurt me if I approach, right, Mavka?"

"Magnar," he corrected, taking a single step back while dragging Delora with him. *"My name is Magnar."*

Even though he'd never confirmed whether or not he would cause her harm and had even stepped away defensively, a warm and bright smile lifted into Reia's features.

"You have a name now? I like it. Magnar suits you." Then she turned that welcoming smile to Delora, and she could see the kindness in the sharpness of her eyes. "And what about your name?"

"Her name is Delora," Magnar answered on her behalf before she got the chance to open her mouth. *"I am sorry I stole from your garden, but she needed food. I did not know where else to go."*

"See?" Reia said as she darted her face to Orpheus' large head next to her. "He needed to help Delora, and if he had asked, I would have been happy to share. There's no reason to fight."

"No," Orpheus stubbornly bit, yanking her more to his side. *"I would never have allowed for him to take from you."*

"Orpheus," Reia warned in a dark tone.

Reia gave a deep sigh when nothing happened, like she was

awaiting something in particular. Then she turned transparent and literally floated through his restricting arm.

Delora gasped and would have fallen on her arse in shock if it wasn't for Magnar.

"A Ghost! She literally turned into a freaking Ghost!"

Reia had been floating just above the ground with her toes skimming it as she moved in their direction, but she paused at Delora's shout. Orpheus came up beside her with a growl, but a single swipe of his hand through her told him he couldn't pull her back into the safety of his arms.

"She doesn't know she can do this?" Her voice sounded distant, as if she was talking from far away, and a frown of confusion marred her features.

"She does. She just hasn't done so yet. Delora has not been with me for long."

She hadn't quite believed Magnar when he said she could turn transparent, but seeing it happen right before her eyes had taken her aback. Her cheeks heated in embarrassment, but she couldn't avert her eyes even if she wanted to.

Reia's hair was floating, as was the bottom of her skirt. Her entire body had turned so white and transparent, including her clothing, that it was difficult to see her.

Delora released the grip she had on Magnar's fur to look down at her hands, wondering how she was supposed to do this as well. It was kind of awesome that she had an ability like this. Not only would she be nearly invisible, but she'd be able to move through things.

Then Delora realised something startling.

The golden flesh of her thighs showed to the point that she could even see the curve of her backside. She squeaked and yanked the shirt she was wearing down so it covered her better.

Shit! I'm not wearing pants, and I'm pretty sure my arse was showing. Delora didn't think she could have met another person in more mortifying attire, or rather, lack thereof. Her cheeks heated further to the point that even her ears were burning.

It usually took Delora a little while to warm up to people. She wasn't naturally a talker, instead rather quiet and reserved. Now that she'd met Reia like this when perhaps she could have met her while standing and not showing her lady bits, she wanted to go inside and hide.

"Well," Reia laughed, while placing her hands on her ghostly hips, "I guess I did first learn how to do this because I died."

Delora's shame faded at the words Reia just uttered. *She... died?*

Seeming to sense this, Reia waved her hand dismissively.

"Don't worry. It's a long story, and it kind of worked out for the better." She went to place her hand on Orpheus' neck, but her arm completely went through him. She tipped sideways like she was expecting herself to be solid. She didn't seem to care as she brought her hand back, looked down at it, then wiggled her fingers. "We'll always come back. After a day or death, we'll return to them."

"I now understand why you were so defensive about me being near Reia," Magnar said to Orpheus. His form started to revert to the one Delora was used to, and his clothing seeped up from his skin until it covered him. "I did not understand she was so precious to you until I found Delora."

Orpheus did the same, coming out of his monstrous form to reveal his black button-up shirt and trousers similar to Magnar's. Like him, his wolven skull and Impala antelope horns didn't change. However, black boots covered his feet, as his were more human formed and could wear them.

"If I have learned to accept it, then so will you."

He neatened the cuff of his shirt by pulling it down before ruffling his entire body as if to make sure everything was where he wanted it to be.

Magnar snapped his jaws in a blatant threat, making a chomping noise when his fangs came together. He lifted Delora by pulling her to the side like a ragdoll being snatched away by a toddler.

With a sigh, Reia's feet sunk to the floor as she began to materialise back into a fully solid body. When she was done, she turned her head to Orpheus before glancing back over to Magnar, another smile brightening her features.

"Well, since we're already here... should we help out?"

Delora looked to Magnar, who shuffled his feet nervously

before meeting Delora's gaze.

Help out? she thought with her brows furrowing. *Help out with what?*

FIFTEEN

Magnar peeked up at Delora, who was sitting upon the steps of the porch, watching him cut and peel back the bark of a thick tree he'd cut down so he could work with it.

Holding the handle of each side and keeping himself steady on the tree stump he sat upon, Magnar sliced his drawing knife up the side of the trunk. The lower layer peeled away with a curl while the dry bark layer flung off in random directions.

He'd already cut this tree down before he'd been vacant from the area, before he met Delora, and was now tending to it so he could use it for the porch. He'd been building everything on the outside first so that it was ready and protected before he started working on the internals of the building.

He worried if he waited too long, the porch flooring would become weather damaged.

Should I make the rooms first? That would make her more comfortable, but he eventually shook his head. No, the porch definitely needed to be completed now that he'd started it.

When his sight drew away from stripping the bark back up to Delora, his orbs turned a reddish pink.

I should have listened to Orpheus. He'd told Magnar to finish the inside, but he'd foolishly fixated on the outside being complete before doing anything within its four walls.

There had been no point before.

"So," Reia butted into his thoughts casually, skipping her way over to him with a watering can in her hands behind her back. She'd been tending to the garden for him. "How are you going to take Delora to the Demon Village now that you've got her soul?"

Magnar gave a huff of irritation. He didn't know how he was going to do that.

He knew he needed to go there, needed to go to that place – and soon. There were tools and items he needed from there to finish the interior of the house.

The Demon Village was a fairly large area filled with Demons who were intelligent like Mavka. They had consumed enough humans to be less violent and rarely hunted them anymore. Instead, they had started mimicking their way of life.

They built the village and then began living in it, selling in it, and participating in events to celebrate.

Those strange Demons had also built homes in an area right near the middle of the Veil and lived there peacefully. They ate meat, no matter the creature it came from, but they were beginning to create families, friendships, and business partnerships. It was hard to see them like the normal Demons Magnar had come across.

There was only one difference between when he'd gone there with Reia and Orpheus, to how he would take Delora there.

"You were human," he mumbled as he sliced his drawing knife up the log he had between his knees. His sight returned to green. "Delora can turn into a Phantom."

"That's still quite dangerous." She tilted her head, her hair falling to one side. "That will make it known you have her."

She was right, and that was something Magnar was worried about.

"I do not know how Orpheus did it," he admitted to her. "To take you to such a place while you were human was remarkably silly. You could have been harmed."

Once more, Magnar let his sight drift to his female, who was fidgeting with the cloth that she'd tied around her waist. Apparently she felt underdressed, but he found she was now wearing too much.

He didn't understand why she felt the need to cover her body.

"You didn't have a problem with it back then," Reia rebuffed as she set the watering can on the ground behind her and placed her hands on her hips. She even raised her brow at him, and he was thankful he'd eaten three humans since he'd met her. "What? Because it benefitted you to have me taken there, you saw no issue with it? I didn't think you were so selfish."

She was being truthful, despite her hurtful words, but she also held a slight smile, like she was joking. He wasn't adept enough in humans to know if what he was interpreting about her was true or not.

All he knew was that who he was then was different to who he was now. Not by much, he was still 'stupid,' as Orpheus called him, but he'd learned much.

"I did not know any better," he answered as he watched Delora's eyes slip to him before she averted her gaze. She immediately brought it back like she couldn't help herself watching them, just as he couldn't help his sight from trailing to her. "I did not understand the significance of what we were doing. You were unprotected without the ability to turn transparent."

"I had you and Orpheus, remember?"

And looking at Delora now, and how he felt about her...

"It was not enough. Just one strike and you would have died. You should not have pushed him into a corner. You should not have made him take you."

Reia's jaw dropped in disbelief. "Are you seriously scolding me for helping you?"

"Yes," he admitted. "I will forever be thankful for the risk you both took on my behalf, even more so now that I understand why Orpheus was so hesitant."

"You seem to like her a lot."

Reia turned to Delora, who froze on the spot with both of them looking in her direction. She'd been a little shy and reserved since the incident around the apple tree. Her face had a been a cute colour of beetroot, but he knew her just enough to know when she was uncomfortable.

He thought perhaps it was because of the fight with Orpheus – that he'd shamefully lost before it even started. He'd been hoping they'd all meet under better circumstances.

It wasn't just Orpheus she was reserved with, but also Reia.

They'd exchanged a few words and did some strange custom of shaking hands, but then Delora had gone inside for a long while. It gave Magnar, Reia, and Orpheus the opportunity to discuss plans for the day.

They were helping him build this cabin like they had been doing from the start.

Delora had come outside to sit on the porch steps not long after Reia had asked Orpheus to procure a couple of items from their home so that Delora could be more comfortable here. Things like a washing bucket so she could properly clean herself, some soap, a few pots and cutlery, a proper blanket, and a pillow. Reia had also asked that he bring food – even though Orpheus tried to deny the last request.

Magnar was now going to have to trade some of the food he was growing, that they didn't have, in gratitude for their help. This was the only thing that appeased Orpheus.

They didn't know Magnar had already planned to give his food to them.

Instead of answering her comment about him liking Delora 'a lot,' as she put it, Magnar ignored her and returned to stripping more bark off. He couldn't stop his orbs from turning a reddish pink in embarrassment and wished he wasn't so obvious with his feelings, which, incidentally, made them more obvious.

A loud, high-pitched laugh began, and he looked up to Reia, who was cackling while pointing her finger at him.

"You do!"

"Why is that so funny?" Magnar growled, his orbs turning to bright red.

She shook her head before rolling her eyes.

"You Duskwalkers can't hide anything with those glowing eyes of yours. I can't believe you tried." Then she came to stand next to him, her shoulder almost brushing his, to stare down at the instruction book he had laying on the ground near his feet. "She's really pretty. How'd you bag yourself such a voluptuous woman?"

A what? He sometimes didn't understand Reia's mannerisms or what her words meant.

"You say *voluptuous,* but she said... fat? What is the

difference?"

He wanted to better understand why his female had been strange about him touching her in certain places so he could argue with her about it in the future.

Reia's brows furrowed. "Nothing, I guess. But one way is nicer to say, almost like sexy. She's a curvy woman, I can't deny that, but some humans think it's a bad thing."

"Hmm," he hummed loudly, almost stopping his task to tap at his snout in thought.

Humans are odd. And he knew they were wrong. There was nothing about Delora's appearance that was bad.

Actually, those plump, bulging hips of hers gave him this strange desire to... gnaw on them.

Reia reached down to grab the furniture and house instruction book he owned – something she had given him – and flicked through it. She came upon a page that instructed on how to build a chair.

"You should make one of these for Delora," she stated, showing him the simple chair with four legs and a grid-like back. She also showed him its matching table on the page after it. "You'll need to make one eventually, and it'll be good if she has a place to sit and eat."

He paused to look down at what he was doing before inspecting the chair. What he had between his thighs was a massive log that was going to be split into sections for the porch roof supports. He'd have to stop this to start the task she was showing him. He needed smaller logs, like tree branches.

"Is a seat and table more important than a porch roof?"

"You can't just expect her to live in an empty house. She'll need furniture eventually. I sent Orpheus home to grab some other stuff, but she should be able to start cooking with some of the quicker growing vegetables in the garden. I don't like eating on the floor, and I doubt she will either."

"But I don't know how to do this," he answered in a dejected tone. He took the book from her so he could look at it properly. "I don't know how to carve wood like this."

Reia turned her green eyes up to him and smiled. It had once stolen his breath, but now he felt as though he was forever holding it, waiting for the day Delora shared her very first with him.

His eyes changed from their usual shade of green to something much darker. He averted his sight to see the chair legs had curving shapes in them. He didn't know how to attach it all together without it falling apart.

"That's okay. Orpheus can show you if you can't do it yourself."

She pointed to the drawn diagram while reading the section of instructions to him.

Reia knew Magnar couldn't read. She had been planning to teach him some words at some point, but he wondered if perhaps he could ask Delora to teach him instead.

As he was pondering this, Reia, who was standing rather close to his face since they were nearly the same height while he was seated, brought her eyes up from the book to look at him.

"You know," she started, raising a blonde brow at him. She was looking at him peculiarly. "You never answered my question about how you met Delora."

Magnar's head tilted. Why was this so important that she needed to ask twice? Delora was here – that was all that mattered to him.

"She fell on top of me," he answered, knowing Reia would pry until her curiosity was fulfilled.

Her head reared back suddenly. She frowned with a pout of confusion puffing her lips.

"What do you mean?"

Magnar lifted his snout slightly and pointed it upwards. "She fell from the sky and landed on top of me the last time I left my cave to come here."

"Like... literally from the fucking sky?" Her tone wasn't filled with amazement, but rather with shocked horror. "How did she get in the sky, Magnar? Why was she falling?"

"I do not know."

"What do you mean, you don't know?"

"I do not know why she fell into the Veil."

Magnar's fur and feathers puffed in apprehension at the face Reia gave him. His head darted to Delora when he realised this may not actually be a good thing.

Why did Delora come to the Veil? He'd never thought to ask before, but should he be concerned?

Delora fiddled with the cuff of the black shirt she wore for the umpteenth time, then rearranged the dirty white cloth she'd tied around her hips so it covered her privates and legs better. It was *never* better. It was like a sarong, and since it wasn't big enough to do from one corner to the other around her hips, she'd folded it into a triangle so its furthest corners could meet.

One whole thigh was completely showing, but it was still better than not wearing anything at all.

She'd been thankful, at first, to see that the other Duskwalker wasn't around – the one she didn't know.

They had been welcoming enough when they'd briefly spoken, until Delora's inability to ignore the fact she was half-naked started to bug her. Reia's outfit was rather cute.

Delora's original opinion of her had been positive.

Now, as she sat here on the porch step watching the pretty blonde and Magnar speaking, Delora felt a hollow pit in her stomach.

They seem to get along really well.

Reia had been laughing and smiling with Magnar, practically leaning against him when she picked up the book he'd laid on the ground to go through it with him.

Delora didn't like it.

She didn't like that Reia was so close to Magnar. She didn't like that she was laughing with him, that she was leaning against him... that she was speaking so casually with him that it seemed to be with ease.

A tightness was spreading in her chest, one she'd felt before and hated with every fibre of her being.

He's my *Duskwalker.* When they both turned their heads to

Delora, she turned hers to the side with an angry pout. *She has her own. Why does she have to be so friendly with mine?*

Delora had never been a jealous woman. She'd never felt the possessive flare of acid running through her veins before, but after what happened with Hadith, how he had betrayed her, it was hard to shake the feeling.

Especially when Reia grabbed one of Magnar's antler branches and shook his head around. He didn't stop her.

She wished she could hear what they were talking about, but she didn't care to approach. She'd been here for a while. If they wanted to talk to her, they would.

Instead, she just grabbed the folded cuffs of her black shirt and held them in a firm grip, wishing for the stomach-twisting emotion in her gut to fade. She knew it was irrational, but it still made her feel spiteful.

Magnar abandoned what he'd been carving so he could go to a tree under Reia's command. She pointed to a thick branch. Delora watched the show of his impressive strength when he grabbed it in one hand while supporting the tree with his other and snapped the branch off in one motion.

He did the same to three others that Reia pointed to before they returned to the stump he'd been using as a chair. This time, he had his back to her.

That hollowing hole in her chest burrowed deeper.

She didn't know what he was doing, but suddenly he didn't even want to face her now that Reia was here!

Could he have perhaps wanted to be with Reia but couldn't because she gave her soul to the other one? She didn't know the answer to that question, but it made her feel like shit that she may have just been some runner-up.

Heat burned in her cheeks, hot and rage-filled, and she narrowed her eyes as she turned her gaze away. She wanted to remain in her spot to show her presence, but she didn't particularly want to watch them anymore.

That gave her the opportunity to watch Orpheus come through the tree line, carrying an array of items in his arms and tied to his back.

He came straight for Delora, but his head had been turned to

Reia, like he couldn't keep his gaze away from her. His orbs, which were usually blue, turned a dark green.

When he came to Delora, he gave a deep huff, one that sounded of irritation. He stopped in front of the bottom step, right near her side, and finally faced her, digging through the large bucket he had in his arms.

Now that she saw all the items strapped to Orpheus that were intended for her, some of her anger faded. Reia was being generous and understanding of her situation to give her all this. What right did she have to feel any kind of negative emotion towards her?

Fuck. My mind is so damn twisted. It constantly felt like a jungle, so dense and full of twisted roots, so deep and vast, that she couldn't find her way out of it. A tangle of paranoia, hurt, anger, and confusion constantly warred within her. She wished she could cut it all down and make way for clarity.

I want it to stop.

She was about to grip at her face in annoyance with her own thoughts, but a large hand shoved itself into her peripheral. Inside it was a ceramic jar that had a piece of twine tied around it to keep the lid attached.

Delora looked up to Orpheus, who was staring down at her from his enormous height. She realised he was trying to give it to her.

She still didn't know how she felt about him after what happened earlier. He'd attacked Magnar, and it appeared as though he'd intended to kill him for stealing.

"What is it?" Delora asked warily, lifting both her hands to take it.

"It is mint, lemon, and honey tea," he answered, slowly bringing his hand away when the backs of her fingers brushed against the dark callouses in his palm. "Reia likes this tea I make for her, and I thought you might too. It should still be warm."

His voice wasn't as deep in baritone as Magnar's, but it was just as rich and smooth.

Delora's eyelids fluttered rapidly. She couldn't believe he'd given this to her.

"Are you saying that you... made this for me? Why?"

Orpheus' orbs changed back to blue, and he tilted his head at her like she'd often seen Magnar do. Perhaps it was a Duskwalker thing. They couldn't convey their emotions through their face, but they could with their body.

"Because you're a human." He lifted his gaze to stare at Reia. "It is hard to live in the Veil, to live with us Mavka. I'm aware that I frightened you earlier, and I know how dangerous that fear can be. I wanted to make amends with you, especially now that we will be seeing each other more often."

Delora was taken aback by how well he spoke and how much forethought he had. He almost seemed... older than Magnar, more intelligent even.

"Why do you say that?"

"Because Reia will want to visit you. She will want to make sure you are comfortable. I can already tell this about her from today." Orpheus nodded his snout in Magnar and Reia's direction. "She has already convinced him to make you a chair."

"Really?" Delora's gaze shot to them to see that they were huddled around the book, and he was holding one of the branches he'd already managed to strip the bark from. "But she doesn't know me. Why would she do any of this for me?"

"Because Reia is good."

Orpheus said nothing more on the subject before going up the stairs to dump everything he'd brought inside. In that time, Delora managed to undo the twine, remove the sandy ceramic lid, and take a sip of its contents.

It eased some of the terrible feelings she'd had swimming in her stomach and was sweet against her tastebuds.

As he was coming out, Delora mumbled, "Thank you. It's actually really nice."

Orpheus nodded, his shoes thudding against the porch steps as he came down them.

"I better help him. He'll make a mistake if I don't." Then he shook his head as he said, "It's not easy to make furniture."

He went straight over to Reia and curled his large hand around her small waist, pulled her to him, and bumped the tip of his snout against her jaw in affection.

Delora's eyes widened when he blatantly licked at her neck,

making her squeal out a giggle as she pushed at his face. They were a lot closer than Delora could have imagined, and she noticed Magnar watching them with a darker colour of green present in his orbs.

Then he turned his head to Delora and twisted it sharply.

Does he want to lick me like that? One side of her lips curled up when she realised she wouldn't mind if he tried to do that.

Now that Orpheus was there to assist, Reia abandoned them to come to Delora. Her back immediately stiffened when she sat next to her about a foot away on the step above her own.

"Did Orpheus apologise?" Reia asked with a firm tone.

Delora brought her knees up so she could lay one arm across them and then place her elbow on it. Then she plopped her chin in her open palm.

"Did you ask him to?" Delora turned her body slightly towards Reia to show she had her attention.

"Nah," she answered with a shake of her head. "I just know him well enough to know he'd feel bad about frightening you because you're human." Then Reia jutted her chin in both the Duskwalkers' directions. "I like the name you gave him. I'm glad he finally has one."

"How come you didn't give him one then?"

Reia lifted her shoulders. "Didn't want the responsibility. I suck at being creative. The only things I know how to make are dresses, and that's really because I *had* to learn. Not because I wanted to."

Delora's brows drew together tightly. "Does that mean you made the dress you're wearing?"

Reia turned her eyes, but not her face, to Delora, then brightly smiled. "Yep. Orpheus got me the fabrics and sewing equipment so I could make them. He also got me some fabric dyes so I can change the white clothing he already had from the offerings he was given."

Delora's lips drew together. She took her eyes away from Reia to watch, just in time to see Orpheus tap the back of his hand against the side of Magnar's head as if he'd made a mistake.

"Offerings?"

"Yeah. I'm not sure if you've heard of him, but he's the

Duskwalker that was going around offering a protection ward in exchange for a bride."

"Yeah, I've heard of him." Then Delora mumbled, "But I thought Duskwalkers were just a myth until I met Magnar."

"Well," Reia chuckled lightly, "they're definitely real, as you can tell."

"Yeah, no shit. I'm guessing that since you've given him your soul, he won't be looking for more offerings?"

"No." There was a long pause, as if Reia was waiting for Delora to say something. When she didn't, she asked, "So, how did you end up in the Veil?"

Delora's chest tightened. "It's a long story."

One she'd rather not reveal to her, or at all.

When her eyes flicked to Reia, she noticed hers had squinted. Delora quickly looked away, making it obvious she wasn't going to say anything more about it.

If she was going to unload the past that felt like a terrible weight within her mind and heart, then she would do that with someone she trusted, someone she was comfortable with. She would do that with the big Duskwalker who had almost fallen from his tree stump trying to reach for the branch that had started rolling away from him.

A cold feeling rushed through her entire being. She wondered if she'd ever be able to shed her fear of being abandoned to actually tell him the truth.

Delora didn't want Reia learning of it first to twist the story. She was a human. She would understand the significance of what Delora had done.

She suddenly wished they would just disappear so that it was only her and Magnar again. Their presence made her feel more pressure, made her feel like she had to pretend. She didn't want to be rude, but this was the longest she'd been awake since she'd arrived in the Veil and her energy was waning.

Losing the will for life was surprisingly draining.

"You said you had clothing dye," Delora started. She let her gaze fall awkwardly back to Reia to find she was still being glared at. "Does that mean you have paint?"

"Paint?" Reia frowned in thought before shaking her head.

"No, I don't. Why?"

Delora bit her lip. Perhaps she was asking for too much since they'd already given her plenty, but now that her mind had grasped this thread, she couldn't let it go.

"How about clay?"

"Sure, but Magnar already has clay for building."

His name coming from her mouth gnawed at Delora. Her jealousy was like a nasty leech that had permanently attached itself like a parasite.

She took a deep breath to settle it, before sighing it out.

"Um, would it be alright if I borrowed some dye then?" Delora turned her head to the sky, her features relaxing at her idea. "I'd like to paint, and I can mix dye with clay. I haven't painted in so long, but if you don't want to–"

"You can have as much as we can spare, Delora," Reia quickly interjected. "We don't have a lot that I can give you because I need it myself, but whatever you need to be happy here. I'll give you what I can."

"Thanks..."

Delora didn't really know how to express her gratitude, but she tried to weakly smile for her. It was awkward, and it fell immediately when she knew it hadn't reached her eyes.

"Of course," Reia chuckled, but her eyes held a sharpness – something dark. "I don't want you turning out like Katerina."

"Who?" Delora asked with a frown.

The smile Reia had wasn't as humble as it had been before.

"I'll tell you the story about Katerina – who she is and what happened to her – when you tell me why you fell off a cliff and landed in the Veil."

Oh shit. Delora's eyes widened when Reia got up and stomped her way to the Duskwalkers, apparently done with their conversation.

It seemed Reia wasn't as docile as she first appeared to be.

SIXTEEN

Delora was hesitant about sitting in the wooden chair Magnar
had made. She bit her lip as she *slowly* lowered her backside
before she eventually plopped herself in it.

She had thought it would break under *any* weight, but now
that she was in it, she knew it was truly sturdy.

The yellow glow of his eyes made her heart soften, and it only
grew in intensity when he placed its matching small table in front
of her. He even gave her a bowl of fruit to demonstrate its
capabilities, and she dug into it enthusiastically for his benefit,
which seemed to please him.

He'd made this while Orpheus and Reia had still been here,
but they'd long ago left, and Magnar had been working on the
porch ever since.

Delora had quietly watched him before she'd asked how they
were going to fill the wash bucket they'd been given. Magnar
had demonstrated a rather nifty, but off-putting spell he could
perform. He'd cut his wrist to produce a droplet of his blood into
the bucket, and it began to fill with heated water.

Thankfully, the water had no strange smell to it, but it did
have a tang to its taste.

She didn't care. It was her first proper chance to bathe since
she'd come to the Veil. The water was hot, the soap she'd been
given pleasant, and she wiped her body down from head to toe
with a patch of cloth.

Magnar had been busy outside the entire time, but she'd
called out to him once she had a makeshift towel around her

body. He'd been more than happy to give her his last remaining clean shirt, and she promised she'd return it when Reia gave her a dress in a day or two. She planned to clean the dirty one she'd just removed and use it as her sleeping gown in the future.

Reia had gotten a rough measurement of her body with the use of string and said she would alter a dress she thought might be close to fitting her. It had been awkward after the abrupt end to their previous conversation, but Reia had still offered to make her one.

Gods, it was nice to feel clean. It somehow made her feel more like herself, more human.

"You smell different," Magnar commented as he sniffed her hair while she ate.

Her chair had been positioned next to one of the walls since it would have looked out of place right in the middle of the empty house.

"It's soap." She lifted her head and almost headbutted his snout. "I told you I was going to have a bath."

"I do not like it." He gave a huff at her hair before standing back. "Do not have baths. I liked the way you smelt before."

"But I was dirty." When she knew he was going to argue, Delora lowered her lids in annoyance. "It's important for humans to bathe. We should do this. It's good for us, makes us feel good, and being unclean is bad for our health."

Magnar let out a grumpy snort before conceding defeat. "Fine, but only because I can still smell your scent underneath your *soap*."

Once she was done eating, Delora made her way over to the nest that now also contained a thin blanket and fluffy pillow inside. It had navy coverings and looked to be made of a good quality fabric, but she wouldn't have cared. She'd always found it difficult to sleep well without something covering her, as if her mind needed a barrier from the world while she slept.

She knelt inside and then leaned over the nest's edge to grab the hairbrush Reia had given to her. She started brushing her hair now that it was dry. Her hair was straight, and whenever she tried to brush it when wet, it felt stringy and snapped easily.

It was a slow process, as this was not only the first time she'd brushed her hair in over two weeks, but the first time she'd been able to wash it. She had to start at the tips and slowly make her way up the length of it.

"What is that?" Magnar asked, coming closer so he could cup his hand around the one she was using.

"It's a brush." She looked over her shoulder at him. "It helps to get knots out of my hair. See?"

To demonstrate, Delora pushed his shirtsleeve up and brushed the fur on the back of his wrist. His black fur immediately appeared glossier, and he caressed his fingers over it before tapping at his snout.

He lifted his head to make it obvious he was staring at her hair when she started untangling it again.

"Can I do this?"

Delora paused with the bristles tangled through some knots. "You want to brush my hair for me?"

His eyes glowed a reddish pink, but he nodded when she took the brush away so he could hold her knotty strands.

"This action looks pleasant. I would like to touch your hair and make it nice for you."

How could such a simple request make her heart stutter?

The brush appeared far too small in his large hands, but Delora showed him how to wield it without causing her any pain. Magnar was careful and cautious, as if he thought he'd rip her bald in one swish of his hand. It made the task take far longer than it should have.

Delora was thankful for that.

It didn't take long for her eyes to shut with satisfaction. Especially when he'd completely worked the knots out and was just merely combing her hair because he wanted to. It pushed the bristles over her sensitive scalp and felt like utter bliss.

Then he grew braver, combing his claws through the strands as well. Delora let out a breathy gasp when the tips scraped behind her hair and down the nape of her neck. A shiver tore down her spine, making her arch.

"I have seen Reia do things with her hair," Magnar said, causing her eyes to open and narrow at the wall. "Will you do these things as well? She calls them *plaits* and *braids*."

"You seem awfully close with her," Delora grumbled, trying her hardest to not sound petty.

She was glad he probably didn't understand the tone in her voice.

"Reia is the first human I ever spoke to. She is the one who convinced Orpheus to help me, and she has been very kind to me. She was the one who told me about humans so that I would not frighten you."

Delora turned to look at him, and he continued to brush her hair like he was unwilling to part with the action.

"I would have eaten you, if not for her." Then he quickly averted his gaze by turning his snout one way and then the other. He scratched at the back of his neck. "Perhaps I should not have said that."

And there was that wall again.

Delora wondered how often Magnar kept his thoughts to himself or watched his words around her. She didn't want him to hold back because he was worried she'd become fearful or apprehensive of him.

"Magnar." She placed her hand on his and started to turn around.

"If you are going to do funny things to your hair, I would like for you to teach me how." He still wasn't looking at her, but she could see the embarrassed glow of his orbs was brightening. "I will learn for you."

He was rambling. Delora knelt in front of him between his spread thighs where he was kneeling in the nest. She placed her hands in her lap, and her nose heated in nervousness over what she wanted to say next.

Delora wanted to be close with Magnar. Orpheus had held Reia, had petted her and nuzzled her without hesitation, and she wanted them to be able to do that as well. She wanted things to flow with ease between them.

"Do you... uh, want to touch me?"

Now that the words had been uttered, her cheeks also grew hot, but she refused to back down.

"Always."

"You can if you want. Wherever you like," Delora said, and

his orbs shifted to bright yellow. His hand came up, but before it could cup the side of her face, she grabbed it with both her hands to stop him. "On one condition. I want you to take your shirt off."

Magnar pressed his fingertips to his chest as he turned his head down and to the side so that he could see past his snout.

"My shirt? But I was told not to show my body to you."

Delora reached forward and let her fingertips brush across the protruding white bones that were over the backs of his hands. She'd noticed that he had more of them than Orpheus did, and even though Magnar was taller, Orpheus appeared more... fully formed.

"I think in the beginning that might have been wise, but you don't need to hide anymore. I promise I won't get upset."

They both needed to take a leap tonight. Magnar needed to partially strip, and Delora needed to let him be curious with her. She hoped that was the answer to bridging a comfortable companionship between them.

She was apparently with him forever. There was no point in either one of them being shy.

Delora had never seen Magnar work the buttons of his shirt. When it appeared as though he was struggling with the tiny things with his large fingers and curling claws, she opted to assist him by carefully sliding her hands under his.

She started from the top, and it was quickly revealed that his body was covered in fur, but his pectoral muscles were lined with little feathers that grew longer and larger around his shoulders. The lower she went, the more it revealed indents in the fur around his stomach, showing just how much the muscles in his lean body shape dipped. He looked strong, his torso longer than a human's would be.

She didn't understand why this was supposed to be off-putting, why he'd been told to hide his body, until she undid the last button and pushed it off his shoulders.

A part of her had known she might see more strange bones outside his flesh, but she hadn't thought she'd see his ribcage entirely, nor his sternum plate. She could also see the balls of his shoulders and the top inner section of his hip bones since the rest of it was sunken.

Magnar had gone frozen under her gaze. She peeked up at him through her lashes before she reached forward and caressed one side of his ribs to show she was okay with them.

"Have you always been like this?" she asked.

She trailed her fingertips over them. His head lifted back slightly, and his fur and feathers puffed as if his body was thrilled by her light touch.

"No. The bones continue to sink beneath my flesh."

"How come you're changing?"

She drifted her fingers lower so she could touch his abdomen, where the fur on his body seemed to be the shortest. He had a belly button, which she was surprised about.

When he didn't answer, Delora pulled back and waited for him to respond. He didn't, and she noticed he was purposefully facing his skull away from her like he thought that was enough to evade her.

When she folded her arms across her chest and gave him a raised brow, Magnar began to fidget more. She figured he recognised that she was getting upset. Perhaps Reia had pulled a similar action.

"I obtain a little more humanity every time I eat one of your kind. My body changes as well. Bones sink in while more flesh grows."

With that knowledge, Delora let her eyes travel over his revealed torso. She figured the reason he was much leaner than Orpheus, although taller, was because, at one stage, his body must have been deformed and near skeleton-like.

She was glad it was at least the state it was now, as this wasn't difficult at all to look upon.

Actually, the longer she looked at his chest, the more she wanted to dig her fingers through the texture of his fur. She wanted to ruffle his feathers and feel his strong muscles beneath her palms.

Instead, she popped the top button of the black shirt she was in. Then she grabbed his hand so that she could place his warm palm against the flat part of her chest right above her breast.

"Touch, Magnar." She pulled his hand down her chest a little to give him courage. "I promised you could."

"You said wherever I like... Does this mean however I like as well?"

He brought his hand back so he could brush the edges of his claws against the underside of her jaw.

"Yes."

Magnar drew the backs of his claws over her shoulders, down her back, and then gripped her arse cheeks with both hands. She let out a surprised squeak when he lifted her up and over his legs until she rested upon the tops of his thighs. Their torsos were squished together when he laid the bottom of his jaw over her back.

A hug? she thought when he brought his arms around her midsection and squeezed. Delora lifted her arms so she could wrap them around his neck to return his embrace and was rewarded with a contented huff.

"I am much bigger than you." He rubbed the side of his jaw against the back of her head. "But you fit in my arms well. I like this. I worry about being near Reia, as she is so small and weak looking, but you are perfect like this."

A spark of tenderness fluttered in her chest like a shy butterfly, and it only moved more rapidly when he pulled back while supporting the back of her head. He drew his tongue over the edge of her jaw, from her chin all the way to her ear.

She didn't expect his lick to elicit a small shiver over her body. It grew in intensity when he licked from her collar bone and then up and over her ear, this time to the point it folded and dipped inside the shell of it.

Delora squirmed on his lap when she felt a throb in the delicate places all over her body. She never realised just how sensitive her ears were before, but even his heavy breath over the now saliva-covered flesh made her gasp with subtle heat.

"I saw you wanted to do this earlier," Delora said, grabbing both sides of his snout to stop him since it was tickling her and sending strange, unwanted signals throughout her body.

"I have seen Orpheus do this many times and have always wondered why." Despite her hands cupping him, Magnar parted his fangs and drew his tongue even harder against her, almost licking the entire front of her neck. "I can taste your scent, and it feels good."

When he grabbed her thigh with his palm, Delora noted he'd sheathed his claws in order to protect her skin. He slid it upwards, and she knew when he dug his fingers under the bottom of her shirt because he wiggled them to get underneath.

She flinched when he grabbed her stomach, but his following huff said he was delighted with the feel of it in his palm, which was rough from hardened callouses. They were coarse but delightful as he brushed them over her side and grabbed her there before going over her back so he could caress her skin.

Magnar seemed curious about every dent of her body, like each one between her vertebrae and each roll up her back and to the sides. Each swipe of his hand, while the other supported her on his legs by gripping her backside, left a tingle in its wake.

He touched her back everywhere, leaving no spot missed.

He even dipped his hand into her sleeve to touch the ball of her shoulder joints, her biceps. He dug down as far as the shirt would allow him to fit before he slipped away to go down the middle of her back again.

I've never had someone learn my body like this.

There were places that felt awkward, like her armpits, but she understood he saw no issue with any part of her body. He didn't have a human's ideology of judgement – it was just another place to touch her.

Although, she did mention that it tickled.

When his hand brushed across her side but high up, Delora knew where his next destination was.

She bit her lips together and clenched her eyes shut. Her breast literally pooled in his palm when he lifted it, and he held it so he could brush his thumb over her nipple curiously.

He swirled it in his palm before moving to the other to do the same, lightly dipping between to tease her sternum and collar bones.

A sharp moan suddenly cut its way past her lips when she felt his tongue there!

Delora opened her eyes to find he'd used his forearm to lift the front of her shirt and had slipped his snout underneath so he could lick her nipple directly. His tongue had been rough and textured against it, sending a shockwave throughout her entire system that shot straight to her pussy to make it pulsate.

She even felt liquid pooling at her entrance. She squirmed a little.

"I thought they would have a different taste when I saw them." She was about to ask him when he'd seen her breasts, only to remember he'd cleaned and changed her when he'd first healed her. "However..." He sniffed around her chest with quick draws and then huffed. "There is a really sweet smell coming from you now. From here."

Delora nearly jumped out of her skin when his explorative hand cupped between her spread thighs. Her entire pussy, from clit to slit, rested in his large palm.

Okay, so she had said Magnar could touch, but she didn't think her body would react like this. That she would get turned on by the simplest of touches because he was being so light and gentle with her.

She also didn't think he'd be able to smell that she was becoming aroused.

Her face flushed hot, but before she could grab his forearm to stop whatever he was about to do, his hand grasped her thigh, and he tugged. Delora went rolling backwards until her shoulders hit the softness of the nest with her arse in the air.

Magnar held her leg up high.

The shirt she was wearing fell above her breasts, her entire body on show for him, and she realised he was inspecting between her legs up close and personally!

"What is this? I do not have anything like this on my body." He tilted his head while sniffing so directly that the hard bone of his snout pressed against her folds. She feared the worst when he swiped his tongue across the side of his snout, almost as if to lick the amount of liquid he'd collected. "But I like the way it smells and tastes."

Delora was shocked, frozen in her upside-down position, barely believing her cunt was right in front of a Duskwalker's face being sniffed. How was she supposed to explain what this was to him? What its function was?

Her heart raced so wildly that she could feel it in her stomach, her wrist, inside her core that he was staring directly at.

Did she *want* to explain it, though?

The longer she was in this position, being inspected so inquisitively to the point he literally used the tip of the forefinger on his free hand and *rubbed* the hard nub of her clit, the more she wanted to explain it to him. Especially since it caused her inner thighs to twitch with pleasure.

She wanted him to know what to do with it.

Delora covered her mouth. *Do I actually want him to touch me like this?*

His orbs flashed a dark purple before returning to their yellow glow of curiosity. She'd never seen them turn that colour before, and he lifted his head and looked around as if with surprise.

Magnar continued to pet her clit. It throbbed more and more with need and want as desire swiftly coiled in her belly like a starved beast desperate for attention.

She didn't know what was giving her this reaction. If it was because it was him touching her or that his reactions were beyond adorable and held no bad intentions in them, that it made her feel like she was suddenly on fire, and she needed him to put her out.

Or if, perhaps, it was because she couldn't remember being touched this delicately before. Every grasp, lick, tug, and caress had been filled with care, like he thought she was made of glass. Yet he knew she wasn't by the simple fact she was laying just on her shoulders, with her arse nearly resting against his chest.

But somehow... it felt *wrong* to be doing this when it was clear he didn't understand.

"You also have a hole here," he said as he brought his finger down between the lips of her folds to dabble at the slitted entrance to her insides.

"Magnar." She needed to stop him so they could speak properly about this.

The next word to fall from her was barely a word at all. It was an 'Eeek!' A squealing squeak when he shoved that big finger inside her so abruptly and without warning that it had her back bowing.

Delora involuntarily shuddered around that finger, a rush of intense, heat-filled shivers dancing along her flesh.

It was longer than a human's, to the point she thought it might be close to brushing her cervix, and it was thick enough to partially fill her.

Delora didn't realise her vision had dazed until he pulled his middle finger from her channel and inspected it.

"It's wet?"

He rubbed the pad of his thumb over the slickness covering his dark-grey flesh and spread it over his middle finger as well.

"Wait!" she yelped when she saw him move.

She reached to grab his hand, but he was quicker than her. This time, he sunk both his middle and index fingers inside her. A full body shudder wracked her this time, and she brought her clenched fists near her chest when she squirmed.

Delora melted as a tiny moan escaped her.

"It's warm inside you," he commented before he started moving his fingers back and forth. "And that scent grows stronger when I play with you here."

It was the strangest sensation when she felt him *digging* inside her. His two fingers moved individually as they twisted, stroked, and delved inside her pussy, but each one had her twitching in pleasure.

Why... Delora let out a moan and she clenched her eyes shut, knowing her face was bright red. *Why does this feel so good?*

I'm not stopping him... And she knew she actually... didn't want to.

Especially when it felt like absolute bliss when one finger curled and gouged right against her G-spot to the point she bucked back into his hand. Her hips waved through the air as a loud groan passed her trembling lips this time.

Magnar paused. She didn't know she'd been skimming right on the verge of an orgasm until he'd stolen it away from her by doing so.

"Delora?" She peeked open her eyes to find his orbs were white with uncertainty. "You are making sounds like you are in pain. Am I hurting you? I thought this smell meant you liked it."

Like he couldn't help himself, Magnar, still with his fingers deep inside her, leaned forward and stroked her clit with his firm tongue. Her pussy walls clenched his fingers.

His head darted back in surprise when he felt it.

"N-no," she rasped, her voice hoarse, high-pitched, and ladened with so much desire that it sounded erotic even to her own ears. "It, uh, feels good, Magnar. Really good."

His orbs flashed yellow, and he lowered her down so he could scoop her up and have her kneel on top of him again. It appeared as though he wanted to be closer to her, because he refused to remove his fingers from her the entire time and was now crushing their chests together.

"I found a place you like being touched?" Cradling the back of her neck with his hand while his arm supported her back, he twisted his head at her in question. "That feels good?"

Now that she had an actual perch and was able to support herself, when he moved his fingers in and out of her, her hips rotated. Her body sought more friction, more of his touch.

Instead of answering, Delora slipped her arms under his so she could wrap them around his thin body. She dug her fingers into his fur and held onto him, burying her face between his firm pectoral muscles.

She moaned when his rough fingers grazed her swelling G-spot.

"That sound means you like this, yes?"

Things were moving too fast, she knew it, but she gripped him tighter in worry he'd stop. *I feel like I'm going to come.* She couldn't remember the last time she'd come because of another.

When her breath hitched, and she moaned again, Magnar realised he'd found the sweetest place for her. He kept ruthlessly attacking it to the point her eyes rolled into the back of her head.

"Right there," she begged, her body bouncing as she tried to buck into his fingers.

Her uncovered hardened nipples grazed against him, making them throb at the sensation of his different textures. Hard bone, dense muscles, and soft, tickling fur.

"Y-yes, Magnar. I like it."

She didn't know when her mind had gone numb, when her thoughts had gone blank, or when she'd let go of all her inhibitions to allow herself to lewdly and wantonly buck into his fingers like she was riding a cock, but that's what Delora was doing.

She knew her face was buried in fur and feathers rather than human flesh. That the delicious smell of vanilla bean and cream belonged to Magnar. She knew the growl that was beginning to emit from him was because he was a Duskwalker.

Delora squeezed her arms around him and gripped his feathers harder in her hands to the point that she knew she must be ripping a few out.

"Don't stop," she rasped as she uncontrollably gyrated. "Please don't stop."

Her cunt was pulsing, throbbing, and quivering. It was so wet that she could feel the easy glide of his fingers that grew more rapid after her pleading. Delora knew she was about to blissfully come around his fingers, and she was absolutely fucking *dying* to.

The scent coming from Delora was beginning to saturate the air, and Magnar huffed it in greedily.

It still smelt like apples and frost, but there was an extra tang to it, something that had his mind tingling. It smelt *naughty*, it smelt hot, and the aroma of it, mixed with the little pleasure-filled cries she gave, had his exterior puffing.

His fur stood on end, his feathers rose, and a vibration down his spine had his body shuddering in reaction to the point his tail shook. It thumped happily against the ground.

His vision flickered to purple, and he looked around in surprise at the colour. This was the first time his sight had *ever* turned to purple, and he had no idea of its meaning.

But every time it changed to it, something stirred in his groin beneath his flesh. He'd also never experienced that sensation before either.

However, Magnar didn't have the thought to focus on these changes within himself.

Delora was moaning against him with her face buried in the fur of his chest, something he was dearly hoping was a good sign. Her body was wriggling on his fingers as he moved them, and her insides were quivering and sucking on them.

He'd never thought touching her inside would make her react like this, especially since he'd thought this was a wound when he'd first healed her only to discover that this slit still remained on her body. As long as she wasn't bleeding, and it was obvious she was enjoying his touch, he didn't care what he was doing.

He just wanted to make Delora happy, and she seemed very, *very* happy right now.

He was touching her, holding her, and she was clinging to him like how he always wanted. Perhaps not like this, not with her making such a pretty sound, but he found he actually liked this more than his fantasies of hugging her.

Her scent was choking his lungs as well as his mind. He was irresistibly drawn to it. He was desperate to breathe it in, to taste it, to have it cover him. He didn't understand his insatiable desire for it, but he was so fixated on making it deepen that he tried to follow her cues.

Magnar had always been a quick learner, so he knew by the hitches of her breath, or the highness of her moan that he'd skimmed a spot she liked. And when her insides swelled around his fingers, he stayed where he was and played.

"Ohhh, *Magnar.*"

The sound of her sweet cry with his name altered his vision to purple completely, and it remained there.

His insides at his groin squirmed. It was a strange sensation, but it also felt pleasurable, tingling with an odd hardness he could feel with a perception of pulsing.

"Oh, gods. I'm going to come," Delora cried breathlessly, her own momentum increasing.

He was curious to know what she meant. He wanted to know what was about to happen, and he moved his fingers faster to see if that would help her.

Delora threw her head against his hand resting behind her neck, arched her back, and screamed just as her inner walls clenched so tightly around his fingers it felt like there was no space for anything more inside her. Then hot liquid rushed out of her, coating his fingers and palm with her juices as she twisted, turned, and bounced.

And that *scent* was now everywhere.

Magnar snarled, before licking at her neck. He desperately needed to taste her, his hand moving faster between her thighs – the place he truly wanted to devour with his mouth, the source of that scent.

Her little body was trembling in his arms, and he gazed at her face with her lips parted on her sweet song. Her brown eyes appeared dazed, but there was something about her expression that had a dark feeling of possessiveness crawling up from the depths within him.

He knew it was special, and he wanted only him to be the one who ever saw it.

Mine...

Something slipped from his own body, something that ached, and he looked down at his groin to find something was tenting his pants.

His mind was then struck.

Something was happening to him, but he hadn't looked down at their bodies yet. His hand was between her thighs, her pink lips were spread around his dark-grey fingers, and he could see everything was wet and glistening from her. He'd never seen such a wonderous sight. His mind froze, and he was unable to take his sight away from them joined like this.

Heat flared throughout his entire body, and whatever was growing from him shot further forward.

Magnar yelped at the pain he felt. What had come from him was squished within his trousers, and the material felt *horrible* against it.

When his purple vision flashed to white in confusion and worry, he lowered Delora from his thighs. He'd been intending to do it gently, but the movement made it scrape against the inner material of his clothing like sandpaper.

He accidentally pushed her off him harder than he intended to with a yelp.

"Magnar?" Delora asked with a frown marring her forehead.

Her lips were parted as if she was panting heavily, and her cheeks were a light pink – not from embarrassment, but rather because she was warm.

He flinched when the pain worsened.

He wanted to apologise. Instead, he rushed out of the house when the ache in his body grew until he could no longer ignore it.

Once outside and to the side of the house, he clawed to undo the front of his trousers and nearly sighed with relief when he released what was bothering him.

He knelt down and twisted his head in bewilderment. He held the phallic thing that was jutting between his hip bones. He'd never known that the line down the centre of his groin could split apart and reveal a dark-purple rod that had a near-black tip.

Four tentacles wriggled around the long and thick girth of it with seeking tips from the base of the slit that had opened. The tips of the tentacles flared in a spade shape, and they had little nodules inside them.

He curiously poked the side of the hard, not squirming part, coming from him.

"What is this?" he muttered, bringing his finger away after poking it to find it was actually covered in a slick liquid.

The head was a roundish oval shape, but the rim of it had bumps around it. There were three double sets of smaller bumpy nodes going down the top and sides of the hard, phallic rod, and a deep indent going from underneath him.

He tried to sniff it. He couldn't reach that far, but it smelt sweet from what he could tell.

He wasn't quite sure what to do with this new thing on his body.

And the longer he did nothing, staring at it questioningly, the more the air got to it. The liquid that had been covering him, like it was a protective layer, started to dry.

Magnar jerked back.

"It stings." Then he backed away again as if he could escape his very own body part. "Why does it sting?!"

He yelped when it dried further and gripped it to make it stop burning. That only covered part of it, and the head that was exposed swelled due to the terrible stinging sensation that wouldn't ease, and instead became rather distressing.

He gripped it with both hands as sharp whines echoed into the night around him and then he started *shoving* it back inside.

It hurt, creating this horrible pressure in his groin due to the hardness of it, but he kept trying to get it back inside, where it instantly felt better within the shelter of his body.

The tentacles that had been seeking something curled around the rod protectively. That eased the worst of his pain, but he couldn't get the last quarter inside his body until it went soft from his distress.

Magnar sat back on his haunches while staring at the line of fur that turned inwards right between his hips. Now that it was gone, he no longer felt any sensation there – neither good like in the beginning, nor bad like the ending.

He gave an irritated huff at his body.

Magnar promised himself that the strange and painful thing that had come from him would never be allowed to emerge again.

Yet, the moment his mind tried to turn to something positive, like how Delora had *come* – as she called it – around his fingers, and he lifted his hand to sniff her liquid, his sight flickered to purple.

His groin began to squirm, and his seam started to open!

An acute whine came from him, and he shoved his hands against it to keep it shut. He let his sight wander around the yard.

Thinking about her scent, her noises, the faces she pulled, was making his body stir.

"Does... that mean I cannot touch her again?"

But he wanted to, badly.

He curled his tongue so he could lick his fangs from the outside, the insatiable need to taste the honey that gushed from her gripping his mind like a frenzied animal refusing to let go of its prey. He *need*ed to taste her.

Now he wondered how he was supposed to do that without *this* coming from him.

SEVENTEEN

Delora curled herself up in the new blanket she'd been given until she was well and truly *burritoed* inside of it. She even tucked the pillow in the opening to support her head as she tried to hide from the world.

I can't believe he suddenly left like that!

She felt all sorts of tangled emotions. Anger, embarrassment, shame, guilt... but she hadn't felt that way until he'd withdrawn his fingers from her and bolted out of the room like she was on fire.

Instead, Delora had been huffing against his chest, floating in some blissful state of euphoria after coming directly into his hand.

She had wanted to break down the barrier between them. She didn't know it would lead to him delving his fingers inside her pussy, but she had felt undeniably closer to him because of it. Delora had *liked* it.

She'd never had someone focus solely on her pleasure rather than just getting her turned on so they could receive their own. And the way Magnar had held the back of her head and licked affectionately at her neck while asking her if she liked what he was doing had made her heart race.

Now it beat with dread on each thump.

What if I was the only one that liked it? Had she misunderstood how he was feeling? Was pity the reason he'd done that with her?

But she also felt guilt and shame because she'd let him

continue, all while knowing he was just... learning? Delora knew he had no idea what he'd done and had run on pure instinct. Maybe he'd done it for her, but that felt extremely one-sided.

Although she found him quite adorable and sweet, it was the equivalent of taking advantage of a naïve idiot. She was angry with herself that she let it go so far, that she hadn't stopped him because she had enjoyed it and wanted it.

I hope I didn't ruin things.

She cuddled her midsection while fearing the worst. Especially when she struggled to fall asleep because he didn't return.

Even when the sky brightened, Magnar was vacant of the area. She made sure to stay within the border of his ward, but she knew after exploring all of it in search of him that he was gone.

There was a bucket filled with fresh water and some food she'd been given, so she had plenty to keep herself well.

He'd never been gone for this long before, and without him there, Delora had little else to do but think. And she didn't want to think. Her thoughts were never positive.

Staring down at her hands while sitting on the porch steps so she could see when he came back, Delora felt the urge to try to turn ghostly. She'd never attempted before, freaked out by the whole idea. Now that she had no one to watch her with possibly judgemental eyes, she felt brave enough to give it a go.

It was better than sitting here depressed, after all.

"Okay... so how do I do this?"

She turned her hands downwards, so her palms were facing the freshly carved steps, before turning them back up, willing her body to change.

That's all it took.

The moment she wanted to turn transparent, pictured it, she began floating about an inch off the porch steps in the same position she'd been sitting. Her arms cartwheeled at feeling no support or assistance. She ended up going upside down so that the upper portion of her body went through the steps while her legs were kicking in the air.

"Go solid! Go solid!"

Once more, it was just that easy.

She floated out of the steps, turned solid, and landed on her face with a distinct thud.

Her eyes watered in pain from bashing her nose and the way her neck kinked when her head hit the porch stairs. Delora slid before the rest of her body fell over her head. *OW!!*

"What are you doing, Delora?"

A shriek left her at Magnar's voice, not realizing he'd been there to see her fall on her face. Laying on her back, she covered her reddening cheeks to hide, wishing to turn back time to five seconds ago.

"You're back?" She gained the courage to look upon him – to find he faced anywhere but in her direction. "Where'd you go?"

There were two dead birds hanging from one of his hands, dangling beside his thigh, and she eyed them with caution.

"I find birds are easy for me to catch in comparison to land creatures, which is why I have so many feathers myself." He raised his arm and shoved them in her direction. "You need meat, so I went to hunt for you."

"You left to get me food?"

She would have been relieved by that, but every time his head started to move in her direction, he would dart it away.

"I went to visit Orpheus, but he and Reia were not home. I thought they may be hunting, so I tried to find them but could not. I remembered you had little food."

When she didn't take the birds, he placed them on the ground next to her and stepped to the side.

"I have work I need to do." He began to walk away while nodding – but more to himself than her. "Yes. I still need to make the supports for the porch roof."

Delora looked down at the birds at her feet with disgust. She didn't know where to start as she'd never plucked a chicken in her entire life, and she also didn't know what species of bird it was.

Is this even safe for me?

Her eyes drifted to Magnar, who had taken a seat on the stump and was carving at the large log he'd been working on the day before. His back was to her, and Delora's heart sunk.

I'm not really hungry, though. Yet she couldn't remember the last time she'd eaten. It definitely wasn't today.

As much as him being distant was bothering her, she reached forward to grab them by their feet. The two birds were large and mostly brown. *I've gutted a chicken, so I can at least do that.* And plucking them didn't look *too* hard, just disgusting.

With that, Delora carefully placed them on the porch where they were safe and collected large rocks from around the yard. Groaning noises could be heard from her as she picked up a few fairly large rocks that were a little too heavy for her to carry.

She eyed Magnar in her peripheral. She intentionally made it a difficult task in order to get him to help her, but she only noticed his body shake before he darted his head the other way.

He, who was usually always curious about her, didn't even ask her what she was doing.

By the time Delora had made a large ring of stones and collected enough dry branches to place in the middle to make a decent campfire, her face tingled with the urge to cry. She was stifling it, refusing to allow herself the release, to shed a single tear.

Okay, I fucked up. She searched the inside for the matches and then tried to light the fire. Her self-made campfire was about three metres away from the porch steps. It was far enough away so the house couldn't catch fire, but close enough she'd be able to feel its warmth.

He's not talking to me. He won't even look at me.

Delora plonked herself on the steps and carelessly worked on pulling the feathers out of the birds.

But it's not just my fault! It was mostly her fault. *He put his fingers literally inside me without warning!* Delora knew she probably could have stopped him. *You're supposed to ask a girl for permission to finger her...* Yeah, but she'd gyrated on his hand like a fucking cat in heat regardless.

Delora plucked the second bird faster when it felt like a bug had nestled its way under her skin and kept biting at her heart.

I-I should apologise to him. But then she would have to explain why she was apologising, which would mean she would have to explain what they'd done together. *Ugh. It wouldn't be this hard if he were a human.*

Her eyes pulled away from her task to land upon him.

It wouldn't be this hard if he were a human, but it was doubtful the situation would have come about in the first place because deep down inside, Delora had a funny feeling she wouldn't be this comfortable with another human, especially a man. She never would have allowed them to hold her, touch her, or even do something as simple as brush her hair.

Humans usually had ulterior motives. Magnar had none.

I wonder when I started finding him attractive.

She drifted her eyes over the large antlers sticking out of his bony skull, wondering when she had started not only caring for him but liking him enough that she'd begun to feel desire.

What had once been off-putting about his face and shape now made her think of him as almost... holy. Like a divine druid spirit that perhaps Witches, in the long distant past, may have danced around in hopes of prosperity, fertility, and faith.

There were still parts of him that made her wary, like his dangerous claws and teeth, but the more comfortable she grew around him, the more it made her let down her guards.

Delora sighed at the plucked birds before she used a knife to gut them. Then she carved the end of two sticks until they were neatly pointed and shoved them into the birds so she could rest them near the fire to cook.

I wonder what would have happened if he didn't run away.

Would she have asked for more? At the time, she'd been content in his arms while feeling her body thrumming around his fingers. She couldn't remember the last time she'd come so hard, even by her own hands.

His inexperienced touch had ignited her.

That nasty bug in her chest bit even harder. She placed her feet on a higher step so she could rest her arms across her knees and cuddle into them. She watched the birds cooking with a glare.

Their smell was surprisingly pleasant, and her stomach *finally* grumbled in emptiness.

Delora let out a humourless laugh. She'd gone through all this effort. She'd collected the rocks and branches, started the fire, and even fully prepared the birds and staked them, and she no longer felt like fucking eating.

I just want to go to sleep. Like before, when she didn't care what Magnar did, where she was, or what happened to her. She just wanted to escape how she felt, especially since it was somehow even worse than before.

Once they were done cooking, Delora pulled the birds away from the fire and wrapped them in cloth. She'd try to eat them later, but right then, her stomach was too twisted into knots to even try.

The sky was growing darker. It always seemed to be dark inside the Veil with all the trees around the house. She didn't think it would be night any time soon, but the constant shadows made night fall long before the sun had truly set.

Delora looked at the remaining water she had in the wash bucket from when Magnar had done the strange spell with his blood to conjure it. It was cold now, but she wiped herself down anyway and immediately regretted it.

It wasn't as soothing as it had been when it was warm. She shivered as she dragged the bucket outside and tipped it onto the fire to snuff it out.

"Hey, Magnar," Delora called out. It was a last bid to get his attention. "I'm, uh, going to go to sleep."

Silence was what she received for a long while, and Delora only knew where to find him in the growing shadows because of his glowing green orbs. His antlers made it appear as though he was a moving tree sometimes.

He turned his head over his shoulder just enough to see her. "But you did not eat, Delora."

She lifted a hand and rubbed at her biceps, hugging her arms to her torso. Her gaze fell to the side, to the extinguished campfire, and then remained there. She didn't understand why she was relieved that he'd actually responded, but her nestling worries didn't ease.

"I don't really feel like eating."

"But you must eat." He dragged his snout through the air in the direction of the campfire. "I hunted for you, and I brought you back meat. It will make you stronger."

Her face paled.

She wished she hadn't said anything. She hadn't expected to be guilted this way. She knew he didn't mean to come across that way, but she didn't want to be questioned about food when she sincerely thought it would feel like lead in her gut.

"I'll eat it later," she conceded, the lie tasting sour.

Delora made her way inside and lit a few candles so she could see through the night if she woke. She'd been given a few candle plates and was thankful for that. She didn't want to burn all of Magnar's hard work to the ground.

Her back went ramrod straight when she heard the familiar sound of three-toed hooves climbing the porch before they crossed it. She cringed as the door creaked open, and she turned in time to see him stepping through the doorway.

The real cause for alarm was that his orbs were white. She knew they only ever turned that colour when afraid or worried – generally for her sake.

He bent over to pick up the meat she'd wrapped in cloth to preserve it, at least for a little while, from the table she'd placed it on.

"You did not eat any of it."

A frown crinkled her brows deeply. *How would he know that?* He would have needed to have been watching her to know she hadn't taken a bite out of them. Had he been?

Caught red-handed, Delora's cheeks heated when he opened the cloth to show the birds were fully intact, aside from her sloppy attempt at preparing them.

She brought her eyes away to look at the log walls of the cabin as though they were fascinating.

"I'll have them later."

She doubted the meat would last more than a few hours before it went bad, as she had no way to store them correctly. He'd gone out of his way to get these for her, and she would be wasting it, but she didn't feel like force-feeding herself. Which was strange considering her old way of comforting herself was with food.

Did becoming a Phantom change me? Not just in the ways she'd already learned, but even more than that?

That brought on the realisation that she still craved food, but she didn't particularly feel starving, even when she didn't eat for a while. Her stomach would grumble eventually, but that was only after about a day.

She hugged her midsection when she realised her weight had not changed despite her new eating habits. *Am I permanently like this?* If she were, that meant her size, her height, and even her age would stay the same.

She touched her cheek. *To be young forever?*

The idea of growing old had once frightened Delora – mainly because of Hadith's cruel comments – but if she was permanently like this, then she no longer needed to worry.

While she had been deep in thought, Magnar came closer with a piece of meat in his fingertips. He was crouching, his head tilted to the side, and approaching slowly as if he thought she was a skittish animal that might run.

"If you are too tired, I will feed you," he offered, his orbs still a stark colour of white. "Humans need food to be strong. You will not get better if you do not eat and drink."

Even from the beginning, Magnar's main priority was to make sure her needs were met. Was that why he was here when he had not cared to speak with her all day?

He raised his fingertips to her mouth, pressing the white meat to her lips. Delora felt pathetic when tears collected on the lengths of her eyelashes, and she gripped his wrist with both hands to stop him.

There is more to taking care of a human than feeding them. She wasn't a pet bird in a cage that only needed water, sun, food, and a little free time. Delora *wanted* his attention.

It made her feel alive. It made her feel like her presence was *wanted*. The desire to disappear faded when Magnar was near. When he'd been gone or ignored her, it had doubled its pressure to the point she feared she'd sink into the ground.

And she *knew* it was pathetic of her.

"Delora," he warned, but she shook her head.

"I-I'm sorry if I upset you," she said quietly, bringing her hands forward to cup him around his snout.

His head darted back at her touch, and Delora bit her bottom lip as a painful surge throbbed through her heart.

That was until he pushed his snout back through her awaiting palms and set the food down carefully. It gave him the freedom to place his hands over her own as they cupped his face.

Magnar had ducked away in shock, as she didn't usually reach for him like this. But she knew by the darkening of his orbs as if they had 'closed,' and the fact she could now feel him rubbing into her hands... he was enjoying it.

"I like this," Magnar nearly purred into her palms as he nestled into them. "It pushes your scent into my nose, and your hands are warm enough that I can feel them."

The food forgotten, he reached his arms around her knees to pull her closer and force more of her body around his snout. The tip was directly against the opening of her shirt right between her breasts, and his breath fanned inside to stroke both at the same time.

Heat immediately rushed through her entire body as a shiver, and she gasped. Then his tongue came out to dab between the valley of her breasts as if he wanted to taste her. It sent an electric shock straight through her body.

They both backed away from each other like a force had driven between them. She slipped out of his arms as his snout came away from between her hands.

His orbs were glowing a bright purple. Turning his head to the side, he covered them up with a hand like he didn't want her to see. His jaws parted, and he let out a raspy huff. Then his body quaked with a shudder that went from the base of his skull to the bottom of his spine, causing his tail to wiggle.

But Delora had backed away because that small amount of touch had sparked her like a thunderbolt. His lick had reminded her of it swiping over her nipple and sensitive skin the night before, and her inner walls had clamped with want for his fingers to delve again.

Magnar covered the tip of his snout with his entire hand, pressing his palm over his nose hole to stifle the scents around it.

"You have that sweet smell again," he said, his voice huskier than normal, darker even.

A horrible emotion tore through Delora. She wrapped one arm over her stomach and gripped her elbow, turning her eyes away from him. Things had been going well. He was talking to her, holding her... and then her body had decided to grow aroused by just that.

Why does he keep giving me this reaction?

EIGHTEEN

After a few seconds passed of Magnar holding the end of his snout, Delora watched as his orbs faded back to their usual green.

He slid a little closer.

"What does this smell mean?" he asked, reaching forward to tap against her pelvis. "Yesterday it was because I was touching you, but just then I was only holding you."

Delora didn't know if her face paled or reddened at having to explain this to him. And she knew she needed to. She couldn't keep this information from him since he had such a good olfactory ability.

"It, uh, sometimes happens to humans. I liked being near you and that you licked me, so I got excited." Delora gripped the bottom of her shirt and shoved it down with both hands as if that would help to stop it radiating from her. "It's called arousal, or that I'm becoming aroused or turned on."

"Aroused?" He tilted his head in that way she knew meant he was curious but didn't understand.

Delora's eyes darted to the side as if her mind was trying to find an escape from the conversation. They eventually fell back on him.

"It's difficult to explain to someone who doesn't feel desire."

His head tilted the other way, a little sharper than before, and the sound of dry bones rattling together clacked from him.

"But I feel the desire to hold you."

Delora shook her head, making her hair sway around her shoulders.

"It's a different kind of desire."

"But it means that you like me?"

When Delora stepped back to create space between them at the invasiveness of his question, Magnar crept forward to follow her. His head followed her movements, and those orbs, holding no emotion in their floating, rotating, fiery vortexes to indicate what he was feeling, were watching her.

She knew he was awaiting a response.

"Yes. I like you, Magnar."

His orbs flashed bright yellow before going back to their usual green. She *knew* they would change.

"And Delora likes my touch? Likes to be held by me so much that she creates this scent?"

She didn't know why he phrased it that way, but she nodded. When he finally released his snout and reached out to place his arms around her thighs to draw her between his crouched knees, Delora staggered away from him in a rush.

The moment his claws scraped over the back of her thighs, her knees had almost caved in.

"I'm sorry, but I can't." Her arousal was deepening, just his voice and the barest of touch sparking her greedy body. "I'm sorry," she repeated.

"Why are you apologising?"

There was a predatory energy coming from him now as he slowly, at her pace, began to follow her retreat.

Because it feels wrong to do this with you. She didn't know how to say that without hurting his feelings.

Not only was he a Duskwalker, but he also didn't understand. She didn't know what to do.

Delora covered her face, wishing for the answer.

She yelped when her ankle and her feet came out from under her. She landed on her arse before she was dragged across the ground.

"Where are you going, Delora?"

Delora let out a gasp when the shirt rode halfway up her back and everything from the under curve of her breasts to her feet was uncovered. Magnar then grabbed the bottom of the shirt and shoved it higher so that it was around her throat, completely exposing her breasts.

"Hey!" She tried to get out from under him when he lifted a hand so he could brush the tip of his forefinger claw against her nipple, creating a sharp sensation against the sensitive pad of it.

She squirmed when she felt the slick of her arousal growing between the lips of her labia folds.

His eyes changed to purple, and he dragged her back towards him with a quick snarl.

"Stay," he demanded. "I want to touch."

"I don't think we should do this."

Delora lost her argument when he swiped his tongue over her entire breast. It was large and flat, but a little rough. He travelled it from the under curve, over her nipple, and then circled it along her areola.

"But I like the smell of your *arousal.* It makes you feel good."

When he went to lick again, Delora shoved her hand against the tip of his snout and pushed it away.

"But you've been avoiding me all day! I thought you didn't like this."

Magnar shot his arm forward and pinned hers to the ground next to her shoulder to stop her from pushing at him. He placed his other hand on her thigh to drive her legs apart, and she could tell he'd taken in a deep draw of her scent by the huff and shudder that followed.

"Because every time I looked at you, I wanted to touch you. I wanted to taste your skin." He leaned his head down and *bit* around one of her breasts, sinking all of his front fangs into the mound of it. Then he licked around and over her nipple, covering it in saliva. "But my sight would turn purple, and my body would feel strange. I did not like it."

His orbs were currently holding a purple that was deepening by the second.

He raked his claws up the line of her inner thigh, and she let out a raspy gasp, almost throwing her head back. Those sharp tips on the ends of his fingers always seemed to do funny things to her insides. Along with his fangs literally sinking into her right breast, they both felt... wrong, dangerous, and deliciously *naughty* when they cut against her.

"Then why are you doing this if–"

"Being aroused means you want to be touched, yes? I want to make you feel good." He pulled his head back, nibbling once around her nipple before nuzzling it. "Your scent deepens when I touch here."

"Magnar, you don't have to do this for me."

Confusing emotions were bubbling within her, and her mind felt frazzled. Every touch was making her skin burn hotter, making the pool of desire at her entrance deepen. Her blood raced faster in need, but she didn't understand *why* he would do this. What did Magnar get out of it?

Was it out of pity for her? Self-gratification for him?

She *wanted* to do this, to have him touch her, but she also wanted him to like it. She didn't know why, only that she did, and his glowing purple orbs seemed to pull her further under.

"I will be good," he promised, not that she understood why he felt the need to make it. "I am in control."

He ran two of his fingers, with claws retracted, from her entrance all the way to her clit, making the hard nub move to the side under his caress.

Her face instantly flustered when he lifted them to inspect the drip of her arousal that coated them. He'd collected a lot.

"You're wetter than you were last time."

"No!" she shouted when he lifted his hand with his tongue poking out. "Don't lick it!"

It was too late.

Magnar swiped his tongue curiously over his fingers to taste her.

The growl that followed was deep, rumbling, and chest vibrating, making her skin prickle with goosebumps. His orbs flashed a *dark* green, then back to an even deeper purple. She watched his entire body puff beneath his shirt.

"More," he snarled.

Delora was yanked again until her lower back was resting against his thighs. Then his long, firm, and rough tongue was shoved inside her so deep that it bottomed out against her cervix. His fangs parted around her.

Her entire body melted. Her brain turned to goo inside her

skull. Her shiver shook her entire nervous system to the point everything tingled, everything clenched – her toes, her hands, and her pussy around the firm organ. *Everything* throbbed.

She twisted her hips the opposite direction his tongue swirled, and then the other way when he changed directions. Her toes curled, never feeling such a flexible, wiggling sensation so deep inside before.

He seemed to want to collect every drop of her slick before his tongue drew away. His orbs morphed to black when he leaned his head back, licked the inside of his mouth, and groaned. The hand around her thigh holding her up clamped tighter, his fingertips digging in.

Magnar gave a huff when he turned his head down and opened his sight.

"*This* is what you taste like?" A rumble came from his chest, one that sounded like it was vibrating within. "Had I known you had tasted this delectable, I would have tried to do this sooner."

When he darted his head forward as if to lick her again, Delora grabbed his antlers with both her hands and held firm by locking her elbows.

She wanted to tell him to wait, but she couldn't. The words wouldn't fall from her, like they were clogged in her chest, refusing to burst. A part of her didn't want him to stop.

She knew if she did, that he would, just like when she'd told him no in the past.

But she couldn't handle him doing that again. Her body had almost had an entire meltdown, and she needed to think. *He put his tongue inside me!* And the saliva he left behind was thick and spreading between her folds. She squirmed to ease the tingling she felt from it.

"More. *I* need *more,*" he demanded, with a snarly undertone present in his voice.

His strength won against hers.

His flat and large tongue licked from her backside, making her jump in surprise, before he dipped it over her entrance and then clit. Her hips moved in a wave from side to side when he stroked it just right.

Delora was still gripping his antlers, but now for an entirely different reason. In a death grip, she used them to centre herself when her body arched against his moving tongue, spreading her lips apart. She let out a strangled moan.

She tried to close her legs, and she wasn't sure if it was to preserve her sanity or to escape the intensity of just how *amazing* this felt.

Magnar paused and gave a terrible whine.

His head backed away. He lowered her, his grip on both her thighs tight as he quaked. The second whine that followed told her it wasn't in pleasure, but in repulsion or pain.

His jaws parted, drool dripping from his top fangs, as he huffed loudly. Each breath exhaled with a high-pitch noise.

Delora's hold on his antlers grew firmer, and her brows knotted together at his behaviour. She tried to ignore the naughty throb all her delicate places were giving her, demanding that she tug on him to bring him back down.

If Magnar wanted to stop, she would let him without complaint. It's just... he kept instigating this kind of touch and then would grow strange and distant.

"What's wrong, Magnar?"

The longer he sat on his knees, the more his quaking seemed to worsen. He gripped at his abdomen, his claws digging into his shirt and tearing it.

She was now wearing the only good one he had left.

"It hurts, Delora," he whimpered.

He gave another shudder, this time with his orbs black, and tore at his neck. But he wasn't backing away. Instead, he seemed to be gripping her thigh tightly, like he didn't want to leave her. She winced when she knew it would bruise.

Delora rolled up so she could sit a little, leaning on her elbows, and eyeing his body for some kind of wound. *Did I kick him?* She'd been wriggling a bunch, but she didn't think she actually had the power in her human legs to hurt a Duskwalker, no matter how much she moved.

"Where?"

His orbs flashed white, showing Delora his hesitation, before he turned his head to the side. Purple remained when he clutched at his abdomen again, giving a longer flash of white, as his head arced from the side to look downwards.

She probably didn't need to squint her eyes to see the strange-looking bulge she could see between her open thighs, but her eyes struggled to see *what* she was supposed to be looking at. She refused to accept that she saw something moving against his trousers from the inside.

"Magnar?"

Her mouth went dry when he reached down and pulled on his trousers as though to unbutton them. She didn't believe he was actually opening them to reveal what he was about to, not when she'd felt nothing there before.

She was wrong. Oh, so very wrong.

He didn't even need to do anything. The moment he opened his trousers fully, something hard, long, fat, and *wrong* sprang from them. It was followed by four moving limbs that wiggled fairly similar to how his tongue had inside her.

Delora's jaw fell, and her lips parted.

Right before her eyes, now laying between her hip bones, resting all the way past her navel and slightly higher, was the biggest cock she'd ever seen or even heard of.

The oval-shaped head was such a dark colour purple that it almost appeared black. The colour started to lighten behind the rim of the head, turning into a deep purple until it met some sort of seam. A slit had opened, which is where this thing had obviously come from, and from what she could see, it was also a deep purple inside.

It was surrounded by short fur between his white protruding hip bones.

The four tentacles that were about six, maybe even seven inches long, followed the same pattern of being darker at their spaded tips and grew lighter the further down to his hips.

Delora's eyes bounced from each strange detail frantically. From the head all the way to the large oval bulges at the base that almost appeared to be what she thought were his semen sacs, but were instead imbedded into the undersides of his penis. Her eyes drew a path up the deep groove underneath his shaft, and then down the double lines of nodule bumps that ran down the top and sides of it.

The strangest part was the rim of the head. It had round bumps that were very noticeable.

Nothing about it could really be called human except for the fact it was phallic in shape. Its length was superhuman. It was so many inches long she knew no human would be able to take all of it, and it was so thick she thought she could clench her fist and it would still be bigger.

"You actually do have a cock?" The question fell from her lips but was more directed towards herself in complete disbelief.

Well, it looked like a *cock.* Just a freaky one. It was where a cock was supposed to be. But Delora couldn't wrap her head around the fact it was hard and staring her directly in the eye.

"Cock?" Magnar asked back on a husky breath, seeming slightly calmer now that he had released it. It was more of a monster than he was! Then he touched the side of it and uttered, "Is that what this is?"

Her eyes grew wide, and she managed to tear them away from his squirming tentacles to look at his bony face.

"You... you don't know what that is?"

"Until yesterday, I have never seen this part of myself." Then he laid his hand on her side, bringing her closer and incidentally slipping his cock over her folds. She realised the shine she could see on it was because his shaft had its own lubrication to keep it moist. "But you know what it is. Can you explain it to me?"

Somehow her eyes grew wider, and she lowered her gaze to stare at it. Her pussy's inner walls immediately clenched – in worry or in *need,* she didn't know.

"It-it's a cock. A penis or dick." She licked at her lips to wet them. "It means that you are a man – or a male, I guess."

A shaking moan fell from Delora when his hand slid down her thigh, and he pressed his entire thumb inside her channel.

"And this means that you are a female?"

"Yes. That's my vagina. Or, uh, pussy."

She almost uttered the word cunt, but Delora *sincerely* didn't think she could handle it if this innocent Duskwalker started calling it that particular word.

"Why are we different?"

Before Delora could answer, his orbs flashed white, and he

gave a curt whine as his jaws parted. He gripped his dick with his free hand while the tentacles at the base wriggled faster.

"It hurts," he explained, gripping it so hard she could see that he was squishing in his fist. "I don't like it exposed. When it dries, it stings."

"When it dries?"

Delora inspected the lubricant on his cock. It was now patchy, and the exposed layers of his shaft looked wrinkled.

"Inside here is warm." He pushed his thumb even deeper and then pulled to the side, spreading her cunt open as if he wanted a little peek inside. "And wet, like the inside of my seam."

Purple came into his floating orbs, and he gave a huff, one that was deep and short like a pant. His hips pulled back and then thrust forward. It placed that groove underneath him so perfectly against the hard nub of her clit that it sat right in the middle and was rubbed from all sides.

Ohhh, fuck! She bit her lip and pushed into it absentmindedly, her eyelids fluttering uncontrollably in bliss until his stroke ended.

"That feels better." His antlers created shadows over her as he held her by her thigh, placed his other hand against the ground near her hips, and starting moving back and forth. Wetness from him slowly began to spread. "*Haaa.* This helps."

She bit her bottom lip and tried to push herself against his heavy erection. "It does?"

"But it is not enough."

Realisation dawned on Delora.

He may not know what was going on, but his body did, his *instincts* did. She knew exactly what his cock wanted, what it needed, and when she saw a single, thick drop of semen well at the eye of his cock head, she knew she had to make a decision.

"Delora," he groaned. "I want inside you. I need warmth and moisture. I need you."

"You want to have sex with me," she whispered, wanting him to at least understand what he was saying. At least give it a *name*. "Be intimate with me."

And as much as the cock sliding against her, petting her little clit back and forth while being deep within the groove of the underside of him was strange, Delora knew she wanted it.

She was scared about its size; she knew it might hurt, but she wanted Magnar. Delora wanted to comfort this side of him, to soothe it. The pool at her entrance grew, and she tried to wrap her calves around his hips.

"Inside," he repeated, as if he was no longer able to think about anything else. "Need inside you."

His hips increased in their pace as he lowered himself to curl around her where she lay against the ground. He drew his thumb out just enough so he could slip his hand to her backside to grasp one cheek and lift her into his thrusts.

She could feel the two tentacles underneath him slipping over her backside with seeking tips, tickling her skin and making her bounce upwards in surprise. She hadn't expected them to feel so rough inside, but they were also wet.

Her heart clenched. She placed her forehead against the fur of his pectoral muscles and gave a small nod.

"O-okay. Just... just be gentle, okay?"

Delora lowered her hand. When she grabbed the head of Magnar's cock, he snarled with his eyes flashing red. She yelped and drew back.

His snarl turned into a constant growl, like her touch had ignited an aggression in him.

He grabbed his cock this time, around the base, and drew his hips back. When he came forward, he wedged the tip against the slit of her pussy, and already she could tell it was going to be a tight fit.

The tip was moist with her arousal, his lubricant, and the drips of precum that had leaked from him. That didn't ease his entrance when he started to push in, *hard*.

Her eyes clenched, and she pressed her hand against his pelvis to slow him. *It's so big.* When that didn't work, she tried to bring her knees up so she could push them against his hips, but he was too close for her to wriggle her knees between them.

Delora felt a twinge when her entrance made way over the large, broad head. She knew she hadn't taken it past the rim yet, and already the strain was too much.

Suddenly she felt too small underneath him, too weak, too

fragile. He was taller than her, bigger than her, and so much stronger that no matter how much she pushed at him to make him pause, he only continued to push. He didn't stop shaking, his body clenching against the power of his first thrust.

"I don't think you're going to fit!"

It was like her pubic bone was going to fucking cave in! She tried spreading her legs more, tried closing them, tried lifting her hips to greet him, and nothing seemed to elevate the pressure.

"I think you may need to prepare me first–"

Delora gasped when the head literally popped through before she was finished speaking. She tightened around it, her arms and legs drawing inwards towards her torso, and she fisted the fur on his chest when he pressed it against her.

She felt pain, the fit almost unbearably snug. Tears filled her eyes, and she looked down to find she'd only taken the head. He hadn't even bottomed out of her yet and she knew it was too much.

"You're too big, Magnar."

Was he, though? He was inside, maybe a little uncomfortably for now, but she did truly wonder if she could adjust to something this huge. She didn't know why, but she wanted this to be possible between them.

Maybe I-I just need to loosen up. She did feel pretty tense, and she tried to breathe to soften her body for him.

"*Tight,*" he rasped on a quake. "Wet. I did not know it would be so tight."

The claws against the ground gouged into the timber when he drew his hand back so he could lift it and slam it down next to her head. When he brought himself closer to her, his other arm slipped underneath her so he could hold her to him.

"And you are so warm, *Delora.*"

When he pushed in more, Delora's back arched. Before she could ask him to wait, his big cock had already reached her cervix and was pushing against it, seeking to go deeper when it couldn't.

"Ha," he huffed, squeezing them together, so there wasn't a place between their torsos that wasn't touching. "I can feel your heart beating from the inside."

Just as his quaking body puffed in tension, his cock thickened. She whimpered from it at the same time he let out a whine. But she knew something was happening when his body shuddered further, and his hand gripped her side tighter. He let out the strangest noise she'd ever heard.

Then heat, liquid heat, started soothing her insides. Delora almost thought her body turned into jelly in his arms. Her vision dazed as it split in two when she thought heaven had formed where they were joined to give her comforting bliss.

His cock was pulsating in heavy bursts, thickening before going down, before swelling. Over and over again.

"A-are you coming?" she whispered, trying to resist the delicious desire to moan at the seed she could feel was bubbling inside her channel, filling her with each squirt.

Magnar's haunting, beautiful groan, was her only answer. In just one thrust, the pleasure of her body swallowing his had made him come.

It spilled out of her, dripping down the curve of her backside to drop against the ground, but she didn't care. Magnar rocked slightly, spreading it around, and teaching her much smaller body to mould around his girth.

And when it ceased, they lay there momentarily panting. Their breaths were the only sound other than the silence that echoed around them. Delora bit her bottom lip as her face twisted into one of emotional anguish.

She may have been able to take him, but even now she could feel it was snug. She felt *stuffed*, overfull, stretched to capacity. Delora was pinned on his length and girth, and she looked down to see she'd only taken him halfway.

This isn't possible between us.

If he started moving right now, Delora knew the comfort she felt from his hot semen, like it had soothed her stretched inner muscles, would dissipate.

He's a Duskwalker. He's not human.

"Something came out of me," Magnar stated, his voice radiating from his skull while his breaths continued to huff. He sounded bewildered. "I have never felt anything so pleasurable that my entire body tingled afterwards. You feel phenomenal like this."

He rubbed the corner of his jaw against hers. Rumbling came from him as he swiped his tongue across her face by starting from her jaw, running over her lips, then running over to her temple. Unable to help herself, her body shivered when he dipped it over her ear, causing her to gasp.

Delora was learning that was a real sensitive spot for her, and she wondered if Magnar had realised this as well. Especially when he circled it before licking the underside of her jaw to go across to her nape. He kept licking at her, almost appreciatively, affectionately, dabbling his tongue against her flesh. She started to squirm.

"S-stop licking my neck, Magnar," she begged on a whisper. "It tickles."

But it wasn't tickling her skin. Her pussy was beginning to react, clenching and quivering in certain strokes to the point she could feel his semen trickling out of her, creating this strange tickling sensation within.

Magnar brought his arm out from underneath her so he could raise himself on straightened arms and lick at her chest instead. It started high first, but as he turned his head down and dragged that tongue across one of her nipples, his antlers began almost circling around her head. She had to watch out that she didn't poke her eye out, making it difficult for her to see what he was doing.

She sighed in relief when he started pulling back, her face twinging in a little pain, but she could bear with it for a moment.

His claws tapped against the wooden floor. They had done this in the middle of the house with nothing beneath them. Perhaps that was for the best so that they hadn't created a mess in the nest.

The only warning Delora got was the slight growl that came from him before he *shoved* back in and then huffed wildly with a shudder. She moaned in response, the wrong kind.

When she managed to battle his antlers so she could see what he was doing, she realised Magnar's cock hadn't gone soft. It was still large and fully erect inside her, and he had been staring down at where they were joined with purple orbs. She now knew what the colour signified, his desire, and they were still that intense colour.

"You are so soft inside," he muttered, as he pulled back.

"Please, Magnar," Delora pleaded. "We can't do this. You're too big for me."

"But I want to spill again." His jaws parted so his tongue could come out and lick across his snout predatorily. "I want to fill this part of you." She heard the claws of both his hands gouge into the timber next her, as his growl became more apparent. "And I want *deeper* inside you, inside your little *pussy*."

Magnar thrust back in, and this time pushed hard. She could feel his cock pressing so deeply against her cervix that it forced her body to arch. She gripped the fur on his chest and tugged.

"Deeper, Delora," he demanded with a snarl. "Take me deeper within you!"

"I want you to go deeper but you can't!" She was taking as much as she could!

She gave a surprised puff of breath when he shoved all of his claws of his right hand into her abdomen. They pierced her skin, making her bleed, right around where his cock was inside of her.

The slicing of his claws stung, but the pain, the tearing feeling, and the uncomfortableness Delora had been experiencing inside her pussy before instantly faded. Relief flooded her.

There was a radiating warmth within, one that felt foreign, mystical, and strange. She knew he must be using some sort of spell or magic on her to remove her pain and to *change* her as his cock slipped further inside when it would have been impossible before.

And it felt sublime. There was something about her body making way for Magnar's cock, literally rearranging to fit him, that had her wriggling in absolute fucking delight around that fat and warm dick.

Now that she wasn't so focused on her own body, she could feel he was throbbing so wildly that it felt like a flutter. The changing swells of his cock, like pulsating but far more intense, made it feel like he was slithering inside.

Her toes clenched into curls so tightly that her feet and ankles arched, and she moaned violently. Her cunt grew wetter in a rush, hungrily trying to suck his cock further in.

She may not truly understand how he was doing this, but all Delora cared about was that it felt phenomenal. It was mind-numbing, thought stealing, and it made her hungrier to be filled.

He drew back before he was anywhere near seated deep, and her eyes grew wide with panic. She frantically tried to look down.

"No," she rasped, shoving her hands to his sides to grip the fur that so she could try to pull him back in. *Deeper.* "You're not all the way in—"

The rest of him rammed inside her in a swift motion.

His cock bottomed out simply because he had nothing left to give her.

"Ohhhh!" Delora screamed as her pussy clenched.

Her entire body bowed. Her head thudded loudly against the ground, radiating an ache in it that was immediately forgotten. Everything went stiff. Her arms, her legs, her stomach muscles, and her body as it started milking his cock.

Delora was coming around his shaft, her eyes rolling back so hard that her vision blackened.

She tried wrapping her thighs around his lean waist as she gyrated, moving him slightly in and out of her as he made guttural noises of satisfaction over her. Delora was completely and utterly lost.

Those moving tentacles wrapped around the curves of her backside and over her hips, snapping her snugly into place, but she kept moving despite them. She needed to, had to, as the most intense orgasm she'd ever felt clutched her entire being so fully that she thought her soul between his antlers may have trembled in reaction.

NINETEEN

Magnar felt the clutch of her pussy as it wonderfully squeezed his throbbing cock. He let out a snorting pant as his fangs parted.

"*Fuck,*" he groaned, a word Reia had taught him, and one he'd never needed to utter before.

But the way Delora's body was convulsing around his, massaging the entire length of the aching rod jutting from between his hips. The way it had covered his cock in slick liquid, completely and utterly drenching him to ensure not a single part of him felt dry. The way her scent was sweet like red apples and cold like frost, but was also spiced in a tang he now knew was wicked...

All of it was so blissful that the curse had fallen from him, and it had felt right to say it.

Delora was hot inside. She was wet. Her pussy was so soft and plump that it moulded around him, cuddling his cock while a soothing and comforting beat drummed from her erratic heartbeat. And she was so fucking tight that he knew there wasn't a place he wasn't filling.

She had swallowed him whole, making him feel connected to her in a way he'd never experienced before.

A feral feeling took over him, making his fur and feathers puff beneath his clothing that suddenly felt far too constricting. He reached behind his back and gouged his claws into his shirt, ripping and tearing it from his body to leave him bare except for where his trousers sat bundled around his hips.

Red flashed through the purple of his intense desire, before switching to a dark green. Strong emotions were pulling at his senses, his mind, pulling on his control and sanity.

Magnar shoved his hand underneath her body until the back of her neck was resting in his palm. His middle and index fingers supported her head as he lifted her, while his thumb and smaller fingers wrapped around her throat possessively. He squeezed just hard enough to make her understand that he was in control of it – a place so delicate on her body – while his body was filling hers.

Leaning over her much smaller frame, when she finally stopped coming, Magnar lifted her as he lowered himself so they were face-to-face.

He snarled in warning.

"Mine."

Every part of her would be his.

Her soul was his. Her mind was his. Her heart would be his. Her body, deliciously wrapped around his cock, was fucking his. Her scent, no matter its state, was his to breathe in. That ravenous moan she'd just given him, the one that had been a screaming cry, was only his to hear.

Her beauty, whether it be her face or her naked body, was his to look upon. He'd never understood why clothing had mattered, but he now understood. Her breasts, so large and round and droopy from their weight, were his to look upon, to taste, to sniff, to tease until she created that aroused scent.

Her ears were his to play with, as was her neck.

"You are mine," he said, before he pulled back his cock, only to feel her inner walls sucking on it, like they didn't want to release him. Her lips meshed together on a whimper, her eyes bouncing between his purple orbs while he cradled her neck and head before he slammed his shaft back in. *"And this, my little raven, is my pussy."*

The moment he'd shoved his claws into her belly and used his magic to change her body to fit his, he knew he'd claimed it. He hadn't really understood what he'd been doing at the time, but now he did. And he would never allow another to get so close to her that their body was within hers.

That single stroke had been enough to spur him, and he let her neck go so that he could wrap both his arms around her from underneath. He protected her from the ground as one hand clamped her shoulder while the other wrapped around her outer thigh.

Magnar pulled back and thrust back inside of her, shuddering from the sheer rapture of it.

Delora wrapped her arms around his torso, delving into his fur without hesitation, and tugged on it. He liked that she did, that she was desperately clinging to him like he'd always wanted. But it was so much better now that he knew he could bury himself inside her the way he was.

They were one.

Her stomach moulded around his own and was so soft that he found himself moving in and out of her harder so that it would jiggle more, would brush over him more. He squeezed her, harder than he would have a smaller human, and huffed his contentment.

Her cries were sharp, ear-piercing even, and he allowed himself to enjoy every single one.

 It didn't take long for him to increase his pace, to spear her repeatedly. She soon started clamping erratically around him as liquid gushed from her.

"That!" he groaned, nearly panting to the point he was choking. His voice kept changing in tone, in darkness, in huskiness, revealing how little control he truly had over himself. *"Again. Come again, Delora. I want to smell it. I want to feel it."*

He wanted it to consume him until he was nothing but bone.

All his life, Magnar had experienced insatiable hunger. To eat flesh, to dig into muscle, to bite around organs. He'd thought it was unbearable, but nothing could compare to the hunger to deeply pound into this squirming woman in his arms.

And the more she wriggled in delight around him, the rougher he wanted to be with her. He gently bit around her throat and held her in place with his tentacles around her hips and his arms around her body. Magnar wanted to pin her down, to pin her so completely she would know who the master was.

He'd never held desires like this before, but they overwhelmed him with each stroke of his cock. He could feel his nodules on the sides of his shaft popping in and out of her like little *vibrations.* Each one sent a spasm through his shaft.

The intensity of their combined heat as it grew from friction, their wetness mingling to create a scent that was unique to them, was intoxicating.

And there was this sound. A sucking, slapping, flapping that happened every time he pushed in or pulled out. He'd never heard anything more erotic than those noises accompanied by her breaths and moans and his growls, snarls, and pants.

Before Magnar knew it, he'd curled around her body, leaning on his knees and elbows while supporting her in the air, and manically thrusted his hips. He shoved hard, he rammed deep, and his movements were swift. He held her steady against him as his thoughts were drowned out except for the want to release.

Like a rutting beast, he allowed his body to take complete and utter control, allowed himself to be enraptured in this moment of intense pleasure.

His whimpers were slight at first, but they grew each time his cock swelled with its upcoming release, preparing the bulges at the base. He felt the terrible clutch of his semen swirling in his sacs and the tingling sensation in his spine.

"Haa. Haa." Another whimper followed, but the sound was a mixture of pain and heaven.

His shaft was aching in a way that had his sight darkening, and he pulled his fangs away from her throat so he could lay the length of his snout against the side of her head to be closer to her. His tentacles snapped them together, making it impossible for either one of them to back away, even if they wanted to.

"Oh, my God!" She pulled the fur on his back, ripping a few strands from him, as she arched her back and screamed, "Magnar!"

He snarled her name and tightened his grip on her so she couldn't escape, making her moan cut short. Her orgasm clenched him right as the first burst of his seed released in a powerful squirt.

Her orgasm intensified his own with its wet, clenching spasms. Her body quivered around his like a wave, almost like it was trying to mimic and dance along with the swelling pulsations of his own.

Magnar filled her already seed-filled pussy until he could feel it dripping down his cock when it leaked from her channel. The scent of his sexual release was strong. He liked that it was in her, on her, marking her. He wanted her permanently saturated with it.

It mixed with the smell of copper, of blood, but his mind was too frazzled to even comprehend what that meant.

He was too euphoric.

And when it was over, he laid her against the ground and held her as he tried to piece together his mind. It was like his consciousness had spun off into the ether, and he had to wait for it to float back into his being.

My Delora... He nuzzled the side of his jaw against her hair.

Satisfaction and joy were the tender emotions swirling inside his chest, playing around his heart, as he held his bride in his arms.

That was until he heard a quiet sob.

"Delora?" he asked hesitantly, pulling back slightly to feel she had buried her head against his chest.

She was gripping him like she didn't want to stop cuddling, but his eyes turned white as all the warmth and tenderness suddenly left him in a cold rush.

Magnar pulled his arms out from under her, his tentacles still gripping tightly as his cock was buried, so he could stare horrified at his blood-covered hands. He could see that she'd covered her face behind his palms to cry, and he pulled them away so he could look at what he'd done.

The regret he felt was instant.

The flesh of her right shoulder and arm and her left outer thigh had been sliced into ribbons. Magnar, lost in his release, had dug his claws into her supple body and ruined it. Blood was freely bleeding from her, and the heavy drip of it from his claws was haunting.

No wonder she was crying.

Magnar placed his bloodied hand on her stomach so he could force his tentacles to release and incidentally smeared blood upon her, causing his jaw to tense. Then he pulled his softened shaft from her trembling body.

She is in pain. His hands shook as he stared down at them again in horror at himself. *What have I done?*

The first thing Delora did after a brief afterglow of a lust-filled pleasure haze, was bury her face into the fur on Magnar's chest and begin to weep. It was unintentional; she didn't mean for the tears to burst from her, but she couldn't stop them no matter how much she tried to.

What the fuck am I doing with a Duskwalker?

She couldn't believe that she currently had a Duskwalker's cock deep inside her. It was thumping alongside the drum of his heartbeat that she could feel against her forehead pressed to his chest. It was so intimate being able to feel both, to sense his presence within her in such a way, that it twisted at her heart.

She loved it being there and hated herself for it.

She hated that the warmth of his body was so damn soothing it melted any tension in her muscles. She hated that his quaking groan had made her ears tingle, and that his huffs had lulled her for a little while longer than she should have been hazed afterward. She hated that the smell of vanilla bean and cream and sex smelt so good that she didn't want him to pull away.

She covered her face to hide it from the world further, noticing the soft pitter pattering that sounded against the roof as if it was beginning to rain.

I'm insane. She had to be unhinged to have allowed this. To have agreed to this. To have *wanted* this so much that she'd opened her legs and told him it was okay to sink that huge cock inside her until he literally stretched her beyond repair.

But what Delora hated the most was that she didn't regret it at all. Not one bit.

Hadith would be disgusted with me. Hell, the entire human race would be. They'd call her a perverted freak! They'd throw her in the Veil twice over.

But... Oh my, he'd never made me come like that. Not to the point she thought she'd stop breathing because she was too busy screaming in abandon. Hadith had never made her mind go so blank that all she wanted was to keep being pounded into until she obliterated into fucking dust.

Delora had never been touched so gently, so tenderly, that her body had purred for more affection, making her desperate to have a cock inside her. She'd been so turned on by Magnar that she hadn't actually considered how freaky his cock really was. All she'd felt was relief that he had one to ravish her body with and needed to have it do so.

There had never been a night where Delora had *ever* been that desperate for her very own husband.

She'd long ago stopped hoping for pleasure, thinking it was an impossible endeavour. How was she supposed to know that the best way to be fucked into bliss was to hop on top of a Duskwalker's dick?

Feeling well and truly sated, *that* realisation was more painful than anything she'd come to learn.

Everything she'd ever wanted from her husband was being given to her by a creature that shouldn't even *exist.* Loyalty, affection, pleasure, protection... and warmth. To be treated both delicately because she was a woman who deserved to be treasured like valuable crystal, and to be rutted passionately, hard and rough, because she'd ignited such uncontrollable yearning.

And she knew that Magnar hadn't wanted to have sex with her because she was conveniently here for him to take his lust out on. He didn't even know what his cock was an hour ago – at least she thought it might have been an hour.

She knew his desire was for her, because of her.

"Delora?" he asked with such concern and sincerity in his voice that it broke her just a little.

He *cared* for her. She could hear it in his voice. And here she was, rudely crying because she was so conflicted by what she felt that she didn't know what else to do. His dick was still inside her, and she was crying pathetically because she liked it there. It was currently making her feel exceptionally whole.

She wanted to apologise because he probably thought she was crying because of something he'd done, but this wasn't his fault. He'd been perfect, and that was the problem.

"I am..." he started as he carefully slipped his shaft from her, even when she clung to him in hopes he'd stay. "I am so sorry, Delora."

She knew her face must be a tear-stained colour of red due to the unbearable heat in it. He was apologising, and she felt like a villain because of it.

"I did not mean to hurt you." The unsteady shake in his voice was unmistakable.

Then she let out a cry of pain when he placed his hand over her shoulder, and she darted her gaze to where she felt agony. Her eyes widened in disbelief at her own rendered flesh. Blood was streaming from her shoulder, and she didn't realise she was a little light-headed until she saw it.

At the same time, warm semen slipped from her channel, and her clit throbbed in delight despite her emotional state.

Oh my God. I can't believe I liked him fucking me so much that I didn't even know he'd torn my skin apart!

And now that he brought attention to it, it stung so terribly she knew he'd not only sliced through skin, but he'd also gone all the way down into muscle. There was a numbness she was thankful for, her nerves severed in certain places.

However, after a few seconds of his palm covering her wound, radiating magic came from where they were touching. It spread all throughout her body, and she looked down at her bleeding outer thigh.

The green glittering magic glowed so brightly it was mesmerising. It paused her crying.

It looked exactly like the colour of the protection ward outside, but so much brighter. Within seconds, she watched her wounds close up and fade as if they'd never been there to begin with.

Magnar pulled his hand away from her and began to retreat. He was planning to flee like before.

"Please," she whispered as she reached for him. "Don't leave."

Although she was crying, she knew she'd settle soon. She just needed a moment to be human, to have her mental and emotional freak out to process everything, and she'd settle.

The only glimpse Delora had gotten of Magnar before he retreated from the house was that his orbs were a stark colour of white. His whimpers, like a puppy that had injured its own paw, were the last thing she'd heard of him before he was gone.

Magnar...

TWENTY

Delora sat on the porch with her back against the wall and waited for Magnar to return. It was raining lightly and had been since he left two nights ago.

Watching the dreary world, she twisted her head and rested her cheek upon her folded arms that lay across the top of her bent knees. Many puddles had formed across the yard, but they seemed to glow where the ward was passing through along the ground.

There was minimal light as the sun had set recently.

When is he going to come back?

His absence was broaching a third night. She knew he must have returned briefly at some point since she hadn't materialised to him like he'd told her he would, but she'd never seen him.

Cuddling the blanket around her tighter to keep out the chill, she glared past the porch steps.

I still can't believe that he left again. He'd run away like a coward. *He didn't even give me time to explain.*

Clenching her fists, she vowed that when he returned, she would make sure they spoke this time. The miscommunication wasn't doing either of them any favours, and she just needed to strap on her big girl panties and tell him the truth.

I don't want to tell him, she groaned to herself.

Not only was she worried about his reaction, but she also just... didn't want to talk about it. She didn't want to talk about her past because she'd much rather forget, but leaving Magnar in the dark about it didn't seem fair. She couldn't truly justify a good enough reason not to tell him

He's my friend. Well... more than a friend, considering what they'd done. *Fuckbuddy? Can a Duskwalker be a fuckbuddy?*

She wanted to ease his worries. They were both new to this and learning about each other, since they were so vastly different. Adding in her complicated and painful past made everything harder.

"It would have been better if a different human had fallen into the Veil," she mumbled out loud. "Someone who isn't like me."

Leaning her head back, she lifted her hands so she could stare down at them. Delora wanted to be happy, but she didn't feel that way. Sleeping alone, knowing he wasn't around for the past two nights, had been nearly unbearable.

Throughout the days, she'd tried ghosting so she could get used to it and came to the conclusion that she despised doing it. It made her feel like she didn't exist to the world. And not in the good way, like just disappearing, but like a Ghost that wasn't ready to let go.

She couldn't smell anything, couldn't touch anything. She could hear and see, but it was like becoming a voyeur, which felt disturbing.

Cuddling her knees again, Delora sighed as she waited for Magnar.

"I'm really hungry."

She'd braved the pelting rain to dig through the garden, only finding a handful of small carrots that were ready enough to be picked. She'd eaten the birds the night they'd had sex after she stopped crying, finding that the sex and the tears had left her starving.

Actually, she was hungrier than usual. Her stomach also felt really awful. She was freezing cold, but sweating, and for some strange reason, her breasts started hurting today.

Maybe I'm getting my period? She was usually irregular, so it was pretty much a guessing game on when she'd get it or if she would at all. *Now though? Of all times?*

Great, another problem to deal with. She wondered how Magnar would handle being around her when she was leaking blood. *Would he be grossed out?*

She groaned in dismay. "I *really* don't want to have that conversation with him right now."

The whole 'I bleed once a month because I'm a woman' thing was just the beginning. Then she would have to explain why women do it, which was to conceive, and she'd be *damned* if she was going to have the birds and the bees conversation with a curious Duskwalker.

In due time, she would be happy to explain everything to him, but first they needed to sit down and talk.

She shivered. This place felt emptier than it already was without his presence. She couldn't imagine being stuck here, forever, by herself.

The Veil was such a daunting and haunting place that Delora wondered if she could ever brave wandering it. Even in her transparent form, she didn't like the idea of stumbling across a grotesque Demon.

She was thankful the ward was large enough that she couldn't see them past the trees. It also acted as a barrier to muffle their sounds.

Not once since Magnar had brought her here had she ventured further than the house and its direct vicinity. She refused to go far, despite knowing it was safe. In her own way, she was pretending she wasn't even in the Veil and that the Demons didn't exist.

It was just her and Magnar in the world.

Well, except currently it was just her. All by herself.

"Come on, Magnar," she sighed, turning her head to the ceiling. "Where the fuck are– Hmm?"

Delora darted her gaze back down when her fingers and toes felt oddly numb. Then her heart raced as she let out a shocked breath. She brushed at her wrist and hand when her fingers turned transparent against her will.

It started growing up her hand, then her forearm, and even her elbow.

"Oh shit! What's happening?"

She was turning into an actual Ghost!

Delora worried something terrible had happened to Magnar. Her chest stung at the thought that he'd been injured or somehow died, and that was why her body was fading now.

It kept growing over her body. No matter how much she tried to turn solid, how much she tried to halt it or reverse it, she continued to grow transparent.

Before she knew it, everything went black.

Delora gasped when light rushed into her sight seconds later.

Well... not really light, considering it was night in the middle of the Veil. Her head spun, like her eyes were spinning in their sockets, but she knew she was partially kneeling on the floor in a similar position to when she'd disappeared.

She attempted to mumble 'where the hell am I?' but even she knew it was so slurred and garbled that it didn't make sense. Delora was discombobulated and disorientated.

She turned her head up to see two fuzzy but black beings in front of her, both of them having bright, glowing orbs. One was green, the other blue. The longer she stared, the better she could see.

She shook her head to clear the remaining fog and ease the spinning she felt. It allowed her to see that Magnar suddenly turned to her, attracted to her whereabouts by either her scent or the sound of her life, and stumbled back on his three-toed hooves.

Delora shakily got on one knee and one foot as she reached for the railing, since they were on some fully built porch.

Magnar's eyes turned bright purple. *Ooo! I know what that colour means now.*

As best as she could, Delora gave Magnar a glare. He'd once told her she could never escape him since she'd return to him once a day had passed if he wasn't near, but it also meant *he* couldn't escape *her* either.

And she could see he was planning on running again.

Fucking fraidy cat, she thought as she took a step closer. *What can a Duskwalker be so afraid of anyway?*

"Don't run," she demanded when he stepped back.

Magnar knocked into Orpheus, who let him pass with ease. Before she could grab ahold of him, Magnar covered the side of his face to hide the glow of his eyes and bolted down the stairs and into the rain.

"Magnar!"

Orpheus put his arm forward and held onto the railing of the porch steps to block her chase. Magnar entered the forest that rustled violently from the harsh winds and disappeared.

"Don't," he warned.

Orpheus stared down at her with his normal blue orbs, and she craned her neck back to glare at him instead, meeting the Duskwalker orb to eye.

"What gives you the right to intervene?" she bit as she puffed her chest in anger. She didn't dare touch her torso to his in a show of aggression, but he'd stopped her from going after Magnar. "I need to talk with him."

This was her fault, and she needed to fix it.

Orpheus tilted his head, making not only his skull rattle like dry bones, but also the two bells hanging from his twisting Impala horns chime. They were held on by string and nine beads that started as blue, then black, then purple, before repeating twice more.

Although her Duskwalker and this one shared similar traits, Delora knew without a doubt that they were different. Not only was his skull the shape of a wolf rather than a fox, but their mannerisms were also so different she could see it in his stance.

Orpheus, although shorter, stood much straighter and with better balance. His body looked thicker, as though it was stronger and more developed, and the way he held it was with confidence.

Then there was the fact that their clothing was made exactly the same, but Orpheus' was clean, crisp, pressed, and tidy. It was buttoned perfectly, and his shirt was tucked into his long black pants that hid the tops of his glossy dress shoes.

Instead of leaning over to scare her, Orpheus eventually lifted his head back nonchalantly, as though she and her anger were insignificant to something like him.

"Although you are brave, little human, right now you should be wary of him." He waved his hand towards the front lawn of what she thought must be his own log-cabin home to gesture to the forest just beyond a flooded salt circle not too far away. "And venturing into the Veil will only upset him and endanger you both. He wouldn't wish for you to come to harm because of your foolishness."

It was only then that she noticed the front door to their home was open, and Reia was on the other side, observing them. She must have seen the whole thing.

Delora winced at his words before she let her shoulders slump.

He was right, and she didn't like that he was.

Regardless, she stepped back so she had space to throw her hands forward. "But he keeps running away! He can't flee every time something happens. He needs to learn how to communicate with me."

Running her fingers through her hair, Delora couldn't believe how immature he was being!

"I spent the last two days waiting for him," she grumbled, averting her gaze defeatedly. "I know I materialised here because it's been a whole day since he last came to the house."

He'd probably come to check on her, or maybe just so she wouldn't appear to him. The idea of the latter made her heart shrivel in her chest.

He left me alone. She wanted to hug herself self-consciously, but refused to show her weakness in front of them.

"Right now, what is safest is for him to be nowhere near you," Orpheus stated, retracting his arm. "He is trying to protect you."

"From what?"

Delora just didn't see the problem. So, he accidentally clawed her when they were having sex? Big fucking whoop. That was then, this was now, and she couldn't see why he kept needing to... leave her. *He healed me straight away.*

"From himself." Orpheus turned his head to Reia, showing that his gaze had fallen on her, but she could tell by the stiffness in his rigid body that he was wary. "You have opened his mind and body to desire, and for our kind, the first time is not the easiest."

"I've kinda always wondered what your first time was like." Reia softly laughed, but her forest-green eyes hinted at understanding.

Orpheus shook his head while scratching at the side of his neck.

"It is not the same." He brought his hand down to look at his sharp claws. They were dulled as if he had gone out of his way to file them back. "I never clawed Katerina."

"Katerina?" Delora frowned, remembering Reia had brought that name up.

When she shifted her gaze to Reia, the woman's lips had thinned, and her brows had drawn in, before she replied, "You didn't?"

"No. She never made me cling so desperately that I wanted to get under her skin." His orbs faded from blue into bright flamingo pink, a colour Delora had only seen once before when she'd given Magnar his name. She frowned at the soft emotion. "But I have done that with you."

"Oh. Oh!" Delora gasped, realisation striking like a hammer.

She'd been thinking this whole time that she and Magnar were the only ones that had done something like sex.

Seeming to sense where her mind had gone, Reia smiled knowingly. She wasn't ashamed or embarrassed to reveal this and actually seemed quite pleased.

"Look, I know what you said last time, but who the hell is Katerina, and why is she so damn important?" Delora gave a brief glance in the direction Magnar had gone. "I'm trying my hardest to adapt to this, but it isn't easy, okay?"

"She wanted to run after him, Reia," Orpheus stated as he took a step closer to his human. "They are not the same. Katerina would never have run into the Veil for me."

Reia crossed her arms across her chest and narrowed her eyes in Delora's direction. Her glare fell as she sighed.

"I think you should come inside. It's a long story." Reia turned her back to them to head deeper within the house. "Don't argue about it, Orpheus. She's our guest. Guests can come inside and have tea."

The big Duskwalker huffed out an annoyed breath through his nose hole, but followed in. Yet, surprisingly, he held the door open for Delora so she could enter before he closed it softly behind them.

She was immediately taken aback by what she found.

It smelt of pine, dry herbs, and life. It was also brightly lit by the many candles that lay on almost every surface and the antler chandelier that hung above in near reaching distance of his horns, but so far away for a human, like herself.

The house was similar in design to Magnar's, the walls made of thick, distressed timber logs that all appeared the same diameter.

In a dining sort of area, there was a massive table to allow for Orpheus' height, but it dwarfed both Reia and Delora as she was taken to one of the two seats available. It was obvious they'd never entertained guests before.

"I'd bring in the garden chair from outside," Reia started as she motioned her hand to Delora to sit in the smaller chair while she climbed into the much bigger one with Orpheus' help, "but it's wet from the rain."

Reia asked Orpheus to make them tea, but Delora had stopped listening to look around instead.

Having to kneel to reach the table properly, she noticed an array of items on top of it, like a cutting board that had dill herbs laying upon it with a ceramic jar next to it. There was a mortar and pestle with crushed herbs and bone and jewel ornaments.

The kitchen had a long windowsill with a basin and a wash bucket inside it. Vine-like plants dangled down into the metal basin while glass bottles with different dusty contents gave colour to the counters.

With awe, her eyes drifted back to the chandelier to see that ornaments hung from it. Crystals, rocks, bones, and even just ribbons had been carefully tied to the antlers.

Then finally, on the other side of the room near a long, gridded window, was a fireplace framed by two single armchairs. One was larger than the other, but both looked soft, since they were covered in animal furs. More of that fur had been laid upon the ground, and between the chairs was a round table.

The last piece of furniture was a mostly empty bookcase that held four or five books, two of which looked very old and worn.

Delora didn't realise she'd been gaping at what she found until her passing gaze fell on Reia, who had been watching her reaction. She shut her parted lips and looked down at the table.

But she couldn't feel anything other than wonder even if she had been caught. Not because the house was spectacular, but because Delora wondered if the home Magnar had built for her would one day look similar to this.

There was a wall that obviously separated rooms from the rest of the house, something theirs didn't have yet, and a long hallway that went to a door at the very end. The layout looked different to what Magnar had told her his plans were for when he finally got the chance to build further.

A pang of longing stung her when she thought of him.

Everything was so overwhelming that she barely even registered that she was half-naked in a black button-up shirt in front of them. She shivered, despite feeling warm and lightly coated in sweat. It almost felt like she had the beginning of a fever, but she put that up to adrenaline.

"Katerina is the first human Orpheus took. Quite a few centuries ago, in fact," Reia said, bringing Delora back to why they'd come inside in the first place. Nibbling at her bottom lip, Reia lifted her hands to gesture at the house they were in. "He built her this home, the garden, this yard. He made her furniture and ornaments, and even bought a lot of it. He did everything he could to make her happy."

Delora's cheeks warmed in tenderness. "Kind of like the same way that Magnar is building me a home?"

She hoped it looked even more amazing than this one.

"Yes," Orpheus interjected when he placed two cups on the table in front of them. Both were steaming with a honey-coloured liquid, but it smelt bitter like ginger and mint. "And I was fairly similar in my development as he is when I brought her to the Veil. It's why he often comes to me for advice. He has been planning for a human that would eventually give him a soul to keep."

Her gaze darted to the fiery soul floating between his horns, bright and red with life. Although her own soul now had a few cracks of light in it, it still looked charcoal and dull in comparison.

"You're a little early though," Reia laughed, but it sounded awkward.

Orpheus backed up to lean against the kitchen counter that was a little low for him, as though it was designed for a human.

The cupboards above seemed to be at his height, though.

"We had planned for him to eat a few more humans and gain more humanity before he found one for himself, but we cannot control what happens and when it does."

"Magnar already explained that Duskwalkers gain humanity from eating humans. In the same way that Demons grow stronger by eating us."

"Exactly," Reia said with a nod, making her blonde hair wave around her shoulders.

Delora wrapped her hands around the wooden cup. "This still doesn't explain anything."

"Has Magnar told you about the Demon King or the Demon Village yet?" Reia asked.

Delora's eyes widened so far she thought they might pop out of her skull.

"A what king and what village?" Delora choked, her voice turning higher pitched than normal.

"I guess not." Reia pushed a few strands of hair behind her ear, her eyes turning away like she was uncomfortable. "I know it's a lot to digest, and things will be explained better in the future, but there is a castle in the middle of the Veil that belongs to the Demon King. He has the capability to use magic, strong magic. Centuries ago, he opened a portal to Earth from another realm and brought the Demons here to eat us. He's trying to grow an army. He also made an area for Demons who have gained enough humanity to build a village, and it just looks like any old village you or I could have come from. It's pretty freaky, but it looks totally normal besides *them* being there."

Her lips parted in disbelief. She wanted to say that she was lying just to make fun of her, but when she gazed at Orpheus, he seemed just as serious. His fist clenched, and he appeared more tense than he did before.

"They made my clothes," Orpheus added in. "They also made many of the housing items I cannot make myself, like the cooking hearth."

He waved his hand in the direction of the fireplace in the kitchen that had the metal hanging rods of a cooking hearth. The timber was protected by multiple layers of brick and stone, and in the middle was a mesh metal table with a pot on top of it where the flames could reach it.

"They also provided us with the tools that we've been using to build the house for you and Magnar."

"Where did they get it from?" Delora asked.

She had to admit, this was all very overwhelming to learn.

A Demon Village in the middle of the Veil that was like a human town? It was so unrealistic. Demons were horrible monsters that feasted upon humans with glee. To even *think* they had rational thought beyond eating flesh was hard to absorb.

Humans had been afraid of them for centuries. No one knew where they came from as they hadn't been on Earth for more than a few hundred years, and no one knew why they'd come here. All her kind knew was that the world had been thrown into chaos, and it was dangerous outside the walls of their towns.

"Some of it they made," Orpheus said.

Like fucking arts and crafts?!

"Some of it they stole from humans."

Delora raised her hand to stop them while placing the other against her forehead. "I can't. I'll have to see it to understand."

Orpheus twisted his head at Reia, and she answered with a sigh.

"Let's just move on. I know it's a lot to take in. What we know as humans is so far from the truth, and I'm still learning much of it myself. There's so much more to tell you, and I wouldn't have believed it either if I hadn't seen it with my own eyes."

"Let's just continue on with this Katerina person," Delora pleaded.

No more about this Demon King and village.

"The Demon King hates Mavka," Orpheus stated, making Delora groan. "We kill Demons and refuse to join him." He looked upon his hands as he raised both palms to look at them. "I do not want to be a part of bloodshed or violence. I have no interest in joining his war, and neither does any other Mavka I've come to know."

"But he gave an offer to Katerina to leave with him, and she agreed. She hated Orpheus, despised him even." Reia then looked Delora straight in the eyes, and she could see the burning hostility in them. Not at Delora, but at this apparent Katerina person. "The Demon King kept her alive for nearly two centuries with his magic. When they finally discovered how to kill Duskwalkers, they tried to use *me* as bait to kill Orpheus! They kidnapped me so Orpheus would be forced to come to the castle as a trap. Katerina was planning on stabbing his skull to break it."

"Destroying our skull is the only way to kill a Mavka permanently," Orpheus said while brushing his claws down the length of his wolven bony snout.

"What did you do to escape then?" Delora asked, unsure if she wanted to hear the answer with the way Reia appeared murderous. "From this apparent castle and all-powerful king?"

"She was going to let the Demon King eat me. I also have a funny feeling she let him eat the other humans they stole from Orpheus." Reia sneered. "So, I stabbed the bitch in the torso with my sword."

"You killed someone?" she squeaked.

"I wish I could do it again." Reia bashed the bottom of her fist against the table, making her cup bounce and almost spill over. "Orpheus did so much for her, and she was completely ungrateful. She thought of him as a monster all the way to the end and wanted to make sure he suffered. They tortured him, stole other offerings, killed them, just to ensure that he was alone. She kidnapped me and then *expected* me to sympathise with her."

Delora peeked at Orpheus, expecting to see his orbs darken in blue at the sad things that apparently happened to him. Instead, they were a flamingo pink again.

Delora *really* wanted to know what that colour signified.

"I don't mean to be rude" – Delora pouted, eyeing the worn timber of the table before fiddling with the bottom of her shirt – "but what does this have to do with Magnar and me?"

"What Magnar is going through with you currently, I went through with Katerina," Orpheus stated before he folded his arms and leaned against the low kitchen counter once more with the back of his legs. "However, I didn't have her soul."

"Thank goodness for that," Reia chuckled as she finally

picked up her tea now that it was cooler, blew into the wooden cup and then took a sip. "Otherwise, you would have been trapped with her."

Orpheus chuckled in return, making Delora frown. She couldn't remember if she'd ever heard Magnar make such a deep and pleasing sound.

"That is very true, my little doe. I am forever grateful it is your soul I get to keep for eternity."

Delora's already sore and aching heart sunk further. What her and Magnar had was *nothing* like this. Orpheus and Reia obviously had a very deep and warm bond, and the jealousy that Delora felt didn't incite rage, but instead grief.

Could they have this? Could they form a bond that was just as tender?

Do Reia and Orpheus... love each other? That was such a strange concept considering she was a human and he was a Duskwalker, but it appeared on the surface that they might.

Delora didn't know if she truly wanted that or even knew how. She'd been so horribly burned by love that she thought her insides might be too disfigured to even entertain the idea. There were some wounds that couldn't be healed, and if Magnar was going to flee like a coward whenever things got tough, then she didn't see it being possible that he'd ever be able to make her love him – that's even if he wanted her love or understood what it was.

Orpheus turned his skull in Delora's direction.

"Katerina taught me much about what it's like to be a human." Then his orbs changed into a reddish pink to signify his embarrassment at his next words. "We Mavka don't have body functions like you humans do. We absorb our food so completely and utterly that there is no waste for us to produce. When I looked down at my own cock for the first time, I didn't know what it was or what its function was."

Delora's cheeks pinkened, and she stole a glance at Reia to see if she was uncomfortable – only to find the strange woman was biting her lips shut to stop herself from giggling.

"I-I think it was a reaction to me," Delora mumbled quietly.

"To you?" There was an obvious note of curiosity in his

voice.

"Yeah." She tried to look anywhere but at either of them. *Is it possible to die of embarrassment?* Delora couldn't believe she was forced to have this conversation with two people who were practically strangers. "To my, uh, scent? He was touching me very curiously, and I kind of got carried away."

Orpheus raised one arm from its folded position to cup the underneath of his long jaw.

"I see. My first time feeling desire was solely brought on by my own cravings of wanting to be closer to Katerina after two years of being together." Then he lowered his hand as if to shrug. "I didn't know it at the time, too stupid to realise, but she never truly desired me. She did what I wanted because she was afraid I would hurt her if she didn't, though I never threatened her. I did everything I could to keep her safe. But like Magnar, I was purely moving forward on instinct because she accepted me. I thought she felt the same way since she didn't tell me otherwise."

Then Orpheus stared down at his own claws.

"Sometimes she instigated touch, tried to incite desire in me so I would do things for her when I didn't want to – like leave to hunt. She was using it as a way to control me, which made things all the more confusing. It was only when she left that I understood she hated me."

"What are you trying to say?" Delora asked, her brows drawing tightly together.

Controlling someone through intimacy and sex was exceptionally manipulative. She took advantage of Orpheus' emotions and lack of understanding.

"Our first times are not the same. I didn't have Katerina's soul, so I didn't feel that kind of connection to her, nor was my desire a reaction to hers. If you craved Magnar–"

"I wouldn't say craved is the right word," Delora mumbled in protest.

But wasn't it? At the time, she'd stared at his cock, at all its freaky, squirming parts, and she'd hungered for it to be inside her. She hadn't cared that it was different, only that it could be inside her, fill her, maybe even give her pleasure... and pleasure her it had.

"If you craved Magnar," Orpheus repeated with a dark tone, making her back straighten and become rigid. Oops, she'd interrupted him. "Then his body was reacting to yours. You awakened his desire with your own and then he'd clung to you, hurting you in the process. I never clawed Katerina, but I have accidentally hurt Reia numerous times. I have bitten her, clawed her, been too rough, and it has always been because of something *she* is doing."

When Delora let her gaze shyly flitter to Reia, she found she was being stared at already. Reia was gauging her reaction.

Whatever she saw in Delora's expression made her laugh.

"It's fine. I like it, and it appears so do you."

Delora clenched her jaw and swallowed thickly.

She fidgeted by rubbing at her forearm with her sleeve-covered wrist. "I didn't even know he'd clawed me until he was apologising, then he just ran away before I could say anything."

"He said you were crying," Orpheus rebutted, making Delora wince inwardly.

"That's not his fault." Her shoulders slumped as she turned her gaze to the table. "I wasn't crying because of anything he'd done. He just made me realise I had been missing something I'd always wanted, and I couldn't believe he was the one to make me see it. I wanted to explain that to him, but, uh, yeah."

"Right now, he's afraid he'll hurt you again." Orpheus turned his head to look at the lit fireplace. When he noticed it was low on fuel, he walked over to the kindling and threw some inside, speaking as he moved around the house. "He is worried about being near you."

"But I don't understand why," Delora said as she followed him with her gaze.

"Because he *will* hurt you," he answered. "Because he can't control himself right now. Even just thinking of you is making his sight turn purple. What he wants right now is *more,* and he knows that isn't wise. He needs to adapt to this new emotion, one that is very prevalent now that he understands what it is, what it can do, and how close it can make him be with you. You are the bride of a Mavka, and we are always hungry for something. You've shown him this hunger, and now he craves it terribly."

"They are annoyingly incessant," Reia whispered with her hand cupping around her mouth to quieten her words.

Orpheus' back stiffened after he prodded the fire with a poker, and he turned his head over his shoulder to growl at her.

"I like being close with you, Reia."

In answer, she rolled her eyes before she brought them to Delora, giving her a wink.

"Welcome to the horny Duskwalker club."

And that was it! The final thing to push Delora over the edge.

She covered her face with both hands and let out a whining groan of dismay. Then she shook her head against her palms, wishing she could just disappear so that the embarrassment could end.

They're weird. They're all so fucking weird!

Reia was strange and far too open about this. Orpheus had just explained this all to her in so much depth and detail, and now learning that Magnar kept running away because he was thinking with his dick was too much to bear.

Delora worried her mind would break. How much more could a person be pushed into insanity? She'd already been half-mad when she'd been shoved into the Veil.

The idea of becoming a Duskwalker's plaything was an odd concept, and she wasn't sure if she was delighted or afraid. There was something erotic about Magnar, about being intimate with a Duskwalker, simply because he was so different to her.

He was big and tall, with strong arms that were like a shelter. She wanted him to squeeze her until she popped, hug her all the way down to her very being, her very essence, her very *soul.*

She'd orgasmed because of him, and she wanted to feel that again. She wanted to discover what it felt like to be accepted as she was, even adored like how Magnar seemed to adore her body, then be fucked into oblivion. Sure, there was a tangle of emotion there too, but her long-denied body yearned for pleasure.

Delora knew in the future she wouldn't deny him, but at the same time, she really didn't like the idea of being clawed nearly to death. The wounds he'd given her had been severe enough that he'd cut through muscle, and she was sure the only thing that had saved her from feeling pain had been because she'd been coming when he'd given them to her.

However, a part of her was willing to risk the gamble if she could sink into body trembling bliss and drown in the waves of it again.

"How would you like a bath?" Reia asked, causing Delora to finally lower her hands to look beyond them. "A proper one, with a bathtub and everything."

For the first time, Reia gave Delora a smile, a real one that didn't hold anything dark behind it.

"That actually sounds really nice, to be honest."

Due to the fireplace, their house had no chill in the air, but Delora was still cold from sitting outside on the porch before she'd materialised here. Her fingers and toes ached, and having the chance to wash properly was something she wouldn't deny.

TWENTY-ONE

Delora sighed with contentment as liquid heat surrounded her, warming her body all the way down to her very bones. It stung her toes and fingertips at first to slip into the large wooden tub, but she didn't mind the sting when the rest of her tingled with blessedness.

Situated at the very back of the house, the washroom was moderately sized for this large, log-cabin home, but she couldn't help finding it rather pretty and inviting.

Large amethyst crystals, some almost to the height of her hip, were in two of the furthest corners of the door. On top of them, and near the head of the bathtub, were lit candles that gave just enough light to make it possible to see without being bright and confronting, allowing her body to remain in partial shadows.

There was no incense, but there was a plate of herbs that could be lit to give a nice aroma. The air still smelt sweet, as though it was permanently saturated.

She'd been given some liquid oil to cleanse her body properly, and she allowed herself to soak in this small and temporary piece of heaven.

"I should get Magnar to create a washroom for me first," she muttered, her voice deep with satisfaction as it echoed off the walls.

She would adore having something like this.

She'd forgo a proper bed, a proper kitchen, a proper house, just to be able to bathe in heat when she wanted.

There was a chance she'd never leave the tub.

All Delora could hear was the tapping of the rain outside, the slight trickling of water that lapped at the sides of the tub whenever she moved, her heartbeat in her ears, and her light breathing.

There was a thought that continued to nag at her, though. One that held no animosity, but still made her heart flutter both in anxiety and in bashful shyness.

Do I really think of that house as my home? Although she'd known Magnar had made it for her, she didn't realise she was already so attached to it until she was brought here.

She already missed it.

Hugging her midsection, Delora leaned her head back against the tub's edge. *I'm homesick for arms that don't even know how to hold me.*

Because it wasn't really the house she was missing, but Magnar. There was an echoing loneliness, and it was even deeper after being here and witnessing Reia and Orpheus together. As much as she pictured her new home fondly, she knew there was an emptiness in it. Not because it didn't have furniture, but because there was a very noticeable and distinct barrier between herself and Magnar.

Unsure if the drop of liquid that ran down the side of her face was a bead of perspiration or a tear, she clenched her eyes shut. *I don't know how to get closer to him.*

What she'd already tried had led them to sex, but that distance between them was even greater now. Magnar couldn't even be in her presence, and the only regret she felt in being intimate with him was simply because she'd lost everything else.

"I don't feel so good," Delora whispered to the air, her stomach so tangled in many emotions that it was nauseous. "I want to go home."

She wanted to be comforted inside a nest of branches and furs, between a set of large and slightly elongated arms, where all she could smell was vanilla and hear a heartbeat and breaths that were too strong to belong to any human.

Her protector was gone, and she no longer felt truly safe.

There was another Duskwalker here, and Orpheus had been... nice enough to her. It was obvious he cared about humans, possibly even a little more than he did his own kind. Delora had wondered if perhaps any Duskwalker may have given her the same feeling of having fluttering moths in her torso, but he didn't give her the same reaction.

Sure, it was an odd thing to imagine, considering he had Reia and she had Magnar, but she'd been curious if it was just any Duskwalker that would have made her feel this way.

It wasn't.

There was something about the way Orpheus articulated himself in conversation, how he had the arrogance and confidence to lean superiorly against the counter with his arms folded, that left Delora feeling cooled by his presence. He was too intelligent, too understanding.

She almost laughed to herself.

I like Magnar because he's nothing like a human. Because humans had been nasty and cruel and had shown her they could have ulterior motives. They could betray so easily. Magnar was too raw with his emotions, so open with them because he didn't know what needed to be hidden and what didn't.

Delora would never be left in the dark with him holding terrible secrets because he'd always reveal them to her. Perhaps not straight away, but soon enough that she would know everything eventually.

After debating whether she'd been in the water for too long, Delora eventually emerged from the tub. As much as she had been enjoying it, being alone was making her thoughts whirl. She was also a guest in someone else's home, and she didn't want to be disrespectful of their hospitality.

After she wiped herself down with a long, white cloth she figured was to be her towel, she wrapped herself in it. Then she opened the door slightly and gently yelled past it.

Reia came up the hallway. "Follow me."

She was taken to a door on the right, and the room she entered was small and somehow felt barren of life. A single bed had been pushed into a corner, with a side table next to it. There was a large wardrobe pushed into the opposing corner, with a window nearby that looked new, as if its glass and frame had only recently been fixed into place.

Everything else looked old, but well-maintained.

On the bed was a long dress that had been laid out. The skirt, which came all the way up to the waist and down to her feet, was a dark green, whereas the long sleeve shirt part of it was a crisp white. Both pieces were sewn together, and the dress was able to be buttoned from the navel up. Folded on top of it was a brown girdle that had shoulder strapping and appeared that it would sit under her breasts.

"That's for you," Reia stated as she motioned her hand to it. "Sorry I didn't bring it to you the other day. Orpheus wanted to go for a walk to show me his old cave, and I'd never seen it before. I don't know why; it was pretty empty."

"I don't mind," Delora offered as she held her towel to her chest and walked over to it. "I just appreciate you making me something proper to wear."

"I hope you don't mind that it's made from two different dresses. I didn't really have much that fit your size, so I had to find what I thought would fit and make the rest."

Reia left the room to allow Delora privacy to change, and she swiftly dropped the towel and rushed to place the outfit on. The buttons had already been undone, and the gap around the waist was large enough for Delora to tightly slip it over her pudgy hips. It took a small amount of tugging, but once she got it on, she eagerly did up the buttons.

Then she placed the brown vest around her back and pushed the laces through the holes so she could tighten it and then tie it.

"How does it fit?" Reia asked from beyond the door.

"It's perfect," she answered as she brushed down the skirt to help it sit more naturally.

Reia entered after her response, and her smile was sincere as she eyed Delora up and then down.

"I'm glad. I was a little worried that my string measurements were off." Reia turned for the wardrobe and opened it before kneeling. "What size shoe are you? If you say ten, I can't help you since that's my size and getting shoes in the Veil is impossible unless I go to the Demon Village."

"I'm a nine," she answered, before a frown knotted her brows. "You've been to the Demon Village?"

"Yeah, twice now." Reia shrugged as she unfolded herself to stand while holding two pairs of shoes, one a pair of slippers and the other a pair of boots. "You can have all the shoes in this size, but what would you prefer to wear now?"

Delora eyed the window that was tapping with heavy rain.

"Probably the boots." But she'd prefer to wear the slippers in the future.

She placed the leather boots on her feet and then looked down at her body, seeing herself dressed properly for the first time in weeks. She felt like a real human again, not some forgotten, discarded creature of the Veil.

Just as she touched her matted but clean hair, Reia handed her a brush.

"I think I should just let the proverbial cat out of the bag and say sorry that I've been a bitch to you," Reia muttered once Delora worked the brush through her tangled hair.

Delora gave a mocking snort. "Yeah, kinda."

Reia gave one in return before a smile curled her lips. It appeared she appreciated Delora's honesty.

"I have pretty terrible social skills when it comes to people." Reia plonked herself on the edge of the small bed and watched Delora as she moved to stand near the window, subconsciously hoping to see any signs of Magnar in the stormy and windy weather. "I was considered a harbinger of bad omens."

Delora immediately paused her actions and looked at Reia warily. *Shit, they're considered bad luck to be around.* She swallowed thickly and pressed herself more into the wall.

Reia tsked. "Don't worry. That shit about cursing those around me and bringing death is just superstitious crap. Plus, we're both already technically half dead, so what does it matter anyway?"

Her stiffened shoulders relaxed. "You're right. I'm sorry."

"All good. I'm used to it. I grew up with people treating me like a disease. Orpheus and Magnar were my first friends, and I'm kind of protective of them because of that. I was worried you might be like Katerina and treat Magnar horribly. He's really sweet. I don't want to see him hurt."

"You made a pretty quick assumption about someone you

don't know," Delora said as she worked the last of the many knots from her hair before giving the brush to Reia.

She took it and shrugged.

"Like I said, I have pretty terrible social skills. And I'm not particularly trusting of humans."

"Yeah, well, me neither. I didn't want to come to the Veil, and I didn't come here by myself."

Reia cocked one of her blonde brows. "What are you trying to say?"

Delora looked away, feeling her lingering shame spike in her chest.

"I was tossed into the Veil," she mumbled, once more looking outside with a desperate hope that Magnar would just... come. Would just... rescue her from these people. "With my hands bound and cloth between my teeth, I was thrown away."

"By who?"

"That's none of your business," Delora answered sharply. "And the first person I'll tell my story to will not be you, but him."

"I guess that's fair." Reia clapped her hands together, the sudden loud sound capturing her attention and making her jump. "I like you. I thought you were meek and timid before, but it appears you can be pretty catty when you want to be. I hate beating around the bush."

Well, isn't that obvious.

"I'm working through some stuff," Delora answered honestly before turning to her and folding her arms over her much larger chest. "I didn't willingly come here, and I thought I was going to die when I fell. In some ways, I gave Magnar my soul because I thought it would kill me painlessly, but I also didn't really care what happened to me either."

"Do you regret your decision?"

"No," she stated without hesitation.

"Well, now that I know all this about you, I'll try to make things easier for you. You're both always welcome to come here and visit. You can have some of my food, within reason, and you can have a proper bath whenever you like. I can only imagine how difficult it is to assimilate into a life and a house that is half built." Reia then rubbed at the nape of her neck awkwardly. "I never realised how lucky I was that Orpheus already had all of this until now. I don't know how well things would have gone between us had he taken me to a cave or a house that had nothing inside it. I fell in love with this house before I even grew to care for him."

"That's a lie."

"Excuse me?" Reia asked in disbelief, her eyebrows shooting up her forehead.

"If I feel even just a small fraction of what you do for Orpheus, for Magnar, then I know that your home is wherever he is."

Reia's face softened, her eyes bowing with understanding, and her hand fell to the bed to rest against it so she could lean on it.

"I guess you're right. I did hate it when he wasn't here, and that was before I gave him my soul." Then Reia drew her eyes down Delora's body and then back up before cocking her head. "Are you saying that you're in love with Magnar?"

She took her eyes away from Reia to look around the room.

"No." Delora crossed her arms over her torso to rub her forearms self-consciously. "I don't love him. I don't have what you and Orpheus share. All I know is that he feels... safe." Then Delora snorted a laugh. "I know that's weird, considering he's a Duskwalker."

"You feel safe with him?" Reia gave her a questioning gaze. "I'm under the impression that he clawed the fuck out of you."

"He healed me straight away. And he didn't mean to. Things just got a little heated," Delora quickly said in his defence, pushing a strand of her hair behind her ear that was turning hot. It was alarming to know that others knew she'd been intimate with Magnar. "But there's something about him that feels comforting to be around. I think it's because he isn't human. I like him the way he is."

I like that he would never do something cruel to me on purpose. Delora could forgive an accident, something that wasn't done with malicious intent, depending on what it was.

She didn't mind that Magnar had clawed her. She didn't think she'd mind even if he killed her by accident, as long as it wasn't painful, since she'd come back. She could forgive those, but if he was to betray her...

Her eyes fell on Reia and tried to dismiss the idea that either one of them would do anything sexual together. It was ridiculous, she knew it, but her lingering fear after Hadith had left a scar of irrationality and was something she just couldn't seem to shed.

Delora's stomach chose that moment to grumble terribly, and she placed her hand on her abdomen as if to hide the noise.

"Sorry. I don't know why, but I've been super hungry since this morning."

Reia threw her head back and laughed.

"I can't believe I didn't think about feeding you. I don't actually feel hunger much these days. I just eat because it feels nice, and I know it makes Orpheus feel good to think he's taking care of me. Even though I'm a Phantom now, it makes me feel... human."

Delora kind of felt the same way too, except for today.

Reia led Delora back to the kitchen and poured her a bowl of already-made stew. She didn't question what kind of meat it was; she didn't care. The moment she sat down at the table, she began to eat.

Giving her a moment of alone time, Reia sat upon Orpheus' lap so they could share the large armchair in front of the fireplace.

She first tasted the broth to make sure it was something she'd like, having rarely ever eaten anyone else's cooking. Finding it was tasty, perhaps not to her level of skills but wonderful nonetheless, she took a bite of meat. It went down smoothly.

Her stomach churned at her second bite, but it still felt horribly empty.

By the third bite, which took her longer to chew even though the meat and vegetables were soft, Delora found it hard to swallow.

Sweat dotted her brow, and a cold shiver ran down her spine. It was odd considering she was warmed by her bath and the fire that was billowing from the fireplace.

The moment it went down, it tried to come straight back up.

She got out of the chair while covering her mouth, her eyes darting for somewhere, anywhere, to put it besides her full bowl.

Oh crap. I think I'm going to vomit.

Her gaze found the kitchen basin, and she rushed for it. On the way, Delora gagged at the food in her mouth and bile rose.

She reached the basin just in time to violently expel the contents of her stomach.

"Shit, Delora," Reia gasped behind her. "Are you okay?"

Instead of answering, Delora retched again, this time with her eyes watering. Her sight was murky, but it was just clear enough that she could tell what came out of her was *black.*

When she was done, she stared horrified at the dark goop that had come from her and stumbled sideways a step. Dizziness swam through her. Sweat now coated her entire body, and her breathing turned sharp and shallow.

Reia was in front of her, a blurry blob, and she placed her arms up when it looked as though Delora was going to fall.

"I-I think I'm going to–"

Before she could finish, Delora began to faint.

Caught by Reia's arms, she heard her frantic voice shout, "Orpheus, help!"

She knew by the strength that suddenly surrounded her, keeping her on her feet rather than letting her sink to her knees, that Orpheus was holding her upright.

Right before her consciousness faded, he let loose a loud, long, distinct howl to the ceiling. It was the last thing she heard before her eyes rolled into the back of her skull, and she passed out.

Magnar slowly paced through the Veil with snorting huffs, agitated with himself and his lack of ability to keep his thoughts... sane.

With a light growl, he kicked a stone with his hoof. It rolled across dirt, patchy grass, and sticks to land inside a black murky pool with a disgusting *plop.*

The air smelt rancid, like blood and decay, but sweeter – which so happened to make it that much worse. The fumes puffed in steamy, translucent clouds above the surface of the bubbling water he was walking next to.

It was so dark that there wasn't a single way to see beyond the top layer of the swamp water. Getting too close could mean certain death or, at least for a Mavka, a permanent drowning.

When Magnar had first started walking through this perilous area of the Veil, the Swamp Lands, the water had been relatively calm despite the ongoing rain that continued to shower in hard, angry pelts.

The area was always disturbingly quiet.

Not a bird squawked, not a rat scuttled, and not even a Demon dared to near this place.

Usually, he stayed away from here, as he was sure all of his kind did. There was no point in being here, and the air bubbles that lay on the top of the water's surface would have been only noticeable to something that had keen senses.

He remained a large distance from the shoreline and watched his path to make sure the dirt he was walking towards was truly dirt and not mud on the surface of water.

Those bubbles, only three or four here and there, followed him.

Something was waiting, hoping he would foolishly draw closer. Instead, Magnar just kicked more stones in the direction of the creature, who was the reason the air smelt rancid, taunting it for being such a horrid monster.

Only once in his life had he briefly seen it eat a Demon that had been chasing Magnar through the swamp. He knew it was a mass of writhing limbs, but he still had no idea what it truly looked like. It was black, which meant it was a Demon.

A Demon that could only feast on what lived in the Veil. Cannibalistic.

I should not be here.

But he was because he'd unwittingly come here in his panic to avoid Delora.

I want to be near her. He wanted his greedy sight to take in her beautiful form. His lonely ears wanted to hear the song of her voice. His orbs desperately sought the connection that came from having her pretty brown eyes, like the riches of earth, looking at his own. He wanted his aching lungs to feel relaxed by the aroma of her frosty-apple scent.

He wanted the warmth of her body.

His sight suddenly flashed a violent purple, and he groaned when his tentacles behind his cock seam shifted in eagerness.

The warmth of her body. Magnar groaned again. *The softness of it melting around mine.* His claws clutched low on his abdomen, trying to keep his slit from opening. *Melted until liquid dripped down my bulges and tickled me.*

And the naughty scent of her orgasms still clung to his mind like an infectious disease that refused to be healed from his body.

He couldn't purge the feeling of being within her while she'd been trapped in his arms. He couldn't escape the memory of her moans that still echoed in his ears like a haunt.

Magnar couldn't *stop* thinking about it. The connection he'd felt with her had been beyond anything he could have imagined, and he craved it. His heart beat fast for it. To be so close to her that he was swallowed by her depths.

He craved her accepting him within her plump but fragile body.

Delora had gifted him something, a hunger he'd never known he'd needed. And Magnar did need it, this hunger like a drive he never knew existed.

In some ways, although he'd welcomed no longer feeling hunger and being satisfied, he'd also felt... empty.

Sex? As he'd learned it was called. His ability to release within her? Now this was a hunger he thought was more prevalent than his original need to feed on meat. Instead, he now wanted to nibble and lick the taste of her flesh, her juices. Not in a way that was bloody, but in a way that was messy because she was shaking in abandon.

His entire body, from head to hooves, including his tail, shivered in delight.

He felt his cock trying to extrude.

He clamped his seam shut even tighter with his claws, but he could feel that his tentacles were confused. They slithered around, but they weren't quite used to twirling around his cock so he could have some semblance of control over his own shaft.

And that was why he couldn't be near Delora right now, when all he wanted was her presence. He wasn't used to handling this new part of himself, and although he now understood the multiple functions of his tentacles, he couldn't control them.

One function was for gripping her so she couldn't escape his desperately pounding hips or his seed when he filled her. Another was so he could shield his cock from the air that dried it and stung.

They also had one last function, one that Orpheus had explained to him when he'd been there last. They were also designed to twirl around his cock and hold it in so that it didn't extrude completely because they could only reach so far. They were to protect himself, and only a state of complete arousal would allow the tip and a few inches to be out of its wet safety. By that point, Magnar should only allow it to extend that far when he knew his cock was going to be sheltered inside Delora's wet, heated slit.

At the moment, he had no control of his body or his tentacles, and his mind was so obsessed with his memories that he was growing erect foolishly.

She wasn't even here, and she was tormenting him.

Magnar was trying, and the only thing that allowed himself to soften was the reminder of her blood on his claws.

In his inexperienced desire, he'd harmed the one creature he never wanted to hurt. He'd *promised* her he wouldn't.

His sight turned a deep well of blue, and his hands fell away from his body when it was calm.

I'm a monster to have harmed my precious raven.

With her black hair so dark that it was near impossible to tell where it was laying across the black of his fur. With her cute lips, small nose, and high but rounded cheeks.

How could he hurt something so beautiful? Something he'd sworn to protect with his life? He wanted to heal her of whatever ailed her mind, not bring her more destruction.

Magnar kicked a rock into the disgusting swamp water with a growl.

Bad Mavka. Bad Magnar. He kicked another rock, this time launching it across the space between the bushes until it slammed against the trunk of a red-leafed tree. Leaves scattered against the ground and the surface of the water, leaving more dry and exposed branches.

Idiot Magnar.

But he no longer felt stupid. Every moment with Delora, he was learning. He'd made a mistake, and he just had to make sure he didn't make it again.

Right now, he just wanted her to be safe, and that included from himself. Although she'd shocked him by appearing behind him, he was thankful she had. She was with Orpheus and Reia, which meant she was protected and with people he trusted.

She also wasn't alone.

His orbs had changed to purple when she'd emerged. The sight of her, the smell of her, and even the sound of her voice had called for him to be close with her. If he hadn't left, he didn't know what he would have done, or if he would have been wise enough to think, to stop, to hold back if she asked him to.

I hurt her. She may not want me to touch her like that again. The idea of that made his heart sink like it wanted to flop out of his chest and drown in the waters next to him.

Why can I not be better...?

The sound of a howl, mournful and long, echoed over the large distance. It was a call.

"Orpheus," he stated, turning his head in the direction it came from.

Magnar had once used his own call in the past, much more fox-like, when he'd been facing off a difficult Demon that had cornered him. That's when they'd discovered they could hear and answer the call of their kind over a large distance.

White entered his orbs at the sound of it now.

Orpheus would never call him, unless...

"Delora."

Something was wrong. Either they were all in danger, or there was something wrong with his bride.

TWENTY-TWO

Magnar began to sprint, dropping to his hands to help quicken his pace as he made his way to Orpheus' home.

The rain pelted against his body more forcefully due to his speed. His feet slipped occasionally, but he quickly righted himself so he could continue forward.

His blood was pumping, making his heartbeat thump in his ears while rainwater sprayed from his nose hole as he snorted out his breaths. He was covering himself in mud, but he paid little mind to that.

Minutes felt longer than they ever had in his panic.

He skidded across the ground when he saw a figure covered in white feathers rushing across the clearing in front of Orpheus' home, much like he was. She was heading in the same direction – the entrance to their house.

The Witch Owl, he thought.

She was drenched from the rain, her white cloak of feathers heavy looking as she ran. Her shoeless feet were mud covered, as were her legs all the way up to her knees. The bottom of her cloak and thigh-high white dress were also dirty.

He knew she must not have transformed into a human-sized owl due to the inability to fly during this kind of intense storm, but seeing her in human form had always been strange.

She was dark-skinned, with tight, curly brown hair. Her eyes were near black and only shined a dark brown whenever any light hit them. They were enchanting to look upon in their own way – as though she'd looked into the void, had seen all of its answers and accepted the power of its knowledge.

Which she had.

The Witch Owl, an odd but immortal creature, had stared into the void, and then mated with it.

She was *Mother*. He'd only come to learn this recently, but she hadn't been the one to inform him of this. Orpheus had explained its meaning, but Magnar couldn't understand this relationship.

What was a mother and a father? A parent? One was a human turned Phantom with magic, and the other a spirit of darkness who had granted that magic to her. Apparently, he'd been created by them, as had all Mavka, but he didn't know what a parent was, how they'd been formed, or what the reason was.

All Magnar understood was that, in some way, she was his creator.

He had no memory of her other than her sometimes being a presence near his home. She'd helped him occasionally, but they'd only spoken a handful of times.

She smelt of magic, which was foul and tingled his senses. Eating her wouldn't be satisfying, and because of her overly saturated scent of mana, he'd never, ever wanted to. Neither had Orpheus.

To see her here now meant she had answered Orpheus' call like he had.

Yes, something is definitely wrong.

The Witch Owl paused when she saw him as he made his way to the porch steps. She allowed him to go before her.

"Mavka," she greeted with a deep, yet feminine voice, nodding her head slightly to him.

"Magnar," he corrected with a snap of his fangs.

Just because she could be trusted didn't mean he truly did.

She was powerful, which meant that a betrayal from her could be deadly. She was the one who told him that if his skull was crushed, he would truly die, which meant she knew how to kill him.

The Witch Owl raised a brow at him, but he merely snorted a huff. He had more important things to deal with.

"Reia! Orpheus!" he yelled, bashing on the barrier that kept him from climbing the porch steps.

On each corner of the house hung protection ornaments made of ribbon, dill, bone, and bells. They stopped all but those that lived within the house from entering unless invited in. They were stronger than a salt circle, but much more fragile as they could be knocked from their place, blown away by the wind, or decayed over time.

"Oh, just move," the Witch Owl bit, cutting in front of him to knock at the barrier.

A shimmering sheen echoed her call, vibrating around the outside of the house to show its placement. When she knocked a second time, this time whispering something he couldn't make out, a puff of black magic wisped from her fore knuckle.

A temporary hole in the barrier revealed itself.

"There," she said, waving her hand forward. "Now you may enter their home."

Just as he stepped through the opened barrier and climbed his way up the steps, Orpheus pulled the door open.

"Magnar," Orpheus greeted, his orbs white as if with worry. Then he twisted his head at the Witch Owl who emerged behind him. "Why are you here?"

"Can I not be?" she answered dully. "You called, I answered."

Orpheus' shoulders lessened in their tension when he let out a calming breath. It was obvious he wasn't completely trusting of her either.

"I wasn't trying to be rude. I was just curious, as you have never wanted to come inside before." Orpheus stepped back to allow them both, dripping wet, inside. "But perhaps it is a good thing that you are here."

As Magnar stepped into the warmth of the house, the Witch Owl lowered her feathered hood and shook out her hair. Straighter than normal, due to the weight of the rainwater, it bounced around her shoulders before she swept its damp contents out of her face.

Then she swiped her hand through the air and black mist formed between her and Magnar. Within seconds, they were both clean and dry.

He stepped back in surprise, inspecting his fluffy fur and

feathers. He felt cleaner and softer than he had before the rain had come, as though someone had given him a soapy bath. He itched at his flesh, unused to the feeling.

But something else stole his attention.

Magnar looked around, finding two little females were missing.

"Where are Reia and Delora?" he asked, his own orbs still a stark white.

Although he feared his reaction, his tugging desires still not a won battle, he would have preferred to have been greeted by both.

There were no Demons attacking the house, which meant he feared the worst. That was enough to cool his frazzled, heated body.

"There is something wrong with your human," Orpheus stated, turning around so that he could lead them further into his home and down the dimly lit hallway. "We've laid her down, but she has fainted."

Magnar's chest tightened. Suddenly, the casual pace of Orpheus' steps was too slow.

Delora had never fainted before.

Orpheus opened the door to a small room.

Kneeling on the floor, Reia was wiping a damp cloth against Delora's forehead while she lay limp in the small, single bed.

"I don't know what to do, Orpheus. Her fever won't go down," Reia rasped without looking at them.

She just continued to dabble the cloth against Delora with a grim expression, turning her lips downwards. When she finally brought her gaze to them, she frowned, seeming just as perplexed as Orpheus had been at the sight of the Witch Owl.

"You're here."

The Witch Owl pushed both Magnar and Orpheus out of the way. Magnar stumbled back a step, unsure how to digest what he was seeing.

Delora's usually tanned complexion was pale, sickly even. Sweat dotted her brow to the point that the droplets reflected the firelight from the candles on the bedside table next to her. Her eyes were closed, but it was obvious she was shivering beneath the furs.

She looked unwell, and nothing could make his body feel as chilled as seeing this.

The Witch Owl knelt with one knee on the bed next to Delora's form. She started muttering something. He couldn't see what she was doing because her body was in the way, but he could sense the power of magic thickening the air by the grossly sweet scent of it.

"What is wrong with her?" he asked Orpheus, turning his head to him with a growl. His eyes turned a pale red as both anger and worry warred within him. "You should have kept her safe."

"I don't know what is wrong with her," Orpheus snapped back in a dark and menacing tone. "I've never had a human be sick with this kind of fever."

"But she was in your home!" He pointed his claw at Orpheus, stepping forward with a stomp. "Did you not take care of her?"

"We gave her a bath, some water," Reia answered, making his sight turn to her instead. "But when she tried to eat, she just... started vomiting black."

He cocked his head slightly. "Black?"

"Humans aren't supposed to vomit black, Magnar," she said with a shake of her head. "This isn't normal."

It is not?

"You have mated with her," The Witch Owl finally said as she leaned back and stood up. She eyed Magnar carefully. "You have filled her with your seed."

"This is... bad?" he asked, his eyes turning white again.

He saw no other way from her being sick unless what they'd done together had been poisonous to her body.

"I did not think when I dropped her on top of you that she would give you her soul so readily. Or that you would reach this step so quickly," the Witch Owl muttered while staring at Delora, bringing a hand up so she could tap her bent fore knuckle against her lips. She eyed Magnar warily this time. "I actually thought you'd eat her."

"You dropped her on me?" Surprise was laced in his tone.

The Witch Owl scoffed, her eyes highlighting with humour.

"How else would she have fallen directly on top of you and

not have died?" Her hair bounced around her shoulders as she chuckled deeply. "There is no other way a human would have survived such a steep fall."

Magnar's fur and feathers puffed in aggression as a snarl emitted from the back of his throat. He parted his fangs, allowing the full strength of it to be heard.

"Her body was broken!" Magnar roared, stamping his hoof when he took a single stomp closer. It clopped heavily against the distressed timber flooring. "She was close to death! How could you do something so cruel to her?"

Her humour didn't fade, but it did soften.

"Perhaps I dropped her a wee bit too high," she claimed while raising her hand and leaving a small gap between her thumb and forefinger. When that didn't placate him, she rolled her eyes. "Does it matter? You learned how to heal, and you saved her from her wounds. Did that not make you feel close to her? Make you more understanding of how fragile a human body is and how much damage it can take?"

The tension in his fingers lessened as he thought on her questions.

Yes. Healing Delora had taught him just how badly a human body could be broken without there being any bleeding. It was what allowed him to know that he could harm her with his strength if he held her too tightly.

"I did check to make sure she wasn't bleeding," the Witch Owl muttered in her own defence.

"Externally," Reia bit while still kneeling beside Delora, seeming to have grown furious with her just as much as Magnar. "But that doesn't mean she wasn't bleeding on the inside. She would have died if it wasn't for him."

The Witch Owl held Reia's gaze with a sense of hostility.

"And he could have been her demise." Then she turned her sight back to Magnar. "Either you would have taken a step into understanding a human while it was unconscious in front of you, or you would have gained more humanity by eating her. Both would have been to your benefit. As I said, I thought you'd eventually eat her, but I'm glad to see that she has chosen to give you her soul instead."

"Then what is wrong with her now?" Magnar asked, the conversation of him eating Delora making his stomach knot.

He didn't want to think about the worst that could have happened. The idea that he could have eaten her instead of learning about the wonderful creature she was, who had been so willing in teaching him much, left a hollow place in his heart.

He wanted to see his little raven flourish in the bird cage of his life, not to picture it ending in a bloodbath from his claws and fangs.

"Wrong with her?" the Witch Owl asked with a mocking snort. "Nothing, other than you being foolish enough to lay your seed in her womb."

"Wait," Reia gasped, her eyes growing wide. "You're not saying she's–"

The Witch Owl turned her gaze to Reia. "Yes. She's pregnant."

"Well, fuck." Reia sighed, palming her face.

All eyes turned to Magnar, and he couldn't help his orbs turning a reddish pink under the scrutiny of Orpheus, Reia, and the Witch Owl's gazes combined.

"I do not know what this means," he answered truthfully, scratching at the back of his neck.

Reia rose from kneeling next to the bed to stand. "It means you're going to be a father."

"A creator?" Magnar asked Orpheus with his head tilting questioningly.

"I had difficulty explaining this to him," Orpheus answered to both women, standing in the doorway since the small room was already cluttered. "He doesn't really understand what a child is."

"Yes, I do," Magnar grumbled. "They are the little humans."

"But do you understand that they start small and become big, like me and Delora?" Reia asked, her brows knitting together in concern.

There was a plea in her eyes.

Magnar tried to avert his gaze, but looking away from Reia brought his sight to the Witch Owl. They were too close to him, making it hard to look away without a pair of eyes judging him.

And looking at Delora ill in the bed, which could be because of him, was distressing.

He stepped back nervously.

"Humans do not start out... their size?"

"No, Magnar," Reia whined, distress clear on her features. "We grow." She cradled her arms together in a similar way to how he'd held Delora many times, but it was almost completely different, as what she was showing she was holding was smaller than any human he'd ever seen – or eaten. "We start off as babies. We can't talk, or walk, or see very well. We need to be taken care of completely, as we are vulnerable and can't do anything for ourselves. Then we grow into toddlers who learn to walk and talk, but we know very little. We learn."

She gestured to her hip to show a size he'd seen in a human before, but he'd thought they were just... different.

"Learn? Like me?" Magnar asked.

"Yes, like you," the Witch Owl said. "But you learn fast – small humans do not. They require a lot of patience and are very fragile, more fragile than an adult."

"Does that mean I can teach it?" A spark of joy lit in the centre of his chest. Magnar would enjoy teaching something about the world. "Would it look like... her?"

His sight fell to Delora, and the idea of seeing a small version of her, something that was even more vulnerable, made him feel warm.

I can protect it.

"No," the Witch Owl said with a shake of her head. "By the fact she vomited black, it will most likely be a Mavka."

"So, it will look like me?"

He was less enthusiastic about this, but being able to teach his own about hunting and life, and maybe even about humans so it could find its own Delora, was still enjoyable.

"That depends on what you feed it," she answered. Then the Witch Owl sighed, rubbing at one of her cheeks with strain. "Perhaps this will be good for you to know as well, Orpheus, if you ever decide to take this path, but raising a Mavka isn't by any means *normal*. You are born blind and rely mainly on scent. What you eat dictates what your appearance will be. The pregnancy is also shortened since there is no need for a longer gestation time. You aren't born whole."

"What do you mean, no need for a longer gestation time?" Reia asked.

"Well, they are born without bones or organs, really nothing but their outer flesh and mouth."

"Okay. *Okay...* That's super weird, to be honest." Reia's eyes were widening in what could only be worry. "So, uh, how long then?"

"A full moon's cycle, sometimes a little more."

Reia sucked in a gasp and then choked on her own saliva momentarily. "You're joking, right?! A fucking month?"

"How long is it normally?" Orpheus asked, making Magnar's head turn in his direction.

Humans were such strange and complex things that not even Orpheus knew everything about them. That brought relief to Magnar.

"Nine months," Reia answered.

Orpheus pointed to her belly. "You hold a baby in your stomach for nine months? From what I know, both the mother and the child are very delicate when combined like this."

"It's not a choice," Reia sighed lightly. "That's just how long it takes."

"The child is growing inside her?" Magnar asked as he stepped towards Delora, making both the women part for him.

The Witch Owl spoke behind him as he moved.

"By how unwell she is, I am guessing it has only been two or three days since you have been intimate with her. The seed of your kind is rather feral, just like your father's, and it happens rather quickly if the woman is fertile. Nothing about this is normal for a human, not even at the time of conception."

Magnar knelt next to her and sniffed at her stomach, only now finding she smelt... different. She still smelt of red apples and frost, but there was a tang to it, one that called to his senses to protect both.

Like she felt his presence next to her, Delora stirred. Her face scrunched up before her eyes flickered open, revealing those pools of brown he adored peering into.

"Magnar?" Delora asked weakly, her voice broken and hoarse.

"I am here, my little raven," he stated, raising a hand so he could brush his claws over her to push her damp hair from her face, unsure if the dampness was from the bath they'd mentioned or sweat.

"I want to go home," she softly whined, curling into his hand welcomingly with a cringe. "I don't feel so well."

"The first few days are the hardest," the Witch Owl stated. "Her body is rejecting something that is unnatural, but it will eventually calm down."

Worry crossed Delora's features, and she peeked over his palm to see they weren't alone. She attempted to recoil into the bed, and her face paling even further wasn't comforting to witness.

Although he heard the Witch Owl speak, all of his attention was solely on the shivering human in front of him. He spoke to her, hoping to distract her from the other prying eyes in the room.

"We cannot go home right now." His voice was filled with disappointment for her, even though he was delighted that she thought of the house he was building for her as her home – and that she would prefer to be there than in this warm house. "It is raining."

"Please?" she begged, reaching up to cling to his wrist.

"The cold might do her some good," the Witch Owl said, and he turned his head over his shoulder to look at her. "I must go before the rain ends, but Magnar, I need you to come with me first."

"No." Delora gripped him tighter, which was as feeble as a bunny trying to escape. "Please don't leave again."

Something cold and painful lanced his heart and felt like shards of ice in his veins. He'd left Delora because he'd been worried about hurting her physically, but he hadn't thought she'd care for his absence.

He could see now that he'd been wrong.

She likes me being near. She didn't hate him for what he'd done to her. He wasn't sure if she would like to know what else he'd done, but he would face that shortly.

Magnar didn't know how he felt about this discovery. He was learning too much too quickly, some things pleasurable while other things worrisome. He didn't need to ask if the intimacy they'd shared had caused this; he knew. He could put two and two together.

It was *theirs.* They were the creators, and he felt a connection to it. He was... happy, but nervous because he also worried about how Delora would take learning this.

Reia looked concerned. Would Delora hate this, detest him for this? He didn't want her to feel anything other than fondness towards him.

What would he do if she didn't want to accept this?

Will she cry again? Those tears of hers stung like small daggers in his flesh. He didn't want to be the source of them, not when he was trying to heal her of her invisible wounds she'd told him he could not fight with his brute strength.

Magnar pulled his arm out of her grip, but only so he could brush the backs of his fingers against her cheek.

"I will stay here in this house, but I must speak with her," Magnar said reassuringly. "I will not be far."

Delora nodded, and he backed away so he could stand, looking down at her with a swirl of dancing emotions.

Reia stepped into his place when he moved towards the Witch Owl, who spun on the spot and exited the room. It forced Orpheus to get out of her way.

"Are you thirsty, Delora?" Reia asked as he left the room. "There's some water here for you."

When Orpheus, the Witch Owl, and Magnar entered the spacious area between the living room and kitchen, she placed her hood over her head to cover herself.

"I had originally left your garden untampered with in order for you to learn how to tend to it on your own, but I can see I'm going to need to grow it for you," she said as she checked her hood's placement. "I can only do this when it rains. The only time a Phantom truly needs food is when they are pregnant, and she will need meat as well, as that is what the Mavka will require to grow."

"Will Delora be okay?"

That's all Magnar truly cared about.

The Witch Owl, surprisingly, gave him a sweet smile.

"Yes, she will be fine. But I'm glad to see how much you care for her. She obviously means a lot to you already. And it's comforting to know she likes you." Then her smile faded as she turned her eyes away. "But this should have come later. It has barely been a few weeks since I dropped her on top of you. Neither of you are ready for this, especially not her."

"We will help as much as we can," Orpheus offered, his orbs turning a dark yellow. "I'm curious to see what will happen."

This was new to all of them. Magnar stumbling his way through it shouldn't be shocking, but he didn't like that he had no one to truly turn to for advice about this. The Witch Owl was only reachable when she wanted to be.

Perhaps I can call her the same way Orpheus did.

"She harbours darkness inside her," the Witch Owl said in an ominous tone, her voice deeper than usual. "She will be unstable. She will be as uncontrollable with her emotions as Mavka usually are. Expect lots of tears and anger, but also laughter. Try not to judge her for it or get upset with her – it will only make it worse."

Orpheus and Magnar both huffed in annoyance. It was obvious they both thought they were good at controlling their emotions.

"Once she gets through the first couple of days, she should stabilise. She will need your presence, Magnar."

"I will take care of her," he promised, not that he should need to.

Now that he knew Delora was in a sensitive and fragile state, he wouldn't leave her side again. His desire had been almost non-existent with his worry for her.

"Good." She nodded with approval. "Take her to the Demon Village and get her essential items. She will require them."

"The Demon Village?" Orpheus muttered with a hint of concern. "Wouldn't that be a terrible idea right now?"

She scoffed. "She's only weak for now. In a few days, she will be bright as anything. It is better he takes her once she feels better than when her stomach is big and swollen. She's a

Phantom now. She can walk with you while in that form."

"Hmm," Magnar hummed, bringing his claws up so he could tap one against his snout. "I was already thinking about taking her there since she would not be able to be harmed like that."

"Exactly. You must be quick, though. After two weeks, it will be too risky. The further along in her pregnancy she is, the harder it is to keep her Phantom form for a long period of time."

"I will take her when she is feeling better."

The Witch Owl nodded before heading towards the front door, finished with the conversation even though Magnar still had many questions that only she could answer. That was how she'd always been.

When she was gone, Magnar turned to Orpheus with a tightness present in his chest.

"How am I supposed to explain this to Delora?"

"No idea," he said, raising one arm and shrugging. "I know as much about this as you do."

Well, what am I supposed to do now, then? he thought with a grumble.

TWENTY-THREE

Delora felt the splatters of heavy raindrops against her face as Magnar cradled her in his long arms. She was facing the sky in this position, unable to escape the falling water that was cold as ice against her heated skin.

She still was unbearably dizzy, and each long footfall caused her to bounce in his arms. It churned her stomach that was filled with as much food as she'd been able to handle before they left Orpheus' house.

On top of her body was a pot of stew, a bundle of clothing Orpheus had given to Magnar, and three pairs of shoes for her.

She hugged them closer, worried she'd accidentally drop something again, but her body felt weak. Even her breaths were strained, occasionally quivering out of her chest in pained huffs.

"What's wrong with me, Magnar?" Delora tried to shout since her voice was so muted in strength. There was also the potential he may not be able to hear her over the constant downpour.

The rain created a continuous *shaa* noise around them as it hit the ground, and his footfalls were always accompanied by the sloshing of puddles around his hooves.

"We will speak of this when we are home," he answered, refusing to look away from his path.

Ever since he'd come back from talking with the Witch Owl and Orpheus, Magnar had refused to look upon her until he was lifting her into his arms to carry her home. He hadn't again since.

He'd informed her they should be safe walking through the Veil with the rain, as it would wash away both their scents. It also hid their sounds under its onslaught, and the mist was thicker than she'd ever seen it.

Currently, unless seen up close, they were invisible.

"Please," she sputtered around water. "I want to know."

She was still tired. She thought that when they returned, she might fall asleep again as soon as he laid her down, despite being wet.

When he didn't answer her, she raised her hand as best as she could without letting anything fall from her torso and cupped the side of his snout to drag it down.

He snorted a huff of annoyance, she thought, and shook his head to get her to let go. Delora's brows drew inwards, and she tried to stem her hurt by hiding it from her features. She lowered her hand away from him.

"I-I'm sorry for crying," Delora said with her voice breaking an octave. "Please don't be upset with me."

Magnar's head turned as he shot his gaze down to her.

"I am not upset with you," he quickly said.

"But you won't even look at me."

Or at least, he hadn't been until this moment. Her eyes bounced around all the features of his skull.

"It is difficult to see properly. I am worried I will trip while holding you," he answered, before raising his head forward to look at his path. "I... am not used to walking this straight for so long while holding something precious." His arms curled around her a little tighter. "I am worried I will drop you because of the rain."

"Oh," she said, her eyelids flickering in understanding. She turned her gaze back to the items on her stomach, feeling relief washing over her. "You've been avoiding me for a few days, though."

The only reason she knew his orbs changed colour, since she couldn't see them, was because the light glow around his skull changed to a reddish pink.

"I hurt you," he said with a darkness to his tone. "I was angry with myself for doing so, and yet I wanted to..." He shook his head before finishing what he was going to say, but Delora thought it might have been that he wanted to touch her again.

"But I am realising that I have been hurting you by being gone as well. You are unwell – this matters more, and it is allowing me to focus on what I need to do."

A flash of purple shone, and his claws dug in lightly before it quickly faded and then the glow from his orbs was green once more.

"I will take care of you."

"From what?" Delora pushed, bringing her gaze to him. "What is wrong with me?"

She felt his body cringing by how it curled around her, almost like he wanted to put her down and shy away. Yet, he just continued to walk forward while refusing to answer.

"A person deserves to know what's wrong with them when they ask, Magnar. I know you want to wait until we're home, but it makes me anxious not knowing."

They'd been walking for what must be at least an hour, and she didn't know how much longer it would be. Each minute made her eyes drowsier, and the longer it was, the more she knew her lucidity would slip. The rain was cold and keeping her awake. She wanted to have the conversation now while she could remember it and be coherent for it.

"I do not know how to tell you without upsetting you," he said honestly. "Reia made me feel like this is a bad thing. I do not want to make you sad or have you angry with me." She saw the glow of his orbs turn blue. "I did not mean to do this, Delora."

Her heart rate spiked, making her feel warmer than she already was.

"What did you do to me?" When her question was met with another head shake, her pulse quickened even further. "I-I'll try not to be upset with you."

"I have made you a creator. Or us, creators." He turned his gaze down to her to find her head was shaking in confusion, with her brows drawn together. "The Witch Owl said there is life growing inside you from me."

Her lips parted in disbelief.

"Are you saying I'm pregnant?"

He looked forward through the rain, drops of it running off his skull.

His answer was slow to come. "Yes."

The items on her torso were squished together when Delora swiftly laid her hands against her stomach.

"How is this possible?" she asked herself. "I'm human and you're a Duskwalker. We shouldn't be able to..."

"But you are not human anymore. You are a Phantom. I have made you like me."

Her eyes lifted to her soul floating between his antlers and understanding dawned upon her. *Giving him my soul made us compatible?* She looked down to her stomach once more, digging her nails in.

"I'm going to be a mother?"

Even though her eyes had been filling with water from the rain, she knew the liquid building there now was tears, as they were warm in comparison. She was thankful that Magnar didn't seem to notice because he would have assumed the worst.

Instead of dread, or anger, or disappointment, which may have been the reaction of any other person in her situation, Delora felt a flutter of joy for the first time in years.

I'm... I'm pregnant. If the pain she felt at the same time wasn't so demanding and cruel that it squeezed her heart, she may have started laughing.

It wasn't my fault.

For her entire marriage to Hadith, Delora had never been able to fall pregnant. The blame she'd been given had been hollowing. She knew his feelings towards her had started turning cold because she'd never been able to have his child. It was something he'd wanted, to continue his bloodline, and because of her inability to produce a child for him, he'd deemed her broken, useless, worthless.

It wasn't my fault! It was his *fault.*

His fucking fault, and he'd pushed all that blame onto Delora! There was nothing wrong with her womb, made obvious by the fact that she was now going to bear Magnar's child. It was Hadith's stupid nutsack that couldn't produce fertile seed.

And she was so happy that he couldn't, that he'd never been able to.

When Delora realised Magnar was tense, she pushed aside all

the sadness she felt because of the years of mistreatment she'd unfairly received and focused on this moment instead.

"I always wanted to have a baby," she muttered shyly.

He braved the opportunity to look down at her with his head tilting. "You are not upset by this?"

Delora shook her head. "No. Sure, I'm surprised, and I don't think this is the best time, but I'm not upset."

Delora didn't actually care if this was the best time or the right time or if this was something they shouldn't have even done. She was going to be a mother, something she'd always longed for, and she, in some ways, was a little excited about the fact it was Magnar's.

"You wanted to do this with me?"

"No," she answered. "I didn't even think this was possible between us, but I'm a little curious about it. Will it be human or like you?"

"The Witch Owl said it will be Mavka because you are sick. Your body is rejecting it."

Dread stabbed through her so swiftly it chilled her entire being. She was thankful the rain would be washing away the smell of fear she knew would be coming from her.

"Rejecting it?"

"Yes." He lifted his head to watch his path as he moved through a small section of trees, stepping carefully over twisted roots. "Because it is the first time, she said. Your body will eventually adjust, and you will no longer be as sick in a few days."

Relief eased her muscles, and she stared at her stomach. *So everything will be okay, then? A Duskwalker's child?*

Her lips curled upwards lightly, perhaps her first small smile in a long time, as she touched her abdomen.

"And when you are better, I will take you to the Demon Village."

"Huh?!" Delora let out a gasp as her eyes widened, making her eyelids flutter and blink when raindrops stung them. "You're taking me to the Demon Village?"

TWENTY-FOUR

For three additional days, Magnar tried his best to take care of his unwell female. Not an easy task when she would suddenly vomit black, and he would have to be quick to catch it in a large bowl so that she didn't mess the nest she lay upon. Then he would rub her back while she was bent over the side of the nest walls so she could retch outside of it.

The heaving sounds were distressing, and her dazed eyes afterwards were always a little concerning, but she seemed better for a short period of time following.

For a little while, she'd fall back asleep. It was like she'd used all of her energy to expel darkness from within her. Magnar would watch over her as she shivered and attempted to bury herself further under the covers. Other times she would seem strangled, desperately kicking them off.

There had been a handful of times she begged Magnar to hold her, and even though she felt hot and clammy, she would plead with him that she was freezing and needed more warmth. It wouldn't take long for her skin to flush and for her to start violently trying to get away from his heat.

She'd been a confusing mess to him, but he tried his hardest for her.

After she slept, he would force her to drink by placing a shallow bowl to her lips and then he would work on making her eat.

The rain was no longer present, but the wonders of the Witch Owl's magic had made the garden grow completely. All the plants had sprouted, even the apple tree that was almost as tall as he was. Delora seemed to be fond of the sweetness of the apples, and it was easier to force food into her if it was accompanied by a slice.

She told him it must be some kind of pregnancy craving that she needed them with all of her food, but he wondered if it was because her body wanted something it smelled like. Perhaps it drew comfort from something similar.

As she didn't have the energy to do much else but be unwell, Magnar was forced to make Delora dress herself while he was outside.

He'd managed to change them both from their wet clothing the first night. Magnar had dressed Delora in a dry shirt with little concern. He'd been too focused on helping her to allow his mind to register that he'd had this beautiful human naked in his presence. He was too befuddled about her response to all this and somehow relieved that she'd seemed almost... *happy* about it.

She'd fallen asleep almost instantly the moment he'd laid her down and covered her with the blanket. He'd dried their clothing inside by tying up rope from one wall to the other, then hung their clothing up, much like how he'd seen Reia do outside on their porch.

He was thankful for that as, on the second night, she'd sweated through the shirt while she was asleep.

Magnar, thinking he could do what he'd done when she'd first come into his life, wiped her face with a damp cloth to clean her. He'd been gentle as he brushed it over her cheeks, her forehead, her ears, and even wiped her hair down.

Her eyes, illuminated by dim firelight, had peeked open to glitter at him with a hazy expression.

"That feels nice," she'd told him as she craned her head to the side and allowed him to wipe down her neck with the cool, damp cloth.

Cradling her back with one arm to keep her slightly upright, he'd fumbled with the buttons of her shirt so he could strip and change her now that she was awake. He hadn't made it to the bottom button before the shirt started slipping open to reveal her full and heavy breasts dusted with hardened pink nipples.

Purple had instantly flared into his sight when she moaned when he tried to wipe down her chest. Unable to help himself, drawn to her like a wretched, ravenous being, he'd dipped his head and drew his tongue across one of her breasts just for her to give an unhidden, sweeter moan with her eyes closed.

He hadn't cared about the saltiness of her skin, or her shivering body, when he started lapping at her chest. His washcloth had been forgotten when he leaned over her. Instead, he drew his claws up the inside of her thigh that twitched under his touch. She arched into him.

His cock had stirred, the movement behind his seam so unbearable that his cock and the tentacles, which were supposed to encase it, started to come out as a writhing mess inside his trousers. The head, unsheltered, had been abraded by the roughness of his pants.

The groan she gave him when he spread her thighs and positioned himself between them while huffing wildly at her chest, his tongue an unceasing limb that moved over her stiffened nipples, made him shudder.

"You're too hot, Magnar," she'd cried before she pushed at his chest.

He snarled in response, trying to draw her closer while reaching for the front of his trousers. The throb in his cock was terrible, but the stinging he felt from it drying out demanded that it take shelter within her.

And to experience the rapture of him spending inside her again was like a venom he'd forgotten he'd needed.

"Please," she'd whispered. "I-I need to cool down. I'm getting really dizzy."

Her broken and weak voice pleading with him had sent his orbs white. Magnar shuffled backwards, wincing when he realised he'd dropped her against her bedding.

What am I doing?

Delora was currently unwell, in a daze, and he'd been moments away from rutting inside her.

But he didn't know how to control the nagging in his cock. And the longer he sat back on his hunches, staring at her from between her feet, seeing her legs were spread, and her inviting little slit open to him, Magnar felt an overwhelming desire to grab her leg, drag her over him, and shove his way into her. He wanted to burrow so deep she wouldn't be able to escape him.

And he *knew* it would feel good.

Purple flared, and he shuffled back again before scuttling to his feet.

"Delora," he groaned, clenching his fists beside himself as he gave her his back. "Wash yourself and dress. There is a bucket and a new shirt. I will return."

Then he went outside before he could hear her answer, ashamed of himself for what he'd been moments away from doing. Pacing, he'd gripped his cock through his trousers despite that it hurt, begging for it to go down and back inside his seam.

Only when it did, and he checked on Delora to find she was clean, dressed, and passed out, did he enter the house.

He hated that he couldn't tend to her when she needed him most, that he was useless and incapable of controlling this... strange part of his mind and body that gnawed at him constantly.

On the second day, Reia and Orpheus had started visiting to bring cooked meat.

Orpheus would work around the yard, cutting down trees and shaping them to help quicken the process of the house now that Delora was here. Magnar needed a fully built home for her. Reia would help in any way she could, tending to the garden, teaching him how to tend it now that it was grown, and washing their clothing.

Before they'd left, he asked Reia to help clean Delora since he couldn't. He knew he couldn't. He couldn't even bear to change her any longer.

They continued to return, even when Delora was feeling much better by the fourth day, and she'd started to move around.

She was still weak, but she'd stopped expelling darkness. She was able to keep down all her food and water, eating slowly if her stomach grew upset.

Magnar became confident enough to leave her side to help Orpheus bring inside the logs he'd cut and shaped so they could begin to build the rooms he'd planned for.

He picked up snippets of conversation between Reia and

Delora as he ducked in and out, but he paid little mind to them. All he knew was that his female was beginning to feel better and that he'd need to start preparing for their journey soon.

The Witch Owl told him taking Delora to the Demon Village sooner rather than later was better, but he was apprehensive of doing so. He wanted her safe, always, and the journey to the village was just as dangerous, if not more so, than the village itself.

He didn't know which he was worried about more.

It was a four-day walk for a Mavka to get there. He couldn't go without her since she'd appear beside him within one day, but he wanted her to be comfortable here. There were things in the village she'd need, and he wanted to give her everything – even the world, if he could.

He would take her there if it meant he could finally see her smile.

Delora sat on the porch steps with her elbows on her closed knees and her chin resting on both her palms, waiting for herself to disappear.

She gave a sigh. *This is boring.*

It was only yesterday that she'd fully gained her strength, five days since she'd fallen ill to begin with, and already she was braving going to the Demon Village.

Magnar had been assertive about taking her there now, despite her lingering doubts. They'd barely spoken the last few days, as her lucidity was infrequent and short, and even though she'd told him she didn't particularly want to go, he was adamant about it. Once she was strong enough to walk the entire yard without issue, Magnar had informed her they'd be beginning their journey that very day.

The idea of waltzing into a dangerous territory with an unborn child, no matter what it was, was frightening. She cared more about the harm that could come to it than herself.

At the same time, she knew why they needed to go.

The last week of her pregnancy would make it difficult for her to maintain her ghostly form, which would only be three to four weeks away from now. She couldn't believe that she'd only be pregnant for a freaking month!

Other than feeling better, she saw no changes within her body so far. She thought that might be because her stomach was already rather rounded, and she'd have to be further along to see the difference.

Still, a month wasn't a long time, and she wondered how her body was meant to adjust to such a quick change. Would she, or it, be okay?

The Witch Owl apparently had no issues.

To learn that the woman she vaguely remembered seeing briefly at Orpheus and Reia's house was actually Magnar's mother was insane. To know she was the person who'd birthed all Duskwalkers was even crazier.

Does that mean they're all brothers?

Delora, once better, had asked Reia millions of questions.

The reason all the Duskwalkers were male was because the first human they'd all eaten had been male. Reia believed if a woman had been eaten first, there would be females of their kind.

However, women were either too frightened to travel because of the Demons, especially since there was a chance they could have their period suddenly along the way – something they always were wary about, even in walled villages – or they were smart enough to not get themselves into situations that could get them eaten by a Duskwalker.

"I'm kind of glad there aren't any females," Delora grumbled. "Would Magnar prefer a female of his own kind?"

This wasn't a question she'd ever ask him, and she was glad she wouldn't be faced with this problem if they all continued to eat men.

That would be totally weird since they'd be siblings. She doubted they would have known, since it was apparently new information to them that the Witch Owl was their mother. What an *oops* that would have been.

"Then again," she continued to ramble. "I wonder if Duskwalkers can give each other their souls. Do they even have souls?"

Her thoughts were in line with the idea that they chose their partner based purely on the fact they seemed to want a soul, since both Magnar and Orpheus had wanted to fulfil this need.

It didn't take long for Delora to snort a gentle huff of laughter.

"Magnar has a soul. I just know it."

He had to have one to be so sweet and caring. A creature without a soul, a heart, would be hollow like a nightmare, feasting terribly on flesh.

But Magnar had tended to her all throughout the last few days. Dabbing a cloth to her forehead, giving her food and water, helping her to adjust to the different temperatures she needed.

He even tried to fluff my pillow. Something warm lit in her chest at the memory.

A large gust of wind shook the trees, bringing her mind back to reality. "This sucks. How much longer do I have to sit here?"

The sun hadn't long crested over the trees, the morning truly well and bright, and all she had been able to do was sit here.

Magnar had already left to go to the Demon Village, making her sit here patiently, or rather, impatiently, so that she would appear by his side once he was out of the most dangerous ring of the Veil's forest.

Apparently, the Veil was made up of four rings of life.

The border where the smallest Demons, but the most ruthless and hungry for human flesh, roamed. It was also where their house was. Then the second ring inwards was where the more medium-sized Demons lived; those that were still hungry for human flesh but would only hunt when starved and would eat whatever they got their claws into. The third ring was a mixture of medium and large Demons, those that had started building houses rather than nests and were already starting to mimic humans.

And finally, the inner ring, where the Demon Village was.

It was a lot to wrap her head around since she'd originally dismissed the whole idea as nonsense.

Waiting to disappear was boring, but she preferred this over having to go through the border ring. *I'm not as fearless as Reia.* Just the idea of brandishing a sword and swinging it at a frothing Demon had her blood curdling.

I wonder what we're going to do on our way back, though.

Magnar *had* mentioned that he was going to scout if there were any nests along the way, so he could mark a safe path for their return journey.

"He's a lot smarter than anyone gives him credit for."

Even Delora hadn't thought of something that insightful, but he'd come up with a plan before she'd even voiced her trepidation.

Her sight flittered to the sun that was trying to shower her in light but couldn't reach because of the overgrown tree near the porch steps. He'd left roughly around this time the day before.

Shouldn't be too much longer.

Just as she'd thought, a few minutes later she turned transparent against her will. Having already experienced this, she just closed her eyes and accepted it.

She knew she'd materialised near Magnar when her posture changed from sitting upon steps to being curled on the side of her hip against the cold ground.

Before she could even open her eyes, she felt the familiar rake of claw tips gliding their way from the bottom of her jugular up to the line of her jaw before they drifted to her chin. Ticklish, her flesh rose with goosebumps that forced a shiver down her spine, and her eyelids opened to find Magnar crouching on one knee in front of her.

"Are you okay?" he asked. The comforting glow of his green orbs in the darkness of the Veil's forest was tantalising enough to make her flush.

"I'm fine," she answered, moving to get up by herself before she noticed his hand hovering in the air. She eyed it, then instantly took it so that he could help to her feet. "I'm not dizzy like I was last time."

"You were dizzy?" Before she could answer, Magnar scooped her up into his arms to cradle her and covered her partially with his cloak that was wrapped around his body. "We must leave this area quickly."

His bag rattled as he shifted it to his side. It was filled with assorted sparkling rocks he said he'd found near the stream close to their home, where he fetched her drinking water from. There were also broken bits of amethyst crystal he'd scavenged from a cave Orpheus had shown him, and pieces of obsidian rock he'd removed from his own cave they'd originally been living in.

This was all brought in his satchel bag, as well as food and a water sack for her – all pre-prepared in case she hadn't been able to reappear to him with the one that was strapped around herself.

It had appeared with her, and now she had twice the amount of food and water, which was good, considering she was always hungry.

"Why?" Delora peeked out of his cloak and looked around. She thought her heart would begin to pump rapidly, but surprisingly, she felt not an ounce of fear because of his presence. "Is something wrong?"

"It took me a long time to find the safest return path, as there were many nests cluttered together. We are out of the border ring, but we are still too close."

He walked deeper into the forest, and Delora noted the trees seemed taller. He didn't even need to duck underneath the lowest hanging branches to clear his antlers.

"Will we be okay?"

She looked up, finding that there wasn't a shred of light this deep within the Veil, and the blue mist that was ever present seemed thicker.

Even the air felt more stagnant.

The only colour that was noticeable came from the red and orange of the occasional tree that was losing more and more leaves, to the point its branches were becoming barren. Not all trees, as many more remained green and luscious, but the splashes of colour at least stopped their surroundings from appearing truly dreary. She liked seeing the floor blanketed in life, rather than just dirt, sticks, and stones.

"Yes. Your scent is not human. It will be confusing to the Demons, but they will not be drawn to you. So long as we avoid them and you remain mostly hidden, we should be safe."

Delora inspected the side of his bony skull, pondering a

question. "You can hear really well, can't you?"

For a creature that didn't have ears, he always seemed to be able to hear well. It was also the same for the fact he didn't have a proper nose, but his sense of smell was keener than any animal she'd ever heard of.

"Yes," he repeated. "I will be able to hear or smell anything that comes near, so do not worry. I will always protect you."

But Delora hadn't needed the reassurance.

She was warm and protected in his embrace as he walked them through the thick brush, and she curled into his solid chest trustingly. His strong heartbeat resonated through his flesh as it pounded next to her ear, and she let it give her a soothing drum for their walk.

"When we are deeper within the Veil, where it will be less likely for us to cross a Demon, you should practice using your ghostly form in preparation for the village."

"Sounds like a good idea," she mumbled contentedly, closing her eyes so she could focus on the thumping of his heart and his hoof-steps.

TWENTY-FIVE

Nothing could have prepared Delora for what she discovered at the Demon Village.

The massive trees that seemed to have grown up diagonally from the ground to spiral around the village to protect it from the bright sunshine that shone over it were... beautiful. Especially with the clearing of grass that surrounded everything, as if to trap the creatures within or keep others out during the day.

Flowering weeds created a sea of yellow and green as they danced between the grass stems. They waved with the light wind that breezed over the gradual hill they journeyed down so they could make their way closer.

The castle in the distance behind the village gave her all the proof she needed that there was such a thing as a Demon King, and she kept her eyes off it. She worried that if she gazed upon it for too long, it would somehow bring him upon them.

From what she'd heard, he wasn't a nice guy.

She doubted she'd have strength like Reia did, who told her of the fight they'd had against him and Katerina. The story made it sound as though she had been level-headed and brave.

Delora didn't know how to use a sword, nor could she run very fast.

Her one act of violence had been accompanied by her own enraged scream and lack of any thoughts. To face something as terrible as a magic wielding part-Elf, part-Demon *freak* sounded like too much for her to handle.

I don't want to witness any more violence or carnage.

Delora wanted to live peacefully, and she thought she may have found that chance with Magnar.

Now that she could live within the safety of a protection ward and turn into something intangible when outside of it, her safety was guaranteed.

And she knew she could make the little log cabin, their home, something comfortable with enough time. Delora was patient. She'd been patient all her life.

In her Ghost form, she touched her stomach to feel the pressure but nothing else. *And with you, nugget, I can finally be what I've always wanted.*

Delora didn't care that it would be different to her.

She brought her gaze up to make sure she was still by Magnar's side as he led her to the towering trees that spiralled around the village. They were larger than anything she'd ever seen, the roots arching over the ground to crest taller than her very height. The trunks had to be hundreds of metres high and just as wide as the protection ward back at home.

The trees cast shadows over the ground, highlighting that night was beginning to fall.

Since it was possible to gain entrance at any intersection of the trees, they walked around one of the many trunks to enter the village.

"Stay with me, Delora," Magnar warned when she could see bright light on the other side of the thin, moss-covered tunnel. "You are not producing a scent like this, so I will not be able to track you here. And if you speak, they will know you are not an actual Ghost. Always stay where I can see you."

"Does that mean I can't talk to you?" she whispered, her voice echoing against the wooden walls.

"You can," he answered just as quietly. "But you must be quiet so as not to draw too much attention. However, I cannot respond to you so openly."

Before Delora could ask why, she lost the ability to speak as they walked into bright firelight. Her lips parted as her eyes turned upwards towards the spiralling roof that protected this place.

Cloth tapestries hung from the very ceiling like creatures had climbed to the topmost branches to attach them. They shot downwards through the air before the ends were then lifted to create a convex shape and attached to lower branches on the sides.

They were colourful, displaying vibrant yellows, blues, reds, and greens.

She didn't know what she was expecting, but the multi-level houses weren't what she thought she'd see. Made from brick and timber slatted roofs, they were cluttered together, most having wooden shutters. Delora could see a *Demon* leaning out of one window, shouting towards another on the stone pathway that ran between houses.

Instead of her eyes taking in the many Demons, or even listening closer to make sure it was really music and laughter she could hear, something glittered and stole her focus.

She lifted a transparent finger and tried to follow the tiny glowing bug that danced right in front of her with many others.

"Oh, wow. They're so pretty."

Delora had never seen glow bugs before, but she knew that's what they were as they fluttered through her intangible form before lifting off into the air as a small swarm. More were present throughout the village, hovering all throughout the sky and making the ceiling come to life as though they were moving stars.

"They begin to appear here when night is falling," Magnar said quietly while leaning his head closer.

Her gaze drew away from watching them with wonder so she could focus on the rest of village and its occupants, but any trepidation she'd felt was lost to the mystical welcome she'd received.

It wasn't frightful, and the dreary mist she was used to seeing in the Veil wasn't present here.

As Magnar began leading her from the outskirts to deeper within, the houses became even more cluttered. They had to start walking up cobblestone and clay steps to get to the higher levels of the village.

The first Demon she'd seen up close had her pushing towards Magnar to the point she accidentally wandered inside his body. He made no complaint and kept at a stride that equalled her steps.

It was an involuntary need to move her body as though she was walking, even though she floated off the ground.

The Demon that had her scuttling away had been like none she'd ever seen before. It was taller than her, with a strangely flat face, but had mostly appeared human in shape. It even had patches of pinkish-white skin against the black void she was used to seeing, as though it was truly taking on the characteristics of a human.

As she continued to look around while inside Magnar's body, observing more Demons that walked on their back legs and spoke between themselves, she realised it was just like any other community of sentient beings.

If she had closed her eyes and only listened, she would have thought she was back in the town she'd originally come from.

It sounded no different when a smaller Demon, that looked like a *child,* squealed a giggle as another chased it. Both had pointed ears, big boar-like fangs, and each one had patches of skin colour that were a fawny light brown. They looked so similar to each other, she thought they might have been siblings.

Delora didn't realise she had slipped out of Magnar until she stopped to watch them with curiosity, the shield of his body now lost.

Demons' prying eyes were now free to view her.

Her back stiffened when one with a more lizard-like face meshed into its human features turned its overly large red eyes upon her. Delora froze on the spot and shrunk under its piercing and hostile gaze... until its sight drew away from her as though she was insignificant.

A sigh fluttered out of her until she connected eyes with another before it, too, looked away.

They were unbothered by her there, and they walked through her ghostly form without care.

She looked at her hands. *They think I'm an actual Ghost.* They didn't know she could turn physical.

A black figure stopped to stand in front of her, blocking anyone else from walking through her, and her eyes drifted up to Magnar.

"They don't care," she whispered in shock.

He snorted a huff in response. Then he turned around and walked forward.

Delora quickly chased after his slow steps and watched as many Demons acted skittish, giving him a wide berth. However, others didn't move out of his way when it got more packed with bodies. They often grunted rudely when they barged their shoulders into him, but surprisingly, Magnar kept his cool and allowed it.

He looked awesome while he towered over *everyone.*

His stature was bigger than any Demon within their vicinity, and his antlers made him even more imposing. Even if she got surrounded and had trouble finding him, she always knew which direction to go when she saw his antlers only a body's distance away from her.

Magnar took her to a clothing shop and greeted a very eccentric Demon by the name of Snush, who had ram horns on the side of his head. He paid Delora no mind as he began speaking with Magnar, asking him if he wanted more clothing. He did, and he traded some of the polished stream stones for more button-up shirts and trousers.

She thought he may have gotten a few extra shirts just for her.

Then he brought her to a shoe shop, informing the more bird-like shopkeeper that he needed new slippers since his feet had changed recently. She gave him a pair of shoes that had no heel and no point, and she watched as he sat on a bench and slipped them on, making it look as though he was wearing shoes that were fitted around his hooves.

These two places were more on the outskirts of the markets, and Magnar took her deeper within, where they eventually reached street carts offering an array of different items. Cooked food, clothing materials, and one that was desperately trying to sell candles – of which Magnar bought many.

There were wooden boxed stalls as well that offered jewellery and the supplies to make them.

He stood in front of this place for a long time without saying or doing anything. It was only because he cocked his snout at it that she realised he was silently asking her if she wanted anything.

Although Delora knew she didn't want anything vain like jewellery, she still leaned closer to inspect them.

Some were crudely made, while others were pretty in their own way, although simple. A coldness tingled within her, perhaps a reaction to her dread, when she saw pieces of jewellery that were obviously more sophisticated, knowing they must have been stolen from humans who had most likely lost their lives.

Just as she leaned forward to inspect a silver necklace with a red ruby sitting in the middle of diamonds that formed a circle around it, a black hand with long, sharp nails took a hold of it.

"I'll take this one," a feminine voice demanded, her other hand reaching over the stall's table to give something to the shopkeeper.

Delora *nearly* screamed when a horrifying wail echoed right as the necklace was touched, and a ghostly figure suddenly appeared through the centre of the table. A transparent woman grabbed at her own face and wept.

Thankfully, Delora had covered her mouth before she could produce her own loud, horrified scream. But she did step away from the shop with wide eyes.

"Oh," the Demon woman said with disgust, carelessly tossing the necklace away. It clanked and rattled the others on the table. "It's an anchor."

As soon as the necklace was released, the Ghost's crying settled until it was only sobs before it slowly began to fade away.

"You shouldn't be selling jewellery that has a human's spirit anchored to it," she bit at the shopkeeper.

The female Demon had long black hair that was glossy, even in the light. She was tall, slender, and almost looked human except for her void-like skin. Freckled human flesh was around the corner of her lips, and the opposing side of her cheek before it ran around one of her red eyes.

It seemed none of the Demons could shed the red colour of their irises, and hers seemed sharp.

"Some people prefer them," the shopkeeper argued back. This one was similar to the woman, but had spikes over his forehead. He nodded his head in Magnar's direction. "It seems this Mavka likes to wear haunted anchors."

Both of their stares, as well as Magnar's skull, turned to Delora. She backed away from them until she found herself within the passing crowd.

She knew by the throbbing of her form that her heart would have been pounding with fear if she had been physical.

Then, with her eyes bewildered, she realised she'd lost Magnar in her panic. She turned in a circle to search, and her brows pulled together when she couldn't find him.

Oh my God, where is he? She couldn't be alone here!

She opened her mouth to yell, but immediately shut it. He'd told her to be quiet, to whisper.

A whoosh of fire had Delora backing up when a Demon began twirling fire poi right in front of her. She couldn't identify his form since he was moving so fast. All she could focus on was the large, fang-filled grin he wore as he jumped and swung the flaming balls connected by rope in a wheel rotation in *her* very direction.

He appeared to be moving in time with a drum being played nearby.

The crowd didn't seem to mind as they passed around him. He was so swift in his movements that her retreat put little distance between them before one of those fire pois went straight through her body.

Then he danced through her as he spun in a circle and then continued through the crowd.

I thought he was trying to attack me!

Nearly hyperventilating, even though she couldn't feel her breaths sawing in and out of her, her trembling form searched the area. But she couldn't focus; instead, her eyes darted from one strange-looking Demon to the next.

They were everywhere, coming from every direction. There were too many as she desperately searched.

A body stepped around her until she was inside of their gigantic frame, their cloak and body blocking out her vision completely. She turned her head up and leaned out of them to see who it was, thinking a Demon had stopped right where she had.

She wanted to get out of their body. She didn't want to be close to one for so long that she was floating inside them.

"Careful," Magnar whispered as his head darted one way and then the other. "Do not get lost."

Delora closed her eyes and took in a large breath, her ghostly form shuddering in relief. Magnar patiently waited for her to calm down, allowing Demons to knock into his shoulders in order to give her a few fleeting seconds of relative calm.

"Thank you," she whispered, wishing she could turn physical and wrap her arms around his slender waist for comfort. "Sorry, I was just surprised."

Delora hadn't expected to see an actual Ghost. And it had been terrifying to learn that a human had attached itself to an anchor, knowing that a Demon would have stolen it from what remained of its corpse – if there had been anything left uneaten.

Magnar huffed and nodded, hesitantly stepping back to make sure she wouldn't duck within the shield of his body.

Delora didn't, although she was tempted to, and Magnar moved further down the markets. He stopped at a shop that would allow her to craft her own jewellery or hanging ornaments if she wished to. Since they were so small and wouldn't take up much space in his carry bag, she silently pointed at a few beads and strings in an attempt to distract herself.

At least none of this should suddenly bring forth a Ghost, or, at least, she sincerely fucking hoped not.

She saw there were carved crystal beads, and she'd grown more interested in them rather than the horn and bone beads that had painted symbols on them. Then a store two shops down caught her attention.

She probably shouldn't have suddenly left Magnar's side, but there were bright strips of colour on a white cloth. There were also ceramic jars out the front.

It was like a fire had lit up inside her.

"This," she pleaded quietly to Magnar, who had come up beside her with interest when she started pointing to *everything.*

"Ah, so Mavka like to paint, do they?" a mousey-appearing Demon chuckled. His hair was a curly red, and he had an upturned nose that sat above two long buckteeth. "What colours would you like? I have any colour you could want."

Magnar turned his head in Delora's direction but said nothing.

Delora's eyes scanned over the array of available options, wishing she could take them all. The ceramic pots looked strong, but too many of them together could find them being shattered.

When she knew she'd made her decision, she flittered inside Magnar in hopes only he would be able to hear her as she listed off the five colours she wanted.

"Blue, yellow, red, black, and white," he said to the shopkeeper.

"Ah," the Demon said, humour bowing his eyes and making them twinkle. "Your kind are smarter than I would have thought."

The Demon used a wooden ladle to scoop the colours he'd asked for into large ceramic jars.

"Why do you say that?"

"Because you've chosen primary colours so that you can mix your own." He placed lids on each of the jars and started tying thick twine around their rims to keep them on. "Beginners start by collecting all the colours, so they don't have to mix them. Do you need brushes as well?"

"Yes," Magnar answered when she nodded.

"What kind?"

"All of them."

By the time they were done, his satchel was filled to the brim with her paints and the required tools.

A smile began to play at her lips, and she intended to turn it towards Magnar while they were walking, but it halted when she saw something white on the corner of a rooftop.

Of all the colours she'd seen within the Demon Village, white was the only one that wasn't as prevalent. And given the fact it was shaped like a massive owl that may have been as tall as she was, she paused to stare at it.

Especially since its eyes were already on her, watching.

Before she got lost again, Delora rushed forward, since Magnar hadn't realised she'd stopped to stare at the owl. Once she was beside him again, she looked up to the rooftop she'd seen it perched on top of, finding it was gone.

She didn't see it again until they were further in the markets, and she spotted it sitting on a rather low-hanging branch, which just so happened to be at least a hundred feet away. It was facing their direction, but its head was moving as though it was searching for something.

It flew off, falling between the gap of two houses to disappear. She knew it had touched the ground, but none of the Demons caused a fuss about it to know where it had truly landed.

This place is so strange. And so much was happening that it was hard to keep focused on one thing at a time.

Delora felt as though her eyes were open to the world.

I want to come back here. She felt safe despite knowing she wouldn't be if she turned physical. *I want to explore this place until I know every corner of it.*

What other odd things would she find? Was there more beauty to behold, or would she discover something gruesome was lurking in the shadows?

The crowd grew thicker when they reached the village centre. An area opened up like a ring with market stalls on the outside that gave plenty of room for a statue in the middle of it – a male character that was standing on a podium with his right hand raised.

The man, almost human looking, had long, pointed ears poking up through lengthy hair that waved around his shoulders, making her think he might be an Elf. However, the large fangs that were produced from his snarl told her he must be a Demon.

Since he wasn't wearing a shirt, she was able to see that someone had *lovingly* carved each one of his muscles on his abdomen, biceps, and chest. They also highlighted strange strips over his arms, shoulders, and sides. Genie pants were tied around his knees to reveal bare feet and strong calves.

His right arm was raised with his claws pointing upwards as though he was trying to raise creatures to stand – or maybe from the dead, like a necromancer.

His stance was meant to convey power, calling all those around to join him.

Delora stood in front of the statue that was even bigger than Magnar.

"That is the Demon King," Magnar said quietly, before waving his hand in the direction of a few Demons that were on their knees around the statue. "They worship him for everything he has done for them, including making this village possible."

Magnar raised his hand to gesture to the sky, as though he was trying to tell her he'd conjured the trees around the village.

"He is not that big, though." He turned, his cloak swishing behind him and his hooves echoing against the cobblestone ground as he walked away. "I am bigger."

Delora had the urge to giggle when it seemed as though Magnar was worried about his own masculinity against something like the Demon King, whose face had been surprisingly handsome. Sharp brows, high cheek bones, firm-looking lips.

She stared at him, wondering how such a nice face could be evil, before she followed after Magnar.

He was leading them out of this area without giving her a chance to look over any of the stores, which was odd considering he'd stopped everywhere else.

Eep! She gasped and took a step back when another Ghost appeared so close in front of her that she almost walked into it. She'd been hoping to not see another one!

It silently cried as it followed a Demon that took a bite out of something from its palm. It was male in form, with short hair and torn clothing. Once the Demon was done eating, the Ghost disappeared.

When she saw it again, the same one, she noticed it was quietly wailing at a bundle of something in the clutches of another Demon. It gripped at its face with horrified eyes, peering at the cloth packaging before the Demon shoved it into its own carry bag. Then it waved its hand through the Ghost as if to get rid of it.

The Ghost followed for a short while, before disappearing and reappearing at a particular store.

Its sobs were quiet, barely able to be heard, but it reacted whenever a Demon took something from that particular store.

A woman's screams caught Delora's attention next, and she found another Ghost at a different stall. There was also a second one there that appeared like an old man leaning on a cane, only ever reaching out a shaking, frail hand when a Demon bought something.

Delora's eyes bounced from stall to stall that surrounded her, finding more and more Ghosts that were either screaming, wailing, or tearing at their own transparent forms with terror. They flitted throughout the crowd with their wide-open eyes fixated on certain Demons who only waved at them like they were nothing but annoying insects.

Everywhere. They're everywhere here.

Delora's transparent form wavered, not seeing a single anchor possible here – that was until she saw something that had her retreating.

On the counter of a stall... lay a human arm.

Thud. A Demon took a cleaver to it and slid it sideways to slip the hand it'd severed to the side. A male Ghost yelled in protest. The butcher then wrapped the arm in the white cloth she could see many shoppers had here, before he gave it to a Demon who then traded for it before walking away.

Oh, shit. Oh no. I think I'm going to be sick!

Delora didn't know where to retreat as she realised she was standing in a market place that was selling meat, *human* meat. They were all around her.

"Delora," Magnar warned, when it was obvious she wasn't following him.

She shook her head, stepping back from him as she tried to find a way out. *I need to leave. I need to get away from here.* Despite being transparent and not usually able to feel anything when like this, her abdomen throbbed, and it felt as though something was clutching at her throat.

And one of the Ghosts even looked *eerily* like Hadith.

Her memories of that terrible night flittered into her thoughts.

The sight of blood pooling off her bed, like what she could see on the counters of stalls that had blood dripping down the edges. The wailing cries were like Cindy's. It was too much. It was too similar, like they were all trying to bring her back to that very night.

Are they going to come for me? Could they?

That owl she'd seen before fluttered into the air, and Delora's eyes grew wider when its shape began to turn into a human woman with dark skin when she landed.

It didn't cross her mind that she looked familiar.

Wearing a cloak of feathers, the woman, who was physical in form, walked up to one of the Ghosts and opened a vial in front of it.

Black sand began to wave around the Ghost, and it stopped wailing. It closed its eyes with relief, and within seconds, it turned even more transparent as the sand wrapped around it completely before it began seeping inside the vial. Then it was gone, and the woman walked over to a different Ghost.

For whatever reason, she was collecting them.

What is she doing to them? Was she saving them or doing terrible things to people that had already suffered?

Magnar stepped through Delora so she could no longer see what was around her. She brought her hands to her face and began to sob, trembling when she realised she sounded like all the other Ghosts.

She feared the woman would come to collect her next.

"Please," she whispered to Magnar, her voice a trembling croak. "Take me out of the crowd. Take me away from here."

She was overwhelmed.

I can't do this. I don't want to be here anymore.

TWENTY-SIX

Magnar, his chest tight with worry, turned his head one way and then the other to look for a suitable place to hide them. Although he'd come to this village twice before, he wasn't completely familiar with its layout.

He headed in a random direction, carelessly shoving Demons out of his way to quicken their pace, and took Delora down a narrow alleyway with more intersecting it. He ducked down the third one he found to put them further away from one of the busiest places of the markets.

"Are you okay?" he asked, his sight already stark white. "We should be safe to talk here."

Instead of answering, Delora came out of his body and turned physical. She planted both her hands against one of the walls and started dry retching, switching between material and immaterial.

Thankfully, she expelled nothing, but she eventually sagged to her knees.

Magnar crouched to hide her with his body before he threw the sides of his cloak around her in the hopes of masking her scent beneath his own.

It was like his heart and stomach were trying to switch places when he saw how pale she'd become. He lifted her into his lap and pressed them both against the wall, understanding that Delora was trying her hardest but wasn't coping.

"Why did you bring me here?" she cried. Her voice cracked an octave as she buried her face against her hands and leaned into his chest. Her shoulders shuddered. "Why didn't you tell me I'd see them?"

"See what?" He was unsure of what was truly happening.

She was fine a few moments ago.

"The Ghosts."

Magnar's grip on her tightened.

"I did not think you would be able to," he admitted. "When we brought Reia here, she had never seemed bothered by them, so I knew she could not see them."

"Y-you should have told me everything about this place."

He pressed the side of his skull against her as best as he could to comfort her.

"You need to control your fear, Delora," Magnar pleaded, wrapping his arms tighter around her.

She will draw the Demons to us.

"I'm trying!" Still visibly trembling, she shook her head. "I can't even maintain my form. I feel really sick."

There were droplets of perspiration against her forehead, much like he'd seen when she'd been unwell.

"It is foolish what you're doing. She'll be smelled like this," someone said outside of their embrace.

Magnar darted his head to the side to see the Witch Owl standing beside them.

He gave a curt growl and a snap of his fangs. "I thought you said it would be fine to bring her here!"

At his tone, her eyes narrowed into a stern glare. "No. I said it would be best to bring her here sooner rather than later."

A Demon paused at the end of the alleyway. Sniffing, its head bobbed at the tangle of fear that must be wafting that way. Magnar lifted his head and snarled in its direction, causing the Witch Owl to look behind her.

With a solemn sigh, she dug beneath her cloak and eventually threw a glass vial against the ground. A plume of pink dust mushroomed around them. It was bitter and peppery, making Magnar give an irritated snort, but the Demon shook its head and immediately walked away.

He turned his head to the Witch Owl with yellow orbs to convey a questioning look.

"It is an aroma cloaking potion, but it won't last long. We

have about five minutes before it disappears."

She crouched next to them on the balls of her bare feet and tentatively opened his cloak so she could peek at Delora. His heart squeezed.

He hadn't realised she'd passed out in his arms.

She fainted! Magnar's panic was growing by the second.

"You will need to wake her if we are to move," she told him, her dark eyes drifting over Delora while her lips drew together. "Poor thing. I remember my first time being pregnant with your kind."

"Where are we going? We are in the middle of the village. I will never be able to get her out of here safely."

"To a hotel." She pointed down the alleyway. "There's a place only a block away you can stay until her sickened state wanes."

With a nod, he turned down to Delora and shook her. She didn't wake. He shook harder, and she stirred, her eyelids just parting.

"Here, eat this." The Witch Owl placed something round and blue near her lips, but it smelt sweet as if it was imbued with some kind of magic. "It will settle your stomach so we can move you."

Delora was slow to part her lips but took it, chewing momentarily before swallowing thickly. After a few seconds, the strain in her muscles eased, and she fluttered out a breath of relief.

Then she clenched her eyes shut. The pressure of her body on top of his lessened, and she turned transparent in his arms.

"What's going on?" Delora asked weakly. She turned her gaze to the Witch Owl to frown in her direction. "It's *you* again. Why do you keep showing up when I feel sick?"

"Come. Let's go, quickly," the Witch Owl ushered before making her way down the alleyway, ducking her head out to make sure it was safe.

They were led down a mostly empty street and taken to a large, two-story building. It was wider than the other houses surrounding it, and one of the two front doors was open to invite people in.

"Delora... hide within Magnar. Don't allow yourself to be seen."

She nodded and sunk inside his form.

Magnar wished he could feel some semblance of her there. He wanted to know she was close, even if he couldn't see her.

He made sure to be slow as they entered the building.

A Demon wearing glasses – that had no glass in them – lifted her head from whatever she'd been reading on the counter she sat behind. She raised a brow in their direction. Her features were harsh, with sharp angles cutting across her cheeks and brow bone, and she squinted her red eyes before a long, thin tail swished behind her.

"Give us a room," the Witch Owl demanded, her bare feet tapping against the timber flooring as she stepped closer. Her head was held high, as though the Demon in front of her was insignificant in her presence. "Consider it payment for all the haunted ones I have removed from your premises in the past."

The Demon gave a masculine laugh despite her feminine form.

"You do that anyway. Don't pretend it's a favour." Then she twisted her lips before pushing her glassless spectacles up her nose. She snubbed it in his direction. "I'll house you, but not the Mavka."

Magnar allowed a growl to emit from the back of his throat.

"Savage," she snorted before folding her arms and pointing her nose in the air. "See? Why would I want to lower the quality of my establishment for one of *his* kind?"

"For this." The Witch Owl placed a vial of red liquid on the table. "Consider it his payment."

The Demon pinched the clear vial with her clawed fingertips and inspected it with interest. She looked at them from the side of her eyelids.

"What is it?"

"The blood of a human."

She gave it a huff before chuckling, placing the vial on the counter to let it purposely roll away.

"I can get human blood from anywhere within the village."

The Witch Owl's dark brows shot up. She thudded the tip of

her finger against the counter to stop the vial from rolling off the edge. Then she picked it up and looked at the vial's bloody contents while it was on its side, slowly sloshing it.

"Hmm." She shrugged nonchalantly. "I guess I'll find another establishment that will trade a stay for Priest blood."

She took a step back to leave.

"Wait!" the Demon shouted, reaching over the counter. "That vial contains the blood of a human that can use magic? Do you know how rare that is to obtain unless you're a lowly border dweller?"

"Yes, I do." Her eyes took on a bored expression as she peered at the Demon. "But you said you didn't want it, so we will go somewhere else. I'll find someone who wants to be granted the use of magic."

Magnar eyed the vial, knowing if he himself were to ingest its contents, it would better increase his ability with his own magic. *It would help me protect Delora better.*

"I'll give you a room. I have a few on the top level available."

The Witch Owl chuckled and shook her head. "Not good enough, not for something like this."

The Demon, baring her fangs with puffed cheeks, gave a snarl. "I'll give you the biggest room I have. A private one."

"Agreed." The Witch Owl waved the vial in front of the Demon like a pendulum, and her eyes followed its swing with excitement. "However, I'll only give you this once you take us there."

Magnar stared at the dark-skinned woman, who radiated magic from her very scent, and saw her in a different light. His interactions with her had only been brief in the past, and he'd always been wary of her.

He was now seeing her for what she was.

She was someone who was able to take advantage of the Veil and its occupants. She knew the village so well that she was able to bring them here and bargain her way into getting what she wanted. She had always been able to traverse the Veil safely, whether that be running through it or flying over it in her owl form.

The Veil was dangerous, but she'd been living here for so

long that she was a part of it. The Demons knew of her, and she was a constant presence to them, but they left her alone. They'd accepted her.

They were even more trusting of her than they were of Mavka.

I must learn to be so cunning. That felt like an impossible task.

The Demon led them down a hallway on the bottom level that was brightly lit by flame sconces. They highlighted dark wooden walls and the yellow carpet runners lining the ground. After they passed the stairs to the upper floor, she waited for them at a particular door.

She glared at Magnar when she opened it for them.

He went in first to make sure it was safe, ducking down a great distance to clear his height and then his imposing antlers.

Just as he was turning around, he watched the Witch Owl give the vial to the Demon and shut the door behind them.

A thud behind him had Magnar spinning around. Delora was on her knees in her physical form, and he didn't manage to reach her in time before her entire body fell to the side. She crumbled against the ground.

The Witch Owl darted forward before Magnar could even get to her. Her touch was gentle as she brushed Delora's black hair from her face.

"She did well making it the entire way," she said as Magnar came to her side. "That berry only lasts a few minutes, but she must have been straining to stay awake and in her Phantom form so she wouldn't be detected."

"What is wrong with her?"

He unbuttoned the hood of his cloak from around his antlers and then slipped it off his shoulders so he could wrap Delora in it.

Using it to hide her scent as well as keep her warm since she was shivering, he lifted her into his arms and took her to the double bed resting against the back wall.

He gently laid her upon it, his sight too focused on her to take in anything else around them. He didn't care about the floors, the walls, the ceiling – not when his bride lay limp and unconscious.

"She's overwhelmed," the Witch Owl answered, pressing the backs of her fingers against Delora's forehead. "When you first came to the village, you attacked multiple people and knocked over carts."

"How do you know that?" Magnar's orbs gave an embarrassed glow of reddish pink. "Did Orpheus tell you?"

He'd grown distressed when Orpheus and Reia had left his side. He'd worried something had happened to them.

"Everyone was talking about the antlered Mavka that went crazy. *You* were overwhelmed when you first came here, and you're not even human. You are used to the Veil and the Demons. Delora isn't. I know it is hard for your kind to sympathise, but imagine what it is like for her. I told you her state would be unstable and that you would need to be patient and understanding."

"I am being understanding," he huffed in annoyance.

He didn't mind that Delora was unwell, other than his worry for her. *I do not want her to come to harm.*

Yet he couldn't shake the blame he pushed onto himself. Perhaps the Witch Owl was mistaking his feelings, thinking he was angry with Delora for something he could see she couldn't help.

"The longer it took you to bring her here, the harder this would have been for her. She's new to being a Phantom and holding that state for a long period of time can be draining. And she's not only pregnant, but carrying one of your kind." There was a look in her eyes, one he couldn't decipher. "Her emotions are heightened, and there is obviously something wrong with her mind, given that she was so afraid of the haunted ones."

"She can see them," he stated. "The Ghosts within the village. Why? Reia could not when we brought her here."

The Witch Owl sighed while stepping back. She didn't lower her feathered hood as she looked up to him from underneath it, but he noticed her usually cool expression was furrowed.

"It's a Phantom ability. Reia was human when you came here with her. She may have seen one or two briefly and may have mistaken seeing them for a trick of her eyes, but humans can only perceive them occasionally. A Phantom can always see and hear them. We see all life and all death. It is both a blessing and a curse to be a Phantom, and there are sides to it that are horrifying."

The Witch Owl hid her shudder so well that Magnar just barely noticed it.

"Then why tell me to bring her here at all?"

Magnar looked around the room, his sight drifting over the table fitted with two wooden chairs and a lace stitch cloth draping over it. There was also a round red carpet on the ground that was intricate, most likely made by human hands.

It was warm and safe, that's all that mattered.

"Because she could not do it when she was further along, and it wouldn't be possible once the child was born." The Witch Owl once more turned her gaze to Delora, but there was a softness in her expression. It was filled with care. "She's doing great, and after she has a little rest, she should be fine. Don't take her through the meat market again – that's where the haunted ones linger the most. I only just arrived when you both did. I was hoping to get rid of them before she saw them."

Realisation struck.

"You knew this would happen," he growled.

"I thought something might happen, yes, and I made sure I was here to help. I wanted to be here sooner, but the Demon King is on the move and hunting one of your kind." Her dark complexion was ashen compared to normal. She muttered quietly, "I can't be everywhere. I can only do so much."

That's when Magnar noticed the darkened circles under her eyes and realised she appeared... tired.

He looked upon Delora curled up in his cloak on top of the blanket. She, too, always looked tired. No matter how much she slept, rested, or ate, those dark circles under her eyes were present. They weren't as deep as when she'd first opened her beautiful brown eyes to him, but they were there, like she was being haunted by something.

If he couldn't heal them with his magic, then he doubted the Witch Owl could either.

"I must go." The Witch Owl made her way to the door, eyeing Delora as if she truly didn't want to leave her side. "Let her rest for a few hours. You should sleep yourself. I doubt you did on the way here."

Magnar grunted. He hadn't wanted to rest while travelling here because he wanted to keep Delora safe in the forest.

"You are always here collecting the Ghosts in the village," Magnar stated, forcing himself to look away from Delora. "I have always wanted to ask you why."

"Because he wants them. He cannot collect the souls within this village because of the magic of the Demon King, and he cannot leave the mist of the Veil without weakening."

Magnar followed her to the door, his sight changing to yellow in curiosity. "Who?"

Pausing in the doorway, she craned her neck to look up to him. "Your father."

TWENTY-SEVEN

Delora lazily opened her eyes to find a lit candlestick on the side table in front of her. It produced just enough light to allow her to see.

"Magnar?" she asked, reaching her hand forward to brush his bony snout.

He was leaning on the bed with just his head plonked there, his arms dangling down his sides while he was seated on the ground.

It was only when his green orbs sparked to life that she realised he'd been asleep.

Delora sat up, having to struggle out of the black cloak she was wrapped in like a mummy. She looked around the room she'd only briefly seen before she passed out.

Her shoulders slumped as her brows drew together to create a knot on her forehead.

"I'm sorry. I didn't mean to faint."

It was alarming to know she'd been asleep in a hotel in the Demon Village in her physical state rather than hiding as something untraceable. The original plan was for them to come for only a few hours and leave as quickly as possible.

At least all her unease and sickness were gone.

"It is fine, Delora," Magnar answered, his voice pleasantly groggy. "I needed to rest as well."

He leaned back to sit straight, and her expression fell as she watched him.

"You don't seem to sleep much these days." Delora couldn't

remember the last time Magnar had crawled into the nest to hold her while he rested. "Why were you on the ground?"

The bed she was lying on had plenty of room for the both of them. Perhaps his antlers might get in the way of the headboard and his legs might dangle if he tried to lie straight, but she was sure he could have joined her on his side.

"After you eat, we should start moving again," he said instead of answering, dragging his satchel bag closer and pulling a few apples from it. "I am not comfortable here."

Delora took the apples and began to eat without argument, eyeing Magnar when he rose to stand.

She knew in some ways they'd grown closer over the course of the past week and a half since she'd learned she was pregnant, but in other ways they were even further apart than before. He was avoiding her, only holding her or touching her when he needed to carry her.

The rest of the time, he created space between them. He was there, always nearby, but not as comforting as before.

Is that why I like it when he carries me around? It was the only time she was allowed to be coated in the warmth of his body and take in the delicious aroma that radiated from him.

Her heart constantly felt like it was sinking. As Delora brushed her fingers over the apple in her hand before taking a bite, she wondered how far it would sink before it drowned.

I don't know how to fix it. It was hard to fix something that had never truly been stable to begin with.

Not wanting to delay them any longer, especially since Magnar looked restless, Delora swallowed the lump of heartache in her throat and quickly ate.

They left moments later, once Delora proved she was able to stay in her intangible form without strain. Before long, they entered the busy streets and markets. They'd come here for a reason and still needed to complete their task, despite it being obvious they both wanted to leave.

There were glow bugs flying in swarms throughout the village, showing her night was still present. Thankfully, he didn't take her anywhere that had any of those horrible Ghosts. Perhaps the Witch Owl had collected the rest of them.

The rest of their time in the village was short and with little issue.

By the time they were finally walking through the spiralling tree trunks to exit the village, Magnar was carting many large and heavy items on his back.

The sun was beginning to shine – its light slipping over the Veil's forest - and would most likely start radiating its heat over the clearing by the time they reached the tree line.

I didn't think the sun touched the ground anywhere in the Veil.

"Are you sure you'll be okay to carry all that?" Delora asked with her gaze trailing over Magnar.

A metal rod was resting over the wide berth of his shoulders, each end holding two cooking cauldrons swinging on chains. He'd somehow managed to convince a shopkeeper to help attach the wooden *bath* to his back with other items such as tools, rope, panes of glass protected by cloth, and her paints packed inside it so that they were secure, and he could carry it all. He'd traded additional crystals for the assistance, and the shopkeeper complied just to have them.

Reia had told her to pick out some fabrics for herself so she could make more dresses for her. They were attached to him as well. The last large item on him were slats of timber – something Orpheus told him to obtain.

Magnar looked weighed down, and he was leaning forward as if to compensate for it.

"Yes," he answered confidently. "I am strong. I will be able to carry all this as well as you." Then Magnar made a sound she'd never heard before. He chuckled. He chuckled warmly as he said, "But perhaps holding you will help to balance me, as I am not used to walking with this much weight on my back."

Even though he seemed more confident on his legs than when she'd first met him, she could only imagine the strain this would be putting on his body. He'd told her he used to walk on all fours, as did most Duskwalkers before they obtained more humanity.

After a short distance inside the forest, she turned physical to be collected into his arms. His speed was swift, but it at least appeared as though cradling her was helping.

I can't wait to go home.

She rolled her eyes with a silent groan. Home was a four-day walk, even by a Duskwalker's long strides, and she already knew how boring that trip would be.

Hopefully we don't run into any issues passing through the border ring of the Veil.

The ingenuity with which Magnar marked their return path was clever considering he couldn't have dropped anything on the ground, like Hansel and Gretel.

Magnar had marked an arrow in the direction they needed to go by gouging his claws into the sides of tree trunks.

Delora turned into her incorporeal form to make sure she couldn't be harmed if they were spotted, although Magnar was using his sharp sense of smell to keep track of if there were any Demons nearby. He also pressed the tip of his snout against his markings to make sure they hadn't been created by a Demon who may have been intelligent enough to understand the markings and redirect them onto a dangerous path.

None were that clever.

Magnar's steps were slower than usual, and she thought that might be because he was tired. She knew when they stopped to allow her to sleep for a few hours during their journey back, he didn't rest himself. He watched over her while she was curled into his lap and arms.

Her sleeps had been restless, her nightmares ever present, and any sounds of the forest being disturbed caused her to be alert.

They were *both* tired.

His usually uncomfortable nest currently sounded like a slice of heaven, and she couldn't wait to fall into it.

When the sun began to set on the fourth day, they were finally deep within the border ring.

The Veil wasn't as thick, and the trees appeared stouter than those that were more towards the centre. She'd learned not to grow alarmed by the thumping or scuffling footsteps she could hear in the distance. She stopped reacting to the sounds of twigs snapping and leaves crunching, even the howls and gargling whines.

The Demons knew Magnar was there, but they were too afraid

to come closer to the big, scary Duskwalker whose scent would have indicated he was alone.

That was until he threw his hand up to block her path. Delora accidentally fluttered through the limb in her ghostly form.

"Stop," he demanded in a low tone. His voice was quiet, as though he worried he'd be heard.

He lowered his stance and turned his body to the side. When he placed both his hands on the ground and took a step back as if to shield her, Delora knew something was wrong.

I can't hear anything.

They weren't being charged at, like how most of the smaller Demons attacked. She couldn't even hear minor movement, like someone stepping on forest debris.

It was eerily quiet.

"You have been following us for quite some time," Magnar said to the forest, his statement echoing through the blueish mist with the undertone of a growl. "I have allowed it because you have not attacked, but do not think I have not noticed you crawling closer."

Magnar darted sideways, using his senses to follow someone moving that Delora couldn't even perceive. Her eyes squinted as she attempted to see through the constantly cold darkness. She found nothing.

"I am not here to attack," a voice echoed.

Magnar darted to his original placement, his stance growing more tense.

His body was puffed enough in aggression that she could see it despite his long black cloak covering him. It was pooled around the back of his feet, and she knew the position he was in was one to either attack or defend.

"But it appears I have been caught," the masculine voice uttered, before she saw red eyes coming into view.

The Demon, black and completely void-like in its skin, walked on all fours over a thick and sturdy tree branch that was reaching in their direction.

Oh, shit. It's a Demon. And not the good kind, from what she figured. Not that she really thought *any* of them were good.

She pushed herself closer to Magnar until she was partially

inside him.

"Then what do you want?" Magnar asked, stepping into the Demon's line of view to block Delora from being seen.

"To know which one you are." The Demon, which looked human all the way from the short black hair on its head and down to its feet, flashed his rows of fangs while twisting his head at them. She hated that, despite the shadows, they seemed to glow white and highlight their sharpness. "I thought you may have been the ram-horned Mavka."

Magnar lifted a hand to brush the side of one of his antlers before lowering his hand to the ground once more.

"No. That is another."

"Then you do not matter." The Demon's tone died with disinterest. "But your time will come shortly. He is first. The ram-horned Mavka. That is who I have been instructed to find."

"Why are you looking for him?"

He inched his way to the side when it was obvious the Demon was trying to peer at her. She'd slipped out from behind Magnar from his agitated movements.

Delora didn't move or speak, nor did she take her eyes off the Demon's naturally red ones when they came into view. He narrowed his gaze on her before Magnar blocked him.

"You speak with this haunted one," he commented, crawling to a different tree branch on his hands and feet. "And she speaks back. They cannot usually do this."

"Perhaps they just refuse to speak to Demons," Magnar retorted. "We Mavka have always been able to see them. We are a part of death, as are they. We are connected."

I wonder if that's actually true. That was a question she'd save for later.

The Demon hummed thoughtfully, his sight turning upwards as though he was thinking before he brought it back upon Magnar with a grin. It held obvious malice.

"Connected? Then do you perhaps know where I can find the ram-horned Mavka?"

"I will not help you hunt my own kind!" Magnar yelled, rising on his feet slightly. "Leave us be."

The Demon tsked loudly to voice his annoyance but stepped

back. Not to retreat in fear, but like he intended to leave, regardless.

"You better return to your cave, Mavka." The snicker he gave was wheezing, but that made it all the more horrid. "But it will be your final resting place."

Cave? Delora thought with a frown. *But we moved from there.*

Then he was gone, leaving just as silently as he'd arrived.

Delora didn't know she'd been suppressing her breaths to hide them until she emptied her ghostly lungs completely on a sigh.

Fuck. That was so creepy.

Magnar turned to her, and despite not being able to touch her, he cupped his hand around the side of her intangible face and held it there.

"Are you okay?" His red, threatening orbs turned to white.

"I should be asking you that," she grumbled. "I'm as safe as anything like this, but he could have attacked you."

He shook his head. "He knows I would have torn him apart within seconds had he tried. He was not strong."

"But smart?" she asked, her eyes lifting to where it had been. "He was so quiet. I didn't think Demons could be so stealthy."

"Small in size, but not in the number of humans he has eaten."

Yeah, well, if it hadn't been for the fangs, the red eyes, and the void-like flesh, it would have looked completely human.

Delora was so used to Demons being unthinking monsters. The fact that some lived communally, and could be sly and cunning, made them even more terrifying than the thoughtless ones that charged. The ability to have thought, to be able to strategize, was a powerful tool to have.

If they get any smarter, they could destroy life as we know it.

If the Demons banded together to build an army, with their ability to craft items and possibly weapons as well, they could overrun the human world and take it over.

Reia had mentioned that the Demon King brought the Demons here from another world via a portal he'd conjured. He was building an army to take back to the place they'd originally come from and destroy it. He was trying to incite a war.

But what happens if that place isn't enough for them? Would they then set their greedy and hungry sights upon Earth as well?

"Come," Magnar commanded as he stepped away, drawing her from her thoughts. "We are almost home."

Delora let out a grateful sigh. *Thank fuck for that.*

TWENTY-EIGHT

While seated on the chair at their little round table, the only pieces of furniture in the house, Delora used the end of a sharp knife to dig into a keyhole. She bit down on one side of her tongue in concentration.

The wooden box she was trying to open was smooth, but the metal was rusted due to its age and lack of use. It jingled every time she held it against her chest as she tried to lever the knife tip inside the hole.

No matter how much she tried, she couldn't get it deep enough to turn it. *Come on! Open you stupid thing!*

Delora sighed and placed it against the table with a disappointed furrow of her brows, the under creases of her eyelids bowing.

When she'd seen this at the Demon Village, she'd asked Magnar to get it for her because she thought she'd be able to open it.

It's pretty old. She thumbed the rusted keyhole just as Magnar came through the new door he'd attached to the front of the house.

While she had been busy with this for the last hour, Magnar had been completing tasks now that he had the supplies required to build specific items for the house.

One of them was the new door, which had been crafted from the wooden slats of timber he'd bought. Seven slats wide and two and a half metres tall, they had been fitted together by crossing slats he'd sawed in half and nailed to the back of the boards to secure them together.

She picked up the box and shook it, hearing it make a sound. She *knew* what it was. *I wish I could open it.*

"What is that?" Magnar asked as he opened the door and then closed it, making sure the hinges he'd nailed to the doorframe worked as well as the door handle.

He's been very clever today. It helped he had a book that instructed him with pictures on what to do. Anything he couldn't figure out, he'd asked Delora what the writing next to the diagram illustrations said.

She didn't mind helping him, and she made sure he wasn't uncomfortable about it. He couldn't read well, maybe a few easy words, but it was obvious he wanted to learn.

"It's a music box." She lifted her eyes away from it to him. "If you have a key, it turns a crank inside and starts playing music for you. I used to have one of these when I was little, but I can't get this one to open because we don't have the key for it."

The Demon who had stolen this from a human didn't know that it required a key to function.

"I could open it," Magnar offered, stepping closer with his massive hand out.

Delora rushed to pick it up and cradle it to her chest.

"No, that's okay. I'm going to ask Reia if they have a skeleton key that might fit. They have pretty generic keyholes."

She thought it likely that Magnar would break it by trying to rip it open with his strength. She may be able to jimmy the lock with some picking tools and rework the box so that she could crank its lever from the inside.

He gave a huff before turning away, but he didn't seem bothered since he crouched down to open some cloth wrappings that were by the door. He carefully lifted a perfectly cut, square pane of glass to check it while tapping one of his claws against the side of his snout in thought.

There were carved sticks next to it that were all the same diameter and perfectly cylindrical. Multiple pieces were long, while others were shorter – perhaps the same length as the glass panes – and they all had a slit down the middle of them on both sides for the glass to slot into.

"Would you like some help?" Delora offered as she stood and made her way closer.

"You want to help?" His tone was filled with surprise, and he lifted his snout up and to the side to look at her with an inquisitive tilt.

"Sure," she muttered. "I don't have anything else I want to do."

Not that she really had much she could do other than perhaps water the garden. Now that she was no longer spending her time wanting to depressively sleep, Delora was restless.

She'd spent the last five years cooking, cleaning, and organising a house for a selfish man. She'd gotten Magnar to buy her a broom, but she couldn't actually do any sweeping until he was finished with all his tasks today.

Just when she thought she may have offended him, possibly made him feel incapable, Magnar's orbs morphed into bright yellow.

Before long, Delora was inside the house where she knew the kitchen was going to be, holding a windowpane against the bottom right corner of the window frame he'd made. Magnar was outside on the other side, and their height was almost matched since she was on a raised level.

He pulled the pane she was holding out so that he could press wetted clay into the frame's slot to secure it. Then he pushed it back in.

While she was holding it, he grabbed a shorter, cylindrical piece of timber and nailed it in carefully with a hammer to make sure the glass wouldn't fall when she let go.

They repeated the process for the next window, and Delora wondered if perhaps Magnar was peeking at her just as bashfully as she was at him. They were face-to-face, only a few inches apart, and she couldn't help finding those vortexes floating in front of his bony eye sockets... mesmerising.

Instead of watching what she was doing, her gaze drifted over the long length of his fox snout, the sharp fangs of his muzzle, his empty nose hole. Then she trailed it up the indents of his bony skull to peruse his large antlers that appeared too heavy, yet he held his head up with strength.

He's really stunning in his own way. Her fingers itched with the nagging need to reach through the window and stroke that cool bone.

When they were done with the bottom four glass panes, and they started on the middle row, Magnar leaned his head slightly to the side.

Oops, she'd been caught staring at him.

Delora's cheeks heated terribly. She pushed her gaze to his fingers working clay into the slit of the long bit of timber that ran across the bottom half of the middle section.

He was being mindful of his claws that were caked in clay, and her face heated further when she remembered she'd had those fingers inside her. They were long... and thick, and flexible.

Her eyes darted to his face once more, wondering when she'd started liking the bony qualities of his skull and the monstrous parts of his body. None of it bothered her, but was rather... titillating instead.

Her heart felt as though it was shyly fluttering in her chest, replaced by a butterfly taking flight.

Especially since they were so close and the window they were building together wasn't finished yet, allowing her to greedily take in the heady aroma of his decadent scent. She almost wanted to lean in and sniff him closer, kiss him, perhaps even *lick* him.

Her tongue tingled before she licked at the seam of her lips. Delora bit the bottom one.

Her eyes darted to what she was supposed to be doing, holding the glass for him, as she cleared her throat that felt thick. She squeezed her thighs together to ease the throbbing in her clit, feeling heat and liquid pooling.

Are my emotions being heightened because I'm pregnant? That still meant they started from somewhere.

She didn't know what it was, but that was what she told herself when she realised she was being turned on just by staring at him.

The air was warmer than usual, and the sun behind his back haloed him in a glittering light in certain places, making him look inviting. Dust particles danced around him, sparkling – or perhaps that was just her perception putting him in a mystical scene.

Regardless, Delora couldn't help being drawn to him, wishing she could be closer to him. So close to him, in fact, that he was inside – *Oh, God! What is wrong with me today?!*

"Thank you for helping me with this." His voice held its usual deep baritone, and Delora shuddered when that bass resonated through her body. Her pussy quivered in reaction. "I tried earlier by myself, but it is much easier with two people."

Delora just nodded, not trusting her voice.

I hope he can't smell my scent. He didn't seem to be reacting to it. Perhaps the clay he'd accidentally brushed over his nose hole was hindering his ability to smell her. *Please don't be able to smell it. Or do...*

Fuck!

A sigh of relief fluttered out of her when they were done, the completed window a barrier between them and her ability to sense him.

Delora paled when she looked at the other empty windows in the house. There were four more to do.

The only reason the others were bearable was because her arms were beginning to strain holding them in the air, and the ache was enough distraction from her budded nipples scraping against the inside of her dress.

By the time they were done, the sun was way past midday, already starting its creep over the gloomy forest.

Now that she was moving, she didn't feel the urge to rest.

So, when Magnar worked on relocating the nest she'd originally been sleeping in, his face covered in clay since he'd kept brushing it with his dirty hands, Delora painted the front door.

She'd asked if she could paint it a dark green, and he said he didn't mind what colour it was. She mixed clay into the blue and yellow paint she had in a large wooden bowl to make it thicker and more weatherproof. Then she got to work coating both the inside and the outside of it.

The door was slightly ajar, allowing her to watch Magnar disassemble the nest. As he pulled off the large quantity of furs that lay over it, it revealed the barbaric layer of branches beneath it that made up the walls.

Orpheus had been building the interior of the house with Magnar's vision in mind while they were away.

The bedroom that would belong to Magnar, and she figured herself – since there would be nowhere else for her to sleep – had been made. It took up one quarter of the house by itself, and the walls of it had been erected, with a temporary log-style door fitted to one of them by rope hinges.

Neither one of them had expected Orpheus to move so quickly, but she was thankful, as Magnar had seemed thrilled to see the house had changed so drastically. It was obvious he wanted to finish it so that he could focus on other things – like making it comfortable for her.

None of the logs had their bark like the exterior of the house did, but they were perfectly carved to be the same diameter, showing that Orpheus had worked with care. He'd also started working on the other two rooms, which were much smaller. They were to be her own personal space and a washroom, the empty doorways facing each other.

The logs only came to about the height of her knee, but he'd mapped both rooms to know their complete dimensions. After they were finished, there wouldn't be much left to do structurally.

The sun was almost gone when Delora was doing the final brush strokes of paint against the last window frame she'd been working on. She had decided she'd wanted them green as well.

Food was her next priority.

Magnar had collected all his wood shavings to place them into the firepit outside since he still hadn't made the area for the cooking hearth yet. He also collected any branches he wasn't using, showing her that the day she'd made it, he'd been watching her the entire time to know what to do.

He'd caught a fish for her when he'd gone to the stream to refill her water bucket, and she fried it while making a vegetable and herb soup to go with it.

Once she was done, she placed her nearly empty bowl on the porch step she was sitting on and stared out at the dense forest that was still present within the protection ward.

The mist was thick and blue, as it always was. The area was brightened by the fire that washed heat over her body, casting light underneath the leaves. Deeper within the forest was dark and frightful, but she didn't feel anything other than peace.

She placed her hand on her stomach while she thought deeply.

Delora's stomach had started to swell, and fast. It had been two weeks since she'd conceived, and her belly was noticeably rounder and much firmer to the touch.

She noticed the difference today, as bending hadn't been as easy as it was before. Since they'd only returned from the Demon Village yesterday, and she'd been unwell before that, she hadn't begun to realise these changes.

Magnar had grown a little panicked every time she made any noise of discomfort. It was hard not to find him adorable in those moments.

The Duskwalker that grew inside her was developing. It was unnatural, and there was always the fear of the unknown.

Delora was aware that she would be the first human who had conceived a child with a Duskwalker, since the Witch Owl had mated with something else entirely. The truth was, no one really knew what she was going to give birth to, if it would survive, and what challenges would come with it.

As long as it's okay, I don't care what happens to me.

She'd come back to Magnar if she were to die anyway.

"It's always so quiet here," Delora muttered when Magnar came to sit next to her.

"There are no animals in the Veil," he stated, his head moving across the forest in front of them before he lifted it to look up at the sky. "The Demons eat them."

"But I don't hear many insects either."

"Eaten." He gave a huff. "They eat everything that moves. No matter how large or how small. Nothing is safe from them."

"They say the same thing about Duskwalkers," she pointedly said.

Magnar gave a weak growl that was short and curt. "We *Duskwalkers,* as you humans call us, do not eat bugs. They taste gross."

When he licked at the inside of his mouth, Delora's eyes

bowed with humour. *Of course you've tried.*

Her perspective on Demons had changed since going to the village. *I guess some were... nice.* Some had even treated Magnar respectfully.

It was the mindless ones she needed to be worried about.

But Delora knew all too well that if humans weren't governed by laws, many would be cruel to each other. They would steal from one another, murder, rape, kidnap. Humans couldn't truly stand on a pedestal of morality since their good-naturedness came from the consequences of being punished.

Demons weren't the only thing to be wary of when travelling outside of towns. Caravans were known to be attacked by bandits that lived on the mountain sides. They were people who felt free even though they shared their forests with monsters, but they were willing to take the risk if it could increase their prosperity by gaining riches.

Many of them would steal until they gained enough to pay their way to live comfortably and rich within a town. They often cut off supplies just so they could barter there themselves instead.

Delora had faced such a hardship before when she was much younger.

"Autumn has always been my favourite season," Magnar quietly said, bringing his hands between his knees so he could interlock his clawed fingers together. "But I like it much more now that we are here."

Delora turned to him while tucking a few strands of hair behind her ear. "How come?"

"The fallen leaves used to always come into my cave, and I would have to clean it every day. They cannot come inside the house because of the door, and I like watching the leaves be scattered across the ground." His snout followed the path of a leaf fluttering before it got swept up by a small gust of wind. Others joined it in a flurry before they settled. "Spring smells much nicer, but autumn has its own scent. However, it is the colours I like seeing. They are red, but they are not angry or hunger filled. It is the only season that stops the Veil from looking ugly."

"What about winter?" Delora asked, surprised they were

having this kind of conversation.

Magnar shook his head. "Snow melts easily within the Veil. It is warmer here than on the surface. It is also cooler in the summer as the canyon and trees provide shade from the heat. Autumn is the only season that makes changes."

"I guess I like spring for that same reason," Delora stated. "The world is thrown into a chaos of colours because of all the flowers that sprout. Sometimes the field in front of the town I came from would be covered in wildflowers, and I would be able to see it from higher up on the hill. Some would be blue, others pink or yellow."

His orbs changed to yellow, highlighting his joy at the idea. "I would like to see these flowers with you."

The butterfly that replaced her heart earlier returned, but there was now a kaleidoscope of them swirling in her chest. It brought more of its brethren, as though they wanted to make her feel lighter.

Trust was the biggest thing they had lacking between them. Delora needed to learn how to trust him, but she didn't know how to truly start.

Despite the flutters in her chest, she wrung her hands nervously on her lap. *I... I need to be more open.*

"I was born in Silvermine Town," Delora started, swallowing thickly to remove the clog of emotion that was trying to rise. "My, uh, mother died giving birth to me. We had nurses and doctors, but it's not always possible to save someone since it's hard to get medical tools and supplies."

"You will not have to worry about that," Magnar said, reaching his hand over so he could pat the top of her hair like he thought she needed comfort. "I will heal you if something goes wrong, and if something does, you will return to me like you do when we are apart for too long."

The warmth of his palm on top of her head was soothing, and she appreciated the touch.

"Silvermine is a mining town that was close to the Mountains of Silverton. I'm not sure if you know where that is, but it's pretty far from the Veil. You'd think that would make us safer, but the caves there allow Demons to live in the darkness and they make nests there. But we were safe since we had walls to protect us." Her shoulders fell as she looked up to the sky, wishing the mist made it easier to see the stars that she could barely make out. "My father was such a good man. He loved me, and never blamed me for killing my mother. He tried to give me everything he could so I could be happy."

Delora wrapped her arms around her torso to hug herself, wishing that thinking of her parents didn't make her eyes instantly sting. She blinked rapidly to clear them of liquid, skilfully hiding her sniffle.

"But he was a miner, and that comes with risks. In order to get to the coal shaft, a large team of workers would leave with soldiers so that they could go deep into the mountains. The entrance was sealed with doors, but Demons had managed to get into the shaft a different way. Maybe they even dug their way in over time. Who knows? But my father was killed."

I didn't even get to say goodbye...

"Why would your people do this if it was such a risk?"

"Because coal is so valuable. It was all my town had to trade with as coal can be used to cook and warm our houses. Blacksmiths use it to smelt their metal ore. We were next to one of the biggest known coal veins, and we'd been using it for hundreds of years, trading with it for supplies." Then Delora snorted a humourless laugh. "But, of course, just because men died, didn't mean we stopped mining. They just brought soldiers to clear them out, covered the hole the Demons had gotten through, and went back to work. It wasn't the first time people died, and most mining towns have some of the highest death rates. Not just from Demons, but also from breathing in the coal dust."

There. Delora had told Magnar of where she'd grown up, of her parents.

She knew it wasn't enough.

Her eyes drifted downwards so she could look at the campfire in front of them, watching as the flames flickered and occasionally made a crackling sound.

Delora rubbed her arms self-consciously. *Why is this so damn hard?* It felt like she was baring herself naked, despite the fact that she hadn't said anything that truly mattered yet.

"I... didn't want to stay there after he died. I didn't want to marry a miner because I knew they would die before me. I'd have been afraid for them every time they left. But that's what the people did in our village. Men and woman mined, and everyone else tended to the farms or crafted essential items. We were workers. We traded for the things we could produce. My mother was one of the rare crafters who carved clay or made paintings, and her items were worth much because people liked having something pretty to look at. Something to forget that the world is actually a dark place. A lot of people were upset that she was gone, and I couldn't handle the way people pitied me that my parents had left me alone."

Magnar's orbs turned blue to reflect the emotions she already felt. "This... is a very sad story, Delora."

Delora let out a shaky breath. She'd already started trembling, knowing what was to come next.

"The town chief made an arrangement to trade people with a military village for more soldiers after many died trying to clear out the mine. I volunteered to leave, and that's where I met a man named Hadith."

"What were your parents' names?"

Delora frowned, not expecting him to care so deeply about their names. "Noah and Ava."

"Noah and Ava Theralia?"

Delora's eyelids flickered. *I didn't think he'd remember my last name.* Her features softened.

"Yes. Those were their full names." The fire sparked, igniting ash to float into the air, and she let out another shaky breath. "Hadith chose me because I was young, only twenty, and I guess because I was pretty. I was much smaller then, but that's what my value to him was. He was a high-ranking soldier, and he was really nice in the beginning. I thought I could be happy even though changing towns was really daunting for me. It was so hard to be accepted by everyone, and not everyone did. I was an outsider, and a lot of women thought I had stolen one of their good men from them. The first two years were fine, but things started to change. He started to come home later when I couldn't give him the child he wanted. I was alone a lot after that."

Magnar's head cocked, making it tilt. "Who was this human to you?"

"Huh?" Delora's face turned to him with her brows furrowed deeply. "Oh. I guess I left out that he was my husband." Then her brows knotted together even further. "Wait. I'm guessing you don't know what that means. When two people get married–"

"I know what a husband is," Magnar bit out, his orbs slowly fading into red. "It means you bonded yourself to another human. Made a *family*."

"Well, yeah. It was an arranged marriage between our towns. That's how most towns trade people. It helps to bring in new people so that we don't begin to create inbred families, especially by accident, since many humans can be born over hundreds of years. It can be hard to keep a track of."

Delora didn't seem to understand why Magnar's orbs had changed. She wasn't even up to the part that she found distressing and had feared telling him about. She didn't want to tell him she was a murderer, that she'd done something so callous and cruel, simply because she'd been jealous.

I have to learn to trust him. What was the worst that could happen? He couldn't leave her, even if he wanted to.

Would he... perhaps... seek a new human? Shivers rose on her skin as a chill crept through her. *Is it possible to trade my soul for another?*

Delora considered stopping her story. She'd revealed enough for today, but she also wanted to get this off her shoulders. This terrible weight had been a burden to bear and... she wanted Magnar to understand her better.

"I-I'm sorry I cried that night," she muttered quietly.

His orbs morphed into a more reddish pink instantly. He tensed beside her, fidgeting almost as though he wanted to leave.

"I wasn't crying because you hurt me, but because someone else did, and you made me realise just how much."

Even now, tears dotted her lashes, and she tried her hardest to stem them. Her pulse quickened in her veins, racing as anxiety clawed at her throat – especially when she noticed the feathers sticking out from Magnar began to puff, like they often did with aggression.

The words started pouring out of her faster and faster.

"I was upset because you were treating me the way I always wanted Hadith to treat me. He was my husband. He married me. He was supposed to take care of me, and yet he was mean to me. I was his wife–"

"You are *mine*," Magnar growled beside her.

His orbs turned red, even brighter than before.

"I know, but before I met you–"

"*You are **mine!***" he snarled, his voice booming and distorted with rage. He twisted his body, moving so quickly that a gasp was rent out of her when he pushed her back against the porch and pinned her arms against the timber above her head. "*You are bonded to **me**. You gave **me** your soul. It is mine. I own it. Hold it. Cherish it.*"

Her heart rate accelerated, her torso heaving up and down with quickened breaths from surprise. She stared up at Magnar, who had pinned her down with his legs on either side of hers. Then he leaned over her body with a rumbling coming from his chest, like a vibration of hostility.

The reddened vortexes of his eyes seemed to swirl faster, drawing her in with the backdrop of the night sky and the crescent moon haloed by the murky mist. She was too stunned to move, to squirm, even though this arched her back and put pressure on her swollen stomach.

"Magnar," she rasped.

He has the wrong idea.

She wasn't trying to tell him this to hurt him, to say that she wasn't his.

He brought her hands together and clasped both her wrists easily in one of his large hands so he could bring the other down and around her throat. Cradling it so completely that she could feel his claws around the back of her head, he lifted it with the webbing of his thumb and forefinger cupping her jaw.

He didn't squeeze her, didn't try to choke her, but the positioning of his hand felt dangerous and possessive.

"*Do you want to go back to him?*" His tone was like a warning, like she should be wary of how she answered. He almost seemed to get bigger, and Delora felt undeniably small beneath him. *"Is that why you are sad? Why you will not give yourself to me?"*

"I-I found him with another woman," she quickly uttered. She needed to calm him, to ease him. Delora realised she needed to get her story out now, and quick. "Even after I did everything for him. I cooked and cleaned and tried to make sure he was satisfied, but he would throw things at me and call me vulgar names. I can't even count the number of times I cut my fingers picking up glass because of him."

*"Then I won't let you go back to him. You are **not allowed** to leave me, **cannot** leave me. Your soul belongs to **me**."*

"H-he's dead, Magnar!"

*"**Good**."* Bringing his snout down against the side of her cheek and brushing it closer to her ear, in a quiet yet menacing tone, he uttered, *"Because I would have hunted for him until I tore him apart with my claws."*

She gasped at his declaration, her eyes fluttering open when his warm breath huffed over her ear and made her hairline behind it stand on end.

*"And if you still seek him, I will ask the spirit of the void to permit me into the afterlife so I can **snuff out** his soul so he cannot find you. So you cannot be together. So that you cannot even think of trying to find a way to leave me. So that he cannot come back and be alive in the same plane of existence as you."*

Delora always thought that when she told Magnar her story she would be full of tears. That she'd be choking her words out, fumbling with how to explain this to him.

But Delora didn't feel afraid.

Her body was tingling from the possessive way he was holding her down, shivering in near delight at his aggression. Her breaths were heated, and her nipples had pearled into hard points, scraping against the material of her dress whenever her chest rose and fell.

Delora was becoming *aroused* by this.

She wanted him to stretch her body further by dragging her hands up while her legs lay down the stairs. She wanted him to grab her throat tighter. She *needed* him to demand that she was his, that he owned her, that he wouldn't let her go.

Unwilling to look away from him, his bony, skulled face enchanting her, she panted.

Her heart clenched when he drew his hand away from her throat. She almost fretted. She wanted it to stay there, to clasp her like he'd rather kill her than let her leave him.

"Did you kiss him?" He ran a claw over her bottom lip, teasing it open slightly.

Delora knew the smart thing to say was no.

Instead, she declared, "Yes."

His growl momentarily grew louder, and goosebumps washed over her.

"I cannot kiss you." Magnar drew his tongue across her lips to lick them, forcing them apart even more.

But wasn't that a kiss in its own way?

She didn't even know his hand had gone down her body until the skirt of her dress was lifted. Sharp claws ran up her calf, tickling them.

"Did you let him hold you?" Delora stifled the moan that tried to strangle its way out of her throat when he snaked his hand underneath her dress and slipped those claws over the inner crease of her thighs. *"Touch your body?"* That exploring hand cupped her between her thighs, covering her cunt so completely that not a part of it felt any of the air he allowed underneath her skirt. *"To be inside here?"*

Delora bit her lip, considering telling him a lie just to make him feel better.

"Of course. He was my husband," she bravely answered.

Magnar snarled immediately at the word *husband.* The continuous rumble he was producing became louder because she said she'd let Hadith touch her. Delora's stomach clenched, relishing this, and her insides fluttered all the way to her core. Against his palm, he would have felt her grow slicker within an instant.

His orbs flashed purple in reaction to her.

The way he parted his fangs and licked at his bony snout had Delora throbbing in all the delicate places on her body. He'd given her the reaction she desired, and he even stretched her body up slightly like she'd wanted as he bent over her more, bringing his face closer.

"Mine," he stated. *"Your scent, your voice, your face and body. He cannot have them."*

Delora licked her lips, but then let out a little cry when he brought his hand up and his calloused fingers brushed over her aching, throbbing clit. He paused. He'd never touched her there properly before, but he realised she'd liked his touch since he pressed against it with a downward rub.

Delora's back tried to arch, but she couldn't in the position she was in. Instead, she bucked into his fingers, her thighs tightening around his hand to keep him there.

"They-they threw me into the Veil because I murdered him and the woman he cheated on me with." She couldn't believe how hoarse her voice had gotten. "I-I hated him by the end, hated how he made me feel. I don't want to go back to him, Magnar. *I* killed him."

She didn't know what she was expecting when he halted. He tensed above her, and his hand clasped her wrists tighter.

He leaned even closer until his snout was right against her ear. She was immersed in his scent when the feathers of his neck brushed over her nose and tickled it.

Why does he have to smell so damn good? Her eyelids flickered in contentment when she nuzzled into them.

"Good girl," he rasped, making her eyes roll into the back of her head. *"You brought yourself to me."*

His breath rolled over the sensitive shell of her ear.

"N-no, not there," she whispered.

She tried to get away when he dabbed his tongue over her ear. The sound of his saliva squelching in her ear sounded naughty, and it spread, making his breaths feel even more powerful. She couldn't handle how turned on she was becoming.

"You have that nice smell. The one that says you are aroused." He gave her a deep growl. *"Is that because of me or because we are speaking about him?"*

She would have thought it was obvious since she'd said she hated Hadith, but she thought he may also just want to hear her say it was because of him.

"You," she whispered. Her reward was him circling her clit with a hard press, and she let out a puff of breath. "L-lower, Magnar. Please."

She wanted his fingers inside her. She wanted him to touch her, to make her come. He could properly learn about her clit later, when her mind was a little more sound, when she wasn't aching and desperate.

She'd told him why she was brought to the Veil. Why she was the way she was. She'd been dreading this conversation, but now her heart felt so light, and he was driving her crazy.

If I had known things would end up like this, I would have told him sooner. Because Delora had been craving this. Being close to him. She didn't know what it was about Magnar, but she was inexplicably drawn to him.

When he didn't move lower, just petted her clit like he was fascinated because it made her breath hitch, Delora tried to lift her hips so she could force his fingers there herself.

"Only I can touch you."

His orbs faded from their angry red to purple, the colour erotic and sinful. His body shook like it was ruffled when he finally moved his fingertips down. His claws sheathed when he pressed against the slit of her opening, and Delora tried to spread her legs for him to help his entrance and give him space between her thick thighs.

"You are very wet for me, my little raven."

Wet? Delora knew she was dripping! She could feel the little pool at her entrance was overfilling.

A gasp was torn from her when he slipped two of his fingers in, and her eyes immediately dazed as she shivered with contentment. She didn't know what compelled her to lift her head and kiss his lipless face, but she harshly pressed her lips against the very tip of his snout and stayed there.

He released her hands to cup the back of her head, keeping her to him, and she clumsily moved her lips over the same spot. He drew his fingers back only to slam them back in, rubbing directly over her most sensitive spot. Delora let out a little cry against his fangs, trying to tilt her head back. He refused to allow her to.

Instead, when her lips parted, Magnar licked over them. Every time his fingers thrust in, she arched and felt like nothing but jelly in his hold.

She didn't stop him when he licked over the corner of her lips, or her jaw, or down the pumping jugular on her neck. Not when she was too busy trying to find something to cling to until her arms tangled in his antlers. She gripped them, needing to as the wet squelch of his fingers grew more rapid in her drenched pussy.

"Yes," she moaned, feeling her body bouncing on its own, trying to match his rhythm so she could feel his fingers come in harder, faster, deeper inside. "*Oh,* fuck. Yes."

She was so close, about to tumble into bliss, squirming into his hand. His fingers felt like she was being prodded by something heavenly, touched in a way that had her burning for more and more and more until she was irreparably scalded in the passionate flames of it.

Just as her toes were curling, the winding coil of her orgasm reaching its tightest point before it unsprung, Magnar ripped his fingers from her. Leaving her unbearably empty, hollow, she clenched around nothing.

Delora let out a cry of distress.

"Wait. No," she pleaded. "Don't stop."

She'd been right there, about to come around his fingers, and now her inner walls were throbbing and pounding with desperation. Her nipples itched for attention, and the ache of them grew more noticeable now that she didn't have him spiralling her headlong into oblivion.

"It aches," Magnar groaned. The claws of the hand he'd been fingering her with slammed into the timber of the porch around her before they *gouged* it. "Inside." The claws of his other hand tightened around her head, scraping into her scalp right near the hairline of her face. "I need inside you."

He laid her head down so that he could lean back and tear at the front of his trousers. His cock shot forward to be a hard and jutting rod between his protruding hipbones, while those tentacles writhed like they were in agony.

Her eyes grew wide as she panted at it, the inner walls of her pussy clenching. She knew *that* would feel so much better, would reach places she couldn't imagine, would fill her with its insane thickness so completely she'd feel like she was going to be torn in two in the best way possible.

His hands slammed around her, thudding loudly in her ears, and the bang of them sent a jolt through her – both in delicious thrill, but also in worry.

Her hands flittered to her stomach protectively, and she tried to scuttle out from underneath him.

Magnar growled and grabbed her thigh. His claws bit into her skin when he dragged her back to him with a snarl, her hair brushing over the porch. Then the lips of her folds slapped against the bottom of his cock, slipping along the deep groove underneath him as he spread his lubricant all over her and rubbed her clit in the most mind-numbing way.

She almost lifted into it so that press could be harder – almost.

Delora pushed at his chest. "Wait."

"Stay," he demanded, dragging her back to him when she tried to get away once more.

"Magnar, please."

And the fear she felt suddenly rushed over her like a terrible ice bath being poured over her heated body.

"Why does he get to touch you, and I cannot?"

His orbs flashed a vicious colour of red before they changed to such a dark green they looked menacing. They were usually a calm, inviting emerald colour, and all she could think was that they looked *jealous*.

Magnar thrust against her, gliding that slimy cock over her folds again. It managed to graze her entrance and make that pool there grow with their mingling fluids.

He was angry, he was confused. She could tell he desperately needed to be inside her, to fill her, to shelter his cock inside her heated channel.

Delora's eyelids bowed in sorrow. *Because I don't trust you.*

"I-I don't want you to hurt the baby." She placed her hands on her stomach before she crossed her arms over it protectively. "If you claw my stomach, you could kill it."

If he rent her flesh again, she could bleed out enough that she lost it. If he hurt her stomach, he could damage her womb. If he took her too hard, lost in his inexperienced pleasure, he could damage it from the inside. He was bigger than her, stronger than her, and so many facets of him were dangerous.

Delora longed to do this with him, but she couldn't.

His orbs flashed white, showing her he understood.

"Go inside," he said quietly, releasing her thigh and placing his hands beside her gently.

"Magnar, I'm–"

"*Go inside!*" he roared, his eyes morphing to purple before he shuddered wildly above her. "Go away before I shove my cock inside you." Shaking, he lowered himself as he spread his fangs over the side of her face like he was trying to breathe her in and nuzzle her at the same time. "I need to. I need to feel your pussy around me, to wet me, to hold me. I need to feel your body squeeze mine." He let out a whine, and the very sound of it made her heart squeeze. "You smell *so good*, Delora."

His tongue came out to dip shyly at her cheek, and every second she remained underneath him he inched closer.

The moment his large and hot palm wrapped around her thigh again, Delora scrambled from underneath him before he lost whatever semblance of control he was holding onto and snapped.

He panted at the ground before his face lifted to follow her with his gaze. It was so purple and lust-filled, but he didn't move from his position as though she was still underneath him.

Frozen, he looked moments away from pouncing her.

"Are you going to leave?" she asked as her arse slipped across the ground.

I don't want him to leave again.

"No."

Her heart settled and Delora rushed to her feet to go to the front door, uncaring if she ruined the paint. She didn't mean to slam the door, but it shut with a loud bang before she pushed her back against the wall right next to it.

Oh, Gods, Delora thought, her legs coming out from underneath her. She slid down the wall. *I'm so horny right now.*

Her hand slipped underneath her dress, and she touched the lips of her pussy. It was so wet from both of them, and knowing his lubricant was on her made her skin flush further with heat.

Covering her mouth so he wouldn't be forced to hear her, Delora shoved two fingers inside herself before realising straight away that she needed a third and her pinkie as well.

Her body was changed, different, and his two fingers had been thick and long. Her little human hands were nothing in comparison, but she tried with all her might as she desperately, hopelessly, urgently, started thrusting them.

Delora dug her fingertips against her face as she attempted to stifle her moan. It wasn't enough, she needed more, she needed deeper.

She needed Magnar's help, but she pounded herself.

I want him to fuck me so bad. Her head fell forward, and her eyes bowed when she realised what she was doing, masturbating over a Duskwalker and having to use her whole hand like a fucking paddle. She didn't stop.

I need his big cock inside me. Her body broke out in goosebumps as she slowly brought herself closer to the edge. *Thrusting inside me. Ravishing my pussy.*

The heels of her feet kicked against the ground when her legs squirmed. She pictured his purple cock with a blackened tip thrusting inside her while his fur brushed against her sensitive inner thighs.

I want him to come inside me. All that hot, overflowing liquid had been phenomenal. She'd never forgotten what it'd felt like as it filled her so completely that it spilled out of her, not once but twice.

His tentacles squeezing me so tight that it felt like it was bruising my skin. Clutching her closer and meshing their hips together like he was trying to get even deeper than was possible.

Fuck. I need it all so badly.

I... please... Her toes curled until her feet ached, a cramp terrorising the muscles of her right calf. *Oh, God. OhGodOhGodOhhh!*

The hand covering her mouth pressed even harder, squishing her lips against her teeth when she started screaming. Delora came around her own fingers. Clamping, spasming, quivering, as she poured her own juices right into her palm in a wet mess.

She kept thrusting, drawing it out.

White dots flittered in her vision as sparks of darkness shot across it. She didn't know if that was from the release, or because she was too busy releasing a pathetic, needy cry to breathe.

She eventually slowed. Her breaths were so panted that they strained out of her, but her heart was rowdy and fast.

Everything went lax when she finished. She fell languid against the wall with her legs spread, her knees bent, barely able to see past her stomach with the way she was slumped.

I don't care what he is. I'm so fucking horny for that big guy.

TWENTY-NINE

Magnar placed a large stone down to replace the tree stump he'd torn from the ground. At some point, he'd work on bringing more dirt to the area surrounding their home so he could fill it properly.

Now that the hole was sufficiently filled, he picked up his axe from the ground and began chopping into the side of a tree. He was clearing more of the yard so he could continue building the rooms.

He didn't need to take a break, but he did simply to stare in the direction of the house.

Yellow faded into his vision as he took in the finished porch roof.

Orpheus had joined him early this day, and together they had worked a two-man saw to cut the logs for it in half by their length. Considering their strength was superior to that of a human's and they started this task the day before, they'd managed to finish building late midday.

Orpheus was currently making the railing.

Magnar had considered cutting down the large tree that was right next to the porch since its leaves scraped against the roof, but he decided he wanted to keep it there. It was becoming barren due to autumn, and he liked the way it dusted colourful leaves over the roof and the grass below it.

Since the forest floor of the Veil was often shaded, the grass was patchy, but the more trees he removed, the more grass sprouted. Orpheus informed him he'd eventually require a scythe to maintain it as it often grew to be so tall that it could hide their humans in its stalks.

The idea of trying to play a game of finding her in it sounds enjoyable, though.

His gaze drifted to the side of the house, knowing that Reia and Delora were behind it in the garden doing something... strange.

They'd asked both Orpheus and Magnar to remove the curve of the logs there yesterday so it was flatter, and they had added clay themselves between the grooves where the logs pressed together. It wasn't perfect, still quite bumpy in texture, but they'd seemed pleased.

The clay had dried overnight, and they'd been back there for most of the morning.

They like each other. Reia and Delora were forming a bond.

Magnar was relieved because he thought it would bring them both comfort, but it also annoyed him because it meant Delora's attention wasn't on him.

The darker green of jealousy grew in his orbs.

She used to watch me work from the steps.

He'd liked showing off his strength and skills while he worked. Especially when he'd lift an entire heavy and long tree by himself – after he removed its branches – to place it with the others neatly.

Magnar resumed his task, and Orpheus eventually came over while he was removing the cut tree's branches. He'd finished the railing for the porch, and Magnar was pleased to see the outside of the house was complete.

"What do you think you will make first?" Orpheus asked, nodding the tip of his snout in the direction of the tree stumps he had in a pile.

Magnar brought a hand up to tap one of his claws against his snout.

"Perhaps the counters for the kitchen?" he answered, trying to picture everything he could make with them. "Would that be best?"

Most of them were rather wide, and he'd be able to saw flat sections and then carve them into squares or even circles – depending on what he wanted their shapes to be.

"That's a good start." Orpheus, almost hesitantly, placed his palm on Magnar's shoulder. "You are doing far better than I thought you would, and your female seems to like it here."

Magnar twisted his head at Orpheus. "You have never complimented me before."

All manner of colours flickered into Orpheus' orbs. Reddish pink from embarrassment. A deeper blue from sorrow. Green from envy. They eventually settled back to their normal blue as he withdrew his hand.

"I wish I had someone to guide me. I made many mistakes when I was at your developmental stage, but you learn quickly."

I have made a lot of mistakes, Magnar thought.

He and Delora hadn't spoken about what transpired the other night, but they'd both been a little awkward with each other since. Him more so than her.

"Delora is also different to Katerina, as are you from me. I am... thankful that I can be here for you." Orpheus then turned his head off to the side while rubbing at his neck. "Although I have been thankful for a long time that things turned out the way they did because I now have Reia, it also makes everything I went through worth it since I can help you. I don't wish for any Mavka to go through what I did."

Magnar didn't know what to say. He never expected such words from Orpheus, who was often cold towards him. But an odd warmness radiated in his chest.

Does he care for me a lot more than he shows?

It also revealed that his pain was still apparent.

Orpheus' head turned in the direction he could hear Reia laughing boisterously.

"We are leaving now," Orpheus quickly muttered.

Magnar thought that might be because he had revealed more than he originally intended to and wanted to flee.

They also didn't usually stay long even if there was much left to still do. It was obvious Orpheus preferred to be alone with Reia, whereas Magnar enjoyed the company of more.

I wonder if I would be the same if Delora and I were like them. They weren't as close, weren't as intimate with one another, and with how things seemed to be going, it didn't feel as though they were *ever* going to be.

Magnar couldn't touch her, and he knew that was his own fault. He was dangerous to his very delicate human. He couldn't control his body like he wanted to, couldn't keep his claws sheathed when his cock stirred behind his seam.

In answer, Magnar grunted with a nod.

"We will not be back for a few days. We have been sharing our meat because you cannot leave to hunt without risking your female, so we must catch more."

"Thank you," he grumbled in answer.

Orpheus took a step back and then turned, heading straight for the back of the house. He disappeared.

"Look! It's you!" Reia shouted loudly. Magnar didn't hear Orpheus' response. "Yes, it is!"

Reia squealed. Moments later, they emerged with Orpheus carting the flailing blonde woman over his shoulder as she giggled. Just as they went to the tree line, he watched Reia turn into her Phantom form.

Magnar paused to stare at the last branch he had left to remove, his orbs shifting into a deep blue.

I want to be like that with Delora.

He wanted to be able to freely lick at her neck without either one of them fretting for their own reasons. He wanted to be able to make her giggle or just smile at least *once*. He wanted to be able to hold her in a way that wasn't him cradling her in his arms just because they were travelling.

He wanted... to be playful with her.

I desire to be near her.

Magnar chopped off the last branch and made his way to the back of the house, carelessly throwing the axe near the steps where he would easily find it later.

Things had been strained between them since the last time he'd touched her, but Magnar refused to allow himself to distance from her.

He needed her near. He craved her within his sight, to be able to smell her and hear her lovely voice. To dissipate the worst of the loneliness he felt – some of it still present despite having her soul.

Rounding the corner, he found Delora dabbing a thick brush covered in green paint against the wall. She was reaching up high while straining on the tips of her toes. It arched her back, revealing just how rounded and big her stomach had gotten over the past few days due to her stretched position.

It worried him, constantly. Delora appeared more fragile to him like this, and she often complained of pains and aches. He refused to truly allow her to do anything by herself.

He'd even given her a stump to place her paint bowls onto. Watching her place her hand on her side to support her back while having to lean to the side so she could reach down around her overly rounded stomach, had been both humorous and upsetting. She appeared to struggle to even do the slightest task now.

However, he did find her strange little waddle cute. It was an odd concept, but part of him liked that Delora was filled with part of his essence for now.

Although much of the green she'd been painting was one colour, it looked as though it had some sort of blobby pattern to it. However, there was one image that was clear, as though she'd started it first and had desired to complete it.

At first glance, he'd thought it was a white horse. But upon closer inspection, he realised it couldn't be since it had a spiralling horn on its head and feathered wings arching high on its back. It was standing on the ground, and he could see Delora had already added a different shade of green around it like grass.

"I have never seen this kind of animal before," Magnar stated as he stepped closer, coming between the opening of the garden fence. "Horses do not have a horn nor wings."

Delora lowered her brush and turned to him with a frown, before she drifted her gaze back to the odd horse.

"That's because it doesn't exist," she admitted. "It's a unicorn."

Magnar cocked his head, noticing Delora was covered in streaks of white, green, blue, and brown.

"Then how do you know what it looks like to paint it?"

"Humans like to make up creatures." She placed her wide brush down into a bowl of its matching green and then picked up a thinner brush laying in pale blue paint. She dabbed at a line under its brown eyes, seeming to see some kind of imperfection. "We like to tell fun stories to each other."

"I do not see the point in false stories. There is much to discover in the world that is real."

Delora tsked. "Perhaps for a Duskwalker, but we've been trapped behind walls for almost three hundred and fifty years. We need to do something to keep ourselves entertained."

Magnar snorted a huff, figuring that was a fair argument. He walked over to some other figure that was very different to what she'd been creating.

Made of black, messy lines, it had a long line torso with an upside-down V underneath that resembled an attempt at legs. There was also one long curving stroke that created a horse-shoe shape near the top like arms. Above these stick limbs was a pointy cone shape that had jagged lines along the bottom edge, and two swirling spirals above it.

The last detail, which was the only colour on it, were two splattered blobs of blue.

"What is this?" Magnar pointed to this strange-looking stick figure. "It is not like everything else you have painted here."

In his peripheral, he noticed Delora brought her lips into her mouth to bite them. Then, seeming to regain some sort of composure, she said, "Reia painted that. It's, uh, Orpheus."

Magnar tilted his head while examining it.

Perhaps the jagged lines were meant to be teeth, and the blue blobs were meant to be eyes, but it was a very barbaric image.

"But it looks nothing like him."

Delora released a heavy sigh while shaking her head. "I tried to tell her that, but she was *adamant* that it was perfect, and that she had captured his likeness."

Exchanging brushes, Delora painted strokes of brown downwards over the top of some of the green. He thought she might be trying to create trees in her image, with a field separating them from the *unicorn*.

"You know..." she started, her eyes focused on what she was doing. "Hadith hated it when I painted."

The growl that immediately emitted from deep within his

chest was involuntary, an instant reaction to hearing *that* name. Searing heat warmed his chest with rage, despising that Delora had been bonded to another before. To a *human.*

He didn't need to know what this *Hadith* looked like to know that he had skin rather than fur and feathers. That he had proper eyes for her to gaze into.

He never realised he could hate a name so much.

Unbridled jealousy and envy coursed through him. He knew they would never have faced the issues that he and Delora faced. They were the same. He was a person who didn't have claws or fangs to harm her with. Who could return her kisses with his own lips.

And yet, Hadith had been undeniably weak.

Magnar could have torn him limb from limb and wanted nothing more than to do so after learning how he'd treated Delora.

He wanted to tear his legs from him so he couldn't come near her with malice. He wanted to rip his arms off so he couldn't harm her with his hands. He wanted to gouge his eyes out so he couldn't look at her, pluck his ears from his head so he couldn't hear her voice, and slice out his tongue so he couldn't speak cruelly to her.

And, lastly, Magnar wanted to rip his tiny, little human penis off for *many* more reasons.

He didn't want to hear about this *insignificant* man that no longer existed in the same plane as her.

Whether she'd heard his warning growl and ignored it, or didn't understand what it was, she continued to speak.

"I haven't painted properly since I left my town to marry him. He said painting anything like a unicorn or a fairy was for children, and that I should be ashamed of myself for being so immature. That there were more important things to do than paint little pictures."

Crimson red shifted the colour of his sight, and Magnar's growl grew more distinct and hostile. He stepped closer.

Why does she keep speaking of him?

"But I wanted to paint them because the world outside the walls was so dark and scary and so full of misery." She lowered her brush with a thoughtful expression furrowing her brows. "I wanted to bring colour into the despairing world we lived in, just like my mother. I guess... along the way, with everything I've gone through and because of Hadith, my inner child died. It's nice to finally greet her again."

"Delora," he warned, his claws heavy and tingling on his fingertips, the itch to maim growing within him. But not her, Hadith. She was *his*, and he didn't want her to remember this male, didn't want her to speak of him. If he could, he'd erase her memory of him with his magic. "Cease–"

"Magnar, stop!" Delora yelled, reaching her hands out in his direction with her eyes turned downwards to the ground.

It was too late. Her frightful yell spooked him, and he stomped his hoof down into a bowl of paint, causing his footing to come out from under him.

He hadn't known there were more on the ground, colours she wasn't using as often and couldn't fit on the small stump he'd provided.

Magnar's long arms spiralled in the air right before he landed on his arse with an *oomph*. The bowl of yellow paint flipped through the air, dropping a streak right across his face, before the wooden bowl clunked against the top of his head with a *thunk*.

Luckily, he'd landed in the dirt aisle down the garden, otherwise he would have likely broken many of their vegetables and fruits.

White entered his vision as he stared at the now empty bowl.

I spilled her paint. Would she be upset with him over this? He knew how much these meant to her considering her reaction to finding them in the Demon Village.

The high-pitched sound that came next was foreign. He'd never heard it from her before, but he knew *exactly* what it was before he even lifted his sight to her.

"Pffft!" Delora snorted, right before she started to laugh, her hands on her thighs as though she needed to steady herself or she'd collapse.

Her lips were curled upwards and parted, flashing him even, white teeth, while her rounded cheeks had bowed her eyelids.

Delora, he thought warmly, feeling something tender

swirling within his chest.

Trying to stifle her laughter, she reached her hand out as though to help him to his feet. The moment he lifted his hand to take it, not that he thought she'd do much to pull him to his feet, she retracted her hand and burst out laughing again. She hugged her midsection like she was getting a cramp.

"Oh my God! I'm so sorry, but I swear that was the funniest thing I've ever seen." She released one arm and pointed at him while turning to give him her side. "You literally fell over like they do in the comedy shows they do in the town square. Like you'd slipped on a banana peel! And then the bowl hit you in the fucking head. I can't. I'm sorry, but that's too funny!"

After a few moments, she settled and came over to stand between his feet while offering her hand. Her face was bright with a humour-filled grin, and he could tell she was trying her hardest not to giggle.

Instead of reaching for her help, Magnar lifted his palm and cupped the entire right side of her head.

"Is this what your smile looks like?" He gently stroked his thumb claw from the crease of her nose to her rounded, puffed by humour, cheek bone. "It is so lovely."

He'd seen Reia smile many times, sometimes directed at him, but it had never stolen his breath like Delora's did. It didn't feel like he'd waited eons to see it, didn't stir his heart to beat faster.

It never ignited his sight to morph into bright flamingo pink, and the warmth inside him was more powerful than any flame he'd been near.

His vision brightened in colour when her smile softened into something so utterly tender with her lips shutting. Her pretty brown eyes were fixed on him when she leaned into his palm in welcome, grasping his wrist to hold him there.

Delora lowered herself so she could kneel on the ground between his thighs, all the while holding his wrist, before she let go of him. Her smile didn't fall, but it did ease into something else, perhaps having a hint of sombre in it.

"I'm sorry I've been the way I am." Her eyes moved across the features of his skull, not bothered by any of it as she looked him over. "I was... I was just really hurt, and I didn't know what to do with my feelings. I didn't know how to make myself feel better, and I worried that you would come to hate me. I murdered two people who didn't deserve to die just because I was angry."

"Why would I hate you for something like this? I have eaten your kind. I have killed far more humans than you have."

She lowered her gaze and fiddled with her fingers on top of her lap.

"Because I see it differently. You killed people because you needed to, because that's what... creatures do. They hunt, and they don't care what it is at the end of the day as long as they are fed. You weren't driven by emotion or anything immoral. You didn't know it was wrong. But I did, and I still did it. I hated myself for doing it."

Magnar carefully brushed one of his claws underneath the line of her jaw until he reached her chin. He lifted her face by nothing other than its sharpness.

"But in doing so, you brought yourself to me."

Her smile, which had started to fall, returned.

"You're very charming in your own way, Magnar."

The fur and feathers on his body ruffled under the compliment, having never received one so tender before.

They didn't often have moments like this, but when they did, it reminded him why he liked Delora so much.

As much as he thought she was the most beautiful creature he'd ever seen in all his long life, the kindness she radiated was nothing he'd ever experienced before. Delora was forgiving. He was a Mavka, one that still had much to learn and was lacking in humanity, yet she never made him feel... less because of it.

Not because she'd never insulted him, which she hadn't, but because she tried to make sure he was comfortable in asking his questions to her. Delora allowed Magnar to be himself, and he knew himself to be very flawed.

He often tried to hide it.

He didn't mind that she'd been sad, that she was trying to heal through her pain. She'd given him a purpose in doing so.

Now he was just working on trying to become her purpose. He didn't know how to do this.

She desires me. That was at least something, especially now that he understood what it meant. *It means she likes me very much... right?* Meant she liked his touch and presence?

"Ooo!" Delora quietly squealed before she looked down to her stomach. "I think because I was laughing it moved! Do you want to feel?"

Before he was even given the chance to reject her offer, apprehensive about the whole thing, Delora grabbed his hand and placed his palm against her rounded belly. His entire dark hand spanned it.

Just as he was about to remove himself from somewhere so delicate and precious, something knocked against his pinkie.

He paused and then moved his palm that way. He felt another knock.

"See?" she asked. "How cool is that?"

Cool is not the word he'd use, but rather *surreal*. It was a life that wasn't born, something he couldn't see, but he'd long ago been able to hear it. Since his ears were so sensitive, he'd started hearing its quick little heartbeat two weeks ago whenever he was near her.

Creator. Father? Touching it made it feel more real.

Something warm, almost tender lifted in her eyes as she turned her head down to look at his hand on her rounded stomach. "What gender do you think it will be?"

"Mavka do not have a gender when we are born." At least that's what the Witch Owl had informed him.

Her face shot up with furrowed brows. "You aren't born with a gender? Then how did you come to be a male?"

He brought his hand away from her stomach because he didn't know how he felt about touching it.

"The first human we eat dictates our gender."

"Oh right, I forgot Reia told me that your kind is androgynous when you're born." She looked pensive for a moment. "So, they're a 'they'?"

Magnar's head cocked in puzzlement.

"It will most likely be a male. Human men are more common above the surface forest."

"Yes, but until they eat one, they'll be genderless. That makes them a they and them. They could still end up becoming a female.

I'd rather not call them a he if they could end up becoming a female, or vice versa."

A reddish pink lifted into his orbs. "I do not understand."

A smile began to play on her lips. The fact she'd given him another made his tail lightly tap against the ground.

"You don't have to understand. You just have to accept it." Her smile grew as she asked, "Okay?"

His tail tapped faster. "Okay."

Whatever she wants to call it, I will call it that. Especially if it meant he could continue to receive this pleasant expression.

For long moments, Delora and Magnar stared at each other, neither speaking but also neither having to. Any tension within him eased and allowed him these few brief minutes of contentment with her.

She is so pretty A soft wind brushed her hair over her shoulder and it touched her lips, causing his sight to drop to them. *I would like to play with them.*

He knew they felt nice pressing against the cool bone of his skull.

"You have paint on your face," she told him, a frown appearing across her brow. Then her face brightened as she said, "Can I paint it?"

Magnar raked his claws down his skull and noticed yellow paint coated the tips of them.

"If you would like."

With a giddy bounce on her knees, she reached down near his feet and pulled multiple paint bowls closer. Then she grabbed the thinner brush, dabbled it in the blue, and started making stroke marks across his brow.

Her face was relaxed, and he noticed that the dark circles under her eyes were almost non-existent except for what was natural.

The paint was cold upon his bone, but he didn't mind as he was able to closely take in her red apple and frost scent right as it came off her skin. He almost leaned closer to lick at her heady aroma.

But there was a thought that filled him with melancholy.

"Are you doing this because you do not like the way I look?"

Was she trying to change him to better suit her wants? To hide that he was faceless and only bore a skull?

"Pardon?"

"I do not have skin like you," he stated, reaching up to touch her cheek. "Would you prefer I did not look this way?"

"Magnar," she whispered with a hint of sorrow. "No, not at all. I didn't mean to make you feel this way."

She unexpectedly darted forward and pressed her soft lips to one of his longer top fangs. Magnar touched where she kissed him when she pulled back.

She'd given him what he wanted, and he was taken by surprise that she did. *She kissed me!*

And it had been warm and malleable, making him want another already. He reached back to stop his infernal tail from wagging wildly, growing shy by how excited it was.

"It's just so white, like a canvas, and I wanted to add to it." Then she proceeded to stroke her brush against her own face to give herself some kind of pink whiskers since she'd changed colours. "Humans like to do this sometimes. We like to paint our faces, or each other's, just for fun. But if you don't like it, I can stop."

The tension in his muscles eased.

"No," he answered with a shake of his head. "If you want to use me as your canvas, I would like this."

It would be like how Reia gave Orpheus his horn bells. Then his orbs turned bright yellow. *But better.*

THIRTY

If Magnar knew he'd have to watch his little raven screaming in pain, he may have ripped his cock off before he got the chance to use it.

He fretted, unsure what to do or how to help as Delora let out this deep, grainy, strained, incoherent noise while resting against the outside wall of their nest. She was adamant about doing this where she couldn't make a mess, but she looked so uncomfortable as she lay back.

Thick white candles were lit all around her. They highlighted the sweat dotting her brow, the tears in her eyes, and her flustered, red face. She was wearing one of his shirts, which she often used to sleep in.

All Magnar could do was exchange his weight from one foot to the other, then to each hand he also stood upon. His surrendering, submissive position was low to the ground, as if that could be enough to save her somehow.

Every time she yelled, his fur and feathers puffed in worry.

"Delora, let me call for the Witch Owl," he pleaded when he noticed the liquid and blood between her thighs.

"No!" she instantly bit back when something called *contractions* eased, only to return soon later. He hated that they always returned, were getting worse, and didn't seem to ever end. "I-I don't want everyone coming here."

"But she can help."

His orbs had been white since this ordeal began.

Delora shook her head, taking in quick, short breaths before her face tensed once more and she screamed horribly. She gritted her teeth as she clenched her fists together. Even her toes curled in.

It eased, the contraction gone, and it gave her another moment to speak through her pants.

"If you call for her, Reia and Orpheus might come." He tilted his head, conveying that he didn't understand what the issue was. She turned her exhausted gaze to him. "I don't want to be watched. This... is really private, Magnar. They won't know what to do."

"Reia is human, Delora," he rebuffed as he came closer.

He patted the top of her hair, wishing he could take her pain from her.

He'd already tried, but he'd just ended up making everything much worse when she'd needed to restart. Delora had to go through the whole process before he could heal her.

Magnar didn't know how long this had been going on for. An hour? Maybe more? The seconds felt like minutes, and every one of her tears and noises were distressing. Her grunts, moans, and high-pitched cries. The smell of salt from her tears, her sweat, blood, and some strange fluid that had been clear but also filled with a blackness that she said wasn't normal.

All this pain seemed... *wrong* to him. It didn't seem natural, even though it was apparently something every female of every species had to go through.

Is it always like this? Then why would anyone want to have children?

"She was a harbinger of bad omens!" she shouted, just as another contraction came. She sighed when she was given another break. "They are shunned by other humans. She's probably never seen another woman give birth, and she'll be just as useless as you are being."

Magnar flinched and his heart sunk.

I am being useless. He wasn't helping.

"I'm sorry," she cried, her brow creasing deeply when she understood she'd hurt him. "I didn't mean it like that. It's just... there's nothing you can do. If you call the Witch Owl, everyone else might come, and I just don't want to be watched like a spectacle. Please..." Delora threw her arm forward. "Can-can you just hold my hand?"

Magnar took her reaching hand.

The next time Delora needed to push, she squeezed his hand in a surprisingly strong grip. It was almost painful when his knuckles were forced together, and the bones scraped against each other.

But she was quieter, as if that truly helped, and Magnar was okay letting her pulverise his hand into dust if it soothed her.

She seemed to like having a wet cloth dabbed across her forehead, and he patted her often, switching between doing that and petting her glossy, but damp, hair.

Her heart rate was fast, her breaths even faster, but Delora, his brave, strong, little human, was persevering through this. He felt overwhelming sympathy, but also pride.

"I am sorry for doing this to you," he said quietly.

"Yeah, fuck you," she said, causing him to tense, but the broken smile she gave him made him relax.

He was surprised she was even joking with him, and he was relieved that these new expressions of hers, her smiles, weren't gone or temporary.

She'd ask for water occasionally, but she spent most of her time trying to find a better position. She switched to being on her hands and knees, then crouching, before squatting. She finally got too exhausted and laid back down.

Just when he thought this was taking too long and was about to call for the Witch Owl – despite knowing Reia and Orpheus would most likely come here – Delora let out a grunted shout that was far different and far longer than before.

"Get out of me!" she yelled, then gritted her teeth, straining terribly. "You son of a–"

Her eyes rolled just as something *plopped* and slipped out. He twisted his head one way and then the other at the strange black thing that was between her legs on the cloth she'd laid beneath herself.

"You were supposed to catch them," she croaked in a groggy, panted voice.

How was I supposed to know that? he thought, as he stepped a hand closer so he could lean forward. He examined *them*.

It does not look like a Mavka.

He was surprised when they moved.

It was slow at first, but they lifted what Magnar thought might be their head. They didn't have glowing orbs, nor a skull. Instead, they had nothing but a curved black face with no features except for two slitted nose holes that opened and closed when they took their first breaths.

They were goopy, covered in black slime, and when they lifted what he thought might be an arm, it also had no features. They had hands but no fingers, feet but no toes. They were odd, and the creature looked nothing like him. No fur, no feathers, no claws or fangs.

A clean slate of nothing but darkness.

Then they opened their maw. It revealed that the edges of their seamless mouth had jagged triangular lines that interlocked with their bottom jaw when shut. Inside was a purple tongue that twitched.

They hacked liquid before letting out a horrible shrill.

They turned their head to Delora, nose holes opening and closing rapidly as if they were sniffing wildly. The creature immediately ran for her.

Magnar knew something was wrong.

He didn't manage to stop them before the little newborn sunk their black, jagged maw into the side of her knee to bite at her flesh.

Delora screamed, both in pain and fright.

Having to wrangle the creature off her before they took another bite, Magnar ripped them from her body and accidentally tossed them across the bedroom in panic.

The creature slammed against the wall before thudding against the ground, but the texture his hand had grabbed was just as odd as it looked. Their flesh was both firm, like their outsides were tough, but also squishy like they didn't have any bones or organs.

The reek of fear lifted into the air from her skin like a hot, curling wave.

"Why?" Delora sobbed. "W-why did it bite me?"

Before he could answer, there came another shriek. The creature ran on all fours in her direction with their jagged mouth bared. *It is going to attack again.*

Delora, noticing this too, tried to turn into her ghostly form, but she was in too much pain to maintain that state. Her form flickered between physical and intangible.

Magnar crawled above her protectively and grabbed the creature when they jumped. He held on tight when they squirmed and wriggled in desperation, trying to get to her.

He tried to place his hand on her chest, but it kept going through her only to be pushed out for a split second when she turned physical.

"Stay physical," Magnar demanded.

There wasn't enough time. Delora would turn intangible under his grip when he did catch her in his palm.

"No! They bit me!"

"I cannot heal you like this!"

He wanted to take her pain, wanted to help her. He also needed her to wash herself once she was healed.

They are a Mavka. They are reacting to the smell of her blood. Her fear. The Mavka was hungry, hopelessly trying to get to their bleeding prey.

"I promise I will not let them bite you again."

Delora peeked up at him, and their gazes met.

Her brows were knotted tight, showing him just how freaked out she was. Then she nodded, staying in the form in which he could touch. The creature became more frantic, their shrill cries piercing his sensitive ears, but he held on while he took Delora's wounds.

The pain behind his seam was excruciating, but he didn't care if that was the cost of helping her. He also took her bite wound.

His body shook under all the new aches he felt.

Delora immediately turned intangible, but there was still too much blood staining the cloth to calm the enraged baby Mavka.

"I will take them outside," Magnar said as he got to his hooves. "I am sorry. I know you are tired, Delora, but you will need to wash and get rid of the blood."

He didn't catch her response, only the wide-eyed stare she

gave him before he left.

The moment he was out in the fresh air and in the forest within his protection ward, the creature calmed their aggressive state. However, their shrills didn't cease, and they managed to wiggle out of his grasp. The Mavka was so small that they fit in just one hand with room to move.

They crawled over his form, sniffing him, but they didn't attack. They weren't frantic or trying to go back after her. They kept burying their face against him, nose holes opening and shutting rapidly, before moving to another place on his body.

They gave a strangled whine.

I thought they said newborn creatures could not move on their own. That's what Reia and the Witch Owl told him, and yet this baby Mavka seemed to move fine.

Letting them do what they wanted because he had no idea what he was supposed to do with the newborn creature, Magnar realised they seemed generally upset by something. They seemed lost and confused, as they kept moving, kept searching.

"What are you searching for, little one?"

They paused their whining cries to sharply twist their head.

Then they scuttled to his face, clumsily crawling to get on top of it. Magnar let them, and before long, they pressed the side of their head against the top of his snout. They were right in front of his orbs where he could see them.

"Is this what I looked like when I was born?" he asked himself, his orbs shifting to dark yellow in curiosity.

The creature scampered on the top of his head before pressing the side of their face against him once more. Magnar realised they were listening for his voice, perhaps in memory of him speaking to Delora when they had been inside her stomach.

A strong emotion stirred his heart.

They remember me.

THIRTY-ONE

Delora's brows pulled tight as she took hold of the third skeleton key Reia had given her.

Reia mentioned she'd pulled apart some ornaments to retrieve them, but she said she was happy to if she was allowed to listen to the music box when she came to visit.

If she ever comes back here, Delora thought with dismay.

She didn't know when she'd come to truly value Reia's presence. It wasn't just because she was the only other human in the Veil and, thankfully, a woman since Delora didn't particularly want to be within batting distance of a man, but it was because Delora liked Reia... *actually* liked her.

Reia was far braver and more brash than Delora, but she was funny. The woman couldn't hold her tongue to save her life, and she was remarkably... cute pushing the buttons of her Duskwalker.

Orpheus was a sweet cake, but he was also stern and rough around the edges. If Magnar was possessive, which he was, then she thought perhaps Orpheus was more so.

It made sense considering he'd been seeking a human companion, a bride, for two hundred years. Magnar hadn't waited as long. He didn't have the same tender aches she could see within Orpheus by just his actions alone.

Will... neither of them want to come back?

She knew the crease in her brow was from sorrow and not frustration when she had to toss the third key onto the round table she stood in front of. There was one left after this, and it looked much too small.

Delora didn't want to be here alone with Magnar, with... *it.*

The thing she gave birth to was horrible. Any chance they got, they attacked her, and when Reia and Orpheus had arrived today, they also tried to attack them.

Orpheus had grown enraged when they had managed to wrangle themself out of Magnar's arms and literally shriek while flying through the air at Reia, who turned incorporeal before they reached her. Then they had started trying to climb Orpheus.

Delora had been forced to watch from a distance as Orpheus bent over forward and then arched his body, trying to reach for the creature when they moved over his back. Their weird, jagged maw kept trying to bite through his clothing.

An argument had occurred between Orpheus, who was enraged his female had been in danger, and Magnar, who had tried everything in his power to defend the little bloodthirsty monster.

Magnar was attached to it. He'd even angrily snapped at Delora a few times because of her behaviour – not that she could help it!

Delora couldn't be near them, and therefore couldn't be near Magnar. He was forced to always hold them, otherwise they would come for her. Her heart would nearly beat out of her chest the moment the little monster got close, then they would become rabid, their maw opening and closing like they wanted to eat her alive.

Delora would turn incorporeal and retreat.

The loneliness was echoing, and now she feared she'd never see her newfound friends again.

The familiar desire to sleep all the time returned. It was like she no longer wanted to be present, and everything weighed her shoulders down. Her nightmares had started returning when they'd become almost non-existent since the night she'd told Magnar her story.

All because of that *thing.*

I don't want to hate them. Tears welled in her eyes before they fell, landing straight onto the backs of her trembling hands as she tried to open the music box.

But they look like a fucking Demon. They were void black like a Demon, and she'd seen a few that crawled around in a similar way. Other than the fact they didn't have red eyes – they didn't even *have* freaking eyes – they looked like the nightmarish monsters of the Veil.

Her gaze flittered up to the window in front of her to see if she could find Magnar in the darkness. She'd moved her chair and table so she could sit at it and stare outside throughout the day.

Her heart quivered in her chest when she saw him carving at a slice of tree stump he was working to make into a kitchen counter. He was outside working in the dark of night because she was awake. All she could make out were his green orbs.

It had been days since they'd properly spoken, and she... Delora missed him like a terrible ache.

She missed his enticing scent. His rich, deep, body-tingling voice that rushed through her mind like a wave to her brain matter. The warmth she could feel coming off him, even if they were inches apart – and now that it was growing colder, it was something she craved.

Delora missed the big, goofy Duskwalker giving her attention, *any* attention.

She thought the flutter of hope she felt was real when the key she used made a clicking sound within the music box, but she couldn't turn the key. She pulled the key out, checked it for whatever reason, then shoved it back in.

I want to show him this. To show him what it did, what the sound of music was like. She thought he'd like it.

Delora was desperately searching for a bridge between them that didn't have anything to do with physical closeness. She wanted to show him things, teach him more. She wanted things to go back to how they were before, even if it was awkward and uncomfortable at times.

Things had been strained before she gave birth, and back then she'd been pleading for an answer to making their relationship work since they were stuck together, for eternity apparently. Delora now wished she had the ability to just speak to her past self and tell her to stop being so selfish.

Past Delora had more than what she did now.

I don't know what I'm doing anymore...

Something brushed against the back of one of her ankles.

Delora stiffened as all the hairs over her body stood on end, her skin prickling in dread. Fear clutched her throat as a cold chill crept through her so violently she shivered.

A gasp clogged in her throat, seizing her lungs when she couldn't breathe, and she turned to find that *thing* near her feet.

Delora let out a high-pitched scream just as they gave a menacing shrill that matched the tone of her own voice. She jumped onto the table when they tried to fucking bite her leg, then they tried everything in their might to crawl up the side of the table leg to get to her. To *eat* her! Her own child!

With her arse on the table and her back against the window, tears of fright welled in her eyes as she tried to scamper back. When she saw one soft, black limb curling over the side of the table, she tried to hide her feet and protect them by bringing them closer to her body.

Delora turned incorporeal to protect herself, a reaction she was beginning to have with fear.

She floated through the table, sinking to the timber floor's level, just as it got on top of the table. They searched for her.

They were inside her ghostly torso.

She floated to the side just as Magnar, orbs white, burst through the slightly ajar door. He ran for them.

"You were supposed to keep them away from me!" she yelled, feeling her intangible body waver.

They didn't seem to mind Magnar's long claws stabbing all the way into them when he picked them up. Delora knew they were practically indestructible.

Nothing stops them. No matter how far they were tossed, no matter what she accidentally dropped on them when they managed to sneak up on her – like now when she'd pushed the music box off the table. Nothing could make them stop.

Magnar released the grip he had on the creature. They crawled all over his body like they usually did.

They're like a parasite attaching itself to a host. She shuddered at that thought.

They jumped away from him to land on the table. The snorting huffs they made as they buried their nose holes against the timber to sniff for her made Delora cover her face.

I can't do this. She couldn't weep in this form, but she sincerely wanted to. *I don't feel safe in my own home.*

She barely felt rested. She worried it would attack her while she was sleeping, and every waking moment felt like a nightmare.

The peace Delora had found here with Magnar was gone.

"They just want to be near you, Delora."

He picked them up again, seeing she was distressed watching them try to *hunt* for *her*.

"To eat me!"

She couldn't face him when she lowered her hands, having to turn her head to the side, but she saw in her peripheral that his orbs had changed to a deep blue.

"Because you reek of fear. They do not attack you when you are unafraid."

"Yes, they do," she swiftly retorted.

Did they, though? Ever since the birth, they had never actually gotten the chance to bite her again because she would always see them before they attacked.

Magnar stepped closer and tried to show them to her, cradled in his arms. Delora stepped back, refusing to be near the creature even in her incorporeal form.

"They are Mavka," he explained, the deep well of blue in eyes darkening. Delora hated that it was because of her. She didn't want to make him sad, hurt him, but she couldn't control how she felt. "They are reacting to the smell of your fear. When you are unafraid, when you do not know they are there, they do not hurt you."

The betrayal she could feel rising within had her jaw falling. Her lips parted.

"You've tried." It wasn't a question, but a statement. "You've put them near me when I didn't know."

"Yes."

Her form wavered in unease. "When?"

"They cry for you," Magnar answered, nervously shuffling

his weight between his hooves. "Sometimes, there is nothing I can do to make them stop except bring them to you."

She knew they cried a lot because the sound *haunted* her every hour of the day. Their horrible shrill made her bones clutch.

Delora floated backwards. "When, Magnar?"

Orange morphed into his orbs for the first time. It was a colour that was similar to his reddish pink but seemed far more... negative. She sensed it was something bad.

His head darted one way, then the other, then he took a step back as he shook his head. He wouldn't look at her.

He knows. The feeling of betrayal deepened. *He knows I wouldn't like it. He knows what he's been doing is wrong.*

He was feeling shame; she could see it in the skittish way he was moving.

"When you have been sleeping." Delora's form turned undeniably cold, like someone had run a frosty finger down her spine in her ghostly body. "I bring them to you and–"

He halted his words to touch the top of his skull when her soul between his antlers lost some of its fiery colour. It had been growing brighter over the past month.

Now it darkened, not completely, but enough that a few fissures of lava disappeared.

"You... you..."

Delora turned away from him with eyes wide, unable to fathom just how much knowing that *hurt*.

He'd been putting her in potential danger while she was in a state that was vulnerable and unaware. He'd brought that creature near her without her permission, without her *consent*.

If she had been physical right then, Delora knew she'd be hyperventilating.

How did I not know? He would have needed to sneak in there so as not to disturb her.

"How could you?" Her hands curled into fists, wishing she could feel the tight clench of them. "I trusted you."

"I would never let you come to harm, Delora. I am with you both the entire time, watching them, but all they do is curl against you and sleep." He lowered as though he wanted to bring himself to her level so as not to tower over her. "They... I think they seek your scent because they cannot see. They do not understand where they are. All they knew was you, your scent, because you held them within you."

She thought she felt a pang of pity, but she was still too angry to truly register it.

"That still doesn't give you the right to do something like that without my consent."

"When they are with me, they lay over the left side of my body, where my heart is. They do the same with you, but they do not whine when they do it to you."

Delora unclenched her hands and hesitantly braved peeking at them.

She hadn't realised Magnar had gotten so low that he was being forced to stare up at her. He was making himself smaller than her, giving her the position of dominance of their stance like he was surrendering.

The flames of her anger dissipated slowly.

"They listen to my heart?" she asked curiously.

"They remember my voice from when I spoke to you. That is why they do not attack me. I think... they are looking for comfort." Magnar brought his hand up to gently brush his claws over them, and for a moment, she heard the slightest whimper. They were clinging to his left pectoral muscle over his shirt, right where his heart was. "You are all that they knew. They seek you constantly, which is why you sometimes find them near you."

Her hurt deepened another layer. "And you let them come after me?"

Magnar shook his head. "Sometimes I am deep in my task, and I am used to them moving on me. They are very light. They do not have a scent, and their sounds are quiet. I do not always notice them leaving me to find you. And they always go to you, Delora. No matter where you are. It is your scream that makes me realise they are gone."

Delora didn't know how she felt, learning all this.

The whirlwind of confusion was daunting. She didn't know how to shed her fear, how to give the creature what they wanted.

They came from her, and she was afraid to be anywhere near

them.

The creature was an unknown thing. When Delora had been carrying them, she had been so excited to meet them, hoping they would be as sweet and warm as Magnar. She'd even been going over names to give them.

But all they ever did was try to eat her from the moment they took their first breath.

She'd just come out of labour, something that had been painful and *daunting* on its own, especially because she had to do it by herself with no one to help her. The relief she'd felt once she'd managed to push them out with tears and a scream had been swallowed instantly by them sinking their weird, jagged mouth into her flesh.

Since then, all she'd felt was confusion.

Delora wanted to love them like she had when she'd been carrying them, but she didn't know how.

"Please," she tearlessly cried behind her hands when she covered her face, wishing he hadn't pushed shame and guilt onto her by revealing all this. "Please... just leave me alone."

"Delora," Magnar said, coming forward so he could dance his clawed fingers near her incorporeal form as though he wanted to comfort her. "If you try–"

"I can't," she answered, shaking her head. "I can't do this right now. I'm really, really angry at you for what you did, and really upset. Please give me a few moments. Just take them outside."

"Okay. If that is what you want."

Magnar, while still low to the ground, crawled backwards to give her space before going to the door. He slipped through and shut it softly.

After a few seconds, when she knew they were far enough away, Delora turned physical. Her arms trembled when she placed her hands on the table while standing.

Her brows drew together as she tried to process all this.

It had only been a few days since she'd given birth. She'd suffered no recovery time from it since Magnar had taken her pain for her, but her emotions had been chaotic ever since.

He... I can't believe he would do that. To make Delora lie with it when he knew she would have been against it. *I didn't think he would ever betray me.*

Magnar's innocence was something she adored about him because she regarded him as safe. She could forgive an accident, but this had been done on *purpose.*

Delora's fingers curled into a tight fist, trying to stem her tears. *But he believed it was for a greater good.* She relaxed her hands and splayed them against the table's surface once more.

I guess they never attacked me while he did it.

Delora had never woken up because of them. She'd never known what Magnar had been doing, which meant the creature had done nothing to harm her in those times.

I-I don't want to be afraid of you, she thought as she pictured their odd form. A shiver instantly coursed through her, and she tried her hardest to control it, knowing she had to shed this fear somehow.

She took in a deep lungful of air and then let it quiver out of her, easing her tears and soothing her emotions so they didn't feel so haywire. Post-natal depression was a bitch and was made worse by the fact that *none* of this was fucking normal.

"I just need to get used to them," she whispered, willing for courage. "Like approaching a feral dog, if it smells your unease, it's more likely to attack."

Delora had never dealt with a wild dog before. They also weren't a dog but a human-eating Duskwalker.

Regardless, she couldn't continue to live like this. In this lonely limbo. In this house that felt eerily cold without Magnar's presence.

She took in another deep draw of air and rolled her shoulders back, lifting off the table and wishing for strength before she let it out. Standing straight, she gazed at her own tired and depressed image that stared back at her from the reflection in the window glass.

Maybe if she could at least tolerate its presence, things might get better.

Delora took in a final breath and glared at herself.

She wasn't resilient like Reia, but she wouldn't allow this to take control of her life – one that she hadn't wanted to live before

Magnar. She liked him, she couldn't leave him. They were stuck together through both of their choices. Things had to work, and that meant she had to be brave and face the things that terrified her.

Delora turned to the door and made her way out of it.

Magnar was sitting on the porch steps staring at the licking flames that remained in the campfire from when she'd cooked her dinner earlier. She'd often seen him sit there with them.

He rotated his skull until one of his orbs, still a saddened blue, could be seen. His gaze followed her movements, and she eventually came to sit beside both of them with her head turned away so as to not look at them. She couldn't, worried that she'd instantly start stinking of fear if she looked upon her own baby.

She was already wary of just being this close.

"Don't do something against my wishes again," Delora said quietly. "Don't do something you know I wouldn't be okay with."

Magnar gave a curt whine in response.

"Consent is something that is really important, Magnar," she continued. "It matters in everything we do. When you receive it, it creates trust, and when you do something against someone's will or knowledge, it breaks it. I understand you were doing something you felt was right, and maybe it was, but that still doesn't give you the right to hurt my trust in you. Sometimes trust can't be regained, so be careful."

"You will not trust me anymore?" The dejected and sincere sorrow she heard in his tone made her heart squeeze.

"I forgive you this time." Delora fidgeted with her fingers by interlocking them before she brought them apart, tensing and then splaying them. She didn't know what to do with them, where she should place them on her own lap. "I wasn't hurt. But if I had been, I could have lost my trust in you, Magnar. If I had a nightmare for some reason, something you know I've been having, I would have smelled of fear. You may not have been able to react quick enough to stop them from hurting me, and I would have woken up already scared and then even more petrified. I would have felt betrayed because you had allowed it."

"I am sorry," he answered quietly. "I did not think about your nightmares."

It was lucky that it didn't happen, especially since I've had some the past few nights.

"If I don't trust you, I won't want to be here anymore," she said truthfully.

The only sturdy bridge between them was that she trusted in him. If that fell, Delora wouldn't want to be near him, wouldn't want to be touched. She wouldn't want to even speak or look at him. She needed that bridge to stand on, or she'd fall into the river of failure below it and drown.

"You *want* to be here?" His voice perked up, perhaps in hope or joy.

"Yes, I do. I want to be here with you."

And not once during their conversation, had the creature made that terrible shrill or tried to attack her.

Inhaling through her nose, Delora clenched her eyes shut and finally braved lifting her arm in Magnar's direction. She pressed the very tip of her middle finger against his body. A link, one that was hesitant and wary.

Seeming to understand what she was trying to do, Magnar's body relaxed. His arms shifted as though he may have been clasping the creature against him with his strength.

A few seconds ticked by until she felt it – the smallest, but exceedingly warm, breath against the back of her hand. She quickly fisted it and presented her wrist, knowing being bitten there would cause less damage than her delicate fingers.

When they pressed the tip of their rounded face against her wrist to sniff her, she couldn't help the strike of concern that cut through her.

A tiny growl followed, and she turned incorporeal to hide her scent.

Just breathe. She could do this. They hadn't attacked so far, and she'd been sitting with them for a little bit. *They... they won't hurt you. You're fine. Everything's fine.*

Once more, she turned physical and presented her wrist.

If they do, Magnar will just heal you.

Then she would go inside and try again another day. Or never. It really depended on what happened.

This time, she didn't back away. Nothing happened as they sniffed before they pressed their entire face against her as if they were trying to smear her scent all over themself. Then their small, weirdly soft hands grabbed her fist before they gave her a lick. A tiny, gentle, little lick.

Delora let out a pent-up breath she'd been holding, as if that would have been enough to stop the smell of her fear from wafting from her, and opened her eyes.

She turned to look when they tried to bring her closer. They weren't being nasty or hurtful. Turning her hand and opening it, she allowed them to grasp her fingers as they continued to smell her.

A sense of ease washed over her. Delora leaned a little closer so they could have more of her.

Okay. This isn't so bad.

That was until they started climbing up her arm!

Delora froze. Since they weren't trying to bite her, she let them crawl onto her with her head leaning away. Her heart was racing, but she tried to slow it by regulating her breathing.

Within moments, they were over her shoulder and lifted their nose holes in the direction of her face, only an inch away.

Their flesh was so strange.

Upon closer inspection, they actually didn't look like the black void of a Demon. Their flesh was just such a dark grey that it appeared black. It was like Magnar's, just more transparent. Like their skin was so thin and soft that she could see their dark-purple blood just beneath the surface.

The flesh was thicker around their nose holes and the place she thought their ear holes might be, but the rest of them looked almost... gooey. Like thick slime that appeared as firm as a brick, but when touched, was liquid.

"If you speak–" Magnar started, before they shot their head in his direction. "It will help."

"H-hello," she greeted hesitantly.

They turned their face to her and then twisted their head like she'd often seen Magnar do. Then they scampered on her shoulder, almost as if with joy.

A mix of emotions fluttered through her, and she relaxed even further.

"This is the first time we've been so close since you came out." She wasn't sure what else she was supposed to say, especially since she knew this could still take a turn for the worst.

I feel like an idiot talking to them. I doubt they understand me.

They scampered again, before brushing their face against the side of her throat like they were nuzzling her.

They quickly moved once they darted their head back, and Delora gasped and stiffened. They manoeuvred themself, and she could feel the tips of their fingerless hands were soft and curled backwards against pressure, giving no resistance as they clung to her.

Before she knew it, the creature was clutching over her chest, resting on top of her large breast with their head over her heart. They started vibrating, releasing this soft, quiet sound that would have been missed if she wasn't so close to them.

A purr, delicate and contented.

Now that she was holding them, suddenly they appeared so small and vulnerable and weak.

They weren't so scary anymore.

They were doing nothing but listening to her heartbeat while deeply inhaling, as though they wanted to take in as much of her scent as possible on each draw. Their nose snorted in satisfaction, and their backwards curling hands tried to sink into her like they wanted back under her flesh to be secure and safe.

They were warm, even hotter than Magnar. Demons always smelt awful, like a decaying corpse, but they were scentless against her.

A terrible emotion clutched at her, twisting her stomach and intestines into knots.

"Delora?" Magnar asked when he must have seen the tears beginning to form in her eyes.

"I'm so sorry," she cried, unsure of which of them she was speaking to right then. She felt like she was always apologising as of late.

She wrapped her arms across her chest to hold the little creature closer, before she buried her face against them.

"I'm so sorry," she repeated, this time to them, her baby she had ignored and tried to run away from. "All you wanted was your mother, and all I thought about was myself. You must have been so scared and confused about the world."

Magnar said they always came looking for me.

"You just wanted to be with me, wanted comfort." Her lungs heaved out her sobs as guilt weighed on her. Delora was ashamed of herself. "I'm-I'm supposed take care of you."

They did something that made her sobs worsen. They lifted their face and licked at her tears, almost as if they wanted to soothe her when she should have been doing that for them this entire time.

Magnar tentatively placed his fingertips on her shoulder as though he was worried about touching her. She lifted one of her hands and grasped his tightly, needing him to comfort her, to touch her in any way.

When she brought her gaze to him, his orbs were a bright flamingo pink. He came closer to wrap his arm around her and draw her into his side. He held her tightly and even brushed the points of his claws through her hair to pet her.

"You were frightened, Delora," he tried to reassure her.

"But... if I just stopped being scared, I would have seen they just wanted to be with me. They're a baby. It doesn't matter what kind or what species. They're just a baby that wanted the comfort of their mother."

And with the dissipation of her fear, love bloomed in its place.

The spirit between his antlers brightened, and although it had places on its body that were still charcoal, it was brighter than before.

"I know I keep saying it, but I'm sorry for the way I've been. I keep making all these mistakes," she said as she leaned into him, greedily taking in his embrace. "I've been avoiding you because you've been holding them in my place."

"It is fine, my little raven." He brushed his fingertips over the small creature that had nestled themself over her left breast and was nuzzling her. "All is well now. That is what matters."

He brought his long fox tail around her waist as though he wanted to deepen the cuddle. She gripped the fluffy fur, having wanted to touch it for so long. She was thrilled by how it was soft, glossy, and tickled her palm.

Then Magnar bumped the tip of his snout under her jawbone to nuzzle her as well, allowing her to receive affection from both of them at the same time.

Delora felt lighter. Lighter than she had in a long time.

THIRTY-TWO

Magnar placed the last stone into the protruding crevice he'd created in the kitchen before he set it permanently into place with clay. He was thankful this was the last thing that required clay, as he'd almost expended his resources. He looked over at the fireplace that had used the rest of it.

He was currently finishing the kitchen hearth that Delora would use whenever she felt the desire to eat, although he'd noticed she only ate about once a day. After a conversation between them where he learned that she didn't feel hunger, perhaps a Phantom quality, he became less anxious about her eating habits.

Her sleeping habits had also grown into something better. His orbs shifted into bright yellow at the memories he had of watching her cuddling their little youngling.

Delora no longer had any nightmares. He wondered if she found their youngling comforting to sleep with, feeling their breaths, heartbeat, and warmth, just as they did with her.

They had become an inseparable pair.

He may have grown dismayed by this, even jealous or lonely, if it weren't for the happiness that radiated within Delora's expressions. They were ones she often shared with him, giving him smiles that were becoming more tender each day.

The dark imprint under her eyes was gone, and Magnar often found her lips curled up just slightly as though she was smiling to herself.

Delora is... happy here with me.

His long tail thumped against the timber ground at his thoughts before he stood, instead feeling it tap against the backs of his legs.

With a proud hum at himself for finally completing the hearth, he let his gaze drift over the counters he'd completed days ago and then the shelving underneath it that bore no doors. He liked the open expression of them, and he'd done the same for the shelving above. He doubted she'd be able to reach those, but they were for him, so he didn't have to crouch down every time he wanted something of his own.

The kitchen was complete, the windows had glass and frames, the door was sturdy. All the rooms had been built with temporary doors made out of logs. He'd replace them with more timber planks in the future when he returned to the Demon Village. The fireplace was done, as was the porch outside.

The only thing left to do was furnish their home.

This was a task Magnar was excited for.

Would she prefer an oval dining table or a rectangular one? He brought his hand up so he could tap a claw at the side of his snout. *I want to make her a proper bed.* He didn't know if he'd be comfortable in it, but she'd looked comfortable in the one she'd slept in at the Demon Village. *I would like to lie in one with her.*

The yellow in his orbs softened until blue began to lift into his vision. His shoulders slumped.

I cannot lie with her.

As much as he wanted to, as much as he'd tried, Magnar couldn't.

Feeling her soft, plump, warm body against his own stirred his insides. When the smell of her frosty-apple scent clutched at his mind, stroked it on each draw in of his big lungs, his breaths quivered out of him.

The desire to touch her grew strong in those moments, and he'd find himself squeezing her. Squeezing as movement behind his seam became so intense he'd feel himself starting to extrude as his orbs turned a dark purple.

He'd realised weeks ago that as much as he wanted to rest by her side, he no longer could.

Delora had awoken a dark craving in him.

His abilities were stunted. He could learn by taking in knowledge, but he wasn't getting smarter, only more knowledgeable. He still had the same level of control over his body, his emotions, his thoughts, as he did when he met her.

He scratched at the feathers on the back of his neck. *I need to consume more humanity.*

He needed to eat her kind if he wanted to further develop. He didn't want to have that conversation with her.

He feared she would draw away from him.

He lowered his hand so he could stare down at the claws on both his hands, knowing that he could blunt them, but they would resharpen within a day. It also *hurt* if he cut them too far back and would even seep blood. Magnar had tried everything to find a solution, even some that were painful.

But Magnar knew he couldn't trust himself.

He'd already maimed her body. He was always at the mercy of his desires, still unable to control his tentacles.

She'd denied him last time when they'd been on the porch steps, and he knew it was because she worried he'd hurt her. He couldn't with absolute confidence promise her he wouldn't.

She'd also never approached him for it.

With an irritated huff at himself, Magnar pushed his darkening thoughts away and exited the house.

It had rained yesterday, so his hooves sunk into the mushy ground as he made his way around to the back of their home.

However, she wasn't in the garden.

Instead, she was at the apple tree, trying to reach for one of the higher pieces of fruit on her tippy toes – she'd eaten most of them while she'd been carrying their youngling. Her fingertips grazed the bumpy bottom of an apple when she bounced to her toe-tips.

Magnar came up behind Delora to reach it for her, bumping into her and making her gasp with a startle. She turned to him just as he plucked the apple from the tree with ease.

Her turning to him revealed two things.

Delora had colours smeared all over her hands and face, and their youngling was nestled across her chest.

They lifted their head and sniffed the air in his direction. Then they were moving to greet him, and Magnar reached out his arm when it was obvious their youngling wanted to crawl all over him like they were awake, full of energy, and wanted to disturb something.

Their youngling only ever slept when they were attached to her, but became lively when clinging to him.

They often pulled Magnar's feathers out and *nummed* on them with their jagged mouth. He didn't mind as it barely hurt, and he always regrew them. However, he did look rather odd when their youngling had once completely plucked him. They then proceeded to try and yank out his long fur – which was far more painful.

He'd always give them back to Delora before that started happening again.

"You should have told me you were hungry," he said, offering the piece of fruit to her at the same time their youngling finished crawling up his arm. "I would have gotten it for you."

"I can do things for myself." Her cheeks had turned pink, and she nibbled at her bottom lip. She rubbed her thumb over the red, glossy apple in her palm. "I didn't want to bother you."

"But I would like to help you, Delora. I want to do things for you."

For some reason, her cheeks grew brighter. However, she nodded. "O-okay. I'll, um, ask for your help next time."

Then, with her head down like she was feeling shy, she walked towards the garden. At the same time, she took a bite from the apple, a loud, wet crunching sound filling his ears, before she stopped in front of her painting to look it over.

Along the top edge of the roof was a cloth that he'd nailed up to stop the rain from hitting against her painting. Currently, it was rolled to the side, partially hiding it from view.

"I'm almost done," Delora quietly muttered, since he'd followed her inside the garden.

"I am not surprised," he answered, stopping behind her to look over her work. "You have been painting this since we returned from the Demon Village."

Delora turned her head to him with a smile.

He'd finally gotten what he'd wanted by coming to her, and all the apprehension he'd been feeling earlier melted under her expression. She'd never know just how much he'd needed to see her contentment right then, to remind him that even though he couldn't touch her, she was still his, wanted to be here, and was happy.

"Do you like it?"

Now that her painting was almost complete, he could see that the unicorn was standing in a field with a large waterfall behind it. A rainbow arched its way from the trees on both sides of it, and the sky was bright with either the beginning of dawn or the wash of dusk.

"It is colourful," Magnar answered with an appreciative tone. "I have never seen this much colour all in one place before."

Her relaxed features scrunched up into a bright smile, her lips parted, and she leaned closer and hugged him. She didn't wrap her arms around him since her hands were covered in paint, but she pressed her elbows in instead.

Magnar returned her embrace by crossing his arms over the back of her head and holding her hips, bumping the tip of his snout against the top of her hair affectionately.

"Thank you. I'm really glad you like it and don't mind that I want to do this. It's really nice to feel accepted."

Magnar understood how that felt since she seemed to be doing the same for him, but he was also filled with pride in himself that she felt that way enough to tell him.

"I will always accept you, Delora."

He didn't see how others could not.

She stepped back from her hug, and he could already see she was becoming antsy about continuing. He gestured his hand forward so she would.

"How's the house? I bet you're almost done too."

She bent down to grab a paintbrush, showing him the generous curve of her malleable arse. Magnar licked at the outside of his fangs. He couldn't help himself from staring, especially when it wiggled side to side, tantalising him. He'd also felt it pressing against him moments ago, which was why he'd bumped into her from behind. He was creating any reason to have contact between them, like he was starved for it.

He wanted to dig his claws into that meaty, rounded, plump backside. He wanted to grip it firmly and shove it against him as he slammed into her wet heat again.

She stood, stealing his view of her, and he was forced to clear his throat. He warily stepped back.

You'll hurt her. He couldn't allow his mind to catch those thoughts and spiral himself deeper.

"It is complete," he finally said after he'd steadied his quickened heartbeat. "All that is left is to furnish it."

She deepened a stroke of red on the rainbow she was painting as if she hadn't liked its original depth and then started working that same colour into the sky around a dusk-stained purple cloud.

Her brows drew in tight with concentration. "That'll be fun."

He liked how adorable it was when she scrunched up her features like this. Her little nose crinkling, her brows furrowing, her eyes squinting, her lips pursing. It was one of the reasons he enjoyed watching her.

I hope she continues to do this. Magnar would like her to paint every inch of their house in colours. Even if she had to straddle his shoulders so she could reach higher, Magnar would enjoy taking her weight and watching her work.

"Maybe you can make me a–" Her words were cut short when they both heard a laugh close by.

"Orpheus and Reia are here," Magnar said, only just catching their approaching scents with the wind brushing in the opposite direction.

The surprise that showed in her face as she darted it towards the trees confused him.

Did she not think they would return?

He hadn't realised she'd been concerned about this after their last encounter with their youngling.

After a few moments, both Orpheus and Reia came into view. Reia was in her ghostly form. Magnar found it odd, considering they were within the protection of his magic circle. Reia usually turned physical when she entered it.

Orpheus was carrying a basket, no doubt having food and various items for them. They rarely came empty-handed.

"You guys came back," Delora said when they approached near the garden.

She placed her paintbrush into the bowl of its matching paint and walked closer to them. Magnar came closer as well, feeling their youngling crawling around inside his shirt.

"Of course we did," Reia said, a curl of humour in her lips. "It'll take a lot more than a biting baby to scare me off."

Orpheus let out a small growling huff, and his orbs flashed red momentarily. They quickly returned to their usual calm blue.

"You are against this," Magnar said with his head tilting the other way.

Their youngling halted their movements within his shirt, listening intently to the newcomers. Magnar doubted they could smell Reia and Orpheus through his scent, since they were inside his shirt.

"Not against," Orpheus rebuffed curtly. "Just wary on her behalf because she doesn't have sense when it comes to danger."

"Sure, I do," Reia said in a sing-song voice, her smile turning into a large, knowing grin. "I won't turn physical, not until we know it's okay to be near the mean, *wittle* Duskwalker."

Their youngling popped their head out at the opened V of his dress shirt and sniffed the air in the direction of Orpheus.

Reia bravely came closer in her ghostly form and looked up to them. She squinted her eyelids as though that would better help her to see, before placing her hand over her lips with a thoughtful expression.

"It doesn't have floating orbs for eyes like you guys do," she stated as she examined them.

Their sniffing grew more rapid, and Magnar could feel their youngling's heart accelerating. Magnar didn't know why, considering they wouldn't be able to smell Reia in front of them.

"They," both Magnar and Delora quickly corrected at the same time.

They both darted their heads to look at each other, surprised that they'd spoken at the same time.

"They?" Reia frowned with her lips puckering.

"Since Duskwalkers don't have a gender until they eat a human, that makes them androgynous as babies. That's why we say they or them," Delora said to her.

Reia shrugged. "I guess that's fair. Have you got a name for them yet?"

Before either one could answer, their youngling managed to crawl their way outside of Magnar's shirt. Within the blink of an eye, and quicker than Magnar could react, their youngling let out a shrill cry and leapt for Orpheus.

They went straight through Reia, who stepped back, startled, while blinking rapidly. They attached themself to Orpheus' arm that held the basket, biting into his forearm.

Orpheus grunted in pain before he sharply shook his arm to flick their youngling off him. The basket was lost to the ground.

"Sorry," Orpheus growled, obviously barely controlling his rage. His orbs had turned red rather than white, revealing that he wasn't all that sorry as he covered his bleeding arm.

Magnar let out his own warning snarl, but otherwise wasn't *too* upset. The baby Mavka was basically indestructible and had never seemed to feel pain – even when accidentally stepped on because they liked to get under Magnar's hooves.

Their youngling retched at the blood in their mouth, swiping at their face and tongue. They rubbed their face against the grass, desperate to be rid of it as though they found it truly repulsive.

They do not like the taste of their own kind.

Magnar almost chuckled as he went to pick them up.

Mavka had never been interested in eating each other. Rage had never stirred hunger, only the need to dominate when they fought.

As if they could smell him approaching, their youngling scattered away from Magnar's reaching hands and darted for the basket. They dug under the cloth, their little legs dangling out of it as they clawed inside it for what they wanted.

They were not attacking Orpheus. Magnar barely resisted the urge to chuckle in ease. He'd been thinking something horrible was about to happen again.

They were eating something within the cane basket, and Magnar crouched down next to it to wait for them to finish eating what he could smell was cleaned deer meat.

"You went hunting for us," he commented, happily watching

his little one eating for the first time.

Orpheus came closer to watch as well.

"We thought perhaps Delora may still be hungry, but we were unsure if you would want to risk leaving in case she appeared beside you, but the infant didn't."

Magnar had never considered this risk. He just hadn't wanted to leave either one of their sides – especially now that she and the youngling were inseparable. He enjoyed watching them together. They were his... *family.* He cared for them and didn't want to be without them, even for a moment.

When they'd eaten everything they wanted, his youngling climbed out of the basket to sit on their backside. They licked at their odd maw, smacking it together by opening and closing it while working their tongue.

Then, before their very sight, his youngling suddenly became bigger.

What had once fit in just one of Delora's hands, now enlarged to fit in one of his perfectly. Nothing grew over them – they were virtually the same, just bigger.

"They grew!" Delora gasped, while stepping closer.

Their youngling let out a high-pitched shrill as they ran towards Delora. She hesitated momentarily, being cautious as that was wise around them, but they spun around in front of her and snarled at Orpheus. Their youngling backed up until they were resting over one of her feet.

Delora let out a laugh and bent over, picking them up to cradle them in her arms. They continued to growl at Orpheus, occasionally letting out a mangled bark-like sound.

"Are you trying to protect me?" Delora asked, nuzzling her cheek against theirs. "That's rather sweet of you, but you're a little small."

Orpheus let out a thoughtful hum. "Perhaps that is why they attacked last time."

"They just don't know us," Reia added, before she turned physical.

"*Reia*," Orpheus warned.

She ignored him as she approached.

"May I?" Reia reached out in their youngling's direction with her hand clenched into a fist to protect her fingers.

"Sure." Delora gave a shrug. "If you want to brave possibly being bitten."

Delora made sure she had a tight grip on them.

Both Magnar and Orpheus crowded both females, ready to intervene if something went astray.

"Hello, little one," Reia greeted, bringing her hand closer to let them sniff it.

They didn't care. They didn't know what she was doing, who she was, or that she was safe. They just continued to ward her away, writhing in Delora's arms to be free.

Reia braved running the edges of her knuckles over their nose, letting them know that the scent touching them was being gentle and wasn't going to hurt them.

After a few strokes, they eased their struggles, but didn't quieten their growls.

"Have you named them yet?" Reia had to back her hand away swiftly before she was bitten at.

She lowered her arm, perhaps thinking this had been enough of a start for now. They calmed once she and Orpheus gave them some distance. However, it was obvious they were still distressed by the snarling and whimpering sounds they gave as they curled into Delora protectively.

"I-I think so." A hint of pink began to rise in her tanned cheeks. "I'm not sure though."

Magnar's orbs turned a bright yellow in delight. "You have a name for them?"

Delora's face flushed even further so that the redness began to spread over her ears and down her neck and chest. She nibbled her bottom lip, her eyes refusing to meet any of theirs as they darted around.

"Please don't laugh at me." When no one said anything, eagerly awaiting, she took in a deep breath. "Fyodor."

"Fyodor?" He came to them and stroked the top of his youngling's head carefully with his fingertips. "Does this name have a meaning too?"

Magnar liked that his name meant protector. He liked that was what Delora saw him as. He wondered if she had put just as much thought into their youngling's name.

She nodded. "Yes. It means God's gift."

"You think they are a gift from a God?" Pink floated into his orbs as a warmth rushed through his entire being. "You think they are precious like this?"

"Do you like it?" she asked instead of answering, uncomfortable with everyone's attentive gaze on her.

"Yes. Very much so."

"Fyodor, huh?" Reia gave a grin, attempting to look around Magnar so she could look at their youngling. Then she stepped over to the basket and opened it to look inside. "Seems like Fyodor is a hungry kiddo. They ate all the meat we brought over for you." Then she sighed. "But not a single vegetable. Figures they'd be just like any other child avoiding their greens."

Magnar didn't know if she was joking or not, considering she must know that Mavka wouldn't eat such things.

"Do you think she is right, Magnar?" Delora's nervousness, and perhaps joy, faded as a worried crease spread across her dark brows. "They've never really cried for food like a normal baby, but could they be hungry?"

"If they are Mavka, then they will always be hungry," Orpheus stated matter-of-factly.

Delora looked up at Magnar expectantly, like he'd have the answers she sought when he had none.

He scratched at the back of his neck. Orpheus was right, Fyodor would always be hungry.

However... "Perhaps we should take them hunting."

THIRTY-THREE

Magnar was forced to hold Fyodor while he walked through the Veil's thick and dangerous forest. Fyodor gave little whimpers, sniffing the air in search of Delora who was currently in her Phantom form.

"It's okay, Fyodor," she said to comfort them. "I'm right here."

Their sounds eased, but barely. They didn't like not being able to smell her.

Magnar directed them to one of the safest paths up the cliffside to climb it, taking long and fast steps. Delora was able to keep up with him since she only had to hover.

"I wonder where I was thrown from," Delora mumbled quietly.

Magnar peeked at her from the side, finding she didn't look depressed or upset. Her face was filled with a thoughtful frown as she looked around.

She is healing. Whatever ailed her mind was fading, and it brought contentment to Magnar. He hoped it may be because of him.

That didn't mean he didn't become angered that her own kind had thrown her into the Veil to die or be eaten by Demons. That they had been cruel to her.

If it was not for the Witch Owl dropping her on me, I would never have gotten the chance to meet her.

Nor would he be holding Fyodor in his arms, and he rather liked them there.

Magnar had never shared that he, in some ways, was thankful for all the terrible things she'd gone through. They were unfortunate stepping stones to reaching him.

He knew it was selfish.

He knew it was wrong to think this way.

But without them, she wouldn't have given him her soul.

Once they made it to the top of the cliff and onto the human side of the world, Magnar saw that snow covered the ground, although it was mainly patchy. It was so late into autumn that the world was beginning to frost.

His nose hole snorted out fogged breaths instead of clear ones.

Before them lay trees that were spindly and more spread apart, which was so unlike the thick, clogging forest of the Veil.

"You can turn solid now, Delora," Magnar said as he began to lead their journey.

Delora turned her head over her shoulder to peek at the cliff edge. "Aren't we still too close?"

"It is daytime." Magnar looked up to the bright sunshine that glittered through the leaves above, feeling its subtle heat. He let it warm him in welcome. He often forgot how much he liked the surface world. "I cannot smell any Demons lurking in the shadows nearby, and they will be unable to climb the cliff walls in the light."

At his answer, Delora turned physical, and turned her face up towards the sun as well. Earth was currently cold, so he was thankful she was wearing long clothing and boots.

She still gave a little shiver that eased when Fyodor struggled in his arms, and she took them to hold.

Their heat will warm her.

Now for the hard part. Magnar would need to keep *all* his senses open to what was around them while they traversed further into the forest and away from the Veil.

Animals tended not to linger anywhere near the border by instinct. Hundreds of years had taught them that going near the Veil meant certain death, and any hibernating animals did so in places far away.

When they were deep enough after walking for most of the morning and into midday, Magnar caught the potential scent of something in the area that he thought might be suitable for the little Mavka to eat.

Just beyond the brush, the sounds of a trickling stream filled his sensitive ears. He headed that way, knowing animals tended to congregate around moving bodies of water.

He'd smelled a small herd of deer nearby, but thought that might be awfully large for Fyodor to eat. There was also a fox, something he considered hunting for, but he didn't want to endanger the two delicate creatures he brought with him.

I have not hunted since she gave me her soul.

He'd hoped he didn't turn into a mindless beast and start chasing animals through the forest with bloodthirsty intent.

His orbs flashed a reddish pink momentarily. *I do not want Delora to see me like that.*

No, he'd much rather find something easier to obtain.

Magnar brought them both to where he could smell animals nesting underneath the ground. A small hole only about two inches wide had been dug through the dirt right between the arches of tree roots. He crouched down on his knees, with no care for the dirtying of his trousers, so he could make that hole bigger with his claws.

He was careful not to flick dirt in Delora's direction, refusing to get even a spec on her gown.

Just as he reached his arm in the now bigger entrance hole, the direction of the soft winds changed. A scent fluttered towards him.

Magnar paused as he examined it with quick sniffs.

There are humans nearby. Most likely hunters, since he could also smell deer blood in the air.

In the past, Magnar would have been drawn to the smell of the blood rather than the humans, bleeding meat clutching at his mind like a set of claws gouging into his brain. If the humans caught sight of him and fled in terror, his bloodthirsty, hunger-filled mind would have focused on the more tantalising scent instead.

When Magnar had fed on humans in the past, it had generally been at least two at a time. They rarely left their towns together in large groups to keep their mingled scents minimal.

Since he no longer felt hunger, he wasn't drawn to these things anymore. Instead, he merely took note of them. From what he could tell, they weren't close enough to warrant him abandoning this burrow to find a different source of food for Fyodor.

Magnar heard a deer's bawling grunt, and the smell of deer blood intensified.

He turned his head to Delora. *It appears Fyodor's nose is not as good as mine.* And he could tell she couldn't smell them either.

I do not want to worry her.

Since he couldn't hear any humans shouting or coming their way – they were usually quite noisy with their clumsy footsteps – he didn't feel the need to tell her.

He reached into the burrow and his claws brushed something furry and moving. Distressed squeaks sounded. He kept his sight on Delora to make sure she wasn't growing upset.

She didn't seem to hear them as she leaned over the burrow hole where most of his arm had disappeared into. Her face was filled with interest, holding onto Fyodor closely to make sure they were secure.

Shoving his arm deeper until the ball socket of his shoulder was pressed tight against the burrow opening, he attempted to catch one of the multiple creatures that were jumping over his hand and between his fingers.

He finally caught one and drew his arm back, holding onto the hindleg of a wild, brown hare. The hare squealed as it squirmed in his grip.

Fyodor sniffed at the air, taking in the new scent, but otherwise wasn't interested.

"Do you want to turn away?" Magnar asked, unsure if she would become troubled at watching him kill it.

Delora shrugged. "That looks a little too big for Fyodor."

Magnar inspected it, noticing it was about the same size as their youngling. Perhaps it was too big for such a small creature's stomach, but he'd learnt that forest mice were harder to catch. Their burrows were too small for him to reach into, and they easily escaped through the gaps of his large fingers.

Sensing that Delora cared more about feeding their youngling than what he was about to do to the hare, he reached his hand around its head and snapped its neck so that it would die painlessly and without a scream.

"If they do not eat it all, then they do not eat it all."

Magnar covered the burrow opening with dirt, snow, and sticks to stop the others from escaping in case they wanted to take the rest home. He'd opted to carry a satchel in case they found anything they wanted to take back with them.

He laid the hare down on the grass right next to a large patch of snow and stepped back while crouching. He gestured to it.

Delora struggled to pull Fyodor off her, who desperately clung to their mother in protest. She managed to pry them off and put them on the ground next to the hare.

Fyodor turned their head up to each of them with their slitted nose holes opening and closing, before they slowly scuttled over to the rabbit. They sniffed at it curiously.

They bumped it, pawed at it, then stepped on it, before they finally sat on top of it by straddling its body.

"Why aren't they eating it?" Delora muttered with her brows drawing tight.

"Perhaps they do not understand."

Magnar pierced its furry flesh with his claw, opening up its stomach slightly.

One sniff of the newly blood-filled air, and Fyodor leapt for it. Clawing at its body to hold it still, they bit into one hind leg. They pulled until they easily tore it off, showing their hidden strength. Then they lifted their head back with it clamped in their maw, opened their jaws surprisingly wide, and began to swallow it whole.

Magnar and Delora watched together as Fyodor did this with each of its limbs. Delora scrunched up her face like she found it disturbing, perhaps disgusting, along with the tearing, ripping, and slurping sounds that could be heard.

Fyodor's mouth opened wide to take in its long body, swallowing that completely before they worked the head in.

Nothing was left uneaten, as if it didn't matter that the size of the hare matched their own. It was merely absorbed.

Once they were done, smacking at the inside of their mouth, they sat on the ground with their little legs splayed out in front of them. Then they turned their head up to Magnar, then Delora, and gave a happy quivering shrill that sounded almost like a burping giggle.

Delora laughed while Magnar chuckled, neither one of them having heard such a sound from them before.

With Fyodor's face pointed towards Delora, their size instantly shifted. They grew two times bigger.

That wasn't the strangest part.

Their outstretched hind legs morphed into something else entirely, almost longer at the feet until Magnar realised they became rabbit-like. Bones started to form all over their body, each one, like the vertebrae of their spine and their leg bones and toes, able to be seen in the dark-grey flesh of their skin. Their hands grew into an actual shape, rather than blob like, with the backs revealing bones and fingers. Around their torso, a ribcage began to rise through their flesh until even their sternum and shoulders could be seen.

Then, finally, white began protruding through the top of their head, slowly lifting until a rabbit skull, with fangs – making it look more predatory than the hare they'd originally eaten – was revealed. The sharper canine fangs that Magnar had were instead closer together, and they sat almost at the very tip of their snout.

They let out a huff through their new nose.

The sound they gave was new, more like a *bawk*, and then they began to purr. They turned to go to Delora.

That was until their newly formed skull began sagging to the side, far too large for their body, and it slumped to the ground with the rest of their body attached to it.

Fyodor grew agitated that they couldn't hold the weight of their own head by themself. They started dragging it backwards as they tried crawling to the side, their flipper feet stumbling over themselves.

Fyodor made a noticeable mark in the mixture of dirt and snow.

"My poor baby." Delora attempted to stem her laughs when she picked them up. "Perhaps we shouldn't have let you eat the head, but I didn't think you'd grow a skull!"

Fyodor's head slumped backwards, exposing their neck, and Delora lifted it for them. She didn't seem to notice that the new, round, tuff tail at the bottom of their spine was wiggling.

"I also didn't think you would suddenly grow bones or actually feel solid. You're so much heavier now!"

As much as Magnar had been awed by the experience, it left him wondering if this was how his body had started taking shape. He looked down to his hooves and wondered if perhaps the Witch Owl had fed him a deer leg first, and that's why his legs had turned out this way.

What other animal parts am I made up of?

Obviously, he'd eaten a fox to gain his skull… and a deer's antlers. But what body did he eat first? What hands? Magnar knew the fur that grew over his body was part fox, while much of him was covered in feathers.

I wanted Fyodor to look like me. A part of his heart sunk. *I should have hunted for the fox.*

If he had known they'd absorb the hare completely and begin to take on its physical characteristics, he would have made a different decision. *Had I known...*

"They look so cute!" Delora squealed loudly, bringing Fyodor closer so she could cuddle them by pressing her cheek against the top of their white rabbit skull. "I thought you all just took on predator skulls, since both you and Orpheus have one."

I thought so too. But his disappointment eased with how thrilled Delora appeared holding their much larger youngling in her arms. She even swayed side to side.

She turned her face to Magnar with a bright smile, one that warmed his insides and made his sight begin to morph to purple. *I like it when she looks at me like that.* Those expressions were compelling, addictive even.

It fell as she looked past him.

He ducked around to find a deer staring at them way past the trees. It had an arrow stuck out of its back, and it froze on the spot as if it was afraid moving would reveal that it was there.

Magnar had been too absorbed in Fyodor's new changes and Delora's excitement that he hadn't been listening out for their surroundings.

The blood that had tracked from its wound had mostly dried, revealing that it had been a while since the humans had shot it. Thankfully, it was far enough away to not send Fyodor into a hungry rage.

They may also be full. Magnar had no memory of what it was like being at their stage other than knowing a comforting scent. Most likely the Witch Owl's.

"There's an arrow sticking out of its back," Delora said quietly as she stepped closer to Magnar. Her eyes were wide, showing the whites of them more, as she looked around warily. "It looks really fresh. Maybe we should leave."

"I cannot smell any humans directly nearby," Magnar answered just as softly. "But perhaps you are right."

They had done what they came here for. Remaining any longer would be foolish. Hunters were good at hiding their sounds so as not to startle their prey, but Magnar could smell two humans in the distance coming closer.

He turned to Delora.

"Do you want me to grab more rabbits?" He gestured his snout towards the burrow. "I can take a few more so that we have food for them."

"Sure," she said while worrying her bottom lip. "But they did kind of get really big all of a sudden. Maybe we should watch how much they eat."

With a nod, Magnar stepped closer to the burrow.

Just as he was about to crouch down, he released an *euk* sound as he stumbled to the side. Pain lanced his throat. He covered the small holes that had begun to seep blood down both sides of his neck, as if whatever hit him had gone all the way through his flesh and come out the other side.

Red instantly flared into his sight, and he let out a snarl.

"Magnar!" Delora screamed, rushing closer to check on him.

His fur and feathers puffed. He pushed her back just in time before a second arrow could pierce into her shoulder. He purposely took the weapon into his side when he bounced forward. She fell onto her backside with a gasp.

Magnar turned his head in the direction the arrows had come

from. He'd mistaken the human scents for far away when they were actually just diluted by masking aromas.

As much as he was in pain, there was only one thought that crossed his mind. One that caused his sight to go to such a deep and hostile colour of crimson that it nearly blinded him.

They almost shot Delora! His snarl deepened in his throat and turned more rabid – only to cut short when he heard the whistle of another arrow shooting from his left. *They could have shot Fyodor's new skull.*

His youngling now had a glaring vulnerability, making them even more precious.

He raised his hand and fisted the shaft before the arrowhead could even come anywhere near his flesh.

Turning slowly towards their attackers, his form started to change. More fur and feathers grew from his body while his clothing sunk beneath his skin. He was forced to rest his weight on his hands due to the changing curvature of his spine becoming more fox shaped.

"Protect yourself," Magnar snapped at her, his voice growing deeper and distorted as saliva began to dribble between his fangs when he opened his jaw in warning.

He hadn't needed to warn her.

Delora had already turned incorporeal in shock. She currently hovered just above the ground as though she was sitting.

"Why are they attacking?"

Magnar didn't answer, not when another arrow was loosed, and it went right through her ghostly form to embed into the ground right next to his hand.

His heart gave a kick in rage, hurtling heated blood faster throughout his body.

He lifted both arms and slammed his fists into the ground before he let out a dark and bellowing roar. *If Delora had been physical, that one would have pierced her!*

Magnar leapt forward, his lungs pumping so erratically in his chest that he thought it might burst under the pressure. His snorting puffs were heavy and harsh, burning like acid in his lungs under each intake of breath as he searched for those nearby. Those that had dared to even *attempt* to hurt his precious bride.

The only reason he knew he was approaching one was because of the subtle breathing that came from them. They were hidden under a white cloak that camouflaged them within the snow. They smelled of bark and dirt, nearly completely hiding their human scent from him – *nearly*.

Before the human could think better of their situation and choices, starting to shuffle to their knees to get up, Magnar swiped his claws as he ran over the top of them.

Blood sprayed from their decapitated head as it flung to the side. *How dare they attack my bride!*

Perhaps a lowly Demon might have been deceived by such a trick, but Magnar was a Mavka. All of his senses were better than a Demon's. They thought he was just like them... trying to draw him closer to the people who were purposely shouting with deer blood on them. A trap.

One that wouldn't work because he had her soul.

From what he could tell, there were at least six humans, seven if he counted the one he'd just killed.

Demonslayers, he thought with malice.

He'd made a foolish mistake in thinking they were only hunters.

Demonslayers were far more cunning about the way they hunted their prey – since their prey liked to hunt them in return. They often travelled in large groups and hid their human scents under nature, whether that be by smearing their bodies in bark, dirt, sap, or anything else that would cloak them. They also sheltered themselves in animal furs like the one who had been laying upon the ground.

They tended to move slowly, reducing the amount of noise they made in order to get into position so they could hide in the trees, or even behind or inside of shrubs.

Usually they were more patient than this. They would hunt a deer and flay their bodies throughout the day so they could hang it up at night, luring Demons out so they could be slain.

But Magnar could walk in the daylight. They must have spotted him when they were hunting for their bait.

He was large, often easily seen even from a great distance. Perhaps they had someone silently scouting, who heard him and

Delora speaking and had relayed their information to the others.

Magnar had come across Demonslayers before – in the middle of a hunt while they mercilessly fought against Demons and often won with few casualties.

He'd only fought them once before, and that was because the scent of those that had been killed had drawn him closer. He usually took one or two since he would begin to eat, growing protective of his meal, while he fought. That gave the others a chance to quietly flee.

But Magnar knew he wouldn't stop killing until every human in this vicinity was dead. His rage wasn't mindless, it was calculated, thought out to make sure that nothing and no one could follow him in order to protect Delora and Fyodor.

"Go for the girl!" he heard one shout in a low voice.

"She's a human, sir," someone answered.

Stay away from her! Magnar headed in the direction of the voices.

"I don't care what she is. She made that Duskwalker go to Ackermeadow Village and take that young boy. She's with him, she chose her side, and now she can die along with him."

Magnar tilted his head at that.

Delora had never made Magnar do such a thing, but he knew *exactly* who had. Reia and Orpheus had brought the human they were talking about to his cave and gave it to him to eat to help increase his humanity. Chad, Magnar believed was his name. He'd had no qualms about eating the screaming, fear-filled man at the time.

He definitely didn't once he'd learned Chad had tormented his friend.

Now he understood their want for vengeance.

These Demonslayers had almost harmed his youngling, and his treasured bride – they were planning to use her against him.

"Sir, I don't think we are ready for something like this. It's a Duskwalker. He's already killed one of our men!"

"This is your first official mission, and if you are to die now, then the guild wouldn't want to lessen their strength with your weakness!"

I will destroy them.

"Shit!" someone yelled, just as they loosened an arrow.

Magnar purposely ran straight into it, while someone else rolled to the side to dodge.

The human who had shot the arrow was still hiding in the bushes, and it embedded into Magnar's biceps as he leapt for the shrub. Then, the painful bite of a dagger sunk into his side just as he closed his fangs around his head and squeezed.

I will destroy them all!

He shook his prey, thrashing his head around as the woman screamed and finally gave him the first whiff of fear. These were Demonslayers, unafraid until they were certain of death.

Her brain matter mushed through his fangs when he finally clamped them shut. She went motionless.

"Magnar!"

He spun on all four limbs and galloped straight in the direction he heard Delora shout.

"What the fuck?" the Demonslayer chasing her grunted. "Why can't I grab her?"

"Don't know," another answered, just as Magnar dodged a tree to get around it. The two men came into view. The Demonslayer's eyes widened when he saw Magnar coming for them, before he narrowed them into a glare. He pulled his sword from its sheath. "Watch out!"

Both Demonslayers dove for the ground and rolled out of his swiping reach, landing on their feet to put themselves into a defensive stance. Magnar slid across the ground and roared in their direction.

An arrow pierced through the fur of his back, but he stepped backwards when the Demonslayers rushed forward with their weapons raised.

Beneath the bearskins both were wearing, sleek black clothing covered their bodies completely, except for their eyes.

Magnar grabbed the bladed edge of the sword one man was holding the hilt of, while the other managed to slice him across the stomach as he ran past him. Then he spun and slashed across his back. Magnar's spine arched due to the pain, but he only focused on the Demonslayer in front of him. He yanked the sword towards himself, taking the human off his feet who immediately let go of his weapon.

His stumble allowed Magnar to slash him down his face with his claws.

Neither smelled of fear, only sweat now that they were moving swiftly. It allowed him to know that the Demonslayer that had cut him was currently running towards him from behind.

Magnar turned just his head in a bird-like fashion to look over his back. His body followed, slower in movement, but it allowed him to evaluate his next move for when he fully turned around.

He dove forward to be on his stomach. He missed the sword sailing through the air above his head, then he lunged forward to sink his fangs into his leg and pull.

Instead of finishing the kill, he spun the human and threw him at the other. They both fell into the stream behind them with a splash.

Another Demonslayer came into view.

There were at least another three left beyond this, but it was hard to tell with their basic cloaking aromas.

One continued to unleash arrows that just narrowly missed him. He was thankful for that as his body was rippling in agony from the multiple puncture wounds he had, the arrows jutting out from his body like multiple sail fins, and the severe slashing wounds he had across his torso.

But his pain was diluted in his seething rage, his feathers puffed out in aggression until he was a ball of unbridled *hate*. Delora was gone, most likely hiding behind the trees.

His thoughts were silent, only instinct called.

A rope snagged around his ankle when he leapt to grab the third human who had come to this area between the trees, but it hadn't been enough to save them from his claws. Instead, it aided him. Rather than grabbing ahold of the Demonslayer, Magnar was yanked off his feet.

His claws raked down the Demonslayer's torso, gouging the front of him, and ensuring his death would be long and painful rather than quick.

He turned and swiped his claws through the old, frayed rope to free himself, but nothing happened. He tried again but was unable to cut it as two Demonslayers yanked him across the ground. He reached forward and lifted it, before dragging the two humans forward under his strength.

Magnar gnawed on it.

Another arrow launched and landed just above his arse, making him yelp.

The rope refused to snap, and when it didn't, he realised he was trapped in it. It was enchanted with some kind of spell. Magnar growled before looking up at the humans who were quickly getting to their feet.

Since one was still trying to hold it, about to yank him across the ground again, Magnar pulled with all his strength while on three legs. The human flew through the air with her arms flailing.

She slid across the dirt and snow on her front to land right in front of Magnar's hands.

"Fuck," the female Demonslayer bit, her eyes squinting with a glare as she looked up to him.

Magnar's breaths were heated and huffing loudly. He gave a snort in her direction.

"*Fuck indeed*," Magnar sneered, right before he stabbed his claws down into the back of her neck. Her forehead thudded against the dirt.

Before he could sever her head, a sword cut into the side of his arm, crippling it and making his body dip before he could balance himself.

"This was only meant to be a Demon capture mission," the new Demonslayer yelled through gritted teeth, his voice much older than the others. He raised his sword and slammed it down through Magnar's torso, cutting through him from behind until it came out of his stomach. "But I thought when they told me they found a Duskwalker, that my juniors were ready, and we were lucky. But no. No matter how many arrows we unleash, no matter how many times we wound your fucking kind, you just won't stay down."

The Demonslayer, the one who had originally ordered for the others to target Delora, raised his sword. This time he aimed for Magnar's already torn throat.

He wasn't wrong, though.

Magnar had at least nine arrows jutting from his body, and his fur was coated in as much of his own blood as the humans he'd slaughtered, but he didn't feel any of his energy waning. He didn't feel lethargic except for how his wounds pained him when he moved in certain ways.

The only way to stop a red-eyed Mavka was to cut off its head. To remove its thought before the body literally disappeared into black sand.

Nothing could stop a Mavka.

They weren't alive enough to be weakened by mortal injuries, and they weren't dead enough to stop breathing. They were the creatures of limbo, of dusk and dawn, of life and death. The blood pumping within them didn't give them life, it only gave strength.

The Demonslayer raised his sword again and slammed it down just as Magnar turned onto his side and raised his arm to stop him. He took it through his forearm instead. His arm slapped against his chest, taking the worst of the blow and stopping the rest of the sword point from going so far as to pierce his heart.

The human had no idea if he just did the same to his skull, he might kill him – depending on if he was strong enough to pierce through his nearly indestructible skull.

"Even a Demon will die if you shoot it enough," the Demonslayer said through gritted teeth, spittle spraying, while trying with all his might to push down before he twisted the sword. "But you? Your kind just will not cease! You slaughter until you are the victor! Until you've eaten *everything.* Why won't you just fucking die?!"

"Because humans are weak," Magnar snarled as he reached up with his free hand and grabbed the hilt of the sword to clamp the human's fists to it. *"Because Demons are weak."* He rose to his knees, already towering over the Demonslayer before he even made his way to his hoofed feet. *"And you are both the same. Nothing but food. Nothing but stupid. Nothing but prey for us."*

The Demonslayer tried to yank his hands free, his stance strong, but it was nothing compared to the strength of a Mavka.

"Damn you! Let go of me!"

"My suffering only makes me stronger. Whereas yours is pathetic."

"Your kind is worse than the foul Demons that terrorise us humans." Another arrow was unleashed from the side, and it sunk with a *thwap* into Magnar's back. He just chuckled at it. "Your kind don't deserve to exist!"

Magnar released one hand and wrapped it around the human's throat, easily lifting him off the ground so they could face each other on the same level.

"Monster!"

"I am fine being a monster." Magnar darted his head forward and clamped it around the Demonslayer's entire head. His voice radiated from his mind as he said, *"If it means I can protect those I care for."*

If the world wanted to treat him a certain way because of the way he was born, something he couldn't control nor change, and *dare* to harm the few creatures in his life he wanted to care for and protect, then Magnar would give it what it wanted – an ugly, ferocious monster.

The roar he heard within his skull was unafraid, only filled with anger, and hatred, and bravery.

The sound was cut short when he clamped his fangs shut and pulverised his entire skull. It splattered a burst inside his mouth.

When he dropped his headless body to the ground with a thud, his upright position put strain on the rest of him, but he refused lower himself to all fours despite being in his most monstrous form.

"Will you face me, or will you run?" he asked the remaining Demonslayer.

He eyed the direction he knew them to be since they were covered in sweat and a tiny hint of fear. All their companions were dead. They were the last one remaining. They must know that Magnar wasn't going to let them live.

"Screw this," he heard a man grumble, before the sound of footsteps tapped against the ground in the opposite direction.

With a roar, Magnar landed on his hands. He sprinted after the last man and caught up to him in only a few strides. The human's breaths were sharp, sawing in and out of him as he fled, but nothing could outrun a Mavka on all fours – *nothing.*

He died with Magnar's claws embedded into his spine.

THIRTY-FOUR

Delora, with her eyes clenched shut, flinched every time she heard either a yelp from Magnar, or the brutal sound of a Demonslayer dying.

Although she knew he was doing this to protect her and Fyodor, it was still unsettling to know he was killing her kind. It wasn't a battle, but a fucking *slaughter*.

There was no remorse, no hesitation, from either party.

She was lucky she'd turned incorporeal, otherwise she would have been captured, and either killed or used as bait. The scream that had come out of her had been a startled one since she'd been hiding behind a tree and hadn't thought she'd be found. She was transparent, for goodness' sake!

She didn't know what to do but call for Magnar's help when she started being chased. Delora had run, wishing she could support Fyodor's limp head as she sprinted.

Delora hadn't known that if she turned intangible while holding Fyodor their body would become ghostly too.

Unfortunately, their skull remained solid and weighed heavily. Although she couldn't perceive them in her arms, she squeezed them to her torso so as to not lose them. They'd most likely scuttle off and try to join the battle because of all the blood.

Currently, they seemed to be in a sleep state, unmoving and unaware of anything.

At first, she'd thought they were dead!

She'd turned physical just to put her ear to their chest to make sure they were alive. They'd woken up immediately and fought her to get to all the blood nearby.

When she'd turned incorporeal again, they reassumed their sleep state.

Nothing could have been more relieving than to know she could protect them herself. Not completely, since their skull was exposed, but as long as she remained out of danger, they were safe.

It made sense she could hold them like this, considering she'd carried them in her womb.

But Delora wished this would hurry up and end.

Although this had been going on for only a short period, it felt like time had stopped flowing. Everything had slowed down. Seconds painstakingly ticked by, forcing her to digest every disturbing sound.

A woman's dying scream reminded her of the last one she'd heard, the one she'd caused, and the grunts and yells of men reminded her of when she'd drove a kitchen knife into Hadith's back.

"It's fine," she whispered, glad she wasn't physical, otherwise she thought she might have vomited.

She *needed* to move past this. She didn't want it to linger in her mind anymore. Delora didn't want it to be a part of her any longer.

"Everything is fine. It's over, you can't change what you did. He's doing this to protect you, to protect us."

There was no way the Demonslayers would have let them walk away with a friendly wave goodbye. From the moment they unleashed their first arrow, the one that had gone all the way through Magnar's neck with a *squirt* of purple blood before it sunk into the tree beside him, it was always going to be a fight to the death.

The Demonslayers had started the fight. *This is their fault.* Delora and Magnar had no interest in them until the humans had made them their targets.

We'd just been minding our own damn business. We weren't hurting anyone!

"Monster!" she heard one of the Demonslayers yell. The seething, dark tone had her heart shrivelling inside her chest.

He's not a monster.

He was charming and kind and so caring that he'd wormed his way into Delora's heart despite that he looked... wrong, odd, and a little scary.

She wanted to help. She wanted nothing more than to grab a sword and protect Magnar as much as he was trying to protect her, but she couldn't. She didn't have any fighting skills, and she needed to keep Fyodor safe.

If their skull breaks, they'll die. But the same thing was true for Magnar as well. *Fuck. What will happen to me if he dies?*

Would they go to the void where all deceased souls went, or would they go somewhere else? Perhaps nowhere, no longer existing in any plane?

Would Fyodor be killed since they were so young and needed assistance just to lift their newly formed and heavy skull?

If humans discover them... they would poke, prod, and torture them until they knew everything about them.

Delora had new fears, ones that involved the people she cared about.

The fighting came to an abrupt halt.

For a long while, it was silent.

The wind was so unnervingly soft that even the leaves didn't rustle together. She found that much more unsettling. There was not a single shout, nor footstep.

All she heard was the echoing noise of a high-pitched, quiet whine that sounded on every exhale.

Her face scrunched up as her eyes bowed in understanding. She knew it was over, and all that remained was Magnar and the agony he must be in.

He sounds like he's in so much pain.

"Delora," he gently called, unable to smell her like this, unable to find her.

Part of her didn't want to step out from her hiding place. Not because she was afraid. She just didn't want to witness the gore and bloodshed. The human blood that must be covering him. All his wounds. She didn't want to face the reality that people were dead because of her.

But Delora wasn't that cowardly.

She stood up from where she'd been squatting inside of a shrub to hide herself and Fyodor completely so another Demonslayer couldn't see them.

"O-over here," she stuttered.

She slowly made her way closer to where she could hear Magnar to meet him. She caught a glimpse of his blood-coated face at the same time his orbs moved to her.

"Do not come any closer!"

Delora halted, unable to see over the shrubs and below the lowest branches of green leafy trees separating them.

"Are you okay?"

He must have been standing on all fours since she could just see his head, and his orbs were such a deep crimson colour that she knew something was terribly wrong. His skull turned one way and then the other, looking around his environment.

"I do not want you to see, Delora," he answered, and the tone in his voice told her everything she needed to know. He was worried she'd be afraid of what she saw, perhaps come to fear him. *"I just wanted to know you were safe."*

Despite his apprehension, she watched as he stood. His body morphed from what she knew was his most frightening and dangerous form, to how he normally was.

The big Duskwalker that was gentle with her.

Even if she had come closer and seen the result of his slaughter, she wouldn't have been afraid of him. He was her protector, he was Magnar, and he'd done this to make sure she remained unharmed.

I... could never be angry at him for something like this.

He approached Delora cautiously, and the closer he came, the whiter his orbs became.

Ten arrows were embedded in his body, and she could see he had many wounds by the flared and angry open pockets that littered his torso. They were hidden away by his clothing when it reappeared.

Although his clothing was clean of blood, she could see splatters of it over his skull and hooves. It left drip marks across the snow as they thickly fell from the tips of his claws. *Red* blood, mostly, signalling that it was from the humans he'd killed.

He lowered himself when he was directly in front of her, trying to appear not as big or scary. Her heart stung at him doing this.

It showed that the trust between them was thin.

Despite his extensive injuries, he stemmed his whines until they were barely noticeable, but she could see the way his shoulders shuddered whenever he exhaled. For whatever reason, Magnar was trying to hide that he was in pain.

Can Duskwalkers be insecure like men? If so, she thought that was beyond adorable.

"Thank you for protecting me." She lifted one of her hands like she was going to pet his snout.

She was still intangible, and the only reason she remained this way was so Fyodor would remain asleep and wouldn't go into a craze. She was glad she couldn't smell the metallic tang of blood that must be saturating the air, since it would have been gut-churning.

The tension in Magnar's shoulders visibly eased, and she knew he wanted nothing more than to nuzzle into her nearly invisible hand with the way he rotated his head side to side.

She thought his orbs would turn to their usual green, but instead, they faded into orange. He stepped away with hesitant movements, turning his head to the side as if to avoid her gaze.

"Would you mind stepping back for a while?" he asked, keeping himself small and unthreatening.

Her brows furrowed deeply. "Aren't we going to go home now?"

Delora didn't want to remain here any longer than what was necessary.

His orbs flashed white before they turned an even darker colour of orange. *I... don't trust that colour.* It often signalled his guilt.

He started picking at the grass that was jutting out from the thin blanket of snow. Delora had never seen Magnar nervously fidget like this before.

"Demons will come here."

"Exactly."

Although the sun was rather high, this much blood might

attract any Demons who were hiding in the shade above the Veil. They'd brave momentarily burning in the light just to get to the corpses.

"It would be a waste for them to eat the Demonslayers," he muttered even softer.

Delora's form wavered when a terrible feeling sunk its way through her entire being.

"What are you trying to say, Magnar?"

He took in a large breath before he sighed it out.

"There is much humanity for me here. If I do not eat them, then the Demons will, and they will grow stronger. Their deaths would be pointless."

Delora took a step back as she shook her head.

Killing them was one thing, but *eating* them was different.

She knew he had in the past – they'd spoken about this – but she didn't think Magnar would continue to eat her kind.

"No," she gasped, her head continuing to shake. "Please don't."

She waited for the feeling of disgust to overtake her, but it never did. She wasn't upset that he was going to eat her kind, but what it would *give* him.

He brought his gaze to her almost hesitantly.

"I have to, Delora."

"But why?" she cried, her brows crinkling together deeply.

He braved stepping closer so she couldn't retreat far.

"Because if I do not, I will never be better for you. I will not be able to take care of you properly." He lifted his hands so he could stare down at his claws with a thoughtful head twist. "I want to do better. I want to understand, and I cannot do that if I do not consume more humanity."

"But I don't want you to change," she admitted.

She didn't want Magnar to grow smarter, wiser. She feared, truly feared, if he did, that he wouldn't want her anymore. Currently, he was content with Delora and didn't see any problem with her, but Delora *knew* she wasn't perfect.

She wasn't brave, or strong, or even particularly smart. She was average, she was boring, and she knew she was useless. She was depressed and knew that her trauma often made her act out of character.

She hadn't *always* been a crier.

Delora had little to offer Magnar.

She couldn't help him fight, didn't know how to tend to the garden. She hadn't even been able to help him build the house. All she could do was paint it, but she worried that if he changed, he'd no longer like the bright images she painted – something Hadith had deemed immature. Would he think it was childish when he no longer looked at the world with a sense of innocence?

Would Magnar grow resentful when he realised the soul he'd taken was Delora's, and he was bound to her eternally? Would he regret his decision?

She'd once told him she was a terrible person. She was a murderer, and he currently saw no issue with that. But in gaining more humanity, he would understand, truly understand, how wrong her actions had been.

Things weren't perfect between them, but at least there was *something* there. A fondness in each other's presence.

She desperately didn't want to lose that. It was the only thing that kept her holding on to the want to live in this cruel and dark world. Without it, without this clumsy, silly Duskwalker, Delora thought she'd drown.

He'd become her lifeline.

It was selfish of her, and she knew she shouldn't want him to eat those people because they were human, but the only reason she didn't want him to was because she was afraid of losing him.

"I am always worried of hurting you, Delora. I cannot hold you, and it eats at me." Blue began to shine from his orbs, a yawning depth of colour that signified how much it weighed on him. "I cannot touch you. I cannot be near you for too long. I want to be close to you, but every time I do, I can feel my claws sinking into your skin. There is still so much you have taught me that I do not understand, and I want to understand... for you. It feels like parts of me are missing. There are *thoughts* that are missing when I think. I can feel the blank spaces. I cannot control my mind, my emotions, my body."

"Y-you can learn," she offered. "I-I can teach you."

He shook his head as his shoulders slumped. The backs of his hands fell against the ground to be limp.

"That is not how it works. I am stunted and have known this for a long time, even before I met you. I can remember everything, but that does not mean I understand what I have been shown or taught. This is as far as my humanity goes. It will not get better. It will not develop further."

Delora tried to bite her lip again, but she didn't feel it other than pressure. She wanted to argue, but as much as she tried to think of a good reason as to why he shouldn't do this, the sorrow she heard in his voice silenced her.

"I want to do this for you," he continued, coming closer until he was crowding around her intangible form as if he wanted to stop her from escaping. "I have been waiting a long time for you without even knowing it, but I am not ready for you." Magnar brushed the tips of his blood-stained claws over Fyodor's physical skull. "I barely even understand what they mean, other than I must protect them."

As much as he was saying he wanted to do this for her, she knew that wasn't the truth. He wanted to do this for himself, and Delora couldn't argue with that.

I can't be selfish. No matter her concerns, she didn't want the guilt of that weighing on her conscience.

Magnar deserved to be happy and to make his own choices, even if they weren't what she wanted.

"Okay," she conceded, sincerely hoping she didn't regret it. "If that's what you want, then I give you my permission."

It was obvious he wanted her consent, which was why he'd asked her rather than just doing it.

"Thank you," he rasped, reaching up to brush the backs of his claws through her ghostly cheek. "I will be better for you. You will see."

Delora just nodded, knowing her words would sound mangled.

With her head bowed, she backed away and left Magnar to be on his own – and get out of earshot if she could.

The wait was nearly excruciating. She wished she something else to preoccupy her mind, but there was nothing she could do but stand in the forest. She couldn't kick snow or tufts of grass, since her foot would just pass through them. She couldn't fidget by picking at low-hanging leaves.

All she had were her thoughts to keep her company, and they continued to rotate with conflicting and horrible emotions.

The hardest thing for Delora was trying to figure out what she felt for Magnar. Desire was one of them, but where did the root of her desires come from?

She wanted to be touched, to feel good, to feel like a woman worth touching, but would it have mattered if it was anyone else? Yet, when she pictured his face, his fox skull filled with a purple glow from his floating orbs, something within Delora stirred. Every. Single. Time.

I'm... attracted to him. A Duskwalker. Some strange creature that was violent and ruthless, as he'd just shown her. A human killer – eater.

But every time he got too close to her, and she managed to snag a whiff of his intoxicating scent or feel the overbearing heat rolling off him, Delora's body would sing with want, with desire, for *him*.

I care for him. How deeply, she wasn't sure. All she knew was that she... needed Magnar in her life. But she needed him how he was. To be tender with her, to dote on her with attention and affection.

Her expression crinkled into in a cringe as her eyes searched the ground, as if the answer was there in the dirty snow.

Why won't the paranoia stop? It was always there. It always lingered, and just when she thought she was better, something would happen to make her feel as though her insides were crawling with invasive bugs.

Would Magnar gaining more humanity be the solution she needed? Or would it be the final strike that left Delora in a cold place where she was forced to live a life she didn't want?

I'm so scared. Scared of him changing.

Everything hung in the balance, and those scales could tip until she fell into total despair.

She wished she could take in a calming breath.

He's been a while. Then again, she knew he must be eating seven to eight *humans*. Anxiety filled her all the way to the core.

Delora stiffened when she heard movement approaching her.

"Where are you?" Magnar grated just off to the side.

Her lips thinned, the urge to bite them shut strong.

"O-over here," she squeaked.

If she'd been able to feel her heart, it would have squeezed in panic.

As he approached, she noticed there was no blood on his white skull like he'd cleaned it. Even his claws and feet were clean.

Did-did he wash in the stream? She'd seen it briefly when she'd been fleeing from the Demonslayers.

Magnar's orbs were a flaring colour of red, and the way he was approaching her was menacing. That wasn't what had Delora backing up a step.

It was because he looked... different.

His skull was the same, his antlers were the same, she even thought his height was the same, but she knew the Duskwalker approaching her was thicker, wider.

His black shirt didn't hang so loosely around his torso, his shoulders and biceps looked bulkier. His spine appeared straighter, no longer curved, and his posture was nearly perfect as he stalked closer.

Other than the white knuckles and all his finger joints as well, the rest of the bones around his hands had sunken beneath his dark-grey flesh. His three-toed hooves had separated into five, almost looking as though the hoof sections were just strange toes, while the heel of his foot now pressed firmly against the ground.

He was able to walk properly, to strut.

Although he still had feathers poking out from the neckline of his shirt, they didn't seem as long or puffy.

Magnar had changed physically, and so suddenly that it was staggering.

At the colour of his orbs, Delora wanted to retreat. Red meant anger, or hunger – but he said he didn't feel hunger anymore.

Something's wrong.

"Stay," he demanded, and the sternness of it, the command of it, had Delora frozen on the spot. She opened her mouth to say something, *anything,* but the words wouldn't come out. "Turn physical."

Her eyes darted away for an excuse, any excuse.

"I-I can't. What about Fyodor?" she mumbled weakly. "If they smell all the blood, they'll–"

Magnar shot his hands forward, and the crack of his claws breaking into the tree just behind her had her flinching.

"It's all gone. I made *certain* of that." He twisted his head at her, slowly inching closer to her face. "Turn physical, Delora."

With her eyes clenched shut, her body sunk as her feet touched the ground. She began to turn touchable, fragile, *unsafe*.

A large, warm hand wrapped around her throat to cup the underneath of her jaw, and her heart, that had already been beating erratically, thumped even faster. She clutched onto Fyodor, who began to stir wildly, keeping them still so they couldn't attack her.

Magnar tilted her head upwards.

Then her eyes flung open wide when a wet, yet slightly rough, tongue ran across her lips. *He licked me.*

Shock had her lips parting and then that tongue ran across her lips again, this time dipping in between them to catch her teeth.

Her heart was still beating fast, but her panicked breaths slowed, as did Fyodor's movements, when Magnar drew that firm tongue across her. She didn't know what compelled her to part her lips further, but when she did, the slippery organ sunk into her mouth to lick the inside of it completely, from her cheek, over her tongue, then to the other cheek.

His tongue only darted back so that he could dip it inside again, over and over, and she nearly moaned. There was a sweetness from him that was coating her tastebuds with something tantalising.

There was no copper taste, no blood, as if he'd washed his mouth out in the stream. All she tasted was sweetened saliva.

She pushed her tongue up to collect it a little better, to lick at it, almost drink it, which incidentally caused her to brush his. Magnar gave a deep growl.

Before Delora knew it, he reached down, grabbed the back of her thighs, lifted her and then slammed her against the tree. He twisted his head for a better angle and parted his fang-filled jaws so he could press them slightly around her face. Then his tongue pushed in even deeper.

He licked more incessantly across her tongue, which was beginning to greet his own.

It was the strangest kiss she'd ever received, but she knew that's exactly what it was – a kiss. A deep and *passionate* one.

All her worry and near hyperventilating anxiety faded to leave something warm and fluttering in its place.

Delora closed her eyes in satisfaction and clung to Magnar with a death grip, refusing to let him get away. Since he'd lifted her so she could greet him, she knew she was at least a metre off the ground. She wrapped her legs firmly around the bottom of his ribcage. Her moulding thighs wouldn't wrap around his body completely, but she dug her heels in to get him closer, to have him completely pressed against her body.

Her arms wrapped around his shoulders. One snaked its way under his shirt from the collar so she could grab a fistful of feathers and long fur, while the other grabbed the base of an antler. She kept him to her.

His large hands were now gripping both her arse cheeks to hold her up. She didn't mistake the appreciative squeeze he gave them, and she tried to sink her arse into them so he would grab them harder. She couldn't feel the usual stab of claws when his fingertips dug in *hard,* and knew he must have gained the control to sheath them.

She couldn't taste blood, only that delicious sweetness, but Delora didn't think she would have cared right then. Whatever had driven him to do this was the security she'd needed, and she moaned into his hot mouth, hearing it slightly echo.

"Delora," Magnar groaned in return, not needing to remove his swirling tongue to speak to her, since it radiated from his skull.

She tried to match his long, invasive, and explorative tongue with her much fatter and shorter one, slipping it any way she could. It was messy, and both of them struggled, but neither pulled away.

Instead, Magnar's hands gripped her arse so hard she knew he bruised her skin right before he shoved his tongue even further. She was forced to swallow it.

"Nhn!" Delora gasped, feeling her throat contracting around it.

Her own saliva flooded her mouth, her throat trying to get it to either swallow his tongue whole or push it out, but it didn't relent.

"Fuck." Magnar shuddered, his body quaking as his feathers tried to stand on their ends in her tight fist. "Why does that feel so good?"

He drew his tongue away, giving Delora a moment to breathe as he collected every drop of liquid that had filled her mouth. Then he sunk it back in. She tensed in his arms, but didn't, in any way, shape, or form, try to stop him.

It was uncomfortable in its own way, but she adored it, adored the way he was reacting, that he was doing this. She tried to urge him on by bucking her hips against his torso, wanting him to do it again and again.

She wanted him to fuck her throat with his tongue.

"Do you know how long I've wanted to do this?" he muttered. "To lick you like this?"

Oh, God. I need him.

Her pussy clenched in desire, wishing his tongue was thrusting there instead of breeching her throat. She wanted it swirling inside her, collecting the liquid of her arousal as he stole it. *I want to come around it.* She let out another moan, trying to find friction against her now pounding, needy clit. The entrance to her core was slick and begging for attention.

All it found was the flat plane of muscle just beneath his chest.

A bawking sound caught both their attention. Their heads darted away from each other when they realised the strangled noise had come between them.

Poor Fyodor had been squished between the tight press of their bodies and had been struggling to get free. They pushed their little rabbit skull up and gave them both a very irritated huff.

With panted breaths, her face blistering hot from both arousal and embarrassment, Delora faced Magnar, who was still holding her in the air.

His orbs presented a deep, hunger-filled purple, and he was

staring at her as well, panting in return.

He darted his snout closer and drew his tongue over the corner of her jaw, dabbing it closer and closer until he ran it over her ear. Delora let out a high-pitched cry. A shiver annihilated her senses as her entire body was wracked with goosebumps.

Her head turned to the side to give him as much access as he wanted. He continued to lick at her skin, over her ear, and down the side of her exposed throat.

"I like the way you taste. It matches your scent."

She dug in the heels of her boots and arched into him. She'd been sent hurtling into arousal, and now her body was screaming that he ease it.

Magnar let out a light, rumbling growl as he said, "If they weren't here—"

He paused, like he thought better of what he was going to say. His body tensed, his fingers squeezing her arse like he wanted to keep kneading it in his soothing palms.

What... what was he going to say? She wanted to know what would have happened if Fyodor wasn't here.

Would he have continued kissing her? Would he have touched her... maybe even more? Would he have fucked her right here against the tree out in the open forest?

What did Delora want?

All of it. Right then, she wanted everything with the way her body was aching and tingling.

"We should go home," he eventually said while turning his head to the side. "The shadows are getting longer."

She was almost tempted to tell him she didn't care that the sun was going down. She just wanted him to touch her.

She wasn't that brave. *Maybe one day...*

"Okay," she answered softly after nibbling on her bottom lip in thought, her voice so croaked and lust-filled it shook on both syllables.

Magnar lowered her by sliding her down his body, but she didn't miss the lick he gave to the outside of his fangs, one that slipped over his nose hole as if he was just trying to taste the scent in the air. And oh yes, she felt something hard running over her body as he slipped her over his groin.

It wasn't long, maybe only partially extruded, but she knew that was his cock. He gave a groan when her body clenched for it – like he could *smell* her growing slicker.

Once she was firmly on her feet, her hands on his torso to steady herself since she felt a little dizzy, she stood there gazing up at him. It appeared neither one was ready to leave their position since they were still pressing up against each other. His cock, which seemed much thicker than she knew it to be, was pressing in between her navel and her large breasts.

I wonder what would happen if I tried to touch him...

What if she lowered herself just enough that it sat between her breasts? She fisted his shirt.

She was *so* tempted to.

"I noticed that they become untouchable with you except for their skull," Magnar commented, nodding the tip of his snout at Fyodor.

Delora cleared her throat, as if that was enough to clear her mind, and looked down to Fyodor clinging across her chest. A part of her couldn't believe she'd been contemplating dirty thoughts with them there.

A boob job? Really, Delora? Then again, she thought Magnar may like it. Most human men did. Her breasts were large and soft, and he did seem to like touching her. She wondered if the reverse was true.

"Yeah. I didn't know that would happen, but I think it's because I've never gone into my Phantom form while holding them."

"Do you think you could hold onto them while travelling fast like that?"

Now that the flames of desire were being fanned out by their conversation, Delora let out a small sigh.

"I guess so." She lifted her face once more. "Why?"

"Because, as it stands, I have extensive injuries over my body." Her eyes drifted over Magnar, knowing that his clothes were hiding his injuries. "We cannot stay above the surface for me to heal, but on our journey home, I will attract the Demons by my blood."

"What are you trying to say?"

"We are going to have to run." Delora's face paled. "I will have to shift and run on all fours, and I'm going to need you to hold onto them and follow me in your Phantom form. You won't be impeded by your normal human speed, so you should be able to keep up with me."

"You'll be attacked?"

"Most definitely."

"Okay. Fuck," she grumbled, palming her forehead and brushing her long fringe from her face. "Shit."

That meant she would have to watch him be attacked while they sprinted home. She wasn't fond of having to witness that.

It took Delora a few moments to realise, after digesting this information, that along with Magnar's physical changes, his speaking mannerisms had changed as well.

THIRTY-FIVE

The journey back had been significantly shorter, but Delora would have preferred it to have been long.

While she floated beside him, Magnar sprinted on all fours and was attacked multiple times. He just shook the Demons off when they attached themselves to him and continued forward. He couldn't stop, otherwise he would have been overrun by them.

He was littered with shallow claw marks, but nothing as damaging as what the humans had done – something she'd only seen when he returned and changed his shirt.

The one he'd been wearing had been saturated with blood.

She'd offered to clean his wounds, which he allowed, but there was no need to bandage them. Although they would remain open, they'd stopped bleeding, and any infection would be healed tomorrow.

She'd seen it once before, how black sand had covered his body after the fight with the creepy snake-like Demon, so she knew there wasn't anything to be truly worried about.

But washing his wounds had allowed Delora to see the massive changes in his body. He was definitely fuller, thicker, bigger even. His muscles had flared out, and even though they were still dense, they filled him out, so he didn't look so gangly and scrawny.

Most of his sternum bone had sunken beneath his flesh so that only the top could be seen, and the bones on his arms had been eaten up by the new muscle that had grown. The only major bones on him that were still visible were his hands, elbows, spine vertebrae, and ribcage.

Everything else was nearly gone from what she'd seen with his shirt off.

It was a lot to think about, to absorb.

For the second time since he'd built it for her, she'd used the cooking hearth. She adored this space and knew she'd be able to cook whatever she wanted since he'd gone out of his way to make it large and obtained everything she'd need to cook with. Pots, pans, a proper cooking rack.

She scooped her steaming vegetable soup into her wooden bowl, her brows crinkling in thought. *I'm the only one who seems to be stuck as myself.*

First Fyodor had such a remarkable change, and now Magnar too. Delora was the only one who hadn't changed.

I guess that's not true. I did become a Phantom.

But physically, she mostly felt the same.

A small smile curled Delora's lips when she exited the front door and saw Magnar sitting on the porch with Fyodor. She didn't know how Fyodor ended up in the position where they were seated upright next to him, but when their skull started falling to the side, Magnar reached out to save them.

He held it by grabbing it from above.

Since he'd been sitting on the porch for a long while, Delora plopped herself next to Magnar. Fyodor instantly sensed her and crawled over to be in her lap. She patted their back, and they wiggled for more while giving a little rumble.

With her warm bowl of vegetable soup hovering above her lap so it didn't press against Fyodor, she slowly ate, watching the flames of the campfire near the porch steps.

Fyodor seemed less inclined to cling to her now that they had a heavy skull and a weak neck that couldn't support it. They often placed it over her shoulder and kind of hung themself there in order to support its weight when she was moving around.

She didn't mind. Whatever made Fyodor comfortable would suit Delora.

After a few moments of silence, a little awkward about talking to Magnar now that he'd changed and wondering what that truly meant for her, she managed to brave a peek at him from the corner of her eyelids.

His snout was pointing towards the sky, almost as if he could see clearly through the Veil's mist to look at the stars.

But what started out as a sly glance turned into a full stare.

His glowing orbs were rapidly changing colours. One minute blue, the next a dark green, a reddish pink, and they often changed to orange.

She paused with a spoonful of food near her mouth when his orbs flared red for a long while before fading to orange. Then they started flicking through different colours again.

It was obvious he was deep in thought.

"How come you started the campfire?" she asked, trying to make conversation to draw him back to reality. "I don't need it now that you built me the cooking fireplace."

"I like the way it looks," he muttered quietly as he turned his gaze down to the flames. His orbs continued to change colour, but it at least slowed as he watched them flicker. "I like that it brightens the world. It's always dark here."

Delora chose to stare at the flames with him, watching it crackle whenever a bit of branch or stick snapped under the drying heat. It would spark embers to float into the air, before cooling and dropping back into the fire or around it as grey ash.

In her peripheral, she noticed Magnar's hands had interlocked and they occasionally squeezed each other as though he was filled with tension. She worried he'd cut the backs of his hands with the way the tips of his shiny claws dug into his flesh.

She wanted to pry, but she didn't know if that was a good idea. She didn't want to upset him or make him uncomfortable.

I don't really know him. Conversations between them hadn't always been the easiest. But Delora had shared her story with him, and she wanted to learn more about Magnar, about his thoughts and feelings – especially now, when he may be able to express them better.

"Are... you okay?" she prodded. "I've never seen your eyes do that." She thought at any point they might just start swirling a rainbow. "Is it because of your wounds?"

"I have much to reflect on."

Delora looked down to Fyodor and began stroking the length of their snout, making them fidget happily on her lap. *They're such a cutie.* She liked that they always curled into her touch.

"Do you want to talk about it? You don't have to if you don't want to."

Magnar gave a thoughtful hum but didn't tap at his snout like he usually would when he made that kind of sound.

"From what I can remember, I have been alive for a hundred and twenty years, if not more. I have seen the world lighten and darken hundreds of thousands of times, and there is so much to remember that I have done. But I regret very little."

"That's a long time to look back on," Delora mumbled. "I can't imagine living for that long."

Then again... wasn't there the possibility that she could since she'd given Magnar her soul?

How do I feel about living a hundred and twenty years? Up until now, life hadn't been pretty fair. *I guess it would be okay as long as it's peaceful. And if things between us got better...* Delora thought she *might*, for once in her life, be happy.

"However," he continued, looking up at the sky again and twisting his head as if he saw something moving that she didn't. "I have regrets about... you. That is currently what I am thinking about."

Delora tensed, her knees knocking inwards as if she was trying to shrink inside herself. She wasn't very good at dealing with confrontation or receiving criticism.

She hadn't expected him to come right out and say she was the problem.

Is this it? Perhaps the kiss they'd shared in the forest had been a high from eating, and now he was realising, upon deeper reflection, that Delora wasn't good enough. *I was worried something like this would happen.*

She wouldn't run just because she didn't want to hear the truth, but she did lower her head so her hair would hide her. She bit at her lips to shut them as she fisted the skirt of her dress, trying to steel herself for whatever he was about to say next.

The area suddenly felt *too* quiet. Even the sound of the fire managed to startle her – an involuntary reaction to the trauma she'd received in the past. Loud sounds tended to come with broken glass and possible pain.

"I have not been fair to you," he said, making her breath come out in a mangled, chest-aching rush.

She turned to him with a frown.

"What do you mean?"

"I took your soul without informing you what that would entail."

Delora let out an awkward laugh. "I still gave it to you. I could have asked more questions."

He twisted his head at the sky again, this time the other way.

"I should have learnt more about you, found out why you were so desperate to be rid of it before I asked you for it. Now that you have told me of your past, and I understand what it means, what you have been through, I can see there is much that can hurt a human beyond a physical wound. I should not have taken your soul without explaining what that would mean for you."

"I guess," she answered, fisting the skirt of her dress tighter. "But it's fine. I really don't mind."

With his orbs bright orange, he brought his gaze to her.

"I took away your choice, Delora."

"No, you didn't. You didn't take my soul by force, didn't steal it. Like I said, I gave it to you."

"You threw it at me, to be precise." Delora winced at that. "You weren't giving me your soul because you wanted to be eternally tied to me. You gave it to me because you no longer cared what happened to you, if you lived or died. You were throwing away your soul because your life was meaningless to you, and I see that now."

"I'm sorry," she said as tears of shame began to well.

"Why are you apologising?" he asked. "I should have waited until you were ready. I should have explained everything to you rather than waiting until after you gave it to me. I took your choice away from you by not explaining everything."

"Yeah, but–"

"Would you have given it to me if I had?"

Delora's lips thinned as she thought on her answer, but she

knew it the moment he asked his question.

"No," she admitted, with her shoulders falling. Then she turned her face to him with a beseeching crinkle to her eyelids. "But I'm glad I did, Magnar. I've known for a long time that I'm glad I'm here with you now."

"But I don't understand. Does it not make you angry that you weren't given a proper choice?"

"I would have made the wrong choice, though."

"You still would have had one."

"Magnar, if I hadn't given you my soul, I wouldn't be here right now." Her eyes darted over the features of his strange, yet somehow beautiful face before finally falling over his fangs. They settled there, examining the deadliness of them. "If you had told me everything, I wouldn't have been given the choice either way."

His orbs morphed into a yellow hue.

"What do you mean?"

She averted her gaze simply because she didn't want to see his reaction to what she was about to say, choosing to look at the flames in front of them.

"You would have eaten me. I wouldn't have been given a choice because I would no longer exist in this world. That is the alternative to our situation. Whether it was in anger at something I did or said, or when the snake Demon hurt me, or anytime I've smelled of fear, if I had not given you my soul and rid you of your hunger, you would have eaten me."

His claws clicked against each other as he fidgeted with his hands. He was growing more tense, just as she was.

"Even if that is true..." He fell silent, as if he wanted to argue but couldn't. Then he said, "There are other things that you didn't get to choose, either. Things I didn't get your permission to do to you."

Delora's lips pursed together when she couldn't think of any other choice that had been taken away from her. If he was talking about when they'd touched, she was pretty certain her body had given away just how much she'd wanted it. She'd never said no, except for once, and he'd immediately let her go when she had.

"What do you–"

"I didn't understand what this meant at first," Magnar said while waving his hand in the direction of Fyodor. "I have been thinking of them as a youngling because my connection to them has been disjointed. That we're creators rather than parents. I knew I needed to protect them, that they were small and defenceless, but my care for them was only that, to protect. I didn't ask you if I could do this to you. And this has been... hard on you."

"Babies happen by accident all the time." She tried to laugh it off. "Humans do it all the time. That's the risk we take when we have unprotected sex. We both had a part to play in their creation. I'm at fault too, and... and they're precious to me. From the moment I knew I was pregnant, I wanted them. I've always wanted a child but have never been able to before."

"But... they are Mavka."

"So? They're mine. That's all that matters to me. And they're actually really cute, now that they've stopped trying to bite me."

"It's because you smelled of fear," Magnar grumbled. "That is your own fault."

She gave a little laugh. He was right, and she couldn't deny that. Now that she looked back on it, she'd been remarkably silly.

"But wouldn't you prefer a human child? I cannot give you that."

Delora shrugged and looked down at little Fyodor in her lap. A small smile played across her lips. Sure, they were different from what she'd imagined her whole life, but so was Magnar.

"A part of me is glad you're not human," Delora admitted as she turned her eyes to the sky, wishing she could see the stars but was content with looking up at the night horizon. "My relationship with humans hasn't been all sunshine and rainbows. I know Fyodor isn't what others would deem a normal child, nor is what we're doing, but I'm glad I'm here with you now, and that they were born, even if they frightened me a little at first. Life can be scary, and all mothers struggle at first in some way or another." Then her lips quirked upwards slightly. "At least I don't have to feed them milk. I think that would have annoyed the shit out of me."

"Humans have milk?"

His question wasn't what Delora had expected him to fixate on, and a laugh burst from her.

"Yes, Magnar. That's what breasts are for. That's why women have them."

"Your breasts do that?" His head darted down to blatantly stare at her tits, tilting as his orbs morphed to bright yellow in curiosity. It just made Delora laugh more. "That is... really strange. I am glad you don't do that."

Magnar leaned his head the opposite way when he realised Delora was laughing because of what he said. Even though it was at his expense, he was relieved she found humour in this, and that she was smiling.

From the moment he reflected back on his time with her and realised his mistakes, he'd been worried about speaking with her about them. He wanted her to know that he understood what he did was wrong, that he'd been stupidly fumbling his way through everything, but he needed to know if she regretted it.

Magnar wanted to know the truth, even if it wasn't what he wanted to hear, so he could know where to start in making amends.

It appeared as though he didn't need to.

For whatever reason, Delora held no regrets about what she had done or that things had turned out the way they did. She wanted to be here with him, and that meant... so much.

She is glad that I'm not human, that I'm Mavka.

Bright pink lifted into his orbs, and he covered one eye with a hand, starting to understand the warm, tingly feeling that grew inside him every time he saw this colour. He couldn't put a word to it, but he understood it was because he cared immensely for her. That it was important.

Then Delora did something that had his heart squeezing wonderfully in his chest.

She reached over and grabbed his hand so she could hold it. He stared down at it, the simple touch sending pleasure throughout his entire body.

"What are you doing?" he asked as she laid both their hands on the porch between them.

She tried to push her fingers through the gaps of his own, but her hand wouldn't stretch open that far and only her fingertips reached.

"I'm holding your hand," she answered, smiling at the flames when she looked upon them. "I'm trying to show you it's okay. Humans do this when they want to convey something without having to speak, to show the person they're with that they're not alone or that the other accepts them. However, your hand is too big for me. I should do it the other way."

She unlocked their poorly locked fingers and then moved to hold his thumb. When he did the same to hers, their hands meshed together a lot nicer, even though his swallowed hers so completely that it couldn't be seen.

He looked down at their palms touching, not realising that simply holding her hand could have such a strong symbology.

I wish I had known that sooner. He would have tried to hold her hand when she'd needed comfort.

She'd asked for his hand when bringing Fyodor into the world, but he'd just thought it was because she needed to squeeze the absolute crap out of something.

A tranquil silence fell over them, and Magnar felt the pressure of his thoughts easing, thankful she had braved having this conversation with him. He'd needed it, even if he hadn't shown it.

"Try not to linger on the past," she eventually said. "That's what I'm trying to do. All we can do is learn from our mistakes and move forward. Look to the future. Okay?"

She looked at him expectantly, and he nodded, his snout bouncing through the air.

She answered him with her own nod before slipping her hand from his, even though he didn't want her to. Delora moved to stand, making sure she had a good grip on Fyodor as she did.

"Today has been a really long and eventful day. I'm really

tired, but thank you for this." She gave him a small smile, one that made tenderness burn in his chest. "Goodnight."

She left to go inside, softly closing the door to keep the cool night air out.

Magnar reflected on their conversation and how it'd turned out. Like a habit he hadn't fully shed yet, he lifted his hand to his snout so he could tap a claw at the tip of it.

That's what breasts are for? To make milk for their younglings? And here he had been, stupidly thinking Delora's breasts existed to be played with by him, considering she'd liked it whenever he touched them.

He liked that they were so big they moved under the power of his tongue, forcing him to chase her nipples around. It was like a secret game he was playing with them.

No, he thought sternly. *They are still mine.*

Her scent always grew amazingly sweet and erotic when he did. He liked stroking them with his tongue until she saturated the air with that mouth-watering, gut-clenching, groin-tightening scent.

Can I? Many things had compelled Magnar to lick the inside of Delora's mouth when they'd been in the forest above the surface. He'd had this overwhelming desire to touch her, taste her, swallow her whole – even though he'd made her swallow his tongue.

He'd seen Orpheus lick at Reia's mouth until she pushed him away with a giggle, mostly because Orpheus wanted to make Magnar jealous because he was possessive of his female. He was less so now that Magnar had his own.

He'd had been wanting to try it with Delora because it had looked enjoyable.

But he'd also been testing the limits of his control.

The overwhelming desire to plant his cock in Delora at the time had been strong, but it hadn't made him feel crazed. His cock also hadn't extruded by itself. It had been sheltered by his tentacles, allowing him to become erect without the stinging pain that usually had him whimpering and needy.

His want to be inside Delora had been because he'd wanted to be close with her, not because he'd needed her to ease his pain.

The desire had felt... deeper, different, better.

Magnar brought his sight to the door, wondering if he could be in her presence now without growing desperate.

She is tired. I shouldn't disturb her. But he wanted to hold her more than anything.

With a click of his tongue, his mind was made up. He got to his new and improved feet, thankful he didn't feel any twinges up his legs and back now that they were straight and could support the posture.

Wiggling his toes, he looked down at his feet.

I will need shoes. Ones like Orpheus' now.

He no longer needed slippers for his hooves, since his five toes and the arches of his feet were more human-shaped.

Quietly, Magnar went inside, knowing the fire would put itself out. He made his way to the very back room, trying to keep his steps light even under his heavy frame.

When he opened the door, he found Delora curled up in the nest, wearing one of his shirts. Even though a blanket was covering her, it was easy to see the impression of her body. She was on her side with her knees up, cuddling around Fyodor, who was pressed up against her chest with their head on her arm. Her other arm was draped over the top of them.

Lowering himself next to the nest wall, he brushed the backs of his claws against her face, trying to stir her gently.

Since she hadn't been asleep for long, she woke easily and brought her drowsy, but pretty, brown eyes to his orbs. He knew they would be the only thing she would be able to see in the darkness, making him easy to find.

"Is something wrong?" she asked, her voice filled with sleep. He liked the sound of her voice like this.

"May I lie with you?"

He'd leave if she said no, but he was hoping that wasn't the answer he'd receive.

"Of course." She scooted to give him more room until her back was against one of the walls, dragging Fyodor with her. "This is your bed too, not that you've been using it."

Perhaps Delora didn't know, but Magnar had been sleeping in this room, just... outside of the nest. Desperate to be near her, but unable to be with her.

Carefully, he crawled his way inside and laid down on his side, moving his head until it sat in a way that his antlers didn't bother him.

"Can... I hold you?" He held his breath this time, unsure if she would want that.

His heart thumped heavily in his chest. *Please say yes.*

"Mhm." She gave him a small nod as her eyes drifted closed. "You're really warm. It'll stop me from feeling cold."

Magnar shifted closer until he was able to comfortably put his arms around her. He forced their positions together until she had to let him be her pillow with her face pressed against his firm chest.

Since he was just testing the waters of his new control, he remained as he was, making sure everything was calm within him. When it remained that way, he let out a contented sigh and squeezed her closer, brushing the side of his jaw against her silky hair.

This was more than he'd been able to do before.

He knew she was asleep when her breaths deepened and evened out, and Magnar brought the hand resting on top of her to her face so he could brush her hair back. Then he carefully drew the claw tip of his index finger down the edge of her jaw, his stomach tingling with strong emotions as he gazed at her.

He felt not a single shred of tiredness within her embrace.

She is so lovely.

He drew the side of his fingertip over the length of her cute nose, before brushing the back of a claw over her high and rounded cheek bone. Then he gently stroked down her jaw again, feeling her head turn up, this time in welcome for it despite being asleep.

But it was his thumb he used to brush over her lips, feeling the thinner upper lip before gently brushing the bottom one. He parted the bottom one, growing ever fascinated with the softness.

From the moment he'd tasted them in the forest, knew how delicious her saliva was, how warm her mouth was, how tough her throat was, Magnar had felt an overwhelming urge to lick her lips again. Constantly, over and over and *over* again, and he knew with absolute certainty that he would never grow tired of doing so. He would never be satisfied.

A hunger he was very much delighted in having.

He wanted to lean closer and do so now, the need pestering at him, but he didn't. The Magnar from before, the one with less humanity, would have fallen victim to the nagging in his mind and would have tried until he'd woken her.

Needing to move away from that thought since purple flickered in his vision, he drifted his claw over the column of her throat. She let out a breathy pant and angled her throat slightly.

Magnar licked at his snout.

I like it when she makes that sound.

Even though he wanted to, he didn't go lower on her body. That was too much for him. If he felt how squishy and sublime she was in his palms, he knew he'd want to touch more until he was satisfied, until he relearned every inch of her.

Instead, he raised his claws so he could comb them through her long black hair, feeling the glossy strands tangling him up. He wanted them to loop around his digits until he was permanently captured by them.

Magnar wanted to become their prey.

She hadn't started trying to style her hair in any way because she didn't have any hair ties. *I'll get her a thousand, however many she needs. If she does her hair as beautifully as she paints, then I know it will be just as mesmerising.*

He accidentally nicked her ear with his claw, not enough to cut it, but enough to make her release another shallow breath.

Magnar chuckled lightly to himself.

With a very quiet whisper, he said, "You have such sensitive ears, my little raven. It makes me always want to play with them."

He drew the tip of his claw behind the shell of it, just wanting to hear her make that little sound again and nothing more.

"Magnar," she moaned, squirming against him while shivering.

The air was spiced with an intoxicating scent, the one that informed him she was becoming aroused. It was swift, taking him by surprise, and it clutched at him terribly.

She moaned my *name in her sleep?* That made his gut tighten. Purple flared in his vision, and he drew away from her in hopes her scent would ease so he could remain.

It didn't. Instead, her breathing grew shallow as her chest flushed. She drew the blanket back like she was growing hot, and the tantalising view of her cleavage, her soft and round breasts, nearly spilled from her sleep shirt. He caught a peek at silky thick thighs before she tucked the blanket around her waist.

She moaned in her sleep, licking at her lips before relaxing. Magnar realised her scent was deepening by the second, even though he'd stopped affectionately touching her.

She was aroused, needy. He desperately hoped he'd stirred her into dreaming of him. Of him *touching* her.

Delora had been the alluring champion of each of his dreams since he'd met her. He wanted to be hers as well.

I want to ease her. Delora grinding on him in the forest hadn't escaped his notice, nor had her heady scent of need at the time.

He'd been so close, nearly taking her supple body right there and then.

He thought she may accept his touch now, but he didn't know if he could trust himself yet. Even so, she was asleep. He wasn't going to wake her.

But Magnar could feel his tentacles shifting, could feel them wrapping around his cock when it started slipping from his seam. He was reacting to her scent, her little pants, the sensual view of her laying there so docile for him.

I want to keep laying here with her. I want to hold her.

He couldn't do that in his current state.

Magnar wanted to trust himself, but he didn't know if he could yet.

An idea lit in his mind, one that had him licking at the outside of his fangs. One that had purple flaring deeper in his sight as he moved to crawl out of the bed without disturbing her.

He was determined not to be away from it for long.

THIRTY-SIX

Where does he keep going at night? Delora thought as she watched Magnar. He held onto a table leg he was currently attaching to a dining table he was making and firmly used a mallet to drive in a long nail.

The table was rustic, made up of multiple slices of tree trunks that were secured together by crossing beams of timber beneath it. The outside had uneven edges, but Delora kind of liked it that way. When he asked if she wanted him to smooth it out and make it either rectangular or circular, she'd said no to both.

He's started sleeping with me.

It was nice being enveloped in warmth each night. Sheltered by long and firm limbs while being coated in feathers and fur. Taking in the delicious, soothing scent that had her not-so-subtly burying her head into his nice pectoral muscles.

She liked hearing his strong heartbeat against her ear and feeling the mind-lulling wave of his chest expanding and compressing whenever he took in a big lungful of breath – only to let it out slowly a few seconds later.

The cuddle was intimate and was made more so each night when Delora braved getting a little closer, sneaking him under her blanket so she could inch her ankles between his. She wanted to entwine them.

That wasn't always easy with Fyodor, who now *demanded* to be in the middle of them as though they selfishly wanted both of them to give them comfort.

I wake up in his arms.

Delora couldn't remember the last time she'd awoken in someone's arms.

In the beginning, Hadith had been a big cuddler, and they'd spent many lazy mornings together.

Those days could never compare to the way Delora woke in Magnar's arms, almost angry with herself that she'd need to get up to pee – thankful they now had a chamber pot for her to use. She was considering asking Magnar to make her an outhouse.

Delora would beg him for just a few more minutes, as if she wasn't wide awake, giving any excuse when he said they needed to start their day.

She thought she occasionally felt his wonderful claws stroking her jaw or scraping over her scalp, pulling her deeper into sleep and giving her really pleasant, and occasionally naughty, dreams.

None of this answered why she knew she'd feel a cold spot in the middle of the night. Being enveloped in warmth meant she woke when it was absent.

Last night, he'd woken her accidentally by untangling from her. Delora, half asleep, had felt Magnar slip away. Only to wake with his claws brushing through her hair in late morning.

What is he doing when he leaves?

He'd started lying with her only a few nights ago.

Since then, the house was progressively being furnished like he was a manic who couldn't sit still for even a second. She already had a long couch he'd built from branches and a smaller one to go with it – both of which now just needed fur coverings to make them softer, but were suitable to be sat in.

She had a bench on the porch, so she didn't have to sit on the steps anymore.

He'd made two dining chairs, one for her and one for Reia because he knew having her around made Delora happy. And now he was making a table to go with it.

Speaking of Reia...

A small, pale hand waved in front of her face.

"Earth to Delora," Reia said slowly, trying to get her attention. "Hellooooo?"

"Sorry," Delora mumbled.

She brought her gaze away from Magnar, and perhaps his muscled, round, firm-looking ass that was partially hidden behind his long tail, to look at Reia's frowning face.

I totally wasn't staring at a Duskwalker's ass. Her face started growing warm. *I swear I wasn't.*

Reia was sitting next to her on the outside bench, her blonde hair curtaining around one side of her head and waving over her shoulder. She was giving Delora a frown.

"You seem a little out of it today."

"Not really," Delora tried to laugh off. "Just deep in thought."

Reia's lips thinned into such tight lines they turned white and almost disappeared, and her eyes narrowed into a knowing glare of doubt.

"Liar." Then she sighed. She crossed her arms behind her head to rest against the wall of the house and the backrest. "Then again, not my circus, not my monkeys."

Delora scrunched up her nose. "What does that even mean?"

"Means it's not my problem, nor my business." Her lips curled up slightly. "And you've already bitten my head off a few times for digging for information you don't want to give. You're pretty secretive, you know."

"When you come from the village I did, it was best to just keep your mouth shut or else everyone would know what went on in your house."

Delora could remember *vividly* the day she'd confided in a 'friend' about how Hadith sometimes wouldn't want to have sex with her. It led to everyone thinking there was something wrong with his dick because her 'friend' had told everyone so. This then resulted in Delora getting into a horrible situation where she'd learned that there was nothing wrong with his dick other than the person it was attached to.

She'd just been looking for advice, seeking a way to spice up their relationship outside of the square of her thoughts. Instead, both she and Hadith had been humiliated, and he'd been furious with her.

The following day, those that lived around them confirmed there was nothing wrong with his ability to perform in the bedroom because they'd been heard all night.

Delora shuddered at the memory with repulsion.

"Probably the same for mine," Reia answered coldly. "But I wasn't allowed to talk to anyone, so I knew jack shit about what went on except for what I overheard getting my food. Jill was cheating on Jack. Hansel robbed his sister Gretel for her breadcrumbs. Blah blah blah. I always found gossip trivial and pointless."

"Sounds about right," Delora snorted with a humourless laugh.

"You know... though," Reia said as she rolled her head to the side to face Delora. "You can talk to me. Who am I going to tell? Orpheus?" She poked her thumb in the direction of the wolf-skulled Duskwalker helping Magnar hold the table so he could attach another leg to it. "We don't care what happens between you two as long as you're okay. You're the human in this situation, living in a place like the Veil, secluded from the rest of humankind."

"Thanks," Delora said in a low voice, wishing her ability to trust in people wasn't so broken.

Although she now thought of Reia as a friend, she didn't particularly know her well enough. She didn't know if her opinions or advice would be helpful or what she needed since they had two very different personalities. She also could just one day... change.

People were often not who they first seemed to be, putting on a façade because it was easier than revealing their true nature.

"How's this little one doing?" Reia reached over and brushed the top of Fyodor's skull with a knuckle as they lay in Delora's lap. "They look like a ferocious rabbit."

Delora dropped her gaze down to smile at them. She couldn't help herself when she scooped them into her arms and gave them a tight hug while swaying side to side slightly. They were so cute that she just wanted to crush them in adoration.

"They're good. A bit heavy to carry now, but I think that's making me stronger."

"Will you be alright for a few days without us?"

Delora nodded.

Reia and Orpheus were planning a trip to the Demon Village.

They had originally come just to tell them they wouldn't be visiting for a while, but then Magnar had asked Orpheus for some assistance in making the table since it was awkward to do by himself.

"You asked me if I needed anything. Could you perhaps get me a few cooking items like some proper knives?"

"Yeah, sure. Sounds easy enough. I'll also get some more fabric." Reia's face brightened into a grin. "Making clothing for us both is actually keeping me entertained. It gives me something to do."

Delora's lips curled up as well, knowing she now had a second dress to wear since Reia had brought it over for her.

"You should come over and let me teach you how to use a sword. Hours of endless fun."

"No, thank you!" Delora laughed. "I'm more likely to cut my own leg off than actually be able to kill a Demon."

Orpheus chose that moment to start heading towards them, the table now completed. Magnar was a few steps behind, lifting the whole thing by himself. Reia bounced to her feet and stretched by lifting her arms into the air and interlocking her fingers, going to the tips of her toes as she let out an unladylike grunted groan.

"Alright, let's get this long and boring walk over with," Reia said as she stomped down the steps.

Orpheus snorted a huff but reached his arm out as though he was starved to touch her. He curled his hand around her waist.

There was no goodbye, as there never was; they would return soon enough.

Delora watched as Magnar turned the table on its side, getting two legs through the doorway before turning it in a curve to get the last two through.

She smiled knowingly.

The old Magnar would have been standing at the doorway, wondering how he was supposed to get the table through since it was wide and awkward, most likely scratching at his head in bewilderment.

I kind of miss him being silly. But she was also fond of this new Magnar.

THIRTY-SEVEN

Delora felt the creep of the cool night air brushing over her exposed shoulder when Magnar slowly moved to crawl out of the nest. He made sure to cover her, but Delora was disturbed from her sleep, growing more sensitive to his movements as he disappeared every night.

She didn't know if she'd fallen back asleep or not, but when she opened her eyes, she realised she'd never gotten the chance to see him leave. She was completely shrouded in darkness.

And alone.

Where did he go? What was he doing and why?

She gingerly sat up while making sure the covers remained over Fyodor. They continued to sleep in a ball, oblivious to the world.

Everything was quiet. So quiet in fact that all she could hear were Fyodor's tiny, usually unnoticeable, breaths.

The air was cool but not freezing against her uncovered skin. Delora chewed at the inside of her cheek as she debated with herself if she should brave going to find Magnar.

She'd never asked him what he was doing at night. *Everyone deserves private moments to themselves.*

She could also be looking for someone who wasn't there. Delora didn't want to seem like a lost puppy pathetically looking for its master.

After a fierce internal struggle, Delora made her decision when she looked outside the window. The moon was bright through the mist on a cloudless night. It should be enough to give her some sort of light so she wasn't walking around blindly.

As much as she wanted to take the blanket to stay warm, Delora left it behind so as not to stir Fyodor. She tip-toed her way out of the house, closing the front door gently.

Okay, I'll just circle the yard around the house, she thought to herself. *If I can't find him, I'll go back inside.* She doubted she'd be able to sleep, though.

Or maybe I can ask him where he went when he comes back. She'd tried to do that last night but had fallen back asleep.

Wrapping her arms around herself to keep warm, thinking perhaps she should have put on actual clothing rather than walking around in one of Magnar's shirts, she eased her way down the steps.

Delora didn't spot him out the front. She veered to the left to see if maybe he was at the back, where the garden was.

The moon made the mist whiter, thicker even, which caused the area to seem haunted – like at any moment, a Ghost might peek out from anywhere. The trees looked creepy since many of them had lost their leaves, appearing like threatening claws in the darkness and moving like they wanted to strike.

I've never been outside by myself at night before. Old habits made it hard to not be wary. *It's a lot scarier than I thought it'd be.*

Humans these days were afraid of the dark, considering there was a real chance they may not be alone in it.

A noise made her ears twitch, and her head perked up.

A huff, deep but short, drifted over the wind like it had echoed nearby. Delora hesitated when she knew it had come from within the forest just past the partially cleared yard.

Maybe this isn't a good idea... What if it's a Demon? She chewed at her cheek again. *Stop being such a scaredy-cat. No Demons can get inside the protection ward.*

At least... they hadn't been able to before.

Pulling in a strong, calming breath, Delora headed in the direction she'd heard the noise, trying not to make too much sound just in case it was something she didn't want to stumble upon.

Magnar could be eating something fucking *weird*, for all she knew.

Another huff, one that was deeper this time and even sounded shaky, redirected her path. A lowing snort followed.

And then she found him.

The trees here weren't dense, and it allowed just enough moonlight shining from between the gaps of the leaves to see him clearly.

Magnar's orbs were black, signalling that his 'eyes' were closed, while his snout was pointed towards the sky. His parted fangs released a cloud on his deep, panted exhale. He was lowered to the ground on his knees, and at first, she thought he was just... sitting there, doing nothing.

Why is he...

It took a moment for Delora to actually register what was going on. When she did, heat flared into her cheeks before it spread down her chest and pooled in her gut. She had to steady herself against a tree trunk when her knees trembled.

Her feet suddenly became rooted to the ground.

From the side view of him she had, she could see he had one hand resting upon his knee, while the other had a firm hold of his thick cock. She watched the long length jutting from between his hips being stroked as he slowly, like he couldn't help it, thrust into his fist.

He gave a shuddering groan, one that had his head twisting slightly before he shook.

Oh, my... Gods.

His four long – and thick at the base – tentacles were writhing in the air, but he wasn't concerned about them. He just brought his fist down around them so they could wrap around his hand before he pulled up and away. Then he rubbed the strange head that had noticeable bumps around the rim that could even be seen from a distance.

Her eyes followed his movements, his large hand swallowing something she didn't think she'd be able to fit both her own around.

The sight was completely erotic: Magnar stroking his cock with just a dash of moonlight cascading over him. She had to steady herself against the tree trunk further when she clasped her thighs together.

Delora's nipples pearled into hard points, feeling remarkably itchy and needy against the smooth material of the shirt she was in. The inner walls of her pussy quivered when Magnar let out a little pleasure-filled growl, his hips jerking forward into his hand before they settled back into their slow rhythm.

Part of her wanted to join in what he was doing by snaking her hand between her thighs to touch herself. The other just wanted to blatantly watch the magnificent scene playing out.

She chewed at the corner of her mouth.

I want to see him come.

She wanted to witness what she *knew* would be a fountain of semen gushing from him in plentiful ropes. She knew there would be a wonderful sound to go with it. A groan that would be rumbly, inhuman, and unhidden.

Her pussy clenched again at the thought, her fingertips beginning to throb along with the rest of her body. Her blood pumped with a high.

It's so hot. I wonder if it will steam. Would she be able to see it doing that with how cold the air was?

His antlers were like menacing branches behind his head, his claws glinting in the moonlight, his fangs parted to let out his pants and showing how sharp and dangerous they were.

He looked like a monstrous beast in this position, but he also looked like a wild fertility god.

And his cock was *glistening* with his lubricant, dripping from his knuckles to splatter against the ground. He was obviously so turned on by what he was doing that she could even hear a wet, squelching sound.

She gripped the bottom of her shirt, seriously considering delving her fingers into her folds, when she had to press her thighs together tighter to ease some of the throbbing in her clit.

Then his tongue came out to lick at his fangs like he was enjoying this, was enjoying touching himself, working his cock.

His orbs were black. *Is he... picturing me, or us?*

His hand stopped halfway down just as his orbs flashed purple. His head snapped in her direction.

Delora started at being caught.

She should have known he'd eventually smell her there, maybe even hear her stammering heart and wild pants, but she'd been helpless to do anything but *watch*. She didn't want him to stop.

She thought his orbs would flash to a reddish pink at being caught. Or perhaps that he would back away from her in embarrassment.

Instead, she received a growled, *"Delora,"* just as his hand moved down to finish its stroke.

That bass, the rumble. It was like a resonance that travelled all the way from her ears to her very core.

Delora's knees almost crumbled as her pussy quivered in reaction, shivers and tingles assaulting her entire body. If Delora had the ability to come without being touched, that would have been the moment.

He licked at his bony snout again, this time his purple, lust-filled gaze fixed upon her. His hand started working faster, like he was *excited* she was there, at being able to take in the sight of her.

But that tongue lick felt like an expression of invitation, and her foot took a step closer without a thought, without hesitation.

"Stay," he demanded, his movements halting. He gripped his cock tightly right behind the head, making it swell.

Where her intelligent mind had gone to, she didn't know. She also didn't fucking care. As soon as the thought of putting her hands on his glistening cock came to her, to replace his with her own, Delora couldn't focus on anything else.

She stumbled at his demand, like some place in her subconscious said getting closer was a bad idea, dangerous even, but her feet kept moving.

"Delora," he warned this time, but the depth of his distorted, baritone voice just made her feel more drunk on her own need.

My name coming from him sounds like a sin.

Since she had been coming at him from the side, Delora inched her way until she was in front of him. The predatory way his head followed her movement had her licking at the seam of her lips, suddenly feeling parched.

The closer she got, the better she could see that a bubble of white liquid was pearled at his cockeye. With her closer, it grew until she thought it would begin to spill down the head at any moment.

Her eyes remained fixed to it, and she dropped to her knees right in front of him with her hands reaching out.

"I can do this for you, if you like."

She wanted to. Fuck... no, she *needed* to.

It wasn't like she was giving him much of a choice when both her palms brushed over the tip of his bulbous head. Thick slime and warmth greeted her, but she had no qualms about the liquid when the hardness of him swelled under her light touch.

He let out an expire, one that was pleasure shaken, as she spread her hands over the head and met his fist right behind it. It had such a tight hold that it seemed to be strangling his cock, liquid bubbling between his knuckles. When her fingertips brushed his hand, he pulled it back as though it was pushed away by her weak strength.

She continued to push, even though she wasn't actually putting any strength to it, until they were halfway down. He released his cock when she fully wrapped both hands around it. *I was right.* It barely fit inside the gaps of her curling palms, her fingertips barely overlapping each other.

Wetness and texture greeted her sensitive palms, and she absorbed all of it. The deep groove underneath the entire length of his cock. The paired lines of nodules that ran down three sides of him – the top and sides. The many veins that she could feel and see were throbbing so heavily. They were thick, swollen, and pumping blood so fast into the hardness of his cock that it nearly felt like stone.

Magnar let out a strangled groan as his head fell back, the hand he'd been using to masturbate coming up to smear his lubricant all over the side of her face and neck. It slipped to hold the back of her head by diving into her hair.

He gave her a deep shudder, like her touch was too much to bear.

She was forced to bring her face only a breath away from the tip when her hands descended, feeling every glorious inch he had to offer. His tentacles wrapped around her forearms, clung to her with even more wetness, but she only felt warmed by them, deliciously stroked by them, rather than repulsed.

"Did it feel good stroking your own cock?" she asked with a breathy voice.

She pulled back, tugging hard to get his tentacles to let go so she could do her first stroke back up. Massaging his cock with everything she had, trying to squeeze it with all her strength since it was so hard it gave so much resistance against her – a human – he bucked into her hands when she reached the rim of his cockhead.

"Yes," he groaned in answer, his hips bucking into her hand a second time when she went back down the head.

That bead of white grew.

She thought with how close she was that he would smell... funny. Salty. Or perhaps have a weird tang to the air in front of her nose. All she could smell was sweetness.

Delora licked at her lips before biting the bottom one.

"Was it better than me touching your cock?"

A curt pant sounded right before his cock swelled, enlarged, thickened under her palms, pushing her hands apart until they no longer touched. That bead of white became too heavy as more liquid formed, and it started overspilling, slipping down the groove in the head that followed down the length of him.

He was tense, his entire body rigid, and she could see he wanted to touch her with his other hand when it lifted into the air. Instead, he fisted it and brought it down back to his knee, while the one cupping her head softened its press against her.

"No."

A thrill of delight course through her at that.

She stroked downwards faster this time and went all the way to the bottom, feeling where his slit had opened up and was pushing his cock forward with the base inside it to support its forward position. She found two round, oval-shaped protrusions at the base of his cock that were embedded underneath.

Delora flinched when he pushed his hips up with a rabid snarl. His fangs parted as he darted his face down in her direction, red glowing in his orbs. His claws dug into the back of her head while his other hand shot forward to grab her shoulder.

She froze with her hands on them. "Did I hurt you?"

"Sensitive," he growled, saliva dripping from between his fangs. *"That is where my release comes from. Feels good."*

"Here?" She rubbed her fingertips over them like she was trying to tickle them.

His cock jerked right in front of her face, and he let out a whine. *Ohhhhh, he likes that.* Perhaps touching them so roughly had felt too good, but her softer touch had elicited a better response, one that wasn't so violent.

She wondered if she played with them too much, if he would just spontaneously combust against her face.

She was game for that, but maybe not right now.

Not when that slitted hole at the tip of his shaft was only a breaths distance away. Yet the white pearly drop there, that had a streaking line coming from it into his groove, was calling to her. *Daring* her.

Her own breaths came out more heated as she stared at it.

Delora parted her lips. *Please.* She let her tongue fall over the bottom one. *Please don't taste gross.* Nothing was going to stop her from coming forward and running her tongue over it so she could collect it and spread it over her tastebuds.

She'd been worried that either his lubricant or seed would be disgusting. Giving him a blowjob had never seemed enticing simply because he was covered in slime. She'd thought it would have a weird taste to it.

The moment both touched her tastebuds, Delora's eyes flickered lewdly. Her abdomen clenched with such a heavy spasm that her own arousal leaked from the slit of her entrance.

His lubricant tasted like a diluted version of his scent, and his semen had tasted like fresh forest. Strange.

It sent a rush through her. Delora sunk as much of her mouth as she could around the big head, swirling her tongue to collect every bit of it.

Magnar rumbled, his claws biting into her at what she had done. Her hands were still moving, but he pulled her head back by gripping her hair and tugging.

"Don't lick," he strangled out.

She looked up to see his orbs were glowing a bright purple in the middle but dark on the outside.

"Why not?" she asked with a pant.

"Feels too nice. I will hurt you."

Delora licked at her lips to take in his taste. There was no way she was going to concede to his demand, not now that she knew how wonderful and delicious it was.

"Then keep your hands to yourself," she commanded, before she darted her head forward and stroked the tip of his cock with her entire tongue.

His hands flew away from her, just as he let out a surprised, strangled, fox-like bark. He clawed at his chest, and she could see his abdomen dipped and clenched.

Delora sidled closer and massaged his swollen and throbbing cock as she began licking it all over, seeking every bit of lubricant. It had pooled inside his groove, and he shook when she dipped her tongue inside to follow its path upwards. She didn't even reach the top before her tongue was greeted by dripping semen.

She collected it as she continued her path.

She even dipped the tip of her tongue in the small, slitted hole where it came from, stealing everything before brushing her lips down the sides of the jerking, jutting rod. She felt his nodules against them, and she played with the little bumps, teasing them with her lips, teeth, and tongue.

Her mind had glazed over; she didn't really know or care what she was doing anymore. She was tasting every inch of it and was rewarded whenever his cock enlarged and swelled as more lubricant rose from the very flesh covering him and re-wetted him, giving her more.

It didn't matter that they were outside where the air was getting to it. It was being played with, massaged, which kept him moist and pain-free, except for what had to be a terrible, needy ache. An ache she wanted to deepen until it clutched at him.

At times she could see in her peripheral that Magnar's hands would hover in the air around her head, like he wanted to grab ahold of her. He knew he couldn't. They twitched and trembled around her instead.

He's being so good.

"Does this feel good, Magnar? Do you like me tasting your cock?"

His only response was a menacing snarl.

A part of her wished she could do this one handed so she could snake her hand between her thighs and mimic her movements. Her nipples were hard, aching, and her heavy breasts swaying against her shirt felt remarkable, knowing they were only so sensitive because of how turned on she was.

She wanted to come while she had her mouth around this Duskwalker's cock.

She squeezed tight, trying to make sure he felt it all the way to his core. Her hands worked in unison, stroking back and forth, but she was slow in order to drag this out. She even cuddled into his cock, undoing the top buttons of her shirt so she could mould her breasts around the base of it.

Delora was in no way going to rush this. Especially since she was hoping to blow this inexperienced Duskwalker's mind with what she was hoped was the orgasm of his life.

I wish I could sink my mouth around him.

Delora tried again, spreading her lips over the very tip. She could only get the head three quarters of the way in until the flared rim was just too wide. Just a little more and she thought she could. With how much she was adoring this, she probably would have tried to swallow the impossibly large thing.

"Do you like my mouth on you, Magnar?"

She eyed him as she moved to suckle the side of it, dabbling her tongue to mix with the suction she was trying to give him.

Magnar wrapped one of his fists around his cock, just behind the head, when her hands descended to his release sacs. The little oval-shaped balls embedded into him moved under her tickle.

She could see he was mangling his cock by how much liquid squeezed through his fingers, but he was now pumping his hips. He was fucking his cock into his fist, against her mouth, and her hands.

"De... lo... ra." His haunting groan was broken, gasping, and yet it still had the undertone of a growl, like it didn't actually come from where he spoke. Her eyes flickered in lust.

She wanted to take his lubricant and use it to finger herself, wanted to smear it all over her pussy until she replaced it with her own orgasm. But she didn't dare let go of his cock, not when she could feel those sacs sinking into the sides of his girth, not when his tentacles wrapped around her arms to grip them tightly.

He's close.

Delora knew what was about to happen.

She had plenty of warning, even though he didn't give it to her. She could have backed away. She could have ducked.

Instead, she swirled her tongue in rings around the tip of his cock as she sunk her face onto it.

Her mind glazed over, her eyes went hazy, and her body took over when he let out a bellowing roar. The first strong spurt of his release filled her entire mouth.

Her tongue lapped up and down at him as it worked to move it in the right direction while she swallowed, and swallowed, and *gulped* every time he swelled before more hot, thick liquid shot into her mouth. Her throat had opened to allow it. She gripped his cock, pulled with her hands, and pushed with her face to keep her lips tight on him as he wildly fucked his purple cock into his own fist.

And it was wild, especially with the way he twitched and quivered from his own orgasm.

Heat rushed through her, pooled inside her, and her pussy just answered it with empty need, on the verge of orgasming, but had no assistance to be pushed over that edge.

Every drop was *delicious.* Impossibly so.

She moaned against the tip. *More. Give me all of it.*

Half drowning, Delora gasped for air when it stopped, and she ducked her head away.

Magnar was a limp heap on his knees, the back of one hand resting against the ground while the other still had a tight grip on himself. Huffing erratically as his chest pumped with rapid breaths, his head was turned to the sky with his orbs purple, as if he was just staring up in a bliss-filled daze.

With the few minutes of calm between them, it took a bit for her mind to fully come to the surface.

She covered her mouth and her stomach with her eyes growing wide.

I drank it all. Heat flared in her cheeks. *And I feel really full.* She didn't think she had missed a single drop going down.

Did I really do that?

But, as she stared at his cock that was slowly going floppy and limp, the tentacles swirling around the base as it was going inside, Delora dabbled her tongue at the seam of her lips.

She *knew* she was going to want to do that again.

The feel of him, the taste of him – everything had been addictive.

If I had known he tasted so good, I probably would have done this sooner. She would have shamelessly *lived* off that thick liquid like it was a fucking smoothie.

Magnar's snout fell forward, and he looked at her for a long while with his fangs parted to pant. Then his hands shot forward, grabbing one thigh and arm to drag her closer.

His claws raked down her back in a wonderful stroke, causing it to arch sharply while he licked at the underside of her jaw.

"You're aroused. I can smell it." Delora thought she was about to combust when he rumbled those words against her ear, forcing a high-pitched cry from her. "You smell like you're dripping wet for me, like you need to be touched."

He was right. Delora was aching for it. But her sense of reasoning pushed him back to escape.

"N-no," she rebutted, desperately wanting to falter. "Just you tonight."

"But you tasted me. *Licked* me." He fought to drag her back... and won. His body was ruffled and puffed, making him seem bigger and even fluffier. "I want to taste back. I promise I'll try to be good, that I won't hurt you."

Delora grabbed both his hands with her own and held them tight. She stopped him from gripping her hips tighter and dragging her onto his lap.

"Please, Magnar?" she pleaded, bringing her gaze to him with a crinkled brow.

His orbs flashed blue as he paused. His grip on her softened when his shoulders sagged. She hated that he looked so defeated.

"You don't want my touch?"

Delora's heart stung, but she gave him a smile and brought

her hands to his jaw, lifting herself so she could brush her lips over the very tip of his snout.

"I do. I really do."

She wanted it more than anything.

"Then why?" The purple had faded permanently to drown her sight in that sad, disappointed colour.

"Because I wanted to gift you this," she said as she kissed his snout again. "Gifts should be given without an expectation to receive. I'm making up for all the times you've made me feel good."

That wasn't the whole truth.

I don't want to ruin this.

This was the first time they'd been able to be intimate together without something going... wrong. This was a start. A true start.

If he touched her, he could harden again. As much as Delora ached, she worried what the next step would be.

She knew part of the reason Magnar feared being close to her was because he didn't want to hurt her. If she showed him this was possible, that things didn't have to end with her in tears or in pain, then she was hoping they could do this again.

And she wanted to suck him again. To lick every inch of that delicious cock. She wanted to do it right now.

But the more they pushed, the higher the likelihood that something could go astray.

Just *once,* she wanted this to go well. If she ever needed it, if he ever tried to draw away from her in the future, she wanted proof that things would be okay as long as they took it slow.

Magnar had changed, but neither one knew just how deeply. Sex last time had ended with Delora's skin torn to shreds.

This was enough for now. Tonight had been perfect. She had eased him, and that in itself made her content.

He deserved it, after all.

When the blue didn't lift, Delora leaned back so she could see him fully. Then she flashed him a wicked grin.

"Maybe next time?"

Purple gently lifted into his orbs, and he pointed the claw of his index finger against his chest. "You want to do this again with me?"

Delora braved dropping her gaze to his disappearing cock, sheltered completely by his tentacles, watching it slip back inside. Then his slit closed, the fur there creating a near seamless line.

She already missed it.

Oh yeah, big boy. I really do.

THIRTY-EIGHT

The last thing Delora thought she'd ever have to do was search for Magnar and Fyodor. Usually all she had to do was shout, and Fyodor would come scampering to her voice. And she only needed to call for Magnar, and he'd come.

While she'd been painting in the garden, extending the outside to make it larger and add to the scene, she'd realised Fyodor had crawled off her at some point.

She now understood how easy it was for Magnar to not realise they were moving away, since it had been done to her. The little Duskwalker usually clung to either her back or chest but would sometimes move around her body. When she'd felt them move down her legs, she thought they were going to investigate something in the garden by dragging their head across the ground to reach what had drawn their interest – usually a rare bug.

It'd taken her a while to realise they'd never crawled back up her body, and when she'd turned around... they were gone.

Maybe they're with Magnar? she thought after she'd checked underneath all the thick, luscious leaves in the garden.

She'd called out to both of them when she'd been unable to find either around the house, but got no response.

Did Magnar leave? Her lips pursed. *But he's never done that before.* She doubted he'd do it without coming to speak with her first.

Despite her rational thoughts, Delora started to panic, running around the yard and nearly tripping over her dress until she gripped the skirt and lifted it. She wasn't sprinting, not that panicked yet, but she was moving fast while trying to listen for a sign from either one of them. She also didn't want to run in case poor Fyodor was chasing her, but she thought she would have heard their little shrill cry if they were.

She started moving through the forest.

Fuck. Where'd they go?

"Magnar!" she yelled as she jogged.

Relief soared through her when she heard Magnar's voice in the distance, calling back. She headed in that direction, surprised he didn't come to greet her halfway.

However, her relief was short-lived once she discovered why he hadn't come to her. As soon as she made it to the small gap between the trees right near the border of the protection ward, Delora gasped.

Fyodor! No! She headed straight for them with her face crinkling into tight, worried lines. She couldn't believe this was happening! That Magnar was allowing it!

The horrible stench of rotting decay turned the air sour... and only one kind of creature made that kind of gut-churning, bile-rising smell.

"You didn't hear me calling back to you?" Magnar asked, letting the horrible scene play out before him with his arms crossed.

He even chuckled at it, while worry squeezed her heart and strangled her lungs.

"Oh my gods!" She grabbed the leg of a small Demon and started pulling back, wondering why Magnar wasn't trying to intervene. "Don't eat that!"

She dug in the heels of her boots, trying to get the partially eaten Demon from Fyodor's maw, but the little Duskwalker held strong. Her feet slipped across the ground while they shook their head side to side, trying to dislodge her as they fought for their meal.

"Stop them!" Delora screamed, catching a stronger whiff of the putrid Demon, whose dark, near-black blood was making her gag.

I think I'm going to be sick.

Instead of doing what she'd asked, Magnar wrapped both his

arms around her waist and lifted her off the ground. She accidentally dropped the dead carcass in surprise and watched as Fyodor sprinted off to the side with it.

"Don't interfere with them while they eat, Delora," Magnar said, his orbs white. "Most Mavka are defensive about their prey. They may attack you."

She kicked her legs and bashed at his forearms, trying to squirm out of his gentle hold even though she was at least three feet off the ground.

"But it's a Demon. That's so disgusting!" A shudder of revulsion wracked her as her face screwed up into a cringe. Delora dry-heaved. "What if it makes them super weird?!"

If Duskwalkers turned into what they ate, then she didn't want Fyodor to become anything like a gross Demon.

If they grow a third arm, I might actually puke!

Fyodor, ripping an arm from the Demon, threw it in the air and swallowed it whole. Her stomach churned further.

"Mavka do not absorb Demons like we do everything else," Magnar informed her. "Nor do they particularly make us hungry."

"Then why the hell did you give it to them?"

She covered her face and looked away, curling to the side so she could bury it into Magnar's chest. She wished it would help hide the slurping and crunching sounds. The horrible smell. At least it shielded her sight.

He lowered her until she could feel her feet touching the ground. She staggered.

"Demons make us stronger. We take their strength." Then Magnar released one arm from her so he could wave it in Fyodor's direction. "I am hoping it will make Fyodor bigger."

"B-but I like them the way they are."

Magnar brushed his claws into her hair soothingly, raking the tips across her scalp. Then he used one claw to lift her head to face him by placing it under her chin.

She didn't miss that his other large hand had spanned across the bump of her hip and was squeezing it. Not in a way that was trying to control her, but like he just wanted to appreciate her there.

"Fyodor cannot support their skull, Delora." His orbs began to turn blue right before her very eyes, and her heart always sunk when they turned that colour. "It upsets me to see them dragging it around. That is all I wanted. For Fyodor to be able to walk around without it bothering them."

Delora's shoulders slumped as she bit at her bottom lip. That was a pretty justifiable reason for doing it, especially since watching Fyodor struggle had been bothering her as well.

"You could have asked me. We could have gone back to the surface and gotten them an animal instead." She didn't dare look in Fyodor's direction, and she cringed when she thought she heard the snapping of bones crunching between their fangs. "A Demon, Magnar? That's just... beyond gross. I can smell how bad it is from all the way over here!"

"I didn't think it would bother you." Then Magnar let out a chuckle as he said, "This is normal for Mavka. We eat everything."

She tried to turn her head away defeatedly, but Magnar held strong, so she averted her gaze to the side and peered into the forest.

"I guess, but... I don't know. It just seems wrong to let them eat Demons."

"They will do it in the future," Magnar stated before he turned his head in Fyodor's direction. He let her go to step after them, realising that Fyodor was done and sniffing around for more. They'd been heading towards the protection ward's outer circle, out of safety, right before Magnar picked them up. Their little legs squirmed in the air in protest. "There is no point in trying to stop them from doing it now, especially when it will help them."

He placed them on the ground at her feet. *I guess they* do *look a little bigger.* Their skull was still too big for their body, but at least they were able to lift it to sniff up at her.

They gave a happy chirp, their shrills becoming less apparent as a form of communication the more they grew. Then they tried to climb up her legs.

"Oh no you don't!" She picked them up and held them in the air away from her body with her nose crinkling. "You are *not* going to get Demon blood all over my new dress. Look at your claws. Yuck!"

Delora headed back towards the house. They opened and closed their excited little paws in her direction, wanting closer and reaching for her with another happy chirp.

"I'm going to need new water after this."

She was intending to use what she had left in the bucket to dunk this stinky, messy, baby Duskwalker into, just as soon as she got back.

They were absolutely saturated in Demon blood from their rabbit skull all the way to their long black paws, like they'd been *playing* in it. The smell was even worse up close, and goosebumps rose on her flesh in disgust – forcing her to breathe through her mouth.

"You shouldn't wash them, Delora. They have tried to bite you numerous times for it. I will do it."

Magnar rushed to take them from her, but she yanked her arms to the side. She didn't want him to get dirtied either.

"Fine, but I'm still not giving them to you until they're in water. The smell clings to your fur."

THIRTY-NINE

Magnar chuckled quietly as he stroked his claws through Delora's hair, untangling it from her day, as he thought. Combing her hair while she slept was something he enjoyed doing; it made him feel as though he was silently pampering her.

Despite being rather cranky all day, which had been alarming because she was especially cranky with him, she had *still* permitted Magnar to lie with her while she slept.

She was resting peacefully as she did each night he was beside her. He hoped it was because his presence made her feel at ease. Magnar liked that he was scary enough to chase away her nightmares.

Even after Magnar had scrubbed the wailing Fyodor until they smelt like her soap, she refused to let go of her anger.

And yet... here he was, being allowed to take in the feel of her body as he played with the glossy, tantalising strands of her ebony hair.

She likes me near. Despite her terrible mood, she still craved to be close with him. That made Magnar's insides feel sore in the most amazing way.

With how things had gone the previous night, he'd been hoping that he could instigate something similar before she tried to sleep.

Her lips around my cock... He brushed the bottom one with the pad of his thumb.

Just the memory of it had caused his orbs to flash instantly to purple in desire – even when she gave him an *adorable* glare across the yard.

Licking me.

He almost wanted to push his thumb deeper and brush it against her wickedly naughty tongue. He never even fantasized she could do something like that to him.

She was opening his mind to many things. Even just gazing at her soft body had his own stirring constantly, but Magnar felt in control – mostly.

Every new thing she taught him, the more content she seemed with him, wanted to be in his embrace even while she slept, the more Magnar felt this *falling* feeling in his chest and stomach. He knew his longing for her was deepening.

I want to bond with her.

Not just in soul, but in heart, in mind, and in body. To connect until they were the same, intertwined, unbreakable, and inseparable. One complete and whole spirit.

If he thought it would help, he would have opened his jaws and let her crawl inside him until they were one.

But that wasn't possible, and he didn't think it would help. Only one thing would.

I want to be inside you, he thought as he bumped the tip of his snout against her sleeping face. *I want to cover you in my scent as you cover me in yours. I want to hear your little sounds, feel your body around mine.*

I want you pulling my feathers from me. He wanted to rut her until she had plucked him clean because she desperately clung to him. *I want there to be a sea of feathers covering our bodies when we are done.*

With a lazy gaze fixated on them, he kept playing with her lips.

It wouldn't be a fumbling accident this time. It wouldn't be him learning. He would be sinking into her, knowing exactly what he was doing, what he wanted, and that he was going to appease his *hopeless* craving for her.

I don't know how to instigate this. Was there some strange song or dance he was supposed to perform like he'd seen some animals do? *I don't know the customs for humans.*

He was waiting for Delora, and until last night, he thought

he'd be waiting forever. Even though it had been less than a week since he'd gained more humanity, it had felt like eons. Every moment within her presence burned at him, igniting scalding flames, until he thought he'd evaporate into dust the next time he was allowed to touch her.

She came to me. She had said it was a gift, and it had been the sweetest treat. Magnar's fur and feathers puffed in memory.

He wanted more, would always want more. A new hunger that was unable to be fulfilled. But Magnar wanted to know if he actually *could* be satisfied.

Would there be a point he could reach where he couldn't spend any longer and was nothing more than a bliss-filled heap? Where his mind and body were nothing but radiating pleasure, stroked and wonderfully numbed?

There was only one way to find out, but to find out was to wait.

He stifled his quiet groan. He pulled her tighter against him and stroked his snout against her in a pleading manner. *I don't want to wait.*

And of course, as it had happened every night since he'd started lying here awake with her, purple flared into his sight.

He didn't even need to tease her a little by touching her or stroking near her ear; his own thoughts had sent him hurtling into desire.

Gingerly, he carefully pulled away from Delora so he could leave, intending to return shortly.

Ever since the first night he'd left in order to ease his desire for her, Magnar had felt calmer. He was getting used to his body, learning how to wield it.

Once he had released the pressure of his seed, he was able to return and just hum contently beside her, combing her hair with his own claws so she didn't have to in the morning. He was rather fond of doing this task, especially since it made her pull closer to him.

Just as he got himself free of her limbs and the blanket, her hand shot forward to fist the front of his shirt. He paused, turning his face to her with his orbs orange because he'd woken her.

"Are you going outside?" Her voice was croaked but not

completely groggy, as if she hadn't been deep in sleep.

"Yes." He wondered if this was something he should be embarrassed about. Was it odd that he was doing this to himself? It felt good, so he didn't see a problem with it. "I didn't mean to wake you."

She didn't let go of his shirt, but she did sink under the blanket a little, as if she was trying to hide from him. She even ducked her face underneath, but he'd noticed her cheeks reddening before she did.

"Do... do you want me to come with you?"

There would be only one reason why she'd want to come with him when she knew what he was doing. And the way her scent changed, spicing the air with her tangy arousal, had Magnar groaning.

She wants to touch me again.

Before she could change her mind, he dug under the blanket and lifted her off the ground. It slipped from her, and she was freed as he carried her out of the room with haste.

"Magnar."

He turned his head down to her as he walked down the hallway. *Does she want me to put her down?* He hoped he hadn't misread the signal he'd thought she was giving him.

He didn't even get the chance to respond before she pressed her lips against his snout, which was now facing her.

Shocked, Magnar stumbled a step. *She kissed me...*

Parting his fangs, he answered her kiss by tracing his tongue over those pretty lips.

She parted them, allowing him inside, while wrapping her arms around his neck and pulling herself up. She changed her position until she was straddling him around his lower ribs. It gave him the freedom to hold her up by cradling her entire arse in one of his palms. He dug his fingers in while the other went to the back of her head.

Just as he was getting to the front door to take them outside, she did something that had him slamming her against the door instead. *Fuck!* She'd *sucked* his tongue, bringing it deeper into her mouth herself.

Magnar let out a growl as he thrust his hips uselessly against the air.

She was too high up on his body to give him any friction as his tentacles shifted to wrap around his extruding cock. He still didn't have the control to keep it inside his seam, but the fact he had their protection meant he could become aroused and not fall prey to his own desires.

Her large and droopy breasts, loose inside the shirt she wore, were pressed tightly against his chest. Her stomach moulded around him, and her thighs were a soft cushion as he squeezed her against the door.

He was torn between wanting to dance his much longer and thinner tongue around hers or shoving it down her throat so he could be greeted by it. The smoothness, the tightness, the taste of it. And the way she clenched up last time had felt wonderful.

Her mind-fogging scent was growing stronger, suffocating him on each intake of breath. He felt his senses lessening by the second.

Delora pulled her head back, but he followed. He refused to allow her to escape.

"Stay," he demanded, trying to get her tongue to play with his again. He wanted to lap at it, feel its grainy texture until he knew every single one of her tastebuds personally.

She bit his tongue, making him retract it with his orbs flaring red. His claws unsheathed and dug into her skin.

"Outside," she begged, her breaths panted and high-pitched. "Take me outside."

Yes. Outside. He licked at his snout to answer her invitation. *More outside.*

Magnar backed up just enough to allow him room to knock the doorhandle down to open the door. He heard it close behind him as he strutted across the porch, tracing his tongue over every bit of skin he could reach. Her cheek, the underneath of her jaw, over her jugular. Each time trying to catch her ear just to make her breath hitch – he even squished his tongue against the shell of it.

Not watching where he was going, too preoccupied with the attractive female in his arms, he tripped down the bottom step of the porch. They were sent hurtling to the ground. He took it completely on his knees and elbows, making sure not a single piece of her touched the dirt until he laid her there himself.

He only gave them a moment of separation before his tongue was exploring the inside of her mouth again. He palmed one of her knees to the side so he could separate them, liking the way her thighs stuck to each other and took a while to open.

More. I need to touch every inch of her.

He slid his hand into that gap, down the inside muscles of her thigh, trying to show her he had control of his deadly, but now sheathed, claws.

At least, he hoped he did.

He had been wondering if perhaps she hadn't let him touch her the previous night because she'd been wary of them. He was as well, but he needed to test the boundaries, wanted to, if it meant he could make this female come apart for him.

She moaned around his tongue when he tickled the inside of her thigh just right. Her scent was stronger now that her thighs were parted, and it caused his body to ripple in answer.

His hands changed their direction when she lifted her hips in greeting. He moved over the top of her thighs so he could grab one of her meaty arse cheeks, feeling it rest perfectly in his large palm. It wasn't small, which made it easier for him to hold, for him to play with, as her skin moulded between his fingers.

He groaned at the feeling of it, kneading it tightly.

"You're so soft."

He moved his hand higher to grasp at the bubble of skin that made her hips flare out even wider. He did it to the side of her stomach, being gentler since she'd once warded him away from being able to touch there in the past. Magnar's pants grew heavier at each new place he explored.

"Do you understand how good it feels to just simply hold you?" He liked talking to her, telling her how he felt. The only time he felt comfortable doing so was when she was welcoming him. It made Magnar want to hopelessly ramble at her. "Just having you pressed against me makes me desperate to touch you."

With his tongue still dancing with hers, all she could do was answer him with another moan. But she did peek open her eyes to give him a tender look. She grabbed his hand in her own while it was placed against her stomach, then she squeezed it, telling him it was okay to touch her there.

But Magnar had somewhere else he wanted to go.

Her sleep shirt was pushed up as he slowly revealed her naked body beneath it. He broke away from their *'kiss'* so he could dab his tongue across her jaw, just as his fingertips found the heavy-looking, droopy mounds of her chest. He squeezed one when she gave him no resistance.

He gave a bated breath just as hers hitched, and he swirled his tongue against her hairline just behind her ear when he found her hard little nipple with his thumb. He caressed it side to side.

Delora was haloed in purple from his sight.

I like looking at her like this. The colour suits her.

Especially when she turned her head to the side while biting at her bottom lip, trying to stifle a sound. It was erotic knowing she was under his touch while his vision was heated.

He darted his head down as he wrapped one of his hands around her right breast from underneath and traced his tongue across the rosy bud. The mound jiggled at her shaken expire, her back arching as she pushed it against him.

Grabbing the other, he did the same, holding both while supporting himself on his elbows. He licked across one and then the other, trying to get every reaction from her he could.

Her breath hitched. Her body waved like it either wanted to buck into him or pull away in oversensitivity. Her eyelids fluttered.

He'd been longing to touch her here again, the place he'd first touched that had started everything between them. A place he knew made her desire deepen.

She likes it.

He could have howled in triumph if he wasn't so preoccupied with learning the curves of her chest, her beautiful breasts that were all for him.

"Magnar, please," she begged when he started doing flat, dragging licks around each nipple, tracing the outside to explore the little bumps that formed a rosy ring around them.

When he looked up, he saw the back of her hand covering her

mouth and her earthy eyes watching him.

"What do you need, my little raven?"

He licked across his snout to show her his interest, his tail tapping momentarily behind him.

He was new to this. *She is begging for something.* And Magnar wanted nothing more than to give it to her.

"Y-you're really going to make me ask you for it?" she whispered in a coarse voice. He tilted his head in answer before he drew his tongue around her nipple – not on it, just around it. "I can't believe you're actually teasing me..." Her eyelids crinkled in what he thought might be anguish. "Fuck, please touch my pussy. I want you to make me come so badly."

He lifted to look down, seeing she had spread her thighs completely for him. His vision wavered when he saw her puffy mound and the pink swollen lips just beyond it. They were slick and spread, and his cock nearly shot past his protective tentacles at just the bewitching sight of her.

Touch... or lick?

The moment the thought of pressing his tongue against her pussy flashed across his mind, he was quickly flicking it down her body. Suddenly it felt dry, parched, and he wanted her to wet it.

He licked across her stomach as he lowered himself further, feeling indents like her skin had scars or stretch marks. He adored all the textures of Delora, how parts of her were smooth while others were rougher. So many aspects of her fascinated him, each one beautiful because they belonged to her. He even licked across a little dark mole he found on her side.

Then his shoulders were between her legs, which she had to push open wide to accommodate his massive frame.

He wrapped his arms around her soft and plump thighs to make sure she couldn't close them, couldn't escape him, as he licked at the outside of his fangs. The anticipation was eating at him.

The lips of her folds were parted, a needy, swollen pink, covered in her liquid, and the pool of it at the dip of her entrance was overflowing.

"You smell so good." Magnar shuddered before he even got

a taste, knowing what he was about to do was going to break him. "I have been waiting so long to do this again."

Last time he hadn't savoured her. This time, he would. He would drink from her until his thirst was quenched.

He parted his jaws and flopped his tongue over his bottom fangs so he could protect her for when he shoved his head closer. He ran the whole thing against the entire slit of her folds, starting with the back of his tongue to the very tip.

The feeling of her lips spreading under the pressure of his tongue, the silkiness, indents, creases, and even the hard nub of her clit, had his orbs flickering between purple and black as though they wanted to darken from the wonderful experience. But it was when he actually registered her taste that his sight turned to black, and his entire body puffed out when his flesh prickled.

"Nnhhnn," he violently groaned.

Magnar had to release one thigh so he could wrap his hand around his tentacles, forcing them to hold onto his cock when he almost extruded past their lengths. His shaft was throbbing, aching from the tension, from the mere taste of her.

If he'd swelled any harder, he thought he may have come against his tentacles sheathing him.

He swirled his tongue against her clit, hearing her cry as her back arched. When he did it again, her hips bucked against him and then didn't stop. She started matching him unabashedly as she tried to move against it.

But the moment he licked down to collect the new pool of dew that had formed at her entrance, then speared her with his tongue as his jaws parted over her pelvis, her hands shot down to grab the bases of his antlers.

"Ohhh!" she cried, pulling at him as if she wanted deeper.

He growled as he gave it to her and shoved harder. He twirled his tongue around as he felt every ripple of her insides, and he found there was a place that was rougher and hot. When he brushed against it deliberately, she tried wrapping her free leg around his head with another cry.

Liquid dripped between his back teeth when he began to salivate. He thrust his tongue back and forth, flexing the limb constantly so that she'd feel it squirming inside her.

Her breath hitched, and her thighs shook against him.

She let go of one of his antlers to slap a palm against his snout to push him back when he licked all the way to the end until his tongue folded against her cervix.

"Oh, *God*. I-it's too much."

He considered stopping, but when her pussy clenched his tongue to grab a hold of it and *suck* it in further, Magnar refused.

He'd felt her do that before... but around his fingers, around his cock. He knew if he kept going, what would greet him in a moment would have him nearly frothing with glee. She already tasted wonderful. He could only imagine what her orgasm would be like.

"Give it to me, Delora," he demanded, moving his tongue inside of her rapidly, spearing her over and over with it, curling it so he brushed against every surface of her channel. Her breasts jiggled when she quivered, her pants so shaken he felt it. "Come for me. I *need* to taste it."

His mouth was here, fucking begging for it.

Please. He even gave a curt whine as a plea.

"Oh, fuck. Oh, f–"

Her pussy clenched, and liquid rushed from her. It coated his tongue completely and filled his mouth.

His cock extruded as he snarled, and he clamped his fangs onto her so she couldn't free herself. She was bucking wildly, her abdomen and stomach hollowing as she let out a pleasure-filled scream.

Magnar ripped at his trousers to free his fully extended cock, needing to get it away from the abrading, rough cloth before he grabbed both her thighs firmly. Then he pulled backwards, taking her delicious pussy with him, as he straightened on his knees.

She'd released his antler and face when he hung her upside down against his body, but she didn't get a second to breathe. Not when Magnar was rapidly trying to get her to come again, holding her up with one hand around her thigh while the other moved to cross over her body to support her.

His body and antlers cast a minor shadow as he loomed over her.

Delora didn't seem to mind she was upside down, not with the sharp, broken little moans she gave him. Her shirt, which was too big on her, slipped from her body to drop to the ground, leaving her completely bared to him.

Magnar had never seen anything more heavenly than Delora's thighs parted around his skull, her hair dangling from her head, her lips parted, while he played with her insides.

It took her a moment to realise he'd freed his cock. She only did when two of his tentacles started tangling in her long black hair.

With his sight open and tinted a deep glow of purple, he watched her turn without hesitation and begin to suck on the side of his cock as she cupped the other side of it to push it closer.

Another whine escaped him, her lips and hands like torture on him. Beautiful, wonderful torture.

She licked at the nodules on the side before darting her head underneath to press into the under groove, which made it feel like she was touching the very core of him. Both her hands were stroking the length of it in different places, her left rubbing a circle over the sensitive head while the other just went up and down, caressing him all over.

I am tasting her as she is tasting me. It was rapture sharing in this kind of explorative touch of hands and tongues.

His stomach dipped, spasming, as his cock jerked and then swelled, producing a heavy drop of seed that instantly overfilled and started dripping.

She moaned when it reached her tongue and then the suckling sound that came from her filled his ears. Slurping against his shaft, she kept stealing his lubricant, leaving it to sting until he produced more. But somehow the pain of it felt... good. She was coaxing him to make more, even though he was already rather coated, her taste alone enough to keep his cock lubricated.

She paused when her pussy clenched again, and she squished her mouth against the side of his cock as she sweetly cried against it. He had to lick it from the well of her channel to bring it inside his mouth when she started coming this time, taking it *drop* by *drop* with his scooping tongue.

Her body slumped when she relaxed. He thrust his cock

forward through the air when she stopped touching it, stopped playing with it with her hungry little mouth.

"Keep going, Delora."

He *needed* her to nurse him.

"I'm getting really dizzy," she slurred.

He noticed then that the flush on her face was much darker than usual when she was aroused. The blood seemed to be rushing to her head due to her position.

As much as he was enjoying the tantalising view of her like this, he changed into a position that might be better for her.

Wanting the weight of her on top of him, Magnar moved his legs out from under himself until he was able to lie back. He wasn't going to give up his prize, clamping his fangs into her flesh, but he needed her to keep touching him.

He was too hard, too engorged, for his tentacles to control. He was past the point of being able to stop. If she didn't continue, he would gladly take over with his fist.

He panted against her when she immediately turned onto her side and sucked at the tip with a content little 'mmm' coming from her. She lathered him in precious kisses, stroking her hands in unison down his cock until she reached the ovals embedded into the base. She tickled them.

A curt whine exploded from him as his legs kicked out against the dirt, his tail quivering while his spine arched.

I can't take it when she does that to me.

Every time she stroked them so lightly that it felt like a flutter, he thought he was going to spontaneously ejaculate.

She did it again, eyeing him with a heated expression this time like she *knew* what she was doing to him. He didn't know what the mangled sound that came from him was, but it was like a twisted combination of a whine and snarl.

She'd caused semen to start flowing from his enthusiastic cock in a light, steady stream.

His groin was in agony, and he could barely keep his hips still. He could feel the fur on his tail had puffed, as had most of it covering his flesh. His entire body was excited, not just his cock.

But in her trying to reach the bases with her hands, she was pulling herself away from his mouth. Magnar growled before yanking her back deep between his fangs. She relented until she wanted to start exploring with her tongue further down.

She drew away again, growing fascinated by his cock, in frolicking with it, and sucking and licking it, while her hands moved. She was too short to reach him lower down if he wanted to keep tasting her.

He tugged her back, red flaring into his orbs. *"Stay."*

"Why does your cock have to taste so fucking good?" she asked with a pant, rubbing the seam of her lips over the rim of his flaring cockhead. "It's so big. I wish I could put my mouth– *Oh!* Right there. Yes, d-don't stop."

Since she'd been able to talk when his mind felt like it was in a thousand pieces, he'd dipped his thumb inside her pussy as well, stretching her and stroking that swollen, rough section that made her shiver every time he touched it. The webbing between his thumb and index finger also rubbed against her folds, the nub of her clit, and she stayed where she was as she moved back and forth over him.

Her movements became more frantic, her mouth darting over him before she paused to moan, just squeezing his shaft with her hands. Then everything got tight. Her body as it filled with tension, her pussy that clamped down on his thumb and tongue, and her hands that tried to crush the stone-like hardness of his cock.

If she likes the taste of my cock so much, then she can drink from it again. He popped his thumb from her as she came, filling his mouth and making him quake as it burst against his tongue.

He had to remove his thumb. His claws had started to unsheathe when his cock swelled, and his seed sacs lifted and sunk, hot and tight, against him. He gripped the back of her head and directed her mouth to the tip of his cock, hoping she'd latch onto it like she'd done the previous night.

His body shuddered when the first bubble of semen climbed his shaft, the throbbing unbearable, painful – the pressure was immense.

If he couldn't fill her pussy with it, then he wanted her mouth to be filled. To have his scent in her in some way, for her to possess it.

She cupped the head with both hands and swirled her tongue as if she was trying to coax it from him herself when it was already too late to stop it.

With a roar, her moan joining him, Magnar released spurt after thick spurt from his pulsating cock. He tried his hardest not claw her when his body was shot with tension like he was being hit with a bolt of lightning.

Coming with her at the same time, both of them drinking each other down, Magnar felt euphoria take over. His roar turned into a helpless groan. His sight darkened, his mind blanked, and all he heard and felt was them.

Just them in the aftermath of heat, of need, of *passion.*

Bliss and contentment floated through him.

When he was done, he finally slipped his tongue from her as all the strength in his body gave way. His antlers smacked against the ground when his head fell back, but he didn't mind. He just huffed as he stared up at the twinkling stars he could see through the mist.

They seemed brighter than normal.

For just a few seconds, they both lay there panting. There was a mixture of scents in the air, but the ones that stole him were their scents of sexual release.

That felt amazing. Magnar gave her clit an appreciative last, but lazy, lick. *She is so wonderful, so alluring.*

He didn't know where she got the energy from when she started to move, comfortably crawling over him until she was straddling his waist so she could stare down at him. She was completely on top of him, her knees resting over his protruding rib bones, like she knew he could handle her light, human weight.

He pushed her up and down as he huffed.

With her breasts pressed together but hanging from her chest as her hands pressing against his, she smiled down at him, her messy hair crawling over one shoulder to slip forward.

"Feel better now?" she asked him with her eyes glinting.

Clumps of hair were stuck to the white liquid he could see was coating her lips, cheeks, and chin, like she hadn't managed to catch all of his release this time.

His own snout was glistening in her juices as well, and he

licked across it for a final taste.

She was smiling at him... covered in his release that had even dripped onto her breasts while she sat on top of his rapidly moving torso.

Magnar had never seen anything so beautiful, had never felt the deep tenderness that overtook him in that moment.

I want her. He lifted his hand until he brushed his claws across the side of her neck. *This is not enough.*

He needed her to accept him, to take him, to mesh them together until they were as one as they could be.

Dark green, a possessive flare, flashed in his orbs.

I want more of her. He wanted to consume every single bit of her desire.

Magnar darted forward, rolling them both until she fell against the ground with an *oomph*. She gasped when he grabbed her wrists and pinned them to the ground above her head.

Her thighs were around his waist, but now his cock, which had been softening, was against the slit of her pussy. He pulled back and rubbed it over her with a rumbling growl falling from him.

His tentacles shifted to move around her hips to capture her as best as they could. They wanted the ease of wrapping around her body when his hips were flat against hers because she'd swallowed him completely whole.

"You are mine," he snarled down at her.

She shivered before looking down and undulating against his cock, *greeting* his movement. So, he did it again, and again, wanting her to crave it as much as it already craved sinking into the heat of her.

Licking at the seam of her lips, she let out this high-pitched moan, one that had her quickly panting behind it. She wasn't fighting him, wasn't trying to get away, wasn't struggling to free her hands. She was being compliant, submissive even.

She looked up at him, and the way she nibbled at her lip, her eyes glinting with a hint of *something,* had him shuddering. She bucked into his cock again, this time deeper, since he was growing hard. It swelled so it would lubricate and stay moist.

I want my cock inside her so badly. For her to nurse me, hold me, comfort me with her entire being. His gaze darted down to their bodies slipping against each other before he lifted it to her mesmerising face, feeling lost in the heady expression she gave him. *I want her to crave me.*

"Magnar," she whispered, almost like a plea. "I want y–"

A horrible shrill caught both their attention. A coldness rushed through him just as she let out a sharp gasp.

It was a reminder.

A reminder that even if Magnar wanted this, wanted to connect and be inside Delora, he actually... couldn't.

I want to be with her. He wanted nothing in the way, but it just seemed never-ending. Even after all this, even after tonight and the pleasure they shared, there was still a barrier between them.

The bashing at the door as that shrill continued and grew more frantic had Magnar releasing Delora's hands slowly, unwilling to let her go as he slipped his claw tips down the insides of her wrist. But he knew he had to.

"I should go to them," Delora whispered, turning her head to the side and averting her gaze.

Fyodor. Magnar cared for them deeply, but they were a constant reminder of what would happen if they were to be intimate.

We can touch and taste, but nothing more.

Because... Magnar knew if he was to be inside her, nothing would stop him until he filled her with his seed.

Then there would be a second youngling, and Magnar and Delora could barely properly care for the first. He also didn't think he could handle having to watch her be unwell again.

He didn't want to have to restart their journey.

They could share in pleasure, that had to be enough for now.

Despite the sorrow that overtook him, Magnar leaned down and bumped the tip of his snout at the underside of her jaw.

"You may go to them," he told her, hoping the dark rumbling coming from his tone was enticing. "But every night, my delicious raven, I am going to want a taste of this pretty pussy. I am going to lick it until you come, until you cover my snout in your scent, just so I can breathe it in the next day while I work on the house."

She shivered and rubbed her cheek against him even as she rose to her knees.

"You shouldn't promise things like that," she answered oh-so-sweetly, placing her palm on his disappearing tentacle-covered cock before it was gone. "I can be pretty greedy in return."

Magnar chuckled.

"You can take as much as you like."

In fact, he was hoping she would.

FORTY

While seated on the ground with his legs crossed, Magnar stared up at Delora, who was standing with a thin paintbrush between her fingertips. He felt the cool glide as she stroked the wetted bristles against his skull and the conflicting warmth that came from her holding the underneath of his jaw to keep him steady.

Fyodor was nestled in his lap. Now that they'd grown bigger – almost the size of a human *toddler* – and were able to support their head, they seemed to prefer lying down whenever they could. They still clung to both Delora and Magnar's bodies, but they'd also begun walking around sightlessly and sniffing around while always remaining close.

Magnar stroked his claws over their back. They shook and turned to the side in contentment as he gazed up at Delora with his sight a bright flamingo pink.

The sun reflecting from the side made her right eye brighten to such a light hazel that it appeared as though it wanted to turn golden. The other was a lighter brown than normal, and he was delighted in the fact that she was looking upon him and giving him all of her attention.

He'd asked her if she would like to paint his skull again when he saw she was unsure of what she wanted to paint on the back wall of the house. It was mostly full there, and she seemed to have the colourful picture completed.

He currently sat in the middle of the garden, and he was thankful he'd taken the leap to do this. He'd wanted her to draw patterns on his skull again since the first time she'd done it. It also allowed him to spend time with her up close.

So close, in fact, that he could see her cute brows twitching as she concentrated. Her lips puckered just as she started a stroke before they relaxed.

It felt intimate. It made him feel wholly close to her, but in a way that wasn't sexual. His eyes were bright pink rather than purple, and he had a light, fluffy feeling in his chest. Rather than his body feeling warm, it was like his soul, his very essence, was being warmed instead.

And every time she leaned even closer to dab a bit of paint against him, his heart beat wildly like a drum. Although he wished it would cease its movements, his tail tapped against the ground.

But his heart and mind wouldn't settle, hoping she'd come just a touch closer. It was like his heart was beating manically in anticipation, in nervous hope that she would.

It was becoming too much to bear, especially when she started painting right above his forehead, lifting herself away but still coming closer.

When her lips moved again, he couldn't resist the urge this time. Before she could put the brush against him, he lifted his snout and nudged it forward, pressing his front fangs against them. The plump, warm softness of her lips moulding around his fangs sent a shiver of pleasure throughout his entire being.

She leaned back and covered her mouth with the hand that had been keeping his head still.

"Did you just steal a kiss?" she asked behind her fingers.

"I did."

Even though he knew he shouldn't, he licked his fangs at the ghost of touch he could still feel. He wanted to take the taste of the stolen kiss into his mouth.

"Nooo!" she whined, placing her hand over his fangs to try to stop him. "I told you not to do that until it dries! You'll smudge it."

Magnar grabbed her forearm, swallowing it in his fist, as he pulled her hand back and licked at her palm. Her face twinged as she gave a little gasp before he drew his tongue down the inside of her wrist. Her twitch grew more intense as she let out a strangled noise.

Her face flushed a *cute* red. She stiffened but didn't draw away from him. "T-that tickles."

"You are very sensitive all over, my little raven."

He released her arm so he could slip both of his hands under the bottom of her skirt to drag the very tips of his claws all the way from the backs of her ankles to her thighs. Her legs buckled inwards under his caress, especially when he got to the backs of her knees. He steadied her before she could fall by gripping her lower thighs from behind.

"Magnar." She nibbled at the inner seam of her bottom lip, her scent ripening ever so slightly into something much more alluring than just frosty red apples.

"You are the most beautiful creature I have ever seen," he rasped, beginning the path of his palms upwards again. "I cannot resist wanting to touch you."

He wished she hadn't removed her hand to place it on his shoulder. He wanted to lick it to show her his appreciation for her as he glided his claws over the round handfuls of her arse cheeks that were remarkably soft on the outside, but firm if he grabbed at them. But he didn't knead them. He just continued his path up her sides, passing over her hip dips and then the pudge above it.

"We shouldn't be doing this right now," she whispered, but her tone was weak – like that wasn't really what she wanted.

Her eyes darted down to his lap, to little Fyodor resting upon him. He wanted Delora under his touch, under his tongue, moaning for him whenever he wanted, but their youngling was always with them.

Last night, he'd deliberately, yet slyly, stirred her from her sleep before he'd gotten up, hoping she might want to come with him. The moment she'd opened her eyes, she'd been biting at her lip, lazily staring at him before he even had the chance to get up.

It was unfortunate that they could only initiate touch in this way. She had to be still and asleep before they could start, but any time they'd tried to leave Fyodor on their own when they weren't completely and utterly lulled, they'd let out a cry. Although they hadn't tried, they didn't need to in order to know that leaving Fyodor inside by themself wasn't a suitable option. They'd bash their skull against the front door, begging and fighting to be with them.

Every time it distressed Delora, and Magnar found it hard to concentrate on this beauty when she fretted.

And he could see that trying to touch her while they were around wasn't going to happen.

Magnar, being careful of the paint on his face, bumped the tip of his snout against her jaw and settled his hands around her waist. His big hands almost fit around the dip in her torso, his pinkies splaying over her rounded hips, but it was only his claws that touched each other. If he'd been holding a smaller human, he knew his fingers would be overlapping, and he would've worried the entire time that he'd snap them in half.

"I will not touch further," he promised, hoping she would just let him hold her in some way.

There was something about her form that left him feeling euphoric whenever he was given the opportunity to hold it. It was warm and sensual and felt like utter bliss. Her body was so sensitive that even the slightest movement of his claws brushing over her spine or just under those lovely round mounds on her chest had her shivering into his hold, almost melting for him.

Now that he was allowed to touch, Magnar craved touching more than before. He couldn't be sheathed inside her, a nagging ache that refused to relent, and the only way he could find peace was the heaven of it up against any part of him.

It had been three nights since she'd tasted him for the first time, and there was a lingering scent on her that put his mind at ease.

When he'd first met Reia, she'd smelt of sticks and thorns, fresh and clean. But at some point, after they'd ventured to the Demon Village together, she'd begun to smell of a salty sweetness, something that had become a massive deterrent to him.

It had smelled like a possession, a marking, one that he'd felt all the way to his gut not to interfere with. Magnar hadn't understood it. He only knew that he was not to get too close to Reia, or he should become wary of the one who'd given her this scent mark – Orpheus.

It was the same scent that was now coated over Delora, but it had come from him.

No matter how much she washed her skin, she couldn't rid herself of it straight away. It dulled throughout the day, her natural body oils dampening it until he replaced it again the following night.

For three nights, Delora had been, in some way, covered in his seed. Whether that was internally from drinking it down – he shuddered every time in memory, his orbs flashing purple for a millisecond – or from globs of it missing her lips and coating her face and chest.

It felt like he'd claimed her, even if he couldn't claim her fully. She was his and was now warded away from other Mavka.

"Orpheus and Reia will have reached the Demon Village by now," Magnar stated when Delora relaxed in his hands and began to paint his skull some more. Her hands were a little unsteady.

He wanted Orpheus to return so he could know, could scent that Delora was his, just by being in her presence. Orpheus had Reia, and Magnar knew he didn't want Delora, but he wanted to be able to gloat in front of him that he had reached this stage by himself.

He also *needed* him to return.

I must ask him if there is a way. They hadn't created their own Fyodor, so what could Magnar do to prevent this?

Because, as much as tasting, touching, and devouring his bride quelled the worst of his desires, they were ever growing. He was becoming agitated, not with her, but with this.

Even just last night, after he'd made sure they'd both come, he'd remained hard, aching to nestle his cock inside her warm little pussy. He burned for it, needed to feel her comfort him from the inside, to fill her insides until she knew she belonged to him, until her body moulded to fit his and he'd permanently broken it in for himself.

Will I need to redo the spell? The one that changed her body for him? Would she be delightfully tight and compelling, or wonderfully fitted to him so he could just slam his cock inside her?

A soft growl began to emit from the back of his throat until he lowered his hands, pushing his clawed fingers through the mesh of her thighs. She shivered as she gave a little moan, her inner thighs a place he knew she liked to be touched. But he didn't reach any higher in order to obey his promise.

There was no gap between her thighs and her flesh began to warm his fingertips for him.

What I wouldn't give to release my cock and pull her onto it right now. The idea was a ravenous one that took ahold of him like a roaring inferno, singeing his mind and body with heat. Violent and frantic.

Magnar flinched when Delora rushed forward and pressed a hard kiss to the end of his snout before drawing back.

"I don't know what's bothering you, but your eyes are going red, and you're kind of hurting me with your claws."

Magnar released the press he had but kept his hands where they were, unwilling to let go of her. His sight faded to its usual green, and he cleared his throat to rid himself of the thick, clogging emotion in it.

"I'm sorry," he answered. "I will be still again for you."

The smile she gave him washed away his concerns.

She is so forgiving. Magnar was thankful for that, as much of what he'd done had required forgiveness.

"No need, I'm all done!" Then she turned slightly to set her brush down into a paint bowl before placing her hands on her hips. "Thank you for letting me do this. It's a lot of fun. Maybe next time you can paint mine, but I promise I'll be a better statue than you."

"I would like that," he said, removing a hand so he could brush the backs of his claws over her plaited hair. His sight followed his movements.

She mentioned it had been bothering her whenever she tried to paint.

It was the first time he'd seen her do anything with it, and he liked the long crossing intersections. In order to keep it together, she tied a strip of torn cloth at the end.

It was by pure luck that one of his feathers had managed to fall out and stick to it, which led to him pulling a few more out and shoving them into the plait. She'd been surprisingly compliant about this, which he was utterly appreciative of.

Magnar began to stand, raising himself from below her until he was towering in her presence, but the fearless gaze she gave him was so endearing.

Fyodor, suddenly being woken, rushed to their four paws to semi-walk and semi-hop around.

Delora reached down to grab them by the torso when it appeared as though they were about to knock into a bowl, and she burst out laughing when they squealed.

I like watching them together, he thought, as Fyodor kicked their legs until Delora cuddled them to her chest.

She nuzzled her cheek against the top of their head. "You're such a good Duskwalker. Aren't you, Fyodor?"

Magnar chose that moment to retreat, hating having any awkward separational conversations, as he was unfamiliar with how to do so smoothly. While he was walking away, his sight crossed multiple times as he tried to see what she'd painted over his snout.

He entered the house and went to the doorless shelves above the kitchen counters, reaching into them to obtain his whetstone from its new home. Then he went back outside and grabbed his axe from the edge of the porch steps before sitting down upon them. He used the whetstone to sharpen the blade.

His sight drifted over his protected territory.

I wonder which tree I should cut down next. It may not look like it to others, but he was carefully selecting which ones he removed. He wanted to keep much of the forest as possible, but thinning it out was his goal, so that it didn't look so dense or unnerving.

He liked the comfort of the dark and wanted to be able to watch the leaves change with the seasons. However, he also didn't want his female to have to witness such a foreboding scene, and was hoping to create the illusion they weren't in the Demon-infested Veil.

"Come back here, you little rascal!" he heard Delora yell from the side.

She was running across the yard, chasing Fyodor who had

managed to steal one of her paintbrushes and had run off with it. Magnar chuckled, even when his blind youngling bashed headfirst into a tree.

Unbothered, like Fyodor didn't feel any pain whatsoever – because they *never* did – they shook their head and bashed into it again when they tried to go around it. After the third attempt, right as Delora was about to catch up to them, they managed to dart past it and into the forest.

Magnar knew they wouldn't go far.

Ever since they'd eaten the Demon and gotten bigger, Fyodor was more active throughout the afternoons.

This was the second time they'd run off with something, the first being a spoon she'd been using to cook with. Watching Delora chase them inside of the house had been quite humorous until Fyodor ran into her legs and knocked her over.

Her shin had begun bleeding from a cut Fyodor had created. Delora turned incorporeal and prevented them from going into a hunger-filled rage. Magnar then put them in the bedroom while he took her wound to heal her.

They seemed to have no desire to eat Mavka, even when Magnar had been bleeding in their presence.

His sight darted through the forest as he watched the wisp of Delora rushing around in sporadic directions, the yellow of contentment filling his sight.

If I hadn't cleared the forest a little, she may have caught up by now. Perhaps Fyodor's incident with the tree had taught them to sniff their way around the forest.

Then he couldn't see them for a bit.

He turned his head down to watch what he was doing with his sharpening stone, making sure he didn't damage the blade.

"Magnar!" he heard her call. He rushed to his feet at the panic he heard in her tone. "They're heading for the border!"

His muscles tensed, white entering his vision, as dread clutched at him all the way down to the marrow of his bones.

No! Without a second thought, Magnar carelessly tossed everything to the side and sprinted in the direction he'd heard her voice.

He was fast, pushing off the occasional tree to quicken his

frantic pace. He followed her scent all the way to the border –
where he instantly lost it.

She's turned incorporeal. Which meant he couldn't follow
either of their scents into the forest. *They're not safe out there!*

"Delora!" he shouted, heading past the protection ward and
straight into the Veil.

"This way!"

She was close by, only a few metres past the trees, but out of
sight. As soon as he sprinted that way, his heart racing in his
chest, he saw a flicker of white rushing between the trees.

Delora, his usually wary female, was braving the Veil just to
keep an eye on their youngling to make sure they didn't lose them
forever. To make sure they weren't eaten or stolen by a Demon
that could be lurking nearby.

Despite his orbs being white with concern, he was overcome
with pride. *She is growing strong.*

As soon as he caught up to her, he saw Fyodor darting around
with the paintbrush still in their mouth. They ran through shrubs,
occasionally tripped over roots, but they refused to slow. Within
only a few long steps, Magnar dove and caught them in his arms.
He rolled forward, being careful of his large, branching antlers,
before he landed on his arse with his feet thudding against the
dirt in front of him.

Thunk. Thunk.

The playful baby Mavka gave an excited shrill at being
caught, squirming to get out of his hold. Their little heart was
beating wildly with exhilaration in his large palms while they
snorted wet puffs through their nose hole.

Magnar instantly knew this was going to be a reoccurring
issue with how much fun they'd seemed to have.

"Are you okay?" Magnar asked Delora as she stared down at
both of them with wide eyes.

She wasn't huffing since she was in her ghostly form, but she
looked rather frazzled.

"No," she admitted softly. "That scared the absolute shit out
of me. I know you can't smell them, and what if a Demon
came?!"

"I have them now." He lifted his arms to gesture to them, his tension easing now that he securely had Fyodor. He'd been rather panicked before. "But we should head back quickly."

He could hear rustling nearby, and the foul scent of a Demon on the tail of the wind.

There was no need to run as they made their way back, since Fyodor hadn't managed to get too far away from the border.

Once they were all in the safety of his ward, Delora took the paintbrush from Fyodor's mouth.

"Maybe you should build a fence around the ward so this doesn't happen again," Delora suggested.

"I was just thinking the same thing."

It would be a lot of work, but he was pleased that he would have something to do. Most of the furniture within the house was built, other than a bed and wardrobe for their room, as well as whatever she wanted in the second room. He'd originally planned to build a second, smaller bed in there for her, but she'd told him she didn't want one.

She wanted to sleep with him at night.

As they were walking back towards the house, Magnar put Fyodor on the ground, knowing they wouldn't run now that they didn't have anything to make her chase them with.

I will have to start building straight away. Magnar grew disgruntled at his thoughts. *It will take me a very long time to span the entire ward.*

It would be weeks of work.

I'll have to stop everything else I am doing.

He didn't think Delora would mind, not when Fyodor's safety was her first priority.

The sound of deep huffing caught his attention, one that was quick and snorting. Magnar quickly pulled Delora to his side when the scent of a Mavka, one he'd met but was mostly unfamiliar with, fluttered over a gust of wind.

Thumping paw-steps, four of them as though the Mavka was on all fours, could be heard coming this way – and *fast*. His kind could reach a speed quicker than anything on Earth, and he knew it would be only a few moments before the approaching Mavka would reach them.

That's if he was intending to come this way at all.

"Delora, turn–" Before he could even finish telling her to become intangible, she did it.

At the same moment, a set of white floating orbs appeared in the darkness of the Veil's forest.

The Mavka broke through the tree line and crossed into the ward. It only kept out Demons, which meant his kind were free to come and go, even if they meant harm. A salt circle may have prevented him access, but Magnar, seeing the stark white of his orbs, knew he wasn't here to be malicious.

As soon as he was safely within the ward, the Mavka skidded to a halt across the dirt. He stopped right next to them, his most monstrous form inhaling and exhaling with such deeply sawing breaths that Magnar thought he'd choke or cease breathing at any moment.

He was covered in forest debris. It looked and sounded as though he'd been running for an exceptionally long time.

Then the Mavka darted his head to them, revealing a feline skull with curling ram horns on the sides of it. He had lizard-like spikes shooting from his back over his protruding spine bones, and smaller ones ran down his forearms.

With sharp, thin, feline fangs parted, his tongue moved back and forth as he struggled to breathe.

However, a horrible feeling overcame Magnar at what his sight focused on, something that made him feel hollow all the way down to the pit of his soul.

Dark-purple blood was heavily dripping from a *crack* in his skull. The crack started from the top of his skull between his ram horns before it ran down his face to circle his left eye socket. Blood flicked and dripped from his nose hole in heavy, continuous drops.

He's been attacked.

Someone tried to kill him. Someone who *knew* how to kill Mavka. Someone with the strength to deal such a debilitating blow.

The ram-horned Mavka's orbs turned black before he finally collapsed on his side, either too weak from blood loss or too tired from running to remain awake any longer, now that he knew he was somewhat safe.

He was choosing to trust them.

The only word that came from him was garbled, but it sounded like a name.

"Mayumi."

Then he crumpled completely, limp and unconscious.

FORTY-ONE

Magnar stepped towards the unfamiliar Mavka hesitantly, keeping himself in front of Delora, who had turned physical behind him. He then crouched low in order to get a closer inspection of the Mavka's skull.

There was a spot on his forehead, right behind the brow, where it looked as though something sharp, but small, had punctured it – perhaps a claw.

"Is he okay?" Delora asked, pressing herself against his back while peeking over his shoulder.

"I don't know," Magnar answered truthfully.

Yet, he could feel his heart sinking.

The ram-horned Mavka was breathing unsteadily at a heavy and quick rate, but his skull was cracked. It was currently bleeding profusely and had been for a long time considering the multiple tracks of blood on his face. It may stop bleeding at some point, but... Magnar knew he wouldn't be able to heal this.

He'd met another Mavka briefly in his life, a mere passing over a distance, and his skull had been permanently marred with claw marks. Some had looked *old*.

This Mavka would never heal this wound, not even in a day, and if it continued to break... he would die, permanently. Forever. Never to return.

Fyodor came around to sniff at the injured Mavka's face. Magnar thought they must understand something was amiss with him, considering the blood and his breathing. Especially when their youngling just sat in front of him and whined.

On an instinctual level, Fyodor understood something was wrong.

Magnar didn't know if Delora could tell he was feeling sorrowful, but her small hand rubbing his back between his tense shoulder blades was the comfort he needed.

"Do you know him?" Delora asked.

"No," he answered with a shake of his head. "Not really. I think most Mavka have come across each other as we often wander the Veil, but I've only spoken a few words to them. This one I have met more than the others, besides Orpheus, but our conversations have been brief."

"So, do you consider him your friend?"

She came around to his side and bent her body sideways so she could see his orbs had turned a deep blue.

Her black plait slipped off her shoulder. A feather came loose, dropping into the pool of dark blood that was beginning to form under the Mavka from the extensive wounds he had on his body.

As the Mavka continued to lie there, his monstrous form began to disappear. Unlike Magnar, who had only just begun to wear proper pants and a button-up shirt in the last few months, this Mavka already wore those as they lifted through his flesh. His feet were bare, and Magnar imagined that was so he could wander freely.

"Orpheus and Reia are my friends. You are my bride." Magnar turned his face to Delora. "He is no one. I don't trust him."

Her brows drew together to knot tightly, her lips thinning.

"But he isn't no one, Magnar. In reality, he and Orpheus are your brothers. You all came from the Witch Owl and that void spirit guy. That means you're family."

Family? he thought, once more looking upon the Mavka before him. *Brother?*

His roaming sight paused at Fyodor still sitting there.

If Delora and he were to make a second youngling, they would be siblings. Brothers, most likely, and they would be family. They would have a unique connection. *Like father and child? Bride and Mavka? These are all families? They are all special to me?*

The world was interconnected between relationships, some closer than others, but it warmed him to know that if he really looked upon his past, he'd never been truly alone. He had parents, brothers... he just hadn't known how to understand them.

The reverse was also probably true.

However, this understanding meant that the sinking feeling in his chest was growing more painful by the second.

He didn't want anyone important to him to die – even the ones he didn't know of yet.

"Perhaps that is why Orpheus helped me when he didn't need to. Because he felt a connection to me. You are right, he is more than my friend. He is my family." Then he turned his head and bumped the end of his snout against her affectionately. "Thank you for showing me this."

The corners of her lips wanted to curl, but they only twitched because of the sad reality that lay before them.

Something inside him desperately needed to hold her. He needed the comfort and warmth of her body meshing into his to erase the terrible coldness.

For some reason, I feel... lonely.

Just as he began reaching up with the intention of wrapping his hand around the nape of her neck to draw her closer, the fur and feathers covering his flesh stood on end.

A terrible, foul scent infiltrated the air just before he heard the rumble of *multiple* footsteps coming their way.

"Found him," an unfamiliar voice, dark and deep and cruel, spat from just beyond the protection ward.

It was a new scent, one that had come closer but appeared *suddenly*.

Magnar turned his head to the side and then quickly drew Delora against his back to shield her. He also found himself stepping towards the unconscious Mavka protectively when he saw the person standing before them had dried blood that smelled of Mavka on one of his hands – especially around one of his thumbs.

"Stay," he warned Delora, needing to know she was safe by feeling her pressed against him, before he gave a deep and continuous warning growl.

The Demon King, he thought with a snarl, his sight morphing into a bright crimson.

The sound of thumping feet grew louder by the second before a Demon burst through the tree line.

He joined the Demon King, who stood before them wearing light-blue harem pants that were tied above his strong calf muscles. His feet were bare and curled with small claws.

He wore no shirt, instead adorning himself with golden jewellery, such as a necklace and arm bands that cut into the bulge of his muscles, more on his left than the right. Dark, tanned skin wrapped the meat of his body, while his ears were long and sharply pointed. There were also two dark horns that protruded from his hairline, curling back over his long blueish-white hair.

He answered Magnar's growl by baring his fangs, his dark eyes narrowing into a hate-filled glare of contempt.

More Demons filed in, perhaps six overall.

One of them was familiar, and it didn't take Magnar long to place where he'd seen him. He looked like a human except for his red eyes, void-like skin, and the fact that he was walking on all fours.

That's the Demon who spoke to me when we were heading back from the village. He'd found the ram-horned Mavka he was after, and in doing so, they'd harmed him.

Shame tore through Magnar, causing his orbs to flicker a reddish pink momentarily.

I should have done something. I should have killed him.

If Magnar had, would this Mavka currently be fine and uninjured? But... he hadn't understood the ramifications of not interfering back then.

He'd been focused on making sure Delora was safe.

Magnar's red sight landed on the multiple Demons with Jabez, the Demon King. He had many hunting for his fellow Mavka.

His stomach knotted like a heavy weight in his gut.

Jabez folded his arms across his muscled chest and cocked one of his white brows at Magnar. Then he leaned his head to the side to quietly speak to the Demon Magnar had met in the forest.

"You didn't tell me the antler Mavka had a human."

Tension shot straight through Magnar and clutched at his bones. Delora was under the eyes of the Demon King, and he wanted her nowhere near him. He didn't want anyone unworthy to look upon his precious bride, anyone who could harm her soft skin, or taint her wonderful scent with her own blood.

He reached back with his arm to push her flush against him. There was no point in her turning incorporeal, she was safely within the protection ward, safely against him – that's all that mattered.

She was with him. By his side for him to protect.

"He didn't have one before," the Demon answered with his head tilted to the side, red eyes trying to look around Magnar. "Last time he had a Ghost companion. This one is different."

The snarl that escaped Magnar was even more vicious towards the Demon on all fours. He didn't want a single red eye on her that wasn't his own.

"I also didn't know he'd made a house here," the Demon continued, trying to look through the tree line. "Otherwise, I would have informed you, sire. It is hard to see it past the trees, which is probably why I missed it."

Magnar had been thinning the trees, so he was sure parts of it were visible – perhaps the corner of the house or the step of the porch or its railing.

"I've been so busy chasing after the ram-horned one that I haven't been keeping an eye on them all." Jabez lifted a single arm and used it to give a half-hearted shrug. Then he finally narrowed his eyes back on Magnar, sneering with sharp fangs clenched tightly. "I hadn't realised that you'd moved from that pathetic little cave you called a home. You should have stayed there. Stayed out of my kingdom."

"The Veil is home to all that live within it. You cannot tell me where I can or cannot live," Magnar rumbled back.

"I made it!" he roared, unfolding his arms to display his claws with curled fingers splayed. "If it wasn't for me, it would still be the forest it started out as! If I hadn't used my magic to make the forest grow and the canyon bigger, then none of you Mavka would even have a place to reside that wasn't infested by lowly humans."

Delora clutched onto the back of his shirt tighter with each yell from the Demon King.

"That still doesn't make it yours."

"You know what?" Jabez relaxed his shoulders and swiped back the long strands of his hair that had fallen over his face. It seemed he was used to displaying frequent outbursts before regaining fleeting control. "I don't give a fuck either way. If none of you will join my army, then you will all die eventually." Then he raised a hand to point a claw at the unconscious Mavka upon the ground. "Just give him to me, and I'll let you live your sad, pathetic life with your human, for now. He's all I want."

Magnar darted his head to the side as he shuffled back. He pressed his ankle into his side until he knew his crouched position had partially hidden the ram-horned Mavka from view.

"No," he bit. "You have already cracked his skull. I won't let you kill him."

Delora was doing a wonderful job of controlling her fear, choosing to curl herself into Magnar's back. She trusted him, trusted the protective ward, trusted that she didn't need to be afraid.

If so, if she would have begun to smell of it and sent the Demons in the area into a rampage to get to her. Perhaps she also knew it would affect Fyodor as well and remained calm just for them.

She was being brave, and Magnar felt pride in her for that – especially since she had once been terrified of Demons.

It seemed she was growing braver every day.

Jabez's lips curled in rage before he rammed his fist against the protective ward. It gave a burst of lightning across the transparent green bubble, but it showed no signs of wavering or breaking.

"We don't want to fight," Magnar continued. "Your war is not our own."

"How would you know what I'm fighting for?" Jabez said back. "I'm fighting for the injustice of my own kind. What I'm doing is pushing back against our oppressors for everything they've done to push us into near extinction until we came here. We deserve to live."

"So do we."

Magnar tried to relax his stiff shoulders, hoping to reach some sense of truce with the Demon King – not just for himself, but for all Mavka.

Orpheus had been impeded by Katerina's hatred, never given the opportunity to speak with the Demon King calmly. She had been a barrier, a hateful one.

Magnar didn't have that.

He'd never crossed paths with Jabez. They'd never had a conflict. In some ways, Magnar had been lucky.

Lucky because Delora had literally fallen from the sky to become his – like destiny had intertwined their fates long before they'd met. Lucky because he had Orpheus to guide him on how to be a better Mavka. Lucky because he had Reia to show him how to care for a human by his being near one. And lucky because, other than the Serpent Demon, he'd rarely had altercations with Demons, and therefore, Jabez.

"But that is not what you are fighting for," Magnar continued. "*You* are starting a war with the Elves because of how they treated you. Orpheus has explained everything to me. How you brought the Demons here through your portal, how you made this land habitable for them, gave them the things they needed in order to become strong. You aren't doing any of this for them, but for yourself."

"You have no idea how they treated me," Jabez growled, his hands clenching into fists. "I was put in a fucking cage and experimented on because I was half-Elf and half-Demon. A rarity because no Elf would *willingly* lay with a Demon. But it was Demons who saved me. Them!" He gestured his hands back to the multiple Demons who had surrounded him from behind. "The Elvish people are cruel. They made us what we are and then tried to destroy us because of what we needed to eat in order to survive. I am fighting for the injustice that not only I have received, but they have as well." Then he locked his gaze on Magnar, his eyes sharp and deadly, before he bared his fangs again. "I was not the only one put in a cage."

"If you were truly fighting for the justice of others, you would leave us Mavka be," Magnar tried to argue. "We have done nothing wrong. Why should we die just because we won't fight in your war?"

"Because you fucking Mavka keep killing our kind!"

"Because your kind attack us!" The rise and fall of Magnar's chest grew faster with every minute, his heart pumping wildly in his chest. The calm he'd been seeking was lost to the failure he could see coming. "Demons don't make us hungry. Your kind smells foul. We only eat your kind when they attack because we succumb to the hunger of our bloodlust. To the humans, Mavka and Demons are no better than each other."

"That's what happens in war," Jabez answered coldly, his expression turning nonchalant. "Casualties happen, and whenever someone gets in the way, no matter which side they're on, or no side at all, they die. It's for the greater good. I have asked many of your kind to join me, and I've tried to be accommodating. You have all said no. You have even said it just now. So what value do you have to me other than being in the way? I have left you alone when I could have attacked you at any point because you have always remained on the border of the Veil – until recently, it seems. You're nothing but a Mavka, so how would you truly understand the complexities that I must face as a king that wishes the best for his people?"

Magnar pondered on Jabez's words.

It was true; Magnar had no idea what Jabez had to endure in his self-proclaimed position. The Demon King *could* be fighting on the right side of the war he was creating, but Magnar couldn't shake the *bitterness* that his kind was being targeted.

There were blank spaces in his mind, thoughts that unravelled as they were forming, reminding him he still hadn't obtained enough humanity to truly understand... everything. He was still stunted, so how could he imagine the weight resting upon Jabez's shoulders?

I want to understand.

He wanted to help his kind any way he could, but he didn't want to fight in a war. He didn't want to fight at all.

He wanted to live in peace with his female and youngling. With his friends and brothers, and unravel the mysteries of their bonds.

The path Jabez wanted them to walk was covered in bloodshed. Mavka would be perfect soldiers. They were difficult to kill and near impossible to disempower when enraged.

But Jabez also didn't see that Mavka would kill *everything* in sight when they succumbed to their rage. They fought to protect themselves and everything was seen as an enemy.

They were monsters, true monsters – even compared to Demons. They were bigger, faster, and far more dangerous and cunning – even when underdeveloped.

"Give me the ram-horned Mavka, or I'll find a way to kill that little human you have behind you." Jabez folded his arms across his chest and lifted his chin superiorly. "Whether you give him to me now, or I find him when he leaves your protection circle, he *will* die. The only difference is, if you help me, I may consider letting you and your human live. He's killed many Demons, you haven't, and as long as you continue to leave my kind unharmed, then I shall spare you."

Magnar swallowed thickly.

It seemed the Demon King wasn't aware that he'd killed many Demons since Delora had come into his life. He wasn't afraid for himself, but he worried for his bride and youngling, who would be targeted at any point if they were caught outside the protection ward.

They needed to leave it in order to obtain food. He didn't want the ward to become a prison for them.

Then... something registered in his mind. Something *unforgivable*.

Magnar finally rose to stand, but as he did, his sight turned an even more violent colour of red, the outer rims of them wavering with black. He flexed his fingers, checking the strength he had in them and his claws as he parted his fangs to show their lethal length.

The snarl he gave was deeper than any other he'd released. And he knew by how tight his skin felt over his muscles that his feathers and fur had puffed to stand completely on their ends, making him bigger, more frightful.

"You dare threaten my female?" His voice sounded distorted, and every second he realised further that Jabez had truly

threatened his Delora, the burn he felt in his muscles demanded retribution. ***"I will NOT give you the Mavka, nor will I allow you to harm her. I am Magnar, her protector, and I will protect her with every drop of my blood!"***

Any threat to her was unforgivable.

All the burning heat suddenly flushed out of him in a cold rush, so cold, in fact, it felt like he'd been dunked into ice water. *No. Come back.* His orbs turned a stark colour of white, while a curt whine escaped him.

He'd been too focused on Jabez that he hadn't realised a problem was occurring right before them.

There was Fyodor, slowly scuttling their way to the edge of the ward towards the Demon King.

They were at my side a second ago. They'd been taking a protective stance with Delora, and Magnar thought they would remain there. He'd blocked Delora's view of them by keeping her pressed against him.

I made a mistake. A big one.

His worry didn't ease, not even when Fyodor stopped just within the ward to sniff at the Demon King's feet. He didn't seem to notice they'd come closer, or that they existed, as if he, too, had been purely focused on their conversation. One that had not being going well for either of them.

Magnar was sure if there had been no barrier between them, a fight would have ensued.

Magnar's body tensed further when a Demon, a small one who looked rather impish with a hunched back, crept forward to inspect Fyodor. His head was half sunken, like he'd been bashed in the skull and survived.

Jabez swatted at the impish Demon.

"You dare try to stand in front of me?!" he snarled, baring his claws.

He scampered back with haste before he pointed in Fyodor's direction. "There is a little Mavka, sire."

Magnar lowered himself to all fours in apprehension when Jabez's gaze darted down to the youngling at his feet. Jabez cringed at them with disgust, his upper lip lifting to reveal part of his dark gums when Fyodor leaned closer to sniff.

"Magnar," Delora whispered with a cracked cry. "Please. *Please* go get them."

A light tangle of fear rose from her scent, but thankfully a small gust of wind pushed it in the opposite direction of the Demons, sparing them chaos.

Magnar began to slowly creep forward. He knew if he darted, it might spook Fyodor and make them stumble out of the ward they were just inside of.

"A sightless, hornless Mavka? You're joking," Jabez said as he stepped closer and crouched right before the ward to inspect them. He brought his eyes up to Magnar. "Your kind can reproduce? You made a baby with that human?"

Then he waved his hand in front of Fyodor's face, catching their attention by the scent of it rushing past their snout. Their head followed.

"NO!" Magnar roared.

It was too late. Fyodor rushed forward a few steps, darting out of the protection ward to bite into Jabez's hand.

The Demon King howled in pain, Fyodor's fangs just as sharp and deadly as his own, and stood while grabbing the top part of their snout. Magnar rushed forward before anything could happen.

The distance was too great. Jabez managed to pry their jaws apart, releasing himself from their latching bite.

Jabez's hands curled around each jaw part in front of their snout, keeping it open as he held onto them near his chest to control Fyodor while they struggled. Then he sent Magnar the cruellest, most vicious smirk he'd ever seen, the upper corners of his lips turning upwards as he flashed his fangs.

The malicious glint in his dark eyes had Magnar immediately stopping in his tracks. He began to pace warily.

"Give them to me," Magnar pleaded.

He tried to not show his fear for his youngling, but he knew the white glow of his orbs gave him away.

"Back up, Mavka."

Fyodor gave a shrilling cry, their tongue curling between their forcibly parted fangs. His vulnerable youngling kicked their arms and legs, squirming in the air to get a hold of something so they weren't hanging there by their poor neck.

Jabez's grin grew even wider when Magnar did as he was told, stepping back a few paces to put space he didn't want to between them.

If I attack, he will hurt them.

Magnar knew if he tried, Fyodor would be killed before he even made it halfway to them – and Jabez was just as aware of this.

Why? Why did Fyodor have to walk over there? Why did they have to leave Magnar and Delora's sides? *I am their father... I am supposed to keep them protected.*

A small whine quivered out of his collapsing lungs.

"The playing field just changed, Mavka," Jabez chuckled, parting Fyodor's fangs a little further until Magnar could see the webbed skin that attached their lower and upper jaws together from inside their mouth. There was no pain for Fyodor, there never was, but they appeared uncomfortable. "You can save one, but not both. Give me the ram-horn or this one *dies*."

There was no hesitation from Magnar.

His sight only left Fyodor for a split second as he backed up towards the unconscious Mavka, but it was so he could lay his gaze on Delora. She looked completely and utterly pale, her tanned complexion whitened in distress. Her hands were even cupped to her chest, like her heart might be beating just as frantically as his own.

Their eyes met, and her expression left his stomach pooling with acid. Her gaze flickered over his features. He knew when they reached his antlers, his snout. They fell onto his white orbs that flashed with a deep blue that resonated the grief he felt at what he was about to do.

He didn't want to sacrifice his own kind, but nothing would come between him and his youngling, nor him and his female. His *brother* may be something he wanted to protect, but not at such a great cost.

He... he will most likely die anyway. That's what he told himself, at least. Anything to soothe the cold ache, like ice shards had formed in his very veins, as he grabbed the wrist of the ram-horned Mavka.

It was then that the whites of Delora's eyes turned glassy and pink, tears beginning to well in the liquid line. Her lips trembled, her brows knotted, and there was something in her expression that was harrowing to see.

Her internal agony intensified when he gave another flash of blue in his orbs that lingered a little longer than before. Her expression deepened when she saw the change.

Then she steeled it just as Magnar gave his first tug.

Her face hardened into something stone-cold. Emotions left her, something Magnar had never seen in her, before she turned her head to face Jabez.

"You're going to kill them anyway," she sneered at the Demon King.

Magnar's stomach clenched when his head snapped to Jabez, who cocked his brow. His lips twitched.

"Are you calling me a liar, human?"

She stepped closer to him with her arms spread wide, giving him a submitting and surrendering pose.

"There is no benefit in keeping them alive. They're just one more Duskwalker in your way, one that you can't control. They're young, probably more dangerous than the others who have consumed enough humans to think and understand." She folded her arms across her large chest and then rose one of her own brows. "It's the oldest move in the game. As soon as he gives you the other Duskwalker, you'll just kill them anyway."

"As king," Jabez started, lifting his head as he rolled his shoulders back to offer a superior stance, "I must adhere to my own vows and promises. I have offered a bargain, therefore I must–"

"Bullshit! You're lying! I can see it in your face." Delora then gestured her thumb towards Magnar. "He may not be able to see it, but I'm a human, and I've seen shit like this time and time again."

See what? Magnar thought, his sight falling onto Jabez to look for some tell he was missing.

"It's a trap. Offer to give someone something they need, but the moment you get what you want, you back out of your end of the deal." Delora huffed out a humourless laugh as she gave

Jabez her side. "Humans do it all the time. Why would you, a Demon, be any better than us?"

Jabez's dark gaze fell on Magnar before his eyes crinkled at the corners. He bellowed out a laugh while throwing his head back.

"You got me. And here I was, thinking I could get away with it. I was hoping he'd come through the ward so I could kill him as well. Three Mavka dead in one day? It's not often I feel so fortunate." However, Jabez's humour faded when he turned his gaze to Delora. It started to darken with vexation. "But then you just had to go and ruin it." His eyes flicked to Magnar with his resentment burning brighter. "You're lucky your human was smart enough to save your lives, but that still doesn't save your fucking child."

His biceps tensed as he readied his hands on Fyodor's jaws. Delora and Magnar stepped forward with swift movements, both their hand reaching out before he could start pulling.

"Wait!" Magnar shouted, trying to yank the heavy ram-horned Mavka closer to show him he would do what he'd been told.

"Stop!" she screamed, sprinting closer than Magnar thought she'd dare to go. She brought both hands up and waved them down as if to stop Jabez. "I have a better idea. Why not use them?"

That got Jabez's attention. He paused, relaxing his hold on Fyodor who gave a growl, swiping their hands to reach uselessly upwards. They couldn't reach past their snout.

A stranger was holding them, a threat – that was all his youngling registered.

"Use it?" Jabez gave a thoughtful hum while cocking his head. "Just how would I do that? Mavka aren't able to be controlled. They do what they want without order."

Magnar had no idea what was going on, but he nearly sagged in relief when the grip on Fyodor had eased. Delora stood in front of him a few paces away. He could only see the side of her when she folded her arms and tapped one of her boots against the ground.

"Like I said, *they're* young. Sure, you can't control them, but

I can. I'm their mother, after all. They know me, trust me." He saw her lips curl up into a wicked grin. "Imagine having a baby Duskwalker as your pet. A guard dog, if you will. They look pretty dog-like in their bigger forms."

Magnar's grip on his brother's forearm lessened when he sensed something was... *wrong*.

What... what is she doing? he thought, shaking his head in her direction with confusion. *It sounds almost as if she...*

Jabez gave a chuckle, one that was dark and without humour. "You'll say just about anything to save *it*, won't you? Why would you help me?"

"Because I'm still their mother, no matter what they are."

"You're with one of *them*." He nodded his head towards Magnar. *"*You fucked him and then gave birth to one of his kind. Why should I trust anything you have to say? Your kind has tricked me in the past and killed my favourite concubine in doing so."

Delora snorted a laugh.

"Do you think I asked to be put in this situation? To be taken by a Duskwalker? It was either stay here with him or fucking die. Those were my two options. Not much of a choice was there?" Then she lifted her head to snub the very Demon King. "And do you think I *asked* to make a Duskwalker? I had sex with him, so what? Can't a girl just be horny for a big dick? I had no idea that we would make a fucking baby! One I didn't ask for, and there was nothing I could do once I knew."

"Delora?" Magnar asked, unsure of why Delora was being this way.

He didn't like it. She came across as cold and unfeeling towards him and their youngling. And each word spoken from her pretty lips caused dread to crawl deeper within him, like a burrowing animal.

Her head snapped towards him.

Then she sneered with a nasty tone, *"What?"*

Magnar's body shook in aversion under the haunting stare she gave him. It was lifeless and bold and held no affection.

"I never got a choice about anything, so don't try to get in the way."

Her words cut deeply because... because he knew it was true. Orange lifted into his orbs momentarily, his once-eased guilt returning tenfold.

Delora turned back to Jabez and stepped forward, making the Demons huddle closer to their master.

"You're giving me a third option, one I never thought was possible. Get me the fuck away from here, from him, from this stupid house in the middle of nowhere, and I'll train that baby Duskwalker to be whatever you want them to be. You want a soldier? I'll give you one. You want a servant? You'll have it. You just want them to be a lap dog? I'll teach you how to pet their head just right, so they'll never bark or bite. All I ask is for you to take me to that big, fancy castle I saw in the distance when I was taken to the Demon Village, and I'll be yours. As long as I get to live, that's all I care about." Delora unfolded a single arm to shrug it. "You can do what you want with me, but obviously in order to train them, you'll need to keep me alive."

"Delora," Magnar whimpered. "What are you doing?"

She was making him feel as though he was... nothing to her. That he'd been nothing, that she tolerated him, hated him, didn't want to be with him. Magnar didn't like the way this betrayal tasted, or how it felt like his heart was frosting over and would cease beating at any moment.

"What I have to," she answered without even turning to him, like he didn't *deserve* to be looked upon.

Jabez began to slowly close Fyodor's mouth, but he still held firm so he wouldn't be bitten.

Magnar released the ram-horned Mavka and approached Delora while crouching. He slipped his hand around one of her ankles, desperate to feel her skin against his own. He needed to feel her, *hoping* his touch could change everything she'd just said.

"Don't touch me!" she screamed, jumping away from Magnar's hold.

He stumbled back at the high pitch of her yell.

A whine escaped his strangled lungs as she backed a few steps away. She put more distance between them, bringing herself closer to Jabez.

"Stay away from me. Leave me alone."

"You sound just like Katerina," Jabez said, eyeing her up and down. "But you're a little prettier. I've been wanting a new human. My Demon concubines just don't feel... warm enough. You look fun to play with."

Red flared in Magnar's orbs. The idea of the Demon King touching his Delora sent unbridled rage through him.

"She is mine!" he snarled.

He didn't care what she said, Delora was *his*.

"Apparently not! She doesn't seem to want you." Jabez gave a bright laugh. Then he cooed at Delora, "You want a prettier male, don't you female? One with an actual face."

"You gave me your soul!" Magnar roared. "You cannot leave me!"

He wouldn't *let* her leave him!

"I'm sure he can figure out a way around that," Delora said as she gestured a thumb at Jabez. "It seems like he has plenty of strong magic, enough to make a whole new forest. And just think about your child, Magnar. You better hope I don't come back, otherwise he'll probably kill them."

The engulfing flame of rage fled faster than it entered him.

He didn't know what to do, how to stop this, but her words echoed painful truths. Not even his stunted brain could ignore the reality before him. He was intelligent enough to understand that there was nothing that could be done.

If Delora does not go with Jabez, Fyodor will die.

But that would leave Magnar alone. He'd lose them both, regardless. He didn't want to lose Delora, but the idea of his *child* perishing was horrid.

I don't want them to go.

The aching pain in his heart was worse than anything he'd ever experienced, but he stepped back and surrendered.

He gave up because there was no other alternative.

If he forced Delora to somehow stay, Fyodor would never come back, and he would be stuck with a female that didn't want to be by Magnar's side. She would hate him, resent him, and he doubted there would be any tenderness from her to ease his loss of losing their youngling.

If Fyodor wasn't here, wasn't being used as a bargaining chip to keep Magnar complacent, he knew he would have fought fang and claw to keep Delora. She was meant to be his bride.

So, what did that mean for him now?

"So," Delora said with a smirk to Jabez. "We got a deal, big boy?"

Jabez's eyes turned upwards as he thought for an exceedingly long time, like he wanted to draw out his answer. Like he just wanted to make them hold their breaths.

To make this worse for Magnar.

"You know what, I'm actually pretty pleased with this." He gave a satisfied grin. "I'm willing to give up the ram-horn for my very own Mavka under my command and a new female. You have a deal."

With that, Magnar watched Delora willingly walk over to Jabez and then step out of the protection ward. The Demon King immediately held Fyodor by one arm, as they squirmed and wriggled in protest, in order to grip her forearm in a tight hold.

Magnar was secretly hoping she wouldn't actually do it, that she wouldn't actually go to him, but his tail curled down between his legs now that he saw her there.

"We'll let you go for now, Mavka. But know that in the future, if you seek to come to take her, I'll make sure you pay for it."

Magnar sat down on his haunches. The blue that lit his orbs was so dark he was barely able to see, but all he saw was Delora's deadened stare upon him.

Is this how Orpheus felt?

No wonder he was so defensive and possessive of the one female that wanted to be with him. The echoing loneliness was already too much to bear, and his insides were crawling like he was filled with terrible bugs that wanted to eat their way out of him from the inside.

His sight fell on his youngling.

No, this is much worse. It had to be as he was about to lose Fyodor as well.

They gave loud, shrilling cries that pierced his ears even with the distance between them. Magnar hoped it was because they somehow knew what was happening and were protesting this.

"Ugh," Delora groaned with her eyes rolling. "Just give them to me. They always make that horrible noise, and it'll only get worse."

It was obvious he didn't want to at first, but when Fyodor really started struggling, reaching to Delora for safety, he began to grunt. He was stumbling under Fyodor's panicked, frantic squirming.

"Fine. Here." Jabez tossed them into Delora's arms while he held onto her forearm firmly. Then he backed up, silently motioning for the Demons to become a blockade between Magnar and them. The one with the sunken head came forward to sniff at Delora's feet. She eyed it warily but didn't back away as she would have in the past. "Go back to your homes or nests for now. I'll take the human and baby Mavka to my castle."

They were about to leave. How was Magnar supposed to cope with this? *I am going to lose them.*

Cold drops began to float around his orbs, reflecting the same blue he saw. He knew they were coming from his orbs, but he couldn't stop the liquid as it fluttered and then floated around his skull to disappear.

This hurts. I don't like this. He looked upon the female whose soul he kept, suddenly wishing she'd never fallen from the sky only to betray him.

Her gaze found his, and he wanted to see remorse. Instead, he saw something sharp. A glare, almost.

His insides shuddered at it being directed towards him. It was like a dagger piercing his very essence.

And then she was gone...

Not because Jabez had materialised them away, since he could transport through his magic. It was because she had turned incorporeal in the Demon King's grip and bolted to the side to run into the forest while holding Fyodor.

It took a moment for everyone to realise what had happened.

Jabez lifted his empty hand to inspect it before he turned his face in the direction she'd gone.

"She's like the Witch Owl," Jabez muttered quietly. Then his confusion fled as he turned his furious expression towards

Magnar. "That's what happens when a human gives you Mavka their soul. No wonder the other human came back to life. They're fucking Phantoms!"

Magnar was too shocked to move, staring at the gap of trees he'd seen Delora run into. The ever-constant mist present and foreboding. *She ran away?*

Jabez spoke to the Demons. "Keep him here. I'm going to kill that lying bitch."

With a bellowing roar, Jabez disappeared into thin air with his claws on display. The Demons came closer to the protection ward and gave hisses and snarls, barring the way Delora had gone.

Magnar knew two things.

Delora did *not* want to go with the Demon King.

And she was in terrible danger.

FORTY-TWO

Oh my God! Why did I go this way?! Delora's mind screamed as she rushed through the forest.

In her incorporeal form, she stopped running so she could assess her surroundings, finding that she had absolutely no fucking idea which way to go. Everything looked the same, no matter which way she turned. It was just endless trees, and nothing pointed her back towards the house and its protective ward.

Fuck!

She knew why she'd gone this way, and it was the stupidest reason, considering she could literally float through things. It was that damn Demon who had been sniffing at her feet, blocking her direct path to Magnar.

Her mind hadn't been thinking clearly, her heart racing with adrenaline, while she'd tried everything in her power to not reek of fear. All she'd wanted was to get Fyodor away from the Demon King and escape with them to safety.

That's all her mind had registered – just the way out, *any* way out. Her fear had made her irrational, foolishly so.

But that Demon... Delora shuddered in revulsion.

She was thankful she wasn't physical, otherwise she knew she'd have bile rising to her throat.

It had been extremely grotesque. Its head was sunken in on one side with an eyeball loose from its socket. That eye... it had been dangling down, swaying against its cheek like an organic pendulum, while some weird black liquid dribbled from between its broken teeth.

And the smell of it... it was worse than anything she'd ever experienced. She'd rather hug a rotting corpse.

And it had been sniffing her ankle! It almost *touched* her.

She'd done everything in her power to not boot it into the freaking cosmos, but it had been between her and Magnar.

Delora had just wanted away from it.

There had been a single gap between the Demons who had started to surround her and the Demon King. Her mind had completely spaced out, and she'd acted like she was physical, running for the gap rather than heading to the safest place possible.

As soon as she'd started running, she immediately realised her mistake and headed for the house.

She'd never found it, nor the green glow of the ward under the shadows of the trees.

Where the fuck am I?

She spun in a circle and headed another direction. But every time she changed her path, Delora grew more worried.

I hope I'm not going the wrong way. She could be leading herself further from the house rather than towards it. Keeping herself and Fyodor safe was something she might be able to do in her incorporeal form but... *If a day passes...*

She worried she'd transport back to Magnar without Fyodor, leaving them alone in the forest with no way to track them.

No. I'll get back. I have to get back.

If she'd been physical right then, Delora knew she'd reek of fear and would have tears falling down her cheeks.

I'm stupid. I'm stupid. I'm so freaking stupid.

Then again, Delora had never been the brightest student in class.

She wanted to call for Magnar, but she had no idea what she'd left behind, if he was fighting to come get her or if he wanted to at all.

Please forgive me, she begged, hoping it would reach him. *I couldn't think of any other way.*

Looking at him sitting there in defeat as she went to the Demon King's side had been heartbreaking to witness. There

were strange glowing drops floating from his blue orbs, so blue
they'd looked like the yawning depths of the ocean – something
she'd read was almost unending, and so dark it was impossible
to see down into.

They were ethereal tears – like the bottoms of them were
made of glass.

Delora had hurt Magnar.

I had no choice.

Fyodor had been in danger. Magnar had been in danger. And
she could tell the whole time the Demon King was lying – and
even if he hadn't been, she refused to risk Fyodor either way.

Now I just have to get back to him. She went in a new
direction, hoping that her determination to return to Magnar
would help her find the way. *I'll explain everything. I'll fix it.*

Delora let out a horrified scream when the Demon King
suddenly materialised right in her path.

"Found you, you little bitch!"

He bared his sharp fangs in lethal rage.

She tried to dodge him since Fyodor's body was intangible
like her, but their skull wasn't. The Demon King followed her
movements, swiping at her ghostly body, but his strike passed
through her. She was still free – she just had to remain so.

Delora kept running, her eyes searching even more frantically
for a green glow.

Where is it? Please!

The Demon King materialised in front of her again, his
narrowed gaze even more furious than before.

"You may be intangible, but I can see its skull isn't."

Before Delora could get out of the way, the Demon King
launched forward with a swiftness no human could match.

The Demon King grabbed Fyodor's skull and yanked
forward. Thankfully Fyodor was in a sleep state, but Delora went
with the Demon King's yank so as not to injure them. Her
Phantom body swayed in every direction he went so he couldn't
play tug-of-war with their little body!

Then Delora did something she never thought she'd do.

She turned physical, her feet dropping to the ground with an
oomph, and bit into the Demon King's hand. Fyodor gave a shrill

of panic, unsure of what was happening.

Biting so hard she heard something break around his pinkie knuckle she'd latched onto, pungent, disgusting, dark blood filled her mouth. Bile didn't rise, not when she was too frantic about releasing Fyodor from his grip no matter what, no matter *how*.

The Demon King gave a bellowing roar.

The next taste to assault her tastebuds was her own blood when he slammed his fist into the side of her face. He let go of Fyodor at the same time, giving Delora a chance to back away from him safely.

Agony radiated through her cheek to the point it almost felt like it was shattered. Forks of pain spread over her head until she was forced to experience one of the worst kinds of migraines she'd ever felt. The blood in her mouth was coming from the three upper back teeth he'd dislodged. She almost swallowed them when she was trying to clear the blood from her mouth.

She spit them to the side.

Delora struggled to hold onto Fyodor, who began snapping their jaws millimetres from her face, the scent of her blood sending them into a frenzy. She forcibly held their snout closed before she turned incorporeal once more.

The Demon King stepped closer, *stalking* her with his claws at the ready.

"I could have given you a way out, but instead, you chose your fate."

"Why the fuck would I go with you?" Delora yelled as she backed up. "You tried to kill a defenceless baby! You're a fucking sicko."

Well... he *was* a Demon after all.

"It's nothing but a filthy Mavka! If they will not follow my command, then they all deserve to die." He shot forward to grab Fyodor's skull again. Delora spun away from his grip, so his claws went through her transparent shoulder instead. "But I will have that Mavka! You're right, it's young. Even without you, I'm sure I can control it once it learns what it means to fear me."

Her incorporeal body wavered at his threat.

He was talking about torturing them into submission!

"Just leave us be!" Delora screamed, before she started rushing her incorporeal body into the forest. She moved her legs as if they would help to hover faster. "I won't let you take them!"

The Demon King materialised in front of her.

EEP! She bolted the other way.

"Magnar!" Delora yelled. "Magnar!

She'd been hoping to avoid detection, but now that she was being chased by a cruel madman, she could no longer stay quiet. She was lost, alone, and scared with their child.

I can't do it by myself.

She would run forever if she had to, but she didn't have forever. She had a day, and that's if the Demon King didn't get ahold of Fyodor again.

A bellowing, large-lunged roar came from the distance.

Delora knew that frightening, beastly noise belonged to the one creature she trusted most in the entire world. She headed in that direction.

The Demon King continued to materialise around her, forcing her to dodge him and redirect her path momentarily.

She heard heavy footsteps only a few paces away, but they ran past her rather than in her direction.

For a split second, she turned physical so he could track her scent, and screamed his name again. She was forced to turn incorporeal right as the Demon King swiped his claws into her upper chest as he went for Fyodor. Drops of blood flicked through the air and splattered against the ground.

She let out a cry, and her forms flickered, unable to maintain staying ghostly against the searing sudden pain.

Ow! Ow! Shit! She hissed in a breath whenever her body flashed to physical. *It hurts so much.*

She managed to regain control right before he could catch her with his claws again, narrowly missing Fyodor being grabbed in the process. She didn't care what happened to her. All she cared about was the baby Duskwalker in her arms.

I have to stay alive. I have to protect them. Keep them away from this bastard.

Delora stopped running and instead just backed up from the Demon King, hoping Magnar could track his scent instead. *I need to stop moving. I need to give him a chance to find us.*

The echoing growl she heard off to the side sent relief through her. Its depth, its rolling tone and menacing reverberation, were like a soothing bass.

The moment Magnar broke through the tree line in his monstrous form, running on all fours, Delora turned physical and tossed Fyodor at him within a safe distance.

"Take them!" she yelled, tackling the Demon King when he diverted his attention onto Magnar, now holding their child.

Delora was like nothing but a kitten to the Demon King and was pushed away without even causing him to stumble. She hit the ground hard, her body impacting and rolling before she settled.

He gave a mean chuckle, stepping towards Magnar with his fangs and claws bared.

"So, you didn't kill them all before you came here." It was hard to mistake the sound of multiple steps coming their way. "Guess this is perfect for me. I'll get to watch you die *and* take that baby Mavka. It will be the perfect tool. I can already picture all the Elves it'll kill."

The Demon King shot forward. When Magnar answered his attack with his orbs crimson and another roar, both his arms fixed around Fyodor, who was squirming wildly, Delora rushed to her feet.

She jumped and grabbed ahold of the Demon King's long white hair from behind. She tugged on it, yanking his head backwards with all her strength. Delora even put her heavy weight into it.

She refused to let go, even when he swiped his claws behind his back in her direction.

"Run, Magnar!" It was a desperate, *desperate* plea.

"I can't leave you here, Delora."

Magnar hesitantly took a step forward, like he wanted to attack before stepping back while curling his arms tighter around Fyodor.

"Please, Magnar!"

The Demon King managed to reach back and claw at her arm, rending the flesh nearly to the bone.

Delora refused to lessen her grip despite the cry that left her and the tears of agony that welled. She fisted tighter with her right hand when her left went cold and numb as tracks of crimson liquid raced down her skin.

"I can come back. They can't."

You can't.

Delora didn't know what would happen to her if Magnar was to die, but she didn't care about that. All she knew was this world deserved that big, sweet, sometimes clueless Duskwalker alive to see it for what it was.

That it was colourful. That it had beauty even in a horrible place like the Veil.

Delora disappeared, gut-churning darkness and dizziness taking hold, before she materialised with the Demon King right in front of Magnar. Using his long hair as leverage, Delora jumped up and dug her long nails into his face from behind, missing his eyes but dragging a yell from him.

When Magnar didn't move except to put space between them, his want to protect her like a thorn in her side, Delora clenched her eyes shut tight against the claws that stabbed into her wrists.

"Please protect our child, Magnar. I'm trusting you."

He whimpered in answer, making her heart squeeze.

She heard his heavy footsteps leaving just before the other Demons entered the area.

"No!" the Demon King bellowed when he ripped her hands from his face. "Get him before he enters the ward!"

The Demons ran after Magnar, heading in a slightly different direction as though to cut him off. They gave snarling hisses, and Delora heard movement further within the trees.

They were calling for help.

"You." Holding Delora in the air by one arm, he turned to her with a menacing snarl. "That Mavka is going to make it to the ward no matter what we do, unless my Demons can slow him down. I'll make you regret choosing their side. You'll regret getting in my way."

With her lips quivering, her eyes narrowed into a hateful glare. Delora collected all the blood and saliva in her mouth and then spat it at his handsome Elfish-Demonish face.

The thick, sticky crimson glob of liquid splattered against his cheek, and he flinched in surprise. It continued to dribble in a sticky drop from between her lips.

"Rot in hell, bastard."

Should she have provoked him? Probably not. But Delora had only one task now, and that was to die in order to keep him here for as long as she could.

Magnar had always protected her, and it was her turn to make the sacrifice for him, for Fyodor.

"You think this is noble?" He tsked at her as he brought her closer. She wished he wasn't holding her torn arm as she winced, the weight of her own body hanging from his fist excruciating. "His kind are vengeful. Your sacrifice will mean *nothing* when he realises you are dead, that you have suffered. He will willingly come through that ward to fight me, like the fucking idiots their kind are!"

There was no way to stem her fear, but she just swallowed thickly and remained physical.

No matter the pain I'm about to feel, I will come back.

She wasn't a hero. She'd never wanted to be one. Delora also couldn't fight, and she *knew* a feeble human like herself stood no chance against him.

"Let's see how much pain you can endure, shall we?" The curling, evil smirk he gave her made a cold shiver run down her spine. "You'll beg for me to stop, crying for him to come back and save you." Then he leaned forward to run the tip of his nose against the side of her neck. "And just like the Witch Owl, you'll come back to life, but not before you experience the worst kind of agony I can give you."

Heat spread through her arm like her skin was on fire, and she looked up to see it was bubbling around where his hand gripped her flesh. She bit her lips together to muffle her scream so Magnar wouldn't be forced to hear it.

Instead, she quietly sobbed as she kicked her legs against the magic searing her flesh.

"The next time this happens... When I come for that baby Mavka, I'm going to make sure all you can do is whimper when you look at me."

Root-like vines shot from the ground to entangle themselves around her arms and legs, holding her in the air in front of his snarling features. They wrapped tight, cutting off the circulation in her extremities.

On instinct, she tried to turn incorporeal, but the snapping of her forearm bones made her scream instead. He wasn't going to let her take that form, and she *did* whimper when she brought her head forward from throwing it back to scream. She met his gaze.

She was giving Magnar time.

Did she regret her decision?

With all her heart, not at all.

Running feels wrong. And yet here Magnar was, leaving Delora behind when every fibre of his being demanded he turn around so he could protect her.

His single grip on Fyodor tightened. *I am failing her.*

Running on three legs slowed down his full sprint, but he needed to keep his youngling against his chest. The further he got from Delora and the scent of her blood, the more they calmed against him.

Fyodor relaxed and began gripping against his fur and feathers, allowing Magnar to focus on the Demons that were both following him and coming from the side.

They were quickly approaching, and his heart raced against the overwhelming feelings that rushed through him.

He wasn't going to make it back to the ward before the Demons got to him. *I am going too slow.* He'd waited too long to leave Delora behind to the terrible fate he knew she must be facing. His actions, his hesitation, were going to put himself and Fyodor at risk.

No. She trusts me.

Despite what she'd said to the Demon King, how she had acted, how she had hurt him, she'd run with Fyodor. He didn't know what words of hers were truths or lies, but she'd told Magnar she trusted him to protect them.

That's all he needed for now.

Right before he could make it to safety, the glowing green of the ward illuminating between the shadows of the trees, four Demons intersected him.

Skidding against the dirt to a halt, he huffed in their direction. Three more came up behind to circle him.

I don't know what to do, he thought, as he gave wet snorts of exertion through his bony nose hole.

The Demons let out wheezing snickers, each of them a different size and shape. One of them even had wings that they'd used to reach him faster than the others – although they weren't useful for true flight just yet.

They weren't large enough to match his size, but two were bigger than Delora. That meant they were strong.

He wanted to perk his head up when he heard the rustling of trees in the distance, telling him more were approaching, but he refused to take his attention away from those currently around him.

Holding Fyodor with one arm to fight would leave him at a disadvantage, but he knew he couldn't run through the Demons without risking them clawing at them both. They could attach themselves to his monstrous back, allowing them access when he passed through the ward.

If any harm came to Fyodor, he wouldn't forgive himself.

He'd failed Delora. He *wouldn't* fail his youngling too.

Red eyes came closer as they tried to decrease the distance between them, waiting to see what Magnar would do. They were intelligent, knowing they would lose unless they did this strategically. He'd already killed two of them before he'd heard Delora call for him earlier.

And Magnar barely had a scratch on him.

I must be smart. That was a challenge in itself. *I must remain calm.*

However, Magnar heard something that incited a terrible rage in him. Something that had his fur and feathers puffing until he almost looked twice his size. Something that had his tail quivering in aggression, and his claws and fangs feeling sharp. Something that had his own red eyes glowing darker until he was almost blinded.

Delora's pain-filled scream reached across the distance like a sharp, cold dagger straight into his skull to pierce the goo of his brain. It was more ferocious than any invisible hand that ever tried to coax him into a frenzy, far more brutal, and Magnar let out the deepest animalistic roar he'd ever given.

He let go of Fyodor when they tightly clenched against his flesh. His mind fixated on where they were on his body to make sure they stayed with him, then Magnar launched himself at the four Demons before him.

One yelped in fear before Magnar even got a hand around his back leg when he tried to retreat like a coward. Magnar grabbed him, spun around, and slammed his body down onto another Demon. Then he reared back onto his hind legs and came back down with force, piercing through both their bodies with his fore claws.

He pulled, tearing them both apart sideways until they split in half.

Because of them, because of Jabez, his female was in *pain.* Delora's cry boiled his blood until he thought it would begin to steam through his very flesh.

She would come back, he knew this, but that didn't stop his desperate need for retribution. If it wasn't for the Demons before him, who had tried to aid Jabez, Magnar might have been able to stay with her.

She will come back to me. He rotated his head a hundred and eighty degrees, so he was looking over his back when a Demon jumped on it. *But she should not have to!* He snapped his fangs forward, and they wrapped around the small Demon's head.

He crushed it in an explosion of brain matter.

He swiped his arm to the side to stop another Demon that had attempted to leap on him. It was one of the bigger Demons, the one with the wings, and it used them to evade Magnar's attack. Instead of grabbing it, Magnar managed to rend his claws down its arm and ribcage on one side instead. They *cracked* under his strength.

Fyodor clung to him, their little claws piercing his flesh in order to stay latched to him, and it gave him the freedom he needed to jump into the air. Thankfully, the smell of their disgusting blood wasn't enticing them.

Magnar evaded two new Demons who had tried to run at him from both sides. They collided before he landed back on the ground – right on top of them.

He chuckled darkly at them as they began to hiss and yelp.

"I guess this will make me a target for Jabez," he said down to them, shoving his claws into the face of one whose skull instantly crushed and caved in while he bit the other around the jaw and tore its head off. *"But if he comes for my family again, I won't hesitate to destroy him."*

A Mavka was too fast for Demons in their monstrous form. They could leap higher, move swiftly, and could contort their bodies to evade before giving a return strike that could be devastating.

Magnar gave a dark chuckle.

Just as he'd told the Demonslayer, Demons were weak, like humans. It's why both tended to scamper away from Mavka.

A new Demon came into the fray, a little one, and it didn't last past its leaping jump before Magnar swiped with his palm and launched it through the trees. It hit the base of a tree, its body wrapping around it until Magnar heard multiple bones crunching.

It hit the ground, lifeless.

Something sharp, like a sword, stabbed right through his back. He grabbed a hold of Fyodor and tore them from his body before they could be harmed when it came out the other side.

Magnar turned to one of the final Demons.

It had used the sharp tip of its long tail to pierce his body. He roared at the spikey, lizard-like Demon, who then drew his tail down to widen the wound. The pain Magnar felt was lost to his fury.

He brought Fyodor back to the safety of his body. A Demon just missed them when it jumped over Magnar to get ahold of the youngling he'd been holding in the air.

He reached his hand out when it leapt again and managed to grab it by the throat, pulverising it in his fist. Then he wrapped his other hand around the tip of the spikey Demon's wiggling tail that still protruded through his torso when it tried to slide away.

He dropped the dead Demon and pulled the tail with both hands, slowly bringing the spikey Demon closer to his back. With wide eyes, the Demon turned to all fours so it could claw at the ground to get away. When that didn't work, it even tried to rip its own tail from its body.

But it was too late. Once it was in reaching distance, Magnar turned his body slightly and slashed his claws, ripping open the Demon's throat and half its face. Dark blood sprayed in all directions. It fell against the dirt with a thud, still alive, but it wouldn't be for much longer.

More feral Demons would come and eat it alive, or it would bleed out.

After walking forward to remove the spiked tail from his body, which caused blood to drip from his wound and onto the ground, Magnar turned to the last Demon standing.

It stepped back on its two legs, its body covered in well-tailored clothing. Some of the Demons had been well dressed, indicating they were like the ones he'd met in the Demon Village. Perhaps he'd even seen them there.

It took him a moment to realise it was a female and that a thin tail curled in emotion as she stared at him. Her feline ears were pressed against the top of her head.

"I never wanted to be a part of this," she whispered, her torso heaving with heavy, panicked breaths.

"And yet, here you stand," he answered, slowly stepping his paws and hands closer.

"Some of us have no interest in participating in any of this anymore." The feline Demon began to back up, her tail curling so tight it formed a ring at the end. "We've changed. We don't want war; we don't want to fight. We... some of us want to live in harmony with the humans, even if that means we have to stop eating them."

Magnar's head turned in the direction from which he heard a weak cry. He knew Delora was losing strength against whatever Jabez was doing to her.

"You are a part of the reason why she is in pain."

"You think I want this? I had no choice! If we don't obey his call, he will kill us or imprison us or *worse*." She clenched one of her fists as her red eyes bowed into an agonised expression. "These ones wanted to be here." She gestured to the ground where her brethren lay, dead or dying. "But I'm a skilled tracker, one of the best. That's why I was called upon."

"But you are not the best," a familiar, masculine voice said from the side and above.

Both of them turned their heads to the Demon Magnar had seen too many times in the past month. He leapt from the tree he was crawling upon and landed on the ground between them, his disfigured human-like body walking on all fours.

Magnar gave him a frothing snarl.

The hatred for this Demon in particular called to his darkest side.

"I'm faster than you could ever be," she rebuffed.

"Whether you are faster or not," he sneered back. "You *will* fight with me, or our king will have your head."

Then, with a swift speed, one that was even startling to Magnar, he sprinted towards him with a squealing hiss. Magnar tried to dodge him by pressing himself against the ground, but the Demon managed to grab one of his antlers and pulled himself onto Magnar's body.

He tore down his back with both hands. Magnar tried to buck him off, rotating his neck until he was looking behind him, but the Demon backed up to avoid the multiple snaps of his fangs. The Demon put himself into a spot where Magnar couldn't reach on his back, even with his hands.

He started *digging* into Magnar's spine.

Magnar gave a yelp and a cry, rearing back on his hind legs until he slammed his back against a tree to squish him. The Demon dodged to the side to remain attached, returning to dig in the same spot when Magnar was back on all fours.

That hurts! Magnar couldn't seem to grab a hold of the Demon to get rid of him – no matter how hard he twisted his body and reached.

Then he was gone, and Magnar looked towards where he heard a *thwapping* noise to the side.

Proving just how swift she was, the female Demon had tackled the male that had been attacking him. She gained herself a slash across the face as he thrashed beneath her, but she merely fought him off and delivered an arcing slash across his throat.

She huffed on her knees above him when he stopped wriggling. Now that he was dead, even though it wasn't done by his own claws, some of his anger lessened.

She protected me.

His head reared back in surprise.

"My mate adores the other Mavka's female," she rasped with panted breaths, sitting on top of the Demon with her shoulders slumping. She stared down at his bleeding corpse. "He was so cheerful that night after she came to his bookstore. He'd always wanted to speak with one, to meet the creatures who had written the books he loves so dearly."

She darted her head to the side to look at him. There was pain in her cat-shaped red eyes.

"I was there when she returned just to say... hello. I hadn't cared about the lives of humans before that. They were nothing but food to me. But... now I understand why we have become the way we are, why we are trying so hard to mimic them. It makes me wonder if the Elves are like that too. They're afraid of us because we've slaughtered so many of them. We had no idea of the significance of that, how losing one of your own could... hurt, until we started eating the humans here and understood what it meant to be like them, feel like them. It took a lot of death for us to discover this, and *so* many of us no longer wish to be a part of it."

Magnar had met the cat-like bookstore owner she was speaking of. It was where Reia had obtained his instruction book to build the house and the furniture he'd been making.

Surprisingly, the male bookstore owner was far smaller than her.

"Why are you telling me this?" Magnar asked, stepping to the side. He brought himself just that bit closer to the safety of his ward.

She gave a shrug as she climbed her way to her feline hind legs.

"Because I'm sorry it's come to this. Our king grows more aggressive with killing Mavka because the rest of our kind is developing too slowly. We've been here for over three hundred years, and the Elves that tortured him are dead. He grows impatient to take over that land, to finally end this, and your kind killing ours, some of you giving the humans protection wards for their towns, angers him. But I want you to know that some of us are... changing. A little more each day, every time we eat a human and gain humanity, just like your kind."

"If that is how you truly feel... then leave," Magnar conceded, cocking his snout to the side. He put space between them to show her he was allowing her to leave.

His stance was still aggressive, showing he would gladly go over there and rip her apart within the breath of a second.

But he didn't *want* to hate. He didn't want to be filled with anger. Magnar just wanted to live in peace with his friends and family.

It sounded as though she wanted the same thing.

"I can't," she answered, taking on a half-hearted fighting stance. "If I run, he'll kill me anyway, or torture my mate, who no longer has an aggressive bone in his body. I just wanted you to know before you kill me that I'm not doing this in hatred, or because I want to."

Magnar gave a snorting huff, before both of them perked their heads up at a quickly approaching Demon.

It took him a moment to make his decision.

He sprinted in her direction. She showed him her true intentions when she made absolutely no move to attack. Her fighting stance had been nothing more than a façade.

Magnar wrapped his hand around her neck and squeezed tightly. She gasped, bashing on his large fist and forearm.

"Then sleep," he demanded, cutting off the circulation and her breathing.

This was all he could do for her.

"Thank... you," she strained out, her voice low like a whisper. She went limp.

Magnar carelessly dropped her so he could retreat into his protection ward, ensuring both he and Fyodor were safe from any more Demons.

He barely had a moment to catch his breath before Jabez materialised into the area. A new Demon sprinted into the area at the same time and bashed into the ward. Its body crumpled against it with a shout. Magnar knew it wasn't dead, only unconscious, when it fell against the dirt.

Jabez did nothing but give it a bored expression before he looked at the carnage that lay around his feet. His gaze never changed. He wasn't saddened or angered by the death of his own kind around him.

Fyodor began to squirm with a shrill at the scent that wafted from Jabez. Magnar had to quickly clasp them as a coldness washed over Magnar at the blood, *human* blood, that dripped from his claws. It was also smeared between his fangs and down his chin while droplets of it splattered on his chest, as if he'd been messy.

Jabez gave him a smirk when his orbs flashed white.

"One of my favourite things about you Mavka gaining a human is the way you react whenever I hurt one of them," Jabez said with a dark chuckle. "Sometimes it's worth letting you escape just to see your eyes turn white or blue, or make those strange, pathetic tears you cry. That's the cost of humanity, to feel grief and loss."

"You are nothing but cruel," Magnar snarled, his sight morphing to a reddened hue once more.

Jabez curled one of his clawed index fingers in Magnar's direction, coaxing him to come to him. "Come on, don't you want to get revenge for her?"

Magnar wanted to, his anger just as intense and prevalent, but he stayed where he was as he cupped a hand over Fyodor.

His youngling was a barrier in so many ways, constantly preventing him from the many things he wanted to do.

"No," Magnar bit. ***"I am not stupid."***

Jabez cocked an eyebrow in surprise, no doubt thinking Magnar would already be charging. Then he laughed.

Magnar was already sick of the sound.

"She did eventually cry your name. Magnar, is it?" Jabez lifted the back of his hand and licked across his knuckles, bringing Delora's blood into his mouth. "It was a little weak at the end – she barely had any strength – but it was rather pitiful. She didn't like it when I started eating her alive." Then he lifted his arm to give a half-hearted shrug. "I'm wondering if her being a Phantom will give me some sort of new powers though, which is why I didn't just leave her for the other Demons that came to watch her die. I'm always thrilled when I get new magic."

Magnar knew what he was trying to do. He was trying to reach into the most animalistic, primal side of Magnar so that he would foolishly attack. He was baiting him.

He held Fyodor firmer, using them to anchor his mind as to why he couldn't. Delora had pleaded with Magnar to protect them, even at the cost of all this. He wouldn't betray that just because of foolishness – because he was being a mindless Mavka.

When Magnar didn't do as Jabez wanted, the Demon King roared in his direction.

"Attack me, you useless fucking Mavka!"

"No!"

Magnar backed up and knocked into the unconscious Mavka within his ward – the reason this had all started.

If only he'd gone to Orpheus' home instead. None of this would have happened. Magnar hadn't even been able to call for Orpheus' help because he wasn't nearby.

"Fine! You're lucky you have this ward to save you for now," Jabez yelled. "But I will be watching you, Mavka. If you're within the Veil, I'll always be able to see you, always be able to come to you within the blink of an eye." He bared his fangs at Magnar. "I'm tired of your kind using the things I created to your benefit. If any of you come to the Demon Village again, you won't live to escape it."

Then with a lingering growl, Jabez disappeared.

He left behind the mess Magnar had created, like his own kind and their deaths were insignificant to the greater schemes of his plans.

Everything went quiet except for the groans of the remaining Demons that were still waiting to die, and the noises from the one that had come and started eating its own kind.

After a few moments, Magnar fell on his haunches, worn out and depleted.

He was injured, and his mind and heart hurt terribly.

This was too much for him. He'd never expected to experience anything like this, and *nothing* he'd learned had prepared him for such events. Nothing.

"Delora," he whined with a high-pitched, fox-like cry.

FORTY-THREE

Magnar didn't know how long he sat on the ground, waiting. He'd watched the female cat Demon rise to her back paws and leave at some point while he remained on his haunches.

He didn't know if he was waiting for Delora to return to him, for the Mavka beside him to wake up, or for the Demons to finish eating their own kind.

It was none of those things that happened first.

A transparent figure came into his protective ward from the side, and Magnar raised his head in the direction of the Witch Owl.

Once she was inside the ward, she turned physical, but he noticed the strong, sweet smell of a cloaking aroma hiding her scent. There was red blood caking her white feather-covered dress, and mud on her arms and legs.

Her small, bare feet padded against the ground as she came closer with her eyes crinkled in anguish.

Half her face was torn by deep claw marks, the flesh open and puffy to reveal the white of her cheekbone. Her throat had been narrowly missed, but her shoulder had been torn at, as well as her side and left calf muscle, giving her a noticeable limp.

She must not want the Mavka to awaken and try to eat her, he thought, since her cloaking aroma was so strong it hid the scent of her own blood.

She paid Magnar no mind as she fell to her knees beside the unconscious Mavka.

"I am so sorry," she cried, placing his cracked skull in her lap.

She pressed her forehead against his bony one. "I'm so sorry I had to leave you to fight by yourself. Please forgive me."

He couldn't help looking her over, feeling overwhelming pity for her. He had his own youngling. He understood why she was upset to see her child injured.

This was something he was able to understand on his own; he didn't need anyone to teach him. With one of his hands still laying over them, Magnar clutched Fyodor closer. Fyodor clutched him in return.

"You are injured." He raised his hand so he could grab her arm. "Let me help you."

She lifted her head to frown in his direction. Then she looked down to see her wounds fading.

His exhaling breath squeaked from his newly acquired wounds, but he made no other sound of discomfort. This was little to him. The wound in his chest from the Demon's tail was far more painful, hurting each time he breathed. The hole that had been dug in his back was also excruciating. A few more little ones were nothing in comparison.

"You did not have to do that for me," she said as her brows drew tighter, like she didn't understand why he would help her. "I would have healed myself eventually with the right herbs and medicine, or when I returned home to be healed by your father."

"It is fine," he answered, turning to look at the injured Mavka. "You left him to be attacked?"

Her dark-brown eyes turned glassy and red, but no tears welled, as though she controlled them with her will.

"I had to," she whispered, looking down to him as well. "Please. Please work."

Her hands began to puff with black sand as she held his cracked skull, gripping it tightly to the point it shook, and her dark fingertips turned pale. The black, glittering sand tried to invade the crack in his skull, but it did nothing other than stop the bleeding and heal his other wounds.

She cannot heal herself like this? Then again, it had been similar to the magic that mended his own wounds. Perhaps it only worked for Mavka.

The spell she was doing dissipated as her shoulders slumped.

She pressed her forehead between his ram horns.

"Damnit. I knew it. It's no use once your kind damage your skulls."

Just as Magnar was about to ask her *why* she had retreated rather than staying to help him, considering she was a Phantom and could come back to life, something moved beneath the feathered cloak she wore.

Suddenly, a little black head poked its way through where the base of the hood was around her neck. Sightless and small, Magnar thought it looked exactly how Fyodor had before they'd obtained their rabbit skull.

"There are more of us?" Magnar asked in disbelief.

He'd never known she'd been carrying younglings on her back, hidden underneath her cloak.

A lump began to rise, a second youngling lower on her back, before they merely readjusted their position. They laid down flat once more, becoming completely undetectable.

"When he wants more of you created, I must obey," the Witch Owl said with a sigh, leaning back on her ankles to look up at the trees above them. Magnar thought she may be speaking of the spirit of the void, their father creator. "That's why I'm his, just to do this, to make more of your kind. I only tolerated it at first just so I could live unendingly with the magic he bestowed on me in exchange, but... you are all becoming so special. The older you all get, growing stronger and gaining more humanity, the more I see that you are wonderful." Then a lone tear tracked its way down her cheek as her lips quivered. "But I cannot do this. I cannot protect you all at the same time. I'm one person trying to protect you from someone who has a literal army."

She slapped her hands together and more black sand began to form. She palmed the air when she threw them forward.

Four spiralling circles began to appear, in total showing an image of six Duskwalkers.

One was of Magnar and the ram-horned Mavka in the area they were currently in. A second was of bull-horned Mavka who was walking through a forest that didn't appear to be the Veil – the trees were different. A third circle showed two Mavka in their most monstrous forms who appeared to either be fighting with each other or playing – considering neither one actually went for a damaging blow.

And finally, the last circle showed Orpheus and Reia. Reia was incorporeal, floating next to Orpheus who was in his monstrous form. He was running on all fours, items strapped across his body as Demons chased them.

Jabez ordered for them to be attacked?

"How am I supposed to do this by myself?" The Witch Owl turned her face to him, her tight brown curls bouncing around her head. "I can only fly so fast with my owl spell. I cannot be here and there at the same time. I cannot fight to my own death when I know that will leave these two by themselves in the Veil to be killed."

She reached up to stroke her palm over the nose holes of the youngling who still had their head poking out of her cloak.

Magnar remained silent. He didn't have the answer she sought.

When he didn't say anything, she lowered her gaze to her lap and stroked the skull that lay upon it.

"You should all leave here. Jabez cannot see past the Veil with his magic, not clearly, at least from what I can tell. It's better to risk yourself with the humans than to stay here."

"There is no place in the world for Mavka," Magnar answered, having known this truth for a long time.

He'd known it when the only safe place had been his cave that was situated on the border between the surface world belonging to the humans and the forest that belonged to the Demons. Mavka were stuck in between.

"We do not belong here, nor on the surface. We must endure and protect what we have."

"But if–"

"I don't want to kill humans needlessly anymore," Magnar interrupted with a heaviness weighing on his chest. "Only enough to gain humanity in order to understand my bride. That is all I care for. If we are to go to the surface, they will come for us with their swords and Demonslayers. We are seen as only death, so let us be death for the Demons."

We will not be safe no matter where we go. There is no place for us in this world. Magnar raised his snout so he could look through the leaves to see the purple and orange hue of dusk – a time of both light and darkness.

"I have only just laid my protection ward," he continued. "There is only one place in the world for me, and that is where Delora is safest. And she is safest sheltered under my magic."

A small breeze rustled both his fur and feathers, as well as her hair and cloak, and the quiet echoed between them as they both thought on his words. The truth rung in the silence, and today Magnar realised his place in this cruel and dark world.

He was *other*. A creature that lived within both worlds but also neither. A creature of dawn, dusk, night, and day, that was capable of both life and death, and given the ability to exist in between. A creature that could go anywhere, and if granted access by the spirit of the void, nowhere.

Mavka – Duskwalkers – were in limbo.

There was only one place he belonged, and that currently felt like a desolate hole in his chest. He may be Delora's living anchor, but she was also now his reason for being – and he worried she truly didn't want him.

His sight turned a deep well of blue as he brought his gaze down to Fyodor. She had done everything in her power to save their youngling, that he knew for certain. She cared for their child, had from the moment she'd begun carrying them, but... he was now unsure if she also shared those feelings for him.

She said she didn't have a choice to Jabez. He'd always known that, but he thought all was well when she reassured him she was glad she'd taken this path with him. *Did she lie because there had been no other option but to accept me?*

Why did that make him feel like more of an ugly monster than before?

Without her... I will have nothing.

"Would it be alright if he stays here with you until he awakens?" the Witch Owl asked quietly, breaking Magnar from his sorrowful thoughts. "Will you keep him safe for me?"

"Yes."

"Then I must leave. Now that you have healed me, I must help Orpheus and Reia as much as I can."

The Witch Owl gently placed the ram-horned Mavka's skull on the ground and stood, staring down at him for a long while.

I did not realise she cared so deeply for us. Even though she'd recently gone through a terrible battle, she was unwilling to rest when more of her children were in danger.

She turned away, propping her feathered hood over her head and began to change into a human-sized white owl. Before she even left his line of sight, she took off in flight, darting between the trees before he saw her swoop upwards, like she planned to fly over the Veil.

There was no goodbye from her.

Fyodor lifted their skull and sniffed the air like they often did, but Delora's missing scent caused them to whimper. They curled into Magnar for comfort.

Apprehension grew within him.

His heart quickened with each passing minute he was alone, awaiting her return while utterly dreading it.

I'm tired... and everything hurts.

He stayed with the Mavka in order to watch over him. He didn't know how much time passed, a minute? An hour? But eventually, a transparent figure appeared just off to the side. Delora lay just off the ground curled up in a ball, momentarily unconscious as though she were asleep.

She stirred. The moment her eyes opened, a gasp tore from her, and she hastily looked around. Her eyes widened when they fell upon him, then she turned physical and scrambled to her feet.

She almost tripped as she rushed over, having to catch herself on one hand against the dirt.

Magnar didn't mean to flinch when she was in front of him reaching towards Fyodor. She didn't seem to notice as she looked down and stroked their skull with both hands. Relief slumped her shoulders instantly.

Fyodor gave a cheerful shrill, nuzzling their snout into her hands.

"Thank you," she said with a smile, her brown eyes twinkling with tears but also with appreciation towards him. "I knew you could do it. I knew you would protect them."

Magnar's skin crawled with her closeness. His heart thumped

in his chest in a wildly unpleasant way.

Just as he began to hand Fyodor over to her so he could shrink away from her presence, Delora bounced up and threw her arms around his thick neck. She squeezed him as she buried her face into his long feathers.

"I'm so sorry, Magnar. I know you must be confused."

Squeezing tighter, he tried not to whine when she pressed against his tender wounds. Thankfully, she was fully unharmed.

"I had to say those things, I had to get him to trust me so I could grab Fyodor. If I made it seem like I hated you, hated being here, that he could train Fyodor like some pet, then I could rescue them." She gave a laugh, one that was filled with humour but also sounded dark. "I tried to be like that woman Reia and Orpheus told me about, Katerina or whatever her name was. I thought if he took her because she wanted to escape, then he would try to take me too."

The tension in his body didn't lessen.

When his grip on Fyodor became tighter, like he no longer wanted to let go of the one creature he *knew* wanted to be by his side, Delora unfurled her arms from around his neck.

She was greeted by the dark blue glow of his orbs – his lingering doubts refusing to dissipate.

Delora cupped the end of his snout with both hands to make sure she held his stare, looking directly at him without a single shred of hesitation in her expression. Instead, her brows were furrowed with determination, her lips tight with it.

"I want to be here with you, Magnar. You are so smart and cool and lovely to be around."

"You said I gave you no choice," Magnar rumbled, his stomach twisting. "And I already told you I knew this."

He tried to avert his skull to the side. She held firm, leaning the way he'd gone to follow him when she couldn't win against his strength. She wasn't going to let him look away.

"And I already told you I'm thankful that you didn't." Delora stroked her palm up the length of his snout. "Please believe me. I called for you because I knew you would be brave and strong enough to protect Fyodor when I couldn't. I knew what I was doing when I told you to leave me behind, Magnar. That I was most likely going to be hurt, and I let him do those things so that I could give you time."

A painfully tender ache radiated across his chest.

"What did he do?"

He didn't know why he was asking. He didn't really want to know the truth.

"It doesn't matter," she said softly with a bitter smile. "I just wanted to give you time." When he didn't say anything, her brows drew together tightly. He could see the uncertainty in her expression. "I will always come back to you, but that doesn't mean I have to stay here with you."

He cocked his head slightly.

"What do you mean?"

"If I really didn't want to be here, if I hated it so much, I could just wander the Veil. Sure, I would return to you, but I could just restart every day."

His grip loosened on Fyodor, having never thought of this option for her. *She could have left me.* She would have been like a Ghost travelling through the shadowy forest.

"But I have never wanted to. Even in the beginning when I didn't really want to live anymore, I found comfort being by your side."

Even from the beginning? He was unsure if she was telling the truth or not, but Magnar *wanted* to believe her with every fibre of his being. His lonely heart was desperate for it.

"Then why did you do this?" Magnar asked, the blue in his orbs refusing to leave his sight. "You say there was no other option, but this could have been avoided had I given him the Mavka."

Magnar gestured to him at his side.

"Because I could see you didn't want to," she answered, sitting on her hip as though she was tired from reaching up to him. He was sure she was exhausted. "And I didn't want you to, either. He doesn't deserve to die because of that jerk. I couldn't stand by and watch you give over your own brother to protect Fyodor. I... I didn't want to do nothing like I always do. You have protected me time and time again. It was my turn to make that sacrifice so that you didn't have to bear the pain of losing either

Fyodor or him. I was the only one who could take that risk without lasting consequences."

A warmth began to grow in his gut, helping to rid him of the cold sadness he'd been experiencing.

"You did it... for me?"

"Yes," she answered sternly, her eyes firmly upon him.

He saw not a single bit of doubt in her gaze.

"Otherwise, I could have just stood there and done nothing. I had a choice, and I made one – even if it hurt a whole fucking bunch." Then she scratched at the back of her head and laughed. "My original plan was to run back to you, but instead, I ran into the forest like an idiot."

Green burst into his vision as he chuckled, her words and laughter replacing his hurt. He curled his arm around her so he could bring her closer in a hug that she immediately welcomed.

"Do not call yourself such things, my little raven. You have always been clever."

"That is not true!" she squealed, but she placed her arms around his neck, and this time he fully accepted it, glad she wanted to return his embrace. "I have my moments, Magnar."

Delora's heartbeat fluttered through her chest and radiated through him. Magnar focused on it, needing to know she was safe and alive, and wanted to be with him enough to allow him to be lulled by it.

He forgives me.

Delora hugged Magnar tighter. She refused to linger on what just happened to her, refused to acknowledge it.

She'd already faced so much, and she didn't want the memory of her agony with the Demon King to be any part of her. She refused. She, Magnar, and Fyodor were safe. That had been her goal, and that was all she wanted to remember.

Everything is okay.

Sudden movement caused Delora to gasp and instinctively push into Magnar's side. However, she was also quick to grab Fyodor, refusing to make the same mistake twice. With others around she didn't trust, Delora would never let Fyodor out of her arms – not that they would ever make any form of complaint.

Magnar took on a protective stance by pushing the other side of his body forward, hiding her a little when the ram-horned Duskwalker rushed to all fours in a burst of movement.

His clothing sunk beneath his skin as he turned more monstrous, his lizard-like spikes growing large and more menacing from his back and arms. He huffed as he backed a step from them before he reached a hand up to touch at his cracked feline skull.

The cattish whine that came from him chilled her to the point that shivers broke across her flesh like a wave. The Duskwalker began to shake his head side to side, his orbs so white they appeared like stark voids.

Then he checked his body for his other wounds, which had somehow disappeared. Delora looked to Magnar for answers since she knew this Duskwalker had been heavily injured before.

"It has been a day?" he asked Magnar, slow with his words.

Magnar shook his bony head. "No. The Witch Owl came and tried to heal you of your wounds and the crack in your skull. She was unable to."

That must be why he'd woken up now, considering she thought he'd be asleep for a long time. She also noted the sky was darkening. It had looked brighter when she'd been *eaten* by the Demon King. Delora shuddered.

"No," he rasped in a heartbreaking, quiet voice.

He pawed at the crack again, his face pointing to the side, before lowering to the ground, as he took in this information. His situation.

"If she could not heal you..." Magnar started.

"Then nothing can be done."

His orbs started to lift with a pale colour blue, as though fear and sadness were too strong within him to take priority.

For a long while, he stared at nothing.

His arms began to slip to the ground, the backs of his white knuckle bones resting upon the dirt as his shoulders slumped. It was horrible watching someone realise there was nothing they could do to prevent their own demise and were trying to come to terms with it.

The Duskwalker began to morph back to normal. His clothing rose through his flesh, the bottom of the pants in tatters, but they were otherwise mostly intact. His shirt, however, was covered in multiple claw marks.

He looks terrible. He must have faced so much.

"Thank you," he mumbled before slowly turning his head to them. "For protecting me. For not giving me to the Demon King. And thank you for letting me rest here."

"H-how long have you been running?" Delora asked, squeezing herself into Magnar in case vocalising that she was there was a terrible idea.

"Two days." His head twisted at her, but he made no move to come closer. "I see you have a human who has given you their soul. I'm sorry if I brought danger to you and your bride."

He wrapped his hand around his snout in deep thought, orange flashing in his orbs much like how Magnar's did when he felt guilt.

Despite his issues and the future she was sure he knew he must face, a spark of yellow flashed in his glowing orbs as he sniffed the air in her direction. He inched closer and waved his hand at her lap.

"But what is this? A baby Mavka?"

Magnar raised his hand up to shield Fyodor from view. "They are my youngling."

The Duskwalker cocked his head at Magnar. "*Your* youngling? We cannot breed with humans, it's impossible. We are different."

"She is a Phantom now."

His head darted up to Delora's partially blackened soul attached to Magnar's antlers.

"I see," he said with a thoughtfulness, his hand coming up to rub the chin of his feline jaw. "So that's what happens when we gain a human's soul. We change them, make them more like us? Not that I will ever experience this now."

It took Delora a moment to realise, but this Duskwalker was more intelligent than she thought he'd be. He was more like Orpheus, who knew and understood everything already.

He let out a chuckle so dark and without humour that it almost sounded insane, like a crazy person laughing at the wall.

"At least I got to learn one more thing about the world before I fucking left it."

Delora couldn't stop herself from biting her bottom lip, wishing there was something she could say to ease him.

There's nothing that will make him feel better. No one in the world could have consoled Delora when she'd been dragged to the Veil to be discarded. *I know what it feels like to know your own death is coming.*

She wanted to reach out to him, a part of her wanted to hug him in apology, but she didn't. Instead, she lifted Fyodor in her arms in his direction, seeing he was of no danger.

"Would... would you perhaps like to meet them? If you're Magnar's brother, then that would technically make them your niece or nephew, depending on what gender of human they eat first."

"Ah, so..." he chuckled, this time a little more warmly, "you know the Witch Owl is our mother."

"You already knew?" Magnar asked, his orbs reflecting yellow.

"I remembered her smell from when I was a youngling. She was always there, and I remembered the feeling of her when I clung to her, remembered her scent, her voice." He lifted his head into the air, his mannerisms slow but calculated. "Perhaps it's because she has hugged me a few times after saving me. The Demon King always comes for me, for some reason. It may be because I'm always in the inner ring of the Veil, speaking with the Demons who reside there."

Delora's brows furrowed deeply. "Then why do you go there?"

"Because it was better than being alone in my cave," he firmly stated. Then he brought his head down to her and nodded. "Yes. If that is alright, I would like to meet your youngling since I will never be able to experience my own. I have always been curious about the humans and their families."

Moving out of Magnar's hold, who was apprehensive of letting her go, both she and the Duskwalker crawled closer to each other. They met in the middle, and she placed Fyodor in a slight sitting position facing him.

"May I touch them?" he asked, seeming to sense that this was a sensitive and intimate thing he was doing.

He also looked towards Magnar to make sure that he was accepting of this.

Magnar somehow, deep inside his obtained humanity, understood the significance of everything that was happening. He nodded as he came closer, placing his arm around Delora's back to hold her.

The ram-horned Duskwalker gently placed his hand on Fyodor's skull and stroked it. Fyodor sniffed at his large palm but wasn't enraged or hesitant – perhaps because they'd gotten used to him while he was unconscious.

The Duskwalker's eyes turned a bright yellow as he parted his jaws.

"Remarkable, absolutely remarkable. So, this is what we looked like before we obtained our horns and sight. I never would have thought we started so small and defenceless." Fyodor lifted their hand and curled it around one of his big fingers. "Even our claws are softer when young."

Wow... she thought, looking at him through her lashes. *He's so different to Magnar and Orpheus. He's so friendly.*

Although they were both kind, Orpheus was far more standoffish with Delora, and Magnar was still learning so much that he often looked awkward and out of place. This Duskwalker seemed to fit in perfectly with them, showing no hesitation nor any rudeness – even despite his dark situation.

It almost feels like I'm talking to a human.

Does that mean he is older than them? Or, at least, more developed. *Or has he just travelled more?* Orpheus, from what she knew, had spent the last two hundred years grieving and trying to find a human until he found Reia.

Magnar had rarely left the Veil or his cave up until recently.

"What are you going to do now?" Magnar asked, watching

the Duskwalker inspect their child.

As though he'd just been trying to distract himself, the Duskwalker sighed and pulled his hand back. His orbs gentled in their yellow hue, settling, and Delora wondered if that was their natural colour.

"I think... I'm going to leave the Veil."

"Like go to the surface?" Delora asked while turning Fyodor in her arms so they could be hugging.

"Yes." He raised his hand and touched at the crack running over his skull. "I don't know if I will die. Maybe if I'm careful, I can escape death. But if I remain in the Veil where the Demon King will come for me, then I stand no chance."

"There are Demonslayers though," Magnar reminded him.

"That's fine. They are easy enough to evade. There... is also someone I would like to see first, if I am going to perish."

"Mayumi?" Magnar asked, tilting his head slightly.

A reddish pink flared in the Duskwalker's orbs.

"How did you–?"

"You said that name right before you collapsed."

"Is it a woman?" Delora hoped her prying didn't make it seem like she was overstepping her boundary.

The Duskwalker scratched awkwardly at the back of his neck. It caused his lizard spikes to wobble behind his head as the skin stretched and moved.

"She is no one. She does not know I exist." Then he brought his hand forward to stare at his claws. "I'm sure if she did, she would have tried to kill me by now."

Delora's brows drew together. "What's that supposed to mean?"

"Nothing," he chuckled, reaching forward to tap the tip of a claw at the back of Fyodor's head. "Thank you for letting me meet your youngling. And thank you again for allowing me to rest here."

Delora was grateful Magnar didn't mention he'd almost given him to the Demon King. And she was even more confident that, despite the horrible pain she'd experienced in sacrificing herself, it had been worth it after speaking with him.

She didn't want to mention she'd saved his life; there was no need. She didn't want to birth mistrust between him and Magnar, and she also didn't do it for gratitude.

They all deserve to live. From the bottom of her heart, she knew that. She knew they weren't monsters, but something so much more tender.

"You are going to leave now?" Magnar asked when the other Mavka stood, and he followed his lead by rising to his own feet.

Delora stood as well, since she didn't want to be crowded by giant Duskwalkers who would have appeared even more daunting if she'd remained kneeling on the ground. She allowed Fyodor to roam around her feet but kept a good eye on them since they were all still close to the border.

"I see no point in staying, and I'm sure you want me off your territory."

Magnar awkwardly scratched at the tip of his snout with the very point of a claw. "I don't mind if you stay for a little while longer. You appear to know much, and I would like to speak with you in order to learn what you know."

"I must admit," the Duskwalker said brightly, "the last time I saw you, you were pretty undeveloped. You seemed to have gained much humanity recently. However, as much as I appreciate the offer, I worry that my time in this world is now limited, and I don't want to spend my time in the afterworld with regrets. There is someone I would like to protect, even if they do not know I'm there. If I can spend the remainder of my time doing this, then that is what I'd like to do."

"Well..." Delora started as she dragged her eyes over his torn clothing. "At least let us give you some new clothes. Magnar recently obtained some more from the Demon Village."

"Magnar?" he said, cocking his head in his direction. "You were given a proper name?"

Magnar wrapped his big soothing hand around the back of Delora's neck and shoulders. "She gave it to me. It means I'm her protector."

A small smile lifted the corners of her lips.

"If we are sharing names, you may call me Kitty."

Kitty? She looked over his feline skull with one of her brows raised. *I guess it matches his face, but that's not a name you'd give someone. Maybe he named himself?*

That was one way to have a name, she figured.

"And if you are offering clothing, could I also trouble you for a new cloak? Mine was torn from me and I'd prefer to wear one if I am to travel the surface."

"Sure," Magnar said, just as Delora nodded.

Today has been a long day. It wasn't even over yet, the sun still setting, and she wanted to go to bed.

They all then began to walk back to the house. Kitty was surprised when he saw it – and he lingered a little longer in order to inspect it with curiosity.

FORTY-FOUR

"I fixed it!" Delora squealed, rushing out of the house with Fyodor chasing after her heels. "Magnar! Look, I fixed it!"

Having been off deeper within the forest, Magnar came rushing through the trees. He'd most likely been cutting down more trees to make the fence for the ward or procuring timber for the fireplace.

"You startled me," Magnar said as he came up to her standing by the porch. "When I heard you scream, I thought something happened."

"Oh, sorry," she awkwardly laughed, before lifting her hands to show him. "I fixed the music box, see?"

He pointed to the top of it. "But you have broken it further."

The box was now permanently unlocked, and she opened the lid to reveal the insides. A small metal carousel with three horses sat alongside the base of the music box she'd destroyed in order to get to the cylinder and musical comb.

She'd used one of Magnar's metal cutting tools that he occasionally used to make hammering nails to cut the lever from the keyhole so she could wind it up by her fingers instead.

"No, here. I'll show you."

She dug her fingertips into the decently sized hole she'd made and turned the lever. The metal comb moved slightly when she knocked it to make a *ting* noise.

Once it was wound up as far it would go, she released it, and it began to play a soft melody.

Magnar's orbs morphed to bright yellow as his head twitched

and cocked at each note that was played, making the sound of rattling bones come from him. He took it from her hands carefully and raised it to the side of his head.

"I have never heard anything like this before," he stated with awe in his voice. "I very much like it."

"You do?" She couldn't contain the smile that spread across her lips.

The song stopped playing.

He gave it to her as he asked, "Could you play it again?"

She turned the lever. When his orbs blackened as though he'd closed his sight, Delora realised he was enjoying the sound of the music so much that he was savouring it.

An emotion, tender and heart-aching, bubbled in her chest.

She grabbed his hand, making him stumble forward with shock when she dragged him back. Once the music stopped playing, she turned the lever and placed it on the bottom porch step.

"What are you doing?" he asked when she placed one of his large palms across her side to almost span its entire width, before she grasped his other with her own.

She placed her hand on his biceps as she started swaying them.

"It's called dancing," she said softly, trying to make sure the music was louder than her voice. "Humans sometimes do this together. This is called a waltz. It's a dance lovers would usually do together."

Delora bravely drew her eyes away from their feet and looked up to Magnar as she steered them in a slow circle. She winced when he stepped on the side of her foot.

"I don't know how to do this, Delora," he said with a shaky voice, trying to pull away from her. "I will hurt you."

She tripped over his feet when she crossed her legs the wrong way. He caught her, and she continued trying to get him to sway with her.

"That's okay. I can't dance either, to be honest. We can learn together." She winced again, and he lifted his foot suddenly. "Just try not to step on my toes, okay?"

Knowing that Delora wasn't very good at this either seemed

to ease his tension, and he allowed her to take control with fumbling steps. She knew he was looking down at their feet since his snout was pointed down with his head twisted so he could see past it.

The only time they broke apart was so she could turn the music box again, giving them at least a solid minute of dancing without interruption.

He grew more confident, and his steps became less hesitant.

Delora's smile grew softer. *He always learns so fast.*

He drew her closer by wrapping his arm around her, his clawed fingers curling between the gaps of her own far smaller ones until he swallowed her hand completely. He pressed them together, her hips meeting his thighs as they gazed at each other.

They both sucked – neither one knew what they were doing – but by the fourth time the music ended, both had forgotten about the music and continued to dance long after it silenced.

She noticed his tail flicking side to side.

His orbs faded into a bright pink, and it caused her stomach to pool with heat even though she didn't understand its meaning. She knew it was important, that it meant *something*, but she was still trying to figure out what she felt for him to even to begin understanding what he felt for her.

He makes me feel so safe. Safer than she'd ever been, even when she was a little child surrounded by her father's loving, coal-dusted arms.

"I... like this," he eventually muttered, leaning down so he could press the end of his snout against the side of her head. "I would like to dance with you again."

Delora plonked her forehead against his hard torso with her lips pulling tight.

What the hell do I feel for him? Just dancing with him was making her heart race like it was threatening to run out of her very chest to get to him.

Burying her face against him filled her senses completely with his inviting scent, and it caused her eyelids to involuntarily flutter with euphoria. His warmth was just as intoxicating, causing her skin to flush in enjoyment.

Even his voice was more tantalising than the music box that

had long gone quiet, giving her the ability to hear his tender heartbeat and his deep breaths.

He nuzzled the side of his jaw just above her ear.

It had been days since the incident with the Demon King. Since then, things between them had been closer than ever. Delora felt cherished, especially since Magnar hovered... almost protectively.

She adored it.

They were so wrapped in the moment that neither one of them noticed they were about to be interrupted until they heard a giggle.

Their heads both darted to the side to see Reia and Orpheus approaching. Delora pulled away from Magnar with a roaring blush heating her cheeks.

"Are we interrupting something?" Reia laughed, pulling away from Orpheus, who was dropping a deer from his shoulders to the ground.

"Nope," Delora squeaked before clearing her voice with a grunt. "We were, uh, just dancing. I managed to get the music box working."

"Really?" Reia's features brightened. "You have to show me! I was really starting to get worried that you wouldn't be able to get it to play."

"You brought us meat?" Magnar asked Orpheus.

Orpheus gave a curt nod, leaving the deer where it was so he could approach. Fyodor sniffed around his feet before going to Reia to run around her in greeting, completely comfortable with these two people.

Delora smiled lovingly down at them.

"Yes." Orpheus waved his hand to the side. "I knew you wouldn't be able to leave the ward to go hunting after what transpired the other day. Reia suggested we resume hunting for you until things settle down."

They'd all spoken about that day when Reia and Orpheus had come to visit last.

Magnar nodded in agreement as he placed his hand over the end of his snout. "It's true. I don't plan to leave her side for a while."

Since that eventful day, more Demons tended to loiter around their home. Still infrequently, but more often... and they weren't always the animalistic kind.

They were being watched, carefully.

However, they didn't attack. It was obvious they knew they'd die, especially if Orpheus and Magnar were to team up together.

Jabez, as Delora had come to discover he was named, couldn't see inside Magnar's ward with his magic. Currently, their home was the safest place to be.

"Reia also said she would like to eat dinner here today, if that would be okay with you both. That's why we brought the whole deer, rather than just a few pieces of it."

Magnar looked to Delora for approval, and she smiled with a nod in answer.

"Of course. It would mean you'll be here for longer, and that would make building the fencing faster."

"Show me the music box," Reia said with an excited grin, cutting into Delora listening to the conversation. "I've never heard one before."

With one last look at Fyodor, who was just sniffing at the ground, Delora walked over to the music box sitting upon the lowest porch step.

Magnar and Orpheus continued to speak, but she couldn't hear what they said the further they walked away.

"Are you okay?" Delora asked Reia as she bent down to grab the music box. "Have you guys been safe?"

"Pfft! Do you know who you're talking to?" Reia laughed, her smile crooked and almost devilish. "Not only do I have Orpheus around, who is literally happy to *tear* Demons in half for even trying to hiss at me, but I'm also really good with my sword."

There was always one strapped to Reia's waist.

"I know, it's just..."

Delora didn't want to know they were in danger. Not just Reia, but Orpheus too. She cared for them both.

"How about you? Seems like Jabez will likely target you guys specifically now."

Delora sighed after she opened the music box.

"He probably will." Then she gave a shrug. "I barely even know the Demons exist because of the forest within the ward. I don't really think they can see us, nor hear us."

"I know the other day you said you were fine, but like... Fyodor was almost taken from you."

Surprisingly, her lips curled into a smile.

"But they weren't. Magnar kept them safe."

And so did I. Delora was proud of herself for what she'd done. She never would have been able to do that in the past.

"What happened, happened. I can't change it, nor should I linger on it. I'm done looking at the bad things from the past." She couldn't help her eyes landing on Magnar as a tenderness spread in her chest. "I only want to think about the things that matter."

The moment she finished turning the lever and music started playing, everyone quieted.

Orpheus cocked his head suddenly at the sound, his orbs glowing bright yellow, just like Magnar's had.

Reia's brows furrowed deeply as she turned her ear in the direction of the box. Then she started to hum. Her hum was a few notes wrong, but the tune was similar to the one that was playing.

When it stopped, Orpheus and Magnar approached while Reia gestured her hands out to see if Delora would let her spin the lever herself.

"I don't know the song's name," Reia muttered, bringing the box to her ear when it started playing again. "But it sounds really similar to the one my mother used to sing to me before she died."

"What is that?" Orpheus asked, stabbing a claw in its direction.

"A music box," Magnar quickly answered, puffing his chest in pride – for some reason.

"I see," he answered, his orbs flashing brighter. "May I hold it?"

"Sure," Delora said, and Reia handed it to him.

Her back stiffened when he poked one of his claws inside the box with curious touches, making it jangle. Then he bobbed his head to the side as he rotated the lever slightly, making his horn bells and the music box play at the same time for a short, fleeting second.

He's a tinker, Delora thought, her eyes crinkling in delight. Perhaps if Orpheus had been a human, he may have tried to work as a clock maker or something with little mechanisms.

Reia took it from him, seeing the same potential as Delora did for him to break it. She wound the lever, put it on the porch step, then brazenly turned to Orpheus.

"Come here, you big bonehead. Want to dance?" Reia held her hand out with both her brows bouncing up and down mischievously.

Despite not knowing what he was about to do, Orpheus trustingly reached out to take Reia's hand without hesitation. "Dance?"

She grabbed his other hand and spun them both in a quick circle, making him stumble. Then she put them into a similar position as Delora had done with Magnar.

It was obvious Reia may have danced in the past by how she moved, but never with a partner, as she tripped over Orpheus' feet. They were much messier in their actions since they were more comfortable with each other.

"You stepped on my foot," Orpheus grumbled.

Reia did it again, on purpose from what Delora could tell.

In retaliation, Orpheus picked her up and spun her in the air with her body flush against him. Reia laughed, and Delora brought her gaze to Magnar, who was watching them.

He was tense, his eyes a dark green – much darker than normal.

"Do you want to dance again?" Delora asked, offering her hand out to him.

"Yes," he grated with a roughness, placing his palm in her own.

He brought them into the same position as before, the one where they were closer, but he did try to spin them together like he'd seen. Delora tried to show him how to throw her outwards so that she could spin back into him.

He chuckled, his orbs fading back to their natural green.

"This seems complicated."

"It can be." She swayed them side to side. "I've danced a few times, but not very often. I can teach you more moves later."

Reia turned the lever again, ensuring that she could keep wrangling Orpheus into dancing with her. Finally, for the first time in her life, happiness warmed Delora.

She had friends, people who valued who she was without judgement, and she'd never felt so... free.

Her cheeks began to heat with a shy blush as she looked up at Magnar's fox-headed skull. Her heart took flight. *I think I'm–*

Before Delora could finish her thoughts, both Magnar and Orpheus halted and darted their bony faces in the same direction.

"Do you smell that?" Orpheus asked, pulling away from a disgruntled Reia, who almost fell over when he suddenly stopped moving.

"Yes," Magnar quickly answered. Then he let go of Delora, his gaze sweeping across the yard. "Where's Fyodor?"

Delora paled, feeling dread creeping in to snuff out her happiness completely. She searched also, finding they weren't playing around everyone's feet like they usually would have been.

"What's wrong?" Delora asked, her heart stammering in quick thumps. "Reia? Have you seen them?"

She shook her head.

"I smell blood," Magnar said, letting her go to head in the direction he smelt it.

Some part of her eased. *Fyodor doesn't bleed.* They also didn't have a scent, and their body couldn't be harmed as it just moulded around what was stabbing into them.

"The deer is gone," Orpheus stated.

Delora looked to where it had once been lying on the ground to see it had disappeared. Her eyes widened.

"Wait..."

Delora raced ahead of Magnar, heading slightly deeper into the tree line. She only needed to make it one or two trees deep before she found Fyodor, who had already started pulling apart the deer.

Their size had grown exponentially already, and each bite was making them burst with width and mass.

There wasn't much left, only the upper half of the deer's

torso. Everyone had realised far too late what was happening.

At least they were safe, still...

"No!" Delora shouted, rushing to the head of the deer and yanking on its antlers to get it away from them.

They're too big! They were almost to the height of her hip, and she didn't want them to get any bigger!

Fyodor slammed their clawed hand down on the deer and roared, their blood-coated fangs parting in warning in her very direction. Delora didn't care, she just kept tugging.

Magnar was swift, grabbing Delora around the waist and lifting her off the ground, but she refused to let go of the deer. She kicked her legs in the air in an attempt to get free.

"Let go, Delora," he pleaded, dragging her back and making the deer come with her.

Fyodor snapped their fangs before they grabbed the other side of the deer's carcass, tugging it in the opposite direction. Their snarl was horrible, muffled by the meat in their mouth. It grew more ferocious when they gained another jump in their mass.

They don't even look like a toddler now. They'd completely skipped being a young child.

Orpheus and Reia, who had come to witness, backed up when Magnar eventually managed to get Delora to release her hold. Fyodor stood on top of their meal and snarled.

"Stop them," Delora begged.

"It isn't wise to get between a Mavka and their meal," Orpheus stated. "If any of us approach, they will attack. Do you really want us to hurt them, or vice versa?"

Her face crinkled in worry about how big Fyodor would get. She wouldn't be able to hold them anymore, have them cuddle in her lap.

No, but... She didn't want this.

She liked Fyodor how they were. That they'd been adorable and small.

Forced to watch them eat the deer without being able to interfere, Fyodor grew bigger and bigger. Short fur started to sprout on their outer extremities, before longer, more rabbit-like fur became obvious around their shoulders, back, and chest.

Her ears tingled at the grotesque sound of skin tearing, bones crunching, and slurping. Delora wanted nothing more than to turn away, but she didn't.

They even ate the head. Their skull had grown larger, like the bones they'd eaten had aided the transformation, and they crunched everything with ease.

Black sand began to eat away at two circles on the top of their skull as horns began to form. Those horns then split apart into forking branches with goopy string that stuck to the tips and edges until they dropped onto their skull.

Once finished with their meal, Fyodor stood on their rabbit back legs and the very tips of their toes. And everyone, including the two big Duskwalkers, warily stepped back.

They're huge! Fyodor reached a height at least a foot taller than even Magnar.

Their claws had hardened and were long, even on their toes, but their body looked hollow and gangly. It was malformed and sunken around bone, like their spine, where she thought she may have almost been able to wrap her hands around it.

It made them look empty of organs and muscles.

The only thing that stopped them from truly looking gnarly was their fluffy rabbit fur. She realised then that Duskwalkers grew their width when they ate.

They started pin-sized, but eventually two green orbs, that matched the colour of Magnar's, began to grow in a rotation like a fire vortex.

Fyodor started clacking their fanged jaws together while giving quiet rabbit squeaks that sounded deep and twisted.

Delora tried to step forward despite Magnar's protective hold on her. He tugged her back.

For the first time in their life, her child looked at her with their own eyes. Green, and just as welcoming as Magnar's.

That was, until they turned a stark white, and Fyodor gave a beastly roar.

They swiped their claws in warning as they backed up, confusion obvious by the way they shifted their gaze between them all. She could tell there was a lack of thought, that they didn't understand, as Fyodor gave whelping cries.

All these abrupt changes brought chaos to their mind.

Delora turned incorporeal to get free of Magnar's arms.

"Fyodor," she whispered, her voice breaking when she bravely turned physical in front of them.

At their own name, or perhaps just the familiarity of it, their distressed sounds stopped. Their head twisted almost freakishly upside down as they took a hesitant step forward. On all fours, their flipper back feet somehow not causing them to trip, they sniffed the air right in front of her.

In her peripheral, she could tell Magnar had cautiously stepped close enough that he could rescue her if need be. She was sure the only reason he wasn't interfering was because she had the ability to turn incorporeal.

Delora wasn't afraid. She refused to be afraid of Fyodor, her own child, even if it meant she was in danger.

But she was alone, the only person within Fyodor's sight, and the subtle wind was pushing her skirt in their direction.

They slowly came just that bit closer, and she couldn't stop her eyes from bowing in worry.

A loud squeal broke from her, right after Fyodor's white orbs turned a bright pink, and they pounced on her. She had to put her hands on their snout to push it back, uselessly, when they licked at her face with long, slobbery licks.

"Oh, my God. Gross!" she laughed underneath them. "Someone save me!"

Magnar approached. After a short warning snarl before Fyodor recognised the person they could *see* standing before them had a familiar scent, Magnar managed to get them to release her.

She got up while wiping her face with her forearm. It wasn't enough to rid herself of their thick saliva, and she was forced to use the skirt of her dress to clean her face.

Fyodor sat, but their frame was so big that they were almost the same height as her even though their arse was firmly pressing against the ground. They looked pleased with themself.

Despite their new size, she couldn't help finding them cute – especially since their fluffy rabbit tail was obviously wiggling.

"They're so big now." Delora came closer and held their snout affectionately before she caressed her hands up to the sides of their jaw. She gave an affectionate shake to their head while gripping it. "You're not my little Fyodor anymore."

"I don't think we are all going to fit in the nest anymore," Magnar said with a thoughtful mumble.

Despite how Fyodor was no longer a child and seemed to be the size of an adult Duskwalker, which left a little ache in her chest, she couldn't help but laugh at what Magnar said.

"Maybe not comfortably," she answered with a tender smile. "But I bet it'll be really cosy."

"And warm," Reia chuckled, causing all three of their heads to turn to her and Orpheus. She lifted an arm and gave a shrug. "It's autumn right now, but it's getting colder each day. The more warmth, the better. Right?"

Orpheus, standing just behind Reia, placed his hands on her shoulders. He leaned down to bump the side of his snout against her ear.

"If you really want more warmth like this, we could make our own–"

"Nope!" Reia yelped with a laugh, stepping forward to get away. "Not ready, *yet*."

Orpheus backed off with a half-hearted growl, dropping his hands from her shoulders so he could fold his arms with a huff, like an immature child. He even turned his head to the side.

"However, I must admit, Fyodor does make me more curious by the day." Fyodor sniffed in Reia's direction when she approached, but they seemed to be adapting better now to their changes. They didn't even give her a growl when she lifted her hand so they could sniff the back of her wrist. "It's amazing to watch them grow and understand what it's like for Duskwalkers. The Witch Owl made it seem much worse. Then again... perhaps for her, it was."

Orpheus brought his head forward, but didn't seem inclined to come meet Fyodor as their adult self. Actually, he appeared to be quite wary of Reia being so close, his fur obviously puffed beneath his clothing.

"What do you mean?" Delora asked, her brows drawing tight.

Her forest-green eyes flicked up to Delora's own, and the gaze she held was stern. "You had Magnar and us. I don't imagine she's had anyone to lean on."

"You forget," Orpheus rebuffed, relaxing when Reia dropped her hand to give him her attention. "She's had the spirit of the void."

"Have either one of you ever met him to know what he's like?"

Delora blinked when Orpheus and Magnar lifted their heads in each other's direction and then simultaneously tilted their heads in opposite directions.

"I have not," Magnar stated. "And it appears he hasn't either."

"Not met." Orpheus shook his head before it turned to the side with what she could only imagine was with a thoughtful gaze. "But I have... felt him. He lingers everywhere within the Veil, and it is often believed he is the cause of the black mist."

"There is no point in speculating," Delora butted in, turning to Fyodor, who had been patiently waiting for her to give them her attention. Their green orbs flashed to pink immediately under her gaze. "We don't really know, and I want to go back to the house now."

Delora didn't want to linger anywhere near the ward. There could be Demons watching them, and she didn't want the Demon King to know of Fyodor's new changes.

She eyed deeper within the forest, constantly wary.

They all started to make their way back – all but one of them.

"Fyodor?" Delora asked, thinking they would have started following.

Instead, they'd been staring into the Veil, their head turned completely the other way. It was only when she said their name, or only perhaps because she had spoken, that they turned their face towards her.

She patted her knees, trying to coax them towards her. They stayed rooted to the ground, twisting their head with a lack of understanding.

"Come on. Follow me."

She patted again, and their head only twisted the other way.

Her heart sunk, especially when Magnar came up beside her and wrapped his hand around her waist.

Thankfully, although very slowly, Fyodor walked on all fours to follow.

"I wonder if we can get Fyodor to dance with us," Reia laughed from up ahead in the more cleared area of the yard.

Delora would have laughed as well, but she couldn't ease the black pit welling in her chest.

They didn't come to me straight away.

FORTY-FIVE

"They're going to leave, aren't they?" Delora asked Magnar when he came to sit on the porch stairs next to her.

He sat with his hands clasped between his parted knees.

The area was almost dark. It wasn't quite dusk yet, but the shadows of the Veil's forest made it dim. They always cast a blueish hue to the area, and the mist aided the dreary colouring at this hour.

The light wind made it feel colder than usual, the treetops bristling.

She'd opted to sit on the steps instead of her bench, simply because she wanted to be able to see the yard fully. Fyodor was roaming it, like they often did over the past three days, but every day, little by little, they were going further and further into the trees.

Delora did nothing else but watch them, wary of how far they'd go. Multiple times, she'd been forced to run after them and somehow coax them back. And every time, Fyodor stared off into the forest for a little while before finally following her.

They seem so restless.

Other than when they were sleeping, which wasn't as much as they used to, Fyodor would walk. They paced the yard constantly.

She'd follow, unwilling to let them go, but... she could see it.

They were different. They were no longer a baby. They no longer felt the need to cling to her now that they were big and could see.

Magnar's interlocked fingers clasped tighter, as if her question had shot tension through him.

"Yes," he slowly answered, his voice darker than normal, as if saddened.

Her heart gave a painful ache, like it was trying to break.

"Is that why she is here?" Delora lifted her eyes to the top of their house where the Witch Owl was currently situated in her owl form. "Is... she waiting for them to leave?"

The Witch Owl turned her head in Delora's direction and then did nothing other than stare at her with her bright yellow owl eyes. There was no emotion in her expression, yet it was like she was trying to say a million things with her intense stare.

"I think she is waiting for you to let go."

It was then that Delora's brows knotted so tightly together there was a heavy pressure across her forehead. Her bottom lip began to tremble.

She turned her eyes away from the Witch Owl to bury her face against her hands. "But I don't want them to go."

The soothing, warm caress of Magnar's hand started from her left shoulder blade and ran around her back in a diagonal before it wrapped around her side. He slid her closer. He pressed her firmly against his torso, bringing his other hand up so he could press it against the back of her head and bury it against the side of his firm chest instead.

"I know, but–" he started.

"We only just saved them." Magnar curled his arms around her more as if he was trying to shelter her completely in his big embrace. "What-what if the Demon King comes for them? They'll be taken, or hurt, and... and... oh gods, Magnar. What if something happens to them and we never know?"

"That is why she's here, Delora. She is letting us know she will protect Fyodor."

But Delora already had an inkling that was what the Witch Owl was planning.

The first night Fyodor had grown big, she'd been inside, carefully watching them while cooking her dinner. Delora had seen her approach Fyodor. She would never know what the Witch Owl said to them, but she had patted Fyodor's snout, and after a little uncertainty from them, they'd eventually welcomed it.

She'd been getting them used to her.

"They are no longer happy here, Delora," Magnar said in the gentlest way he could. His voice had been soft, beseeching, but it only made her sob against him. "I don't remember the first part of my life, but I remember spending much of my life hunting. I was always hungry, and I did nothing else but try to rid myself of that pain."

"They're in pain?!" she yelled in outrage.

Why would he tell her something like this?!

Despite her shout, Magnar gave a solemn chuckle.

"Yes and no. It is more like when your stomach grumbles, telling me my little raven has not eaten in quite some time. Mine did that a lot. It's like a constant nagging."

Delora bit at her bottom lip.

I know they're hungry. She knew because whenever she cuddled them at night, she always heard their stomach gurgling. Fyodor made no noise of distress, but they were so thin that it was so loud... and *annoying*.

The past few nights had been difficult for Delora because she'd been able to feel Fyodor slipping away more and more. Not physically, but mentally. Their heart wanted to roam, and the only thing holding them back was... her.

Poor Magnar had started crawling out of the nest on his own at night. It was either because he was too uncomfortable because there wasn't enough room for him after Delora had coaxed Fyodor to come to sleep, or because he was off being... naughty by himself in the forest.

But she had watched him leave one night, unable to move since Fyodor was cuddling her while snoring *loudly*.

She thought if they left she would even miss that too.

"Why are you so calm about this?" There was an accusation in her tone, and she didn't know why she wanted to start a fight with him. Especially since she thought she'd fall apart if he were to pull away from her. Her emotions felt haywire. "Do you not care about Fyodor?"

"Of course, I do." Magnar pulled back only enough so that he could bring one of his hands forward and wrap it around her chin and jaw, lifting her tear-stained face towards his fox one. It was then that she was able to see that his orbs were a deep blue. "I care very deeply, but... this is natural for us. I can feel it deep within that this is something they must do, which makes me... understand. It is like I am watching myself."

"I'm sorry." She lifted up and wrapped her arms around his neck, allowing him to bring her sideways onto his lap. "I've only been thinking about how I feel."

She knew he was right, but she couldn't stop the way this hurt. No mother was supposed to watch their child go from an infant to nearly an adult in the span of a few minutes. There were things she'd missed out on, things she was supposed to witness.

It's not fair.

"It is okay, Delora. I don't mind." He pressed the side of his bony jaw against her hair. "You are hurting, and I don't know how to ease you. If it makes you feel better to be angry at me, then so be it."

Magnar stroked her back in a comforting gesture, which helped to ease her tension. His warmth and deep, soothing voice helped to make this... not as painful. She wasn't alone going through this, nor was she the only one hurting.

Magnar shared her pain, but he was also being strong enough for the both of them, logical for the both of them – which was so odd.

But the way his arms were tight around her, a part of her also knew that he needed her to hold him too, to comfort him.

"Where will they go?" Delora asked, feeling herself finally settling.

She peeked over her shoulder to see Fyodor pacing between the trees before they looked towards her like they were expecting her to start coming after them.

"They will find themself on the surface eventually." A hoot sounded from behind them like the Witch Owl was confirming this. "I think she plans to lead them there. It will be safer."

"What about humans though? The humans will attack them."

It was odd to think of her own kind as the enemy, but if they were to hurt her precious Fyodor, she'd despise them forever.

"They may not look it, but they are strong. We gave them a hare, and hares are very swift. It is not Fyodor you need to be worried for."

Delora backed up just enough to look at his glowing orbs directly. "What are you trying to say?"

His tone was firm as he said, "Any human that crosses them will die quickly, Delora." He lifted his hand so he could hold the side of her head and brush his thumb across her cheek. He was so careful of his long and sharp claw as he wiped away the evidence of her tears on that side. "Our Fyodor is a Mavka, a hungry one at that, and humans don't know how to kill us. No matter if they *are* harmed, they will only come back stronger than they were before. And with the humanity they were granted from those they'd managed to eat before they succumbed."

She knew Fyodor was strong, that they would be fast... but safe? That's all she cared about, and Magnar's confidence managed to ease some of her fears.

Now she just had to deal with the ache of knowing she'd miss her own child.

Delora curled into Magnar while turning her head to watch Fyodor, who dug at the base of a tree for whatever interesting thing they could smell there.

She knew she needed to accept this. Every mother went through this in some way. And although they did, she also knew this was... different. Fyodor wasn't a human about to take their first steps into adulthood by finding their own home within the village – if they didn't choose to leave it.

They were a *wild* Duskwalker. One she could see... wanted to go.

"Do you think Fyodor will miss us? Remember us?" she asked in a quiet voice. When she got no response, she looked up and her attention on him caused his orbs to become a deeper blue. "Magnar?"

"I don't want to hurt your feelings, Delora."

He turned his face away as if to hide it from her. She knew he hated that he couldn't conceal his emotions from her. His orbs changing colours always gave him away.

It was one of the many things about him she found charming.

"They won't, will they?" A sad smile curled her lips. "I think I prefer that."

He turned back to her so he could tilt his head in question. "You do?"

"Yeah... I don't want them to be sad." She brought her gaze to Fyodor once more. "I'd rather them just go be their big Duskwalker self, with no idea who or what they left behind. I just hope we get to meet them again."

"We will." He drew her in impossibly tighter. "I have met every Mavka. It's almost like we sense each other and venture closer without meaning to. Fyodor will find us, or we will find them when we are on the surface."

"I still think your idea of taking me to a human village to get supplies and waiting for me outside of it is really clever of you, Magnar."

He lifted his hand only so that he could momentarily, and awkwardly, scratch at the very tip of his snout self-consciously.

"It wasn't. Reia said she wanted to do that when you weren't around."

"So you just played it off as your own idea?!" She playfully smacked him in the chest. "How rude!"

A reddish pink flashed in his orbs as he waved his head around. "Well... you never asked me where I got the idea from."

"I don't think I want you to obtain any more humanity, Magnar. You're becoming too cunning." Then she scoffed as she shook her head. "At this rate, you'll give Orpheus a run for his money."

"I... don't know what that saying means, but if it makes Orpheus run, then that would make me feel better."

He really doesn't like it that Orpheus picks on him. How could this Duskwalker make her almost giggle when her heart was aching this badly?

"Delora," Magnar said, brushing the corner of her jaw to entice her to look towards the yard.

Fyodor was drifting away, going deeper within the forest before pacing almost out of view.

Her heart rate picked up, her chest quivering over shaking lungs, but a sense of... composure washed over her. She'd known for days that they'd been wanting to leave and had been mentally preparing herself – even if she didn't want to.

That didn't stop her eyes from watering.

"I... I think I'm ready to say goodbye."

"But you are about to cry again," Magnar stated, his tone filled with so much concern for her.

"It's okay." She wriggled just enough that he released her and let her get to her feet. However, she lifted her hand in his direction with her cheeks heating. "But could you... could you please hold my hand? I don't want to do this by myself."

Her anxiety and stress were immediately fought off when he placed his big, warm, and comforting hand in her own.

"I will follow you anywhere, my pretty raven." Magnar stood. "All you have to do is ask."

He leaned his massive, towering height forward just enough so that it was more comfortable for her to hold his hand.

Delora led him into the forest, and Magnar matched her pace while hunched over so they could approach Fyodor.

On all fours, they lifted their head from where they'd been sniffing. Fyodor came to greet them, and Delora raised her free hand so she could hold the side of their rabbit skull.

"You kind of freaked me out at first when you came into my life, but I'm really glad you did." Then Delora leaned her forehead against theirs and watched as their orbs turned black in welcome. "I know I'll miss you a whole bunch, but it's okay. I know you want to go. Just be safe, okay?"

She stepped back and just let the tears freely fall, unashamed of them. She knew Magnar wouldn't judge her for them, and she didn't want to pretend she wasn't sad.

It was okay to be vulnerable.

He squeezed her hand, somehow knowing she needed the reminder that he was there, even though it was hard to miss his overwhelming presence.

Fyodor's snout bounced slightly as they sniffed the air, coming closer before they licked at her cheek. Delora let out a laugh, one that was filled with both humour and pain.

"One day, I'll meet you again and hopefully you'll have gained enough humanity that I can speak with you." She

clenched her jaw when her voice started to tremble, trying to
brave her way through her words. She cleared her throat and
sniffled. "I'll tell you I'm your mum, and that I love you so much,
and I was so happy you were born."

Fyodor just tilted their head at her, not understanding a single
word that came out of her mouth. She didn't care. She knew they
probably wouldn't remember any of this, but a small part of her
hoped they would at least understand the message she was trying
to convey.

"And... and you better let me hug you, Fyodor. Otherwise, I'll
be really mad at you."

She didn't know how her heart could feel both heavier and
lighter at the same time, but at least she'd gotten to say goodbye
in her own way. That was more than many others got in these
dark and Demon-filled times.

She turned her gaze to Magnar.

After a few moments of her staring at him, he eventually
flinched. "Am I supposed to say something?"

Her brows furrowed deeply.

"You don't have anything you want to say to them?"

Magnar scratched at the feathers around his neck.

"I do not know what I'm supposed to say or do." Despite this,
he still lifted his hand and just... patted the top of their head by
gently tapping it a few times, making Fyodor's skull bounce.
"You are odd, and your presence has been confusing for me. But
do not let the spirit of the void take you, otherwise I will go to
the afterlife and scold you for it."

Then he turned his head swiftly to Delora.

"That's what fathers do, right? They scold their children?"

"How would you–"

It didn't take long for Delora to put two and two together. She
rolled her eyes. *Reia must have explained this to him.*

After shaking her head, Magnar's weirdness about the whole
thing somehow making this easier for her, she brought her
attention back to Fyodor. She gave them a sweet little kiss
between their hollow eye sockets that were filled with Magnar's
glowing green orbs.

Her child looked absolutely nothing like her, but she loved

every bit of them.

"Be a good Duskwalker and grow strong. And don't let anyone bully you." Then she turned Fyodor's head towards the forest, towards the Veil they'd been slowly making their way to. "Now go, before I change my mind and keep you here forever."

When Fyodor didn't budge, she nudged them forward until they were on their feet. They were hesitant at first, but they slowly made their way deeper within the forest, constantly looking over their shoulder.

Delora waved, and she thought it was sweet when Magnar mimicked her, probably just to make her feel at ease about doing it.

The moment they were out of sight, two things happened... The Witch Owl flew directly overhead to follow Fyodor, her wings whooshing through the air.

And Delora no longer held back her sadness as a sob broke.

FORTY-SIX

Magnar tried his very best over the course of the night and following day to console his distraught female. He'd tried to soothe her as she occasionally cried deep into the next day after Fyodor's disappearance.

He'd petted her hair while she curled up against him in their nest, played the music box that had brought her so much joy the day before, and he'd made the tea Orpheus had showed him how to create.

Her tears were infrequent and came in bursts, and she seemed to want to do little else but be by his side.

Now, it was past the middle of the night, and he lay silently in the nest, with her asleep – her face a tear-stained pink and smooshed upon his chest – as he thought to himself.

As much as he missed Fyodor in his own way, a part of him absolutely welcomed this because Delora seemed to settle only when he was holding her. And as much as she was saddened, she also tried to comfort him, not realising that, although he worried and missed Fyodor, most of his concern was on her.

Perhaps he was disconnected from truly feeling saddened because of what he was. He may have gained humanity, but it was limited by the fact that he was a Mavka.

Delora's soul had dulled heavily in its brightness with Fyodor gone, but it was beginning to return to its new normal – brighter with life than when she'd first gifted it to him.

There was only one fissure of darkness left in her soul, one that spanned from the right breast all the way down to the left hip. He didn't know how to remove it, and it was the last piece that was stopping it from completely becoming a flame.

She does not handle her sadness well. Magnar brushed a strand of hair that was stuck to her parted lips. *But I do not mind.* He ran a claw under her jaw to tilt her face slightly so he could gaze upon it. *She is beautiful, no matter the state of her face.*

He kind of liked the pinkness in her cheeks and nose. It showed she was so full of life. He much preferred it over the dark circles she used to have under her lifeless, bleak eyes.

He drew a claw over the side of her cheek bone almost in awe. Despite everything over the last few sad days, Delora had felt the urge to kiss him a few times, and each one had made his heart flutter.

She had also welcomed him in return, as if she wanted to be closer with him, when he'd found it too difficult to resist licking across her lips. She'd dance her tongue with his. They had shared this kind of kiss, the only one he could do, but neither had brought it further than that.

It just seemed as though she desired closeness.

As much as Magnar wanted to touch Delora intimately, he didn't want her to think he didn't care for her pain.

When she is feeling better, we can try then. He bumped his snout against her. *I am content to wait for her.*

When dawn grew closer, Magnar allowed himself to rest by closing his sight. He didn't leave like he had before Fyodor left their home, worried she'd become distraught if he wasn't by her side.

He hadn't expected to wake before the sun rose. He knew he must have reached out for her, only to find she was absent from their nest.

It was still the dark of night.

He moved to get up, but there was no need to rush when he could hear breathing coming from further within the house.

Delora was on her knees in one of his shirts, the fireplace lit to keep her warm and provide light. There were also two candles by her side, brightening the wall she was painting in the living room.

"What are you doing, Delora?" Magnar asked as he

approached.

"I couldn't sleep," she muttered quietly, never removing her eyes from the wall. "And I've decided I don't want to cry anymore."

What she was painting was nothing but a mesh of blobs and lines, the beginning of a large piece of art. Currently she was painting a white, semi-triangular shape on top of a black, limbed blob. It was small, but he could see the drawn outline of two other shapes next to it on either side were much larger.

I am glad she has stopped crying. Her face wasn't red like it had been over the course of the last two days, which meant she hadn't cried since waking. *She is healing.*

He knelt down next to her, not wanting to pull her away from a task that was perhaps making her feel better.

Looking over what she was creating, he asked, "What are you painting?"

"Us." She reached to dab the end of her brush in a bowl with white paint, before continuing. "I was worried I would forget what Fyodor looked like. Even if I see them again, I know they'll be big, but I wanted to remember them when they were little."

He realised then that the shapes she was painting was their family, with Fyodor small, and Delora and Magnar on their knees just behind their youngling.

Her dark brows were furrowed together into a knot of concentration, her lips puckered with that same emotion. *She is so cute like this.*

When she noticed he was just gazing at her, she looked at him from the corner of her eye.

"I'm sorry. This mustn't be very entertaining for you. Do you want to help?"

"Me?" His sight fell on the additional colours and brushes in bowls. "I don't know how to do this."

She tried to give him a reassuring smile, but it was obvious it was weak and false.

"That's okay. Here." She handed him the end of a brush that had black paint dripping from it. "Maybe you could paint yourself? Just try to stay inside the line I drew, but even if you go out of it, I can fix it."

Comfortable silence, except for the crackling of fire and their breaths, echoed between them as Magnar worked the brush against the timber. He obtained new paint when it thinned, trying his hardest not to make a mistake.

His orbs would flash a reddish pink when he did, but her reassurance that it would be fine allowed them to turn back to green with ease.

But... Magnar wasn't interested in painting.

He liked watching her do it, but this wasn't a task he was interested in. It held little value to him to paint a wall.

He eventually lowered his hand, and once more became engrossed in the tantalising view of her.

The fireplace cast light against her, brightening some areas of her while others were shadowed. In his own way, he thought of her mixing with varying types of light as art. It always mesmerised him to see her eyes glitter or the way her tanned skin glowed with a golden hue.

He didn't realise he'd gotten paint on his claws until he stroked them under her cheekbone to pet the shadows there.

I marked her. He looked down at his claws, before his sight found its way back to her.

His heart thumped strangely in his chest. He *liked* seeing the evidence of his touch on her – one that didn't cause pain. His sight grew fixated on the black stain.

"Delora," he rasped, his throat clogged with an emotion that left him with a sense of longing. She turned her beautiful brown eyes to him, and they reflected such a warm and inviting colour with the light of the fire glinting in them. They were almost molten, so rich and vibrant. "I... would like to paint you instead."

Her eyes fell to where her placement on the painting was. "Want to switch sides, then?"

He shook his head as he dipped the tips of his claws in a random colour, finding it was green when he lifted his hand to brush it over her temple.

"No. Like how you paint my skull."

It always brought him joy when she did it for him, he was hoping it would do the same for her.

I want to see her smile.

She would never know how addictive he found them. They were no longer new, she'd given him plenty of smiles, but they always caused a fluffy feeling within his chest.

"Oh." Her eyes flittered to the painting she'd been doing, and he realised she still wanted to continue her task, that she longed to. However, she turned on her knees while placing her paintbrush down to give him a complete frontal view. "Sure. I'd like you to try that. I can, uh... always come back to this later."

Despite her words, his orbs shifted to blue – and he wished they hadn't. "You don't want to."

Magnar didn't want to make her do something she didn't truly want to do with him. He could do this later, at least now he knew it was something he would like to try in the future.

She quickly reached forward and clasped his wrist.

"No, please." She tugged herself forward since he was too heavy for her to bring him closer. "I would like for you to paint me. I would have said no otherwise."

There was a beseeching hint to her furrowed expression. He realised that she truly wanted to, not just because he did, but because of her own reasons – ones that mattered to her.

"I only left our bed because I could see you were asleep, and I didn't want to lay awake by myself." Delora turned her gaze to the side while pouting. She grumbled, "I kind of wanted to be with you."

Delora had been very clingy the last few days. Something Magnar welcomed whole-heartedly.

Warmth lit in his chest, and he leaned over to dip his claws into the green paint. He wanted to see the colour of his orbs in their normal state on her. He brushed the backs of them over her cheek.

He shuddered at the smear of it against her smooth skin.

It wasn't long before he was dipping his fingertips in the blue so he could run it above her brow and down the curvature of her nose. She closed her eyes for him, allowing him to do what he wanted.

He smeared red over her lips, feeling the bottom one part under his caress.

There was no plan in his work as he touched her, almost

worshipping the features of her face. Her soft but arching brow, her rounded cheeks, her pouty bottom lip that was much fuller than the top.

Her face was a mess of colours, and he enjoyed seeing every single one of them, knowing how he'd stroked her to create its semi-permanent, yet gentle mark.

She let out a raspy little gasp when he drew his thumb claw from her chin all the way along her jaw, and she even tilted the side of her head for him.

He stroked back down her jugular, and that erotic sweet smell came from her. It informed him she was enjoying this – his touch covered with cold, wet paint – as much as he was. Every new caress brought on a deeper awe within him.

Every part of her was worth praising, adoring, and he wanted to *worship* more of it with his touch.

I want to go lower, he thought as he drew a combination of colours down her sternum where the shirt she was in slightly parted.

Forgetting about the paint on her lips, she licked at them before she bit the bottom one. Like she'd managed to read his very thoughts, his head tilted to her face in surprise when her hands came up to undo the top button. She shifted it down so she could expose the roundness of her shoulders.

His blood raced at seeing them. With anticipation thrumming, he stroked his entire large hand over one, staining her skin with all the colours he'd coated his palm with.

He did the same with the other hand, dipping underneath the shirt to also partially paint the back of her shoulder as he stroked forward and over it, coming down the flat part of her chest above her breast.

Delora opened her eyes, and Magnar paused with her gaze upon him. The parts of her flesh that could still be seen became flushed with heat, and the longer she knelt there staring at him, the more he could smell her *arousal* growing.

Shifting behind his seam caused his stomach to clench, his body reacting to her, to that tantalising scent that he longed to have on his tongue again.

It had been a few days since he'd been able to pleasure her

with his fingers or mouth, and Magnar burned for it. He also desperately wanted her greedy mouth and hands on him again.

She is sad. She will not want to do this with me right now.

Perhaps she was only letting him do this as a distraction, but Magnar didn't mind. He was content in just being allowed to do this.

Delora unbuttoned the rest of the shirt. She slipped it off her body, giving him a naked view of her except for the strip of cloth she had tied around her hips as underwear.

She looked a little nervous. Even he could sense this with the way she fidgeted slightly. Yet she was comfortable enough to expose herself for him, and his sight drew to her large, lovely, and slightly droopy breasts. He shuddered with *fierce* want.

So, what colour did he want to paint them?

Every colour possible.

Magnar was now filled with a sense of urgency. He placed one palm into the blue paint, the other red, and then brought his hands together so he could make them swirl. He didn't know it would turn *purple* in the places they touched and mixed, but a thrill shot through him upon seeing it.

It was the perfect colour for her, for them.

He cupped both breasts, and she flinched at the coldness before pressing them deep into his big hands for more. He leaned a little closer to her, his breaths more panted and huffed than before, as his tentacles moved behind his seam to encompass his cock and prevent it from extruding.

A small battle began within his body as he flicked her pretty little nipples with the sides of his thumbs. His interest in the paint died. Instead, he was now completely focused on touching Delora and her soft and malleable body.

Even more so when she gave him a delectable little moan when he gave a tentative, yet strong, squeeze to her breasts.

His hands slithered away so he could place them over her sides, his claws only inches from touching as he smeared leftover paint over her.

He could feel the texture of her stretch marks, and he stroked his way across a few, wanting to feel them, to give them the adoration they deserved. He did the same with every dip of skin, every mark, every part that was plumper than the rest of her.

"Magnar," she moaned, leaning forward and pressing her lips to the tip of his snout as she wrapped her arms around his neck. His feathers puffed in reaction.

His hands dipped into her underwear so he could leave palm marks on her arse as he gripped it with a shudder wracking his entire body.

He greeted her lips with his tongue, and she kissed at him messily. She caught his tongue a few times with her lips, then she parted them so he could dip it inside.

The paint, he suddenly thought.

She might stop if he didn't have any, and he liked that she was reaching for him.

He blindly searched for bowls of paint to dip his hands into while he curled his tongue around hers, hearing the bowls clack against the ground. He knew he spilt one. He didn't know what colour he coated the backs of her thighs with, but he didn't care. He kneaded the flesh of them.

Magnar never expected her to, but Delora started quickly undoing his buttons before she shoved his shirt off him. He didn't care why, only that it meant they were closer. He helped her before placing his arms around her and drawing her onto his lap as he knelt there on the timber ground.

He grunted when she unbuttoned his trousers and shoved her hand against his seam. The battle within him was instantly lost under her caress, and his tentacle sheltered cock extruded into her awaiting palm.

"Delora?" he asked with uncertainty, pulling his tongue away from between her lips.

"Take them off," she demanded when she tugged at his trousers. As much as he and Delora had been touching as of late, Magnar had never truly been unclothed in her presence. "Off!"

He did as she demanded, lifting them both while keeping a good hold of her with one arm. He slipped his trousers off his body.

He thought she would climb off him to kneel between his thighs like normal when he returned to their prior position, but she remained on him. Instead, she petted his tentacles, coaxing them to release his cock.

She teased her lips and tongue against his fangs until she was successful in persuading him to slip his tongue back inside her mouth. His first foray caused a pant to slip from him.

Magnar froze. His heart even stopped for a moment when she palmed the top of his cock so she could press the underside against the lips of her exposed folds. Delora had untied her underwear at some point while he removed his trousers, catching him off-guard.

I only meant to paint her face. Yet she was the one to bring them into this position, to lower her clothing until she'd removed it – and his own. He began to wonder why.

That was until she bucked against the length of him. He thrust back, all his thoughts rendered quiet. Her clit was nestled in the groove on the underside of his cock, both spots that were sensitive on their bodies, and they both gave a noise of pleasure at the same time.

Magnar didn't care she was smearing paint all over his fur or that he was ruining the marks he'd placed on her body. He just pressed her closer and helped her to move against him.

I like this. They'd never ground against each other until release, but he liked how... almost tender it was.

She pulled her mouth away and looked down their bodies with her head pressed against one of his pectoral muscles. His shaft jerked when he realised she was watching them move.

"Inside me," Delora whispered with a coarse voice. "I need you inside me so badly, Magnar. *Please.*"

His entire body clenched, his cock swelling as it pulsated at her plea. His claws dug into her thighs, perhaps a little too deeply since he smelt a droplet or two of blood.

Fuck. Magnar mentally groaned, shuddering. *I want that too.* He *needed* it, especially since he could feel her pussy slipping over the underside of him like a naughty, terrible little tease. *I want her to swallow me so whole I disappear. I want to thrust inside her until she spills all over me and covers me in her scent.*

Despite his thoughts, Magnar pulled back and cupped the side of her face so he could lift it, forcing her to meet his gaze.

"I will not be able to stop myself from coming inside you."

He knew it was the truth.

Already his tentacles *ached* to cling to her, to force her body upon him so she couldn't escape and neither could he. They ached to make them inseparable until he was done, until she was completely filled with his seed.

He panted at just the thought, at the very memory of doing it. His head swam when he fell deeper into his lust-filled haze.

"Yes," she moaned, grinding against him and almost making him lose his will. "Please, Magnar. I want to feel you come inside me again. It was so hot and wet and *everywhere.* It tastes so good, but it feels so fucking good too."

She shivered deeply. She tried to move faster on him, but also higher, like she was seeking to do it herself, to bury his cock and warm it from the inside.

"Stop," he growled, grabbing her arse and hips to stop her.

He needed to stop her before he just shoved himself so deep inside her he feared he'd break them both.

Delora pulled back, and the expression she gave him was one of unmistakable hurt. "You don't want to?"

When it felt as though she was trying to slip away, Magnar held her tight with one arm and cupped the back of her head with his other hand. His fingers threaded through her long hair.

"We will make another youngling if we do. And... I don't think I can handle that."

Watching Delora all these months had given him a mixture of emotions. He didn't like seeing her sickness when it first happened or her pain when she brought them into the world. Then there were the other battles they'd had to face together – some pleasant, many not.

He wanted Delora to be his, not something that was shared. He'd cared for Fyodor, but they had been needy and clingy, always in the way, always wanting her presence.

I just want her to be all mine.

FORTY-SEVEN

Delora couldn't help feeling rejected.

Here she was offering herself, and Magnar was saying... no. Making excuses *not* to.

She pulled away, feeling remarkably foolish for even starting this.

For Delora, to reveal herself had been a leap done with confidence. With *trust*. She covered her breasts with one arm while the other crossed over to shield her pubic mound. Her heated flesh suddenly felt too uncomfortably exposed.

Magnar held her firm.

"You could just pull out," she muttered, breaking eye contact and looking anywhere but at him.

He gave a humour-filled chuckle, one that was rumbly and deep. He licked at the edge of her jaw, the side turned to him unpainted, but she had a feeling he wouldn't have cared either way.

"Do you really think I would be able to resist the temptation of completely filling your little pussy with my seed once I'm inside you?" Magnar said in a teasing manner, forcing goosebumps to tingle across her flesh at the sound of his voice and his tongue slipping across her. "The moment I'm inside you, have you wrapped around my cock, I won't let you get away from it."

Her stomach fluttered just as her inner walls clenched, wanting to feel all of that. Some of her apprehension eased.

"I want you marked by it, covered in it. I want you to steal it from me and claim it as yours while you hold it for me." He nibbled the very front of his fangs down the side of her neck, being careful with her as they nipped. She gave a raspy exhale, leaning her head back so he could get to her flesh easier. "But I don't want you to return anything. I won't be able to pull away, Delora."

Her face crinkled into agonised lines. "Then how are we supposed to...?"

He wants to. That eased her worries, but there was *always* something in the damn way! *I want to... I want to have sex with him so badly.*

Her body was begging for it, dripping with need and desire for *him*. And she'd felt this every time they'd touched in the recent past, her body thrumming with anticipation of his filling hers, but something had always stopped her from speaking out about it.

Tonight, she'd finally made that leap. To just... blatantly and bravely ask him for it, rather than wonder why he hadn't done so himself.

So why can't we?

"I can prevent it," he stated, and she turned her face towards him when he pulled back. "I spoke to Orpheus, and he told me of a spell I can do to prevent you from baring any younglings until I remove it."

"Yes. Okay." She inched closer. "Do it."

She'd do anything to be able to have him.

"I did not fully get your permission last time when I changed you." He nuzzled his snout against her, causing her skin to prickle with more goosebumps when his heated breath wrapped around her throat. "I wanted to make sure I received it this time before I did something to your body. It may hurt a little."

Magnar raised his hand so he could bite the side of it to draw his own blood. He rubbed his fingers against his palm, smearing it over it until it was coated.

He didn't need his own blood last time. She'd only ever seen him use his blood for magic when creating her baths.

She was so thankful to have a tub now.

Delora turned her eyes downwards to watch, leaning away to

give him room when he palmed her stomach to smear his purple blood on her. Her gaze caught that his tentacles had moved around his cock to protect what they could, but she could tell the darker tip was drying out. It was jutting between them, and she liked seeing it resting against her hip and the side of her stomach folding over it.

She rubbed it so it would moisten, and he let out a little sigh, pressing his cock deeper into her hands.

"Thank you." He positioned the tips of his claws against her flesh, and she knew he was looking at her with the way his skull was positioned. "Ready, my little raven?"

Was she ready to finally have him inside her again?

"Yes."

"Do you know how long I've been waiting for this?" he rasped against her throat when he brought her closer now that his hand was in position. "Have been waiting for you to ask for this?"

He's been wai– Delora gasped when he speared her with his claws, and a strange stinging and pinching feeling radiated from deep within. She fisted his fur but stifled any other noise that threatened to come out.

Last time he'd done this to her, he'd been moving his cock in and out of her, giving her pain and pleasure at the same time. This brought only pain.

A green symbol almost as large as his hand began to glow upon her stomach, showing them both that whatever he was doing was working. When he pulled his claws out, the green glow remained permanently around her navel.

"There," he said. "It is–"

Before he could even finish speaking, Delora grabbed the corners of his bony jaw and shoved the tip of his snout against her lips.

Her pussy was throbbing, her clit tingled, and now that it was done, she didn't want to delay this any longer.

"I need to fuck you. I need to *feel* you," she begged, trying to stroke what she could of his partially exposed cock. "I want you so badly and have for *so* long."

His tentacles released. He thrust against her, and she greeted him back. His hands were quick to hold the back of her head and waist to pull her closer.

She could feel his fur against her shins, knees, and the backs of her feet. How it covered the front of her as she pressed herself against his firm body. She smeared more paint against him.

I can't wait anymore.

She was growing hornier by the second, frustrated by it even, and she was so heated she feared she'd combust.

Delora grabbed the side of his cock right below the broad head, the little nodules greeting her palm, and raised her body higher. Since she was sitting completely on top of him, his tentacles wrapped around her ankles when she hadn't expected them to. They held firm, squeezing her.

"Delora," he groaned when she pressed the entrance of her cunt over the very tip.

Unbelievably hard girth greeted her. Wetness from his lubricant smeared over the lips of her already slick folds. And heat, so strange and hot, warmed her.

The head of his cock wasn't smooth because of the groove that reached to the slitted hole at the top, and she rubbed herself over it just to tease them both.

"Ohh." She gave a little satisfied moan when he started pulling her, impatient for her to sit on his cock.

There was the sting that came from not having something this... unbelievably huge inside her for so long, and the head was difficult to pop inside, especially with its bumps. She gasped, and her stomach dipped in bliss when it did.

So big. She was *stretching* herself for him, taking him, and forcing her body to accept it. *So... warm.* Her eyelids fluttered in euphoria when she speared herself halfway down. *Mine. He's mine. This cock is mine.*

Like he was able to hear her thoughts, once she was wonderfully seated as far as she could be around him, he growled, *"Mine,"* in return.

"Ohhh fuuuck," she cried.

She was trembling around his cock, her body visibly quaking in need. Her head fell back as her lips parted. Her chest rose higher. She continued to keep a grip around his neck just so she could daze out and completely focus on the way he felt inside her.

She started moving on top of him.

There was a wetness from both of them that made it feel like everything was overlubricated, and she *adored* it. His cock pressed everywhere, filling her – yet she wanted it harder, deeper, all of him. He thrust up into her, allowing her just a simple taste of what she needed.

His vanilla bean and cream scent enveloped her senses. She tried to suck in deeper draws of air just to have more.

There was a rumbly sound coming from his chest while gentle grunts trembled on the ends with a light growl. All she felt was heat, inside and out, and his fur tickling her sensitive hardened nipples. His torso sublimely massaged her heavy breasts.

Neither cared about the paint she was rubbing over his torso, especially since Delora already felt lost in her own pleasure.

"Too... *slow*," he groaned before he gripped her arse and waist tighter to yank her down, to start working her on his cock. He swelled, making her gasp and her insides clench him. "Mmm, that's better."

Delora slipped around his cock faster, Magnar drawing her up until her entrance pulled around the fat rim of his cockhead, before he shoved her down hard and fast, ripping a pathetic cry from her.

"*Yes,*" she rasped, trying to buck into him as her nails dug through his fur to stab into his tough flesh. "More."

He thrust up faster and helped to move her so she came down harder.

She gained just enough strength to tilt her head forward slightly so she could look at his strange face, finding his orbs such an alluring colour of purple that it made her shiver.

Why do I find them so pretty?

"Do you know how long I've yearned to be inside your pussy again?" He darted forward so he could draw his rough tongue across her lips. "How much I've ached for this? To have your insides writhing around my cock like this?" He gave a shudder, his body puffing as his cock swelled again. "Every time I have tasted you, I have been moments from shoving inside you. I *burned* for it. I need to feel you come around me, Delora. I need to feel it, taste it, smell that scent on my body as you coat me with your essence."

Oh, God. Her inner walls clamped down, feeling swollen with her impending orgasm just as her eyes bowed in agonised creases. *I...*

"And to have you on top of me..." Magnar released such a haunted groan, his body quaking beneath her as she rode him. "To have you fuck yourself with my cock... Moving on me like you need me as much as I have hungered for you..."

I think I'm in love with him. Her heart squeezed in her chest, radiating with a tender ache that felt... beautiful to have. *I'm in love with Magnar.*

She had to be. Why else would she have *begged* for his cock? For him?

Her head fell forward so she could place it against him, wanting to be even closer than they already were. It was like there was something fluttering in her chest, so light and carefree, while her body sang with pleasure, every gouge of his cock hurtling her closer to the edge.

He feels so good inside me. Like he belonged there, like he had always belonged there.

"I don't know how much longer I can hold back," he said. "I need you to come for me before I give in, Delora."

When she didn't, he placed a hand around the back of her head and pulled it back so that she was forced to place her dizzy-filled gaze on him. Her nose was fuzzy, her eyes wetter than normal as she desperately panted at his ethereal face.

Her heart fluttered in adoration of him. Of his purple, lust-filled orbs, the white bone of his skull that was highlighted by the fireplace and candles nearby. Of his antlers casting a shadow over her, rising threateningly high above his head.

"Come. For. Me." He growled with a flicker of red flashing in his orbs, ramming into her to punctuate each word as she was bringing her pussy down on him.

Her body clamped tight. Her muscles tensed all through her body.

Just as she was throwing her head back to scream when her

orgasm started, heat swelled everywhere from within. She saw her soul burst in an explosion of flame between his antlers.

The deafening, booming roar that sounded from him when her soul turned to a complete flame and she started milking his cock was the only warning she got.

He lunged forward, slamming her against the ground and shoving the oxygen out of her body. Magnar hammered his cock in and out of her wildly.

Delora couldn't make a sound as each thrust knocked the very breath out of her, strangling her lungs under the onslaught. She slipped her legs around him, digging the heels of her feet into the sides of his legs to hold herself to him. Her arms moved to be around his torso instead of around his neck to hold on against his thrusts.

His tentacles slipped around her hips to cling, digging in so tightly they squeezed.

But that wasn't enough for Magnar.

With a distinct thud, he bashed the forking branches of his antlers against the ground. They supported them both when he lifted himself and her off the ground while remaining on his knees.

His arms wrapped even tighter across her arse and shoulders, meshing them together so that she was rendered completely and utterly unable to move.

The freedom of their bodies in the air allowed him to move even faster, slam even deeper.

And those little nodules that spanned down the long length of his cock on three sides slipping in and out of her felt like a *vibration*. It tickled her entrance and deep inside, making her eyes widen when she realised.

Delora came when a snarl broke loose, his thrusts so feral and uncontrolled that it sent her hurtling over the edge again. She was gone, lost to him, to this, to the pleasure and how his gently vibrating cock felt gliding inside her.

She wanted to beg him to fuck her. She wanted to whisper yes, to tell him how good it felt, that it was amazing. But she couldn't.

There was nothing Delora could do but release pleasure-filled cries and tear his feathers from him until she was forced to grab another section of his back so she had something to hold on to. More came loose.

"You are mine!" he warned, his snarl seeming to worsen. *"You will always be mine!"*

"Yes! Yours." She tried to scream it, but her words only came out as a whisper.

His claws dug in, but she only arched into them. Rather than being frightened, she only found them dangerously titillating. It was like he wanted to burrow underneath her skin.

The slapping and squelching of their bodies meeting when he was seated deep was loud in her ears. His movements were too fast to feel like a pound, and they were both so wet that it was unmissable.

She tried to spread her thighs impossibly further around his massive body. He was so deep, further than any human could be, but Delora wanted him to take her until he'd broken her in fucking two. She wanted to feel it tomorrow, to hobble with aches and pains, knowing she'd been passionately rutted, wanted, needed.

"Feels so good," she whispered, unable to buck into him like she wanted. Her nails scored into his back, clutching whatever of his body she could. "You feel so good. *Yes. Please,* don't stop."

Magnar was winding her up so fast she knew she was going to come again. *I-I've never been taken like this.*

Where she was fucked violently, but also held like she was precious. Held so tightly like he feared losing her.

A whimper softened his voice as he rasped, *"De... lora."*

She clenched him, his little whimper causing her to shiver.

Then in the midst of his rapid thrusts, liquid heat filled her core. Her knees buckled as her inner walls contracted around his cock like her very body was trying to suck that liquid in deeper.

"Oh!" she screamed, her moan laced in her very voice. "Are you *coming*?"

He was still thrusting hard, still shoving against her fast. He let out a whine, and she knew that was his way of answering right now as he filled her with his seed as he *moved,* like he was unwilling to break away from how her insides stroked him.

Delora nearly went cross-eyed, squirming her hips against him even though his tentacles were so tight it was almost painful. *It's so warm. Fill me, give me all of it.* She tried to gyrate up and down, to greet him just so that it would feel even better for him, so he would give her even more.

Oh fuck. Oh fuck. The feel of it sent her over the edge, and she bit her own lip so hard she knew she'd drawn blood.

He gave a shudder that wracked his entire body, just before the familiar squelch of that intense volume of liquid started to overfill and pour out of her in thick globs.

When the tickle of it trickled down the curves of her arse and across her pubic mound to slip over her hip, she wanted to feel more, adoring it, loving it, squirming as she came with him.

When his cock stopped swelling repeatedly, he finally slowed. He finally eased. His rapid heart beat against her cheek, faster than she'd ever heard it, and she hoped he could feel hers against his abdomen.

He twitched like aftershocks were combusting within him.

After a few moments of them both holding each other in this afterglow, Magnar eventually lowered her to the ground, like he was growing weak in his satisfaction. He didn't move, didn't stop hovering above her, like he was unable to let her go.

She smiled when her eyes found deep claw marks across his own shoulder and the side of his arse.

"Did you heal me straight away?" she asked, reaching up to pet him just below the wounds.

They weren't deep, so he must not have cut her as badly as last time, but they still looked as though they were painful.

"I'm sorry," he said, his orbs turning to a reddish pink in shame. "I thought I would be able to do this without hurting you, but I was wrong."

His tentacles unclasped as he placed his hands upon the timber flooring to steady himself, his antlers lifting off the ground. He started to draw his softening shaft away.

Without hesitation, Delora grabbed one of those wriggling limbs and yanked on it.

"Where do you think you're going?" she bit, her voice hoarse and broken from crying out. "I know that cock of yours can come a second time."

He paused when he was almost all the way out of her.

"But I hurt you again, Delora."

"And here I am, wanting more of you." She lifted her hips up and then down to stir the overflowing orgasm inside her. Looking down, she watched as she fucked herself with the very tip of his purple cock, gaining herself a little contented groan from him as he grabbed her shoulder. It was like he needed her to stop, was trying to get her to. "I don't care that you clawed me. I barely even felt it. I just... I don't want to stop. I've needed this for so long."

Like he was unable to help himself, enjoying her moving on him from below, he sunk a little deeper.

"What if I–"

"Maybe you'll do better the second time," she quickly rebuffed over the top of him. She turned her head and bit at the side of his arm, trying to coax him with pain to be naughty with her again. "Maybe you just need to practise." She bit his calloused palm when he shuddered in delight and turned it to her. She sunk her teeth into the firm muscle just below his thumb. "To fuck my cunt over, and over, and *over* again until you're used to filling it, coming inside it, making it yours."

"Delora," he rasped, lowering himself while quaking.

Slowly, being coaxed by her teeth, he slipped his hardening cock back inside her until he was buried to the hilt.

Magnar parted his fangs when his cock was sheltered completely in the comforting nestle of her channel, letting out a groaning sigh.

With a few pants, he eventually stated, "Cunt? I don't know this word."

"There's still so much to teach you," she chuckled, her eyes filled with humour, and heat. "It's another name for my pussy."

Her *cunt* – as she called it – was throbbing, hugging him with its swollen warmth and mingled wetness. It was like utter heaven, and he partially laid over her on his thighs and hands, steadying himself through it.

Like it was unsatisfied with just once, his cock was already fully engorged and aching. The need to release again clutched at his groin like a terrible hunger, demanding that he rut her body again. His blood felt like it was filled with fire, pumping heat throughout his entire being and enlarging his muscles, thumping in his cock in heavy beats, and making his fur and feathers puff.

"It's yours, Magnar," she said below him, making him realise he'd closed his sight as he basked in the bliss of her. "And so am I."

He opened his sight to find the edges were a deep purple, haloing her in a haze.

"You are the most beautiful creature in the world," he grated, the words falling from him without thought.

Much of the paint on her body was patchy and smeared, revealing a rosy-pink nipple and the lightly tanned flesh of her other breast, both moving and quivering with each of her panted breaths. She was beautiful with her messy, dark hair, her brown eyes, and soft, giving body. He was totally enamoured by her, even more so when her lips curled up into a smile.

It was that smile that captured him completely.

He worried if he lay down on her, he would crush her. He kept his arms straightened while he spread his thighs, trying to bring himself to her level. It arched his back deeply. His size was far too big between her thighs, but her legs were open wide in welcome, allowing him in so he could wrap his tentacles around her hips.

She lowered one of her hands so she could wrap it around the base of his cock and touch at the spread lips of her pussy.

"You can have me whenever you want," she said as she leaned up. She pressed her lips to his chest and then underneath his long jaw, making his head tilt upwards as he exposed the underneath to her, his long tail quivering. "I want you to fuck me until you know every inch of me. I want you to use me until you're satisfied, until *you're* the one that wants to stop."

"I don't think that is possible," he rumbled, drawing his hips back only to push them forward a second later. She gave a content mew as a reward. "I don't think I will ever get enough of you, my little raven."

Despite his desire to move faster, Magnar didn't. He wanted to draw this out, to savour her sounds, the noise of their bodies greeting.

He wanted to be gentle and see if he could play with her insides, tease and coax her to orgasm rather than forcing it upon her body with speed and depth. Magnar wanted to see how Delora would break apart around his cock when he was finally in control of himself... and her.

He wanted her to yearn for his cock, for her next orgasm. To make her beg and plead for it like she had for him to fill her.

He felt undeniably whole within her, but he wondered if it was possible to intensify that feeling for both of them.

Magnar wanted to learn everything there was about this. And he was thrilled she wanted to show him, knowing that if she started actively trying to, she'd have Magnar at her mercy. *She already arouses me.* Just her pretty eyes on him had his body stirring. He'd be happily doomed.

Starting with a slow rhythm, he lowered himself just enough, fucking her with just the tip, so that he could draw his tongue across all the sensitive parts of her chest and throat. Her little ears made her shiver, and he focused on one just so she would let out a cry.

The moment her lips were parted, he forced her to swallow his tongue when she released that haunting noise, making her body clench in surprise. He didn't realise he'd feel it around his cock as she nearly strangled it with the inner walls of her pussy.

This time, Magnar was going to be playful. He was going to worship her body the way he'd always wanted to.

I want to see her grow as desperate as I have been.

EPILOGUE

Delora lay comfortably on top of Magnar with her arms folded beneath her chin, lazily swirling her index finger through the long fur covering his chest. She gazed up at him resting back against the ground, his snout pointed to the ceiling.

They were laying torso to torso, both covered from head to toe in the colourful paint they'd smeared all over each other.

They'd also knocked over many of her paint bowls, giving them more to play in, as they stained the timber flooring with the evidence of their rigorous fucking. There were streaks of it everywhere, hand marks, footprints, and smears she didn't know what moving body part made.

There were also quite a few puddles of white she *knew* weren't paint. At some point her breasts had been slipping through one of those when he'd taken her from behind. Magnar had grown increasingly more excited when he discovered he could put her in different positions and make her crazed.

The fireplace was nearly empty of flames since neither had added to it. She didn't need the heat; Magnar was warming her. Plus, the sun had *long* ago risen, providing all the light they needed.

With her thighs moulded around his hips while his tentacles circled hers, she was quite content with having his long but softened cock nestled inside her.

Who knew that having sex would make me feel better?

And it definitely had. She was sad, but it wasn't as prevalent as before, considering her body was singing with contentment.

Delora swirled more patterns higher on Magnar's chest, trying to avoid the multiple claw marks he had on his own body from when he healed her throughout the night.

She accidentally lifted herself partially off his shaft and then burrowed herself down on him even further than before, hoping to feel his heartbeat deeper within.

His huffing chest tightened as he groaned fervently. He accidentally slapped her arse when he grabbed it and pushed her down as he pushed his hips up.

A groan fell from her this time.

"No more," she pleaded, burying her face against his soft fur. "I take it back. I'm tired now."

"You're the one who wanted to stay there." She lifted her head when he moved to look down at her. His yellow orbs of contentment flashed purple before he licked at his fangs, his tongue curling over the top of his snout. "Your body feels like heaven. It is not my fault. I warned you I would never get enough of it."

"It's been four times already!" With a half-hearted glare, she pointed to the living room window. "The sun is up, Magnar. It's been up for hours!"

I just wanted to fall asleep with him inside me.

She liked him there, making her feel cherished and whole. Their cock-warming cuddle was intimate, and the heat of him nursed her tender core. She worried that if he parted from her, it would start to ache.

His antlers thudded against the ground, pushing his head slightly forward in an awkward angle, as he returned to rest.

He drew his claws up the side of her thigh just to make it twitch. He also did the same to her spine, and her back arched like a kitten – which made her pussy slip around him.

"I like it when you do that," he rumbled with a chuckle. "Your body is very sensitive to my claws."

"Do it again, and I'll bite you," she warned.

"Will you now?"

He dragged the sharp points of his claws both up her thigh and her spine, and her body trembled violently. Her body arched in waves, moving his cock in and out of her.

Magnar groaned, like that was what he'd wanted all along.

Delora buried her face against him and bit as hard as she could around the bottom of his pectoral muscle, the fur there shorter than the top half. It was a grave mistake on her part – he begun to thicken and harden inside her just as he thrust fast, squishing his still mostly softened cock in and out.

"Magnar!"

The bastard laughed!

"This is fun," he said once he was done. "I hope you bite me more. It makes me want to punish you with my cock."

Delora blew a strand of her hair out of her eyes. "Can we take a break for now?"

"I don't think that is possible anymore."

She could feel by the pressure inside he was almost fully erect now, and Delora planted her face against him.

"No," she retorted half-heartedly.

He whined in answer.

She lifted her head just so she could gawk at him in disbelief.

"Did you really just *whine* at me?" He did it again! But the flare of purple that had lifted into his orbs told her he was just trying to be devious. She smacked his chest. "Whining doesn't get you everything you want. It just makes you immature."

"Fine," he grumbled, licking the inside of his mouth in agitation. He closed his sight so that his orbs were black. "But you cannot leave where you are now. You may rest like this, with us as one."

*Good. S*he resumed swirling patterns into his fur. The action was soothing, and it helped to make her eyes heavier.

But there was something stopping her from falling asleep and had been for a while.

The bubbles of emotions she felt refused to allow her to rest, requiring she spill them or else she might burst. She gnawed at her bottom lip anxiously, the last shred of her insecurity in his presence holding her back.

She had to force the courage from the very pit of her being. It nearly faltered when she parted her lips to speak.

"I... love you," she said quietly, kind of hoping that he didn't hear it.

Silence greeted her.

Then Delora got pissy when she thought he hadn't heard it when he definitely should have. She may have whispered it, but he usually had superhuman hearing abilities.

Did he ignore me? She kind of expected him to ask her about it.

She did notice his heart rate picking up since her hand had been resting over it. "Magnar?"

He lifted his hand and ran his claws through her hair, petting her as the tips deliciously scraped over her scalp. "I love you too, Delora."

"P-pardon?" she stuttered, confused as to why he said it back.

He lifted his head once more and opened his sight, revealing bright flamingo pink orbs. He twisted his fox skull at her.

"I love you too." Her lips parted in surprise this time, and he twisted his head the other way. "You said it to me, but is this not something you wanted to hear?"

She pressed her hands against his torso to sit up with her brows furrowing in his direction.

"Well, yes. It's just... I didn't expect you to say it back." She couldn't stop herself from averting her gaze. "Do you even understand what it means?"

She only brought her eyes back to him because he'd cupped the side of her face and steered it.

"Of course. I asked Orpheus why I kept seeing the colour I currently see now." Her eyes darted between each of his glowing pink orbs. "And he explained the significance of it. I know what it means, Delora. I have known for a long while now that I love you."

"If that's true, why didn't you tell me?"

"I didn't know if that was something you wanted from me. I did not want to pressure you with my feelings, and I have been content with just loving you even if you did not feel the same way."

Her heart squeezed in her chest, and she couldn't stop the tears that welled in her bowed eyes.

"But why? I'm–I was so cold to you."

"I have found you alluring from the very beginning, Delora.

You were broken and in need of healing, but that did not make you any less beautiful or worth caring for. I started to love you when you were sad, but it has only grown deeper with every smile you have gifted me. And in caring for you, it has made me feel as though I have a purpose. You have made me feel as though I am not just some ugly monster who eats everything, but something that is worth your affection." He stroked his thumb across her cheek to steal a tear. "Why are you crying?"

"I don't know." She curled herself back down until she was pressed against him, clinging to his fur with tight fists. "I'm just happy I'm here. I'm so thankful I met you, Magnar. You're wonderful, and kind, and patient, and I guess I'm just relieved that you love me back."

Magnar wrapped his comforting arms around her and squeezed her to his torso, allowing her to cry happily against him. *He loves me.*

"I am yours, my little raven bride." He bumped the corner of his bony jaw against the side of her forehead affectionately, tenderly, and *lovingly*. She felt it all the way down to her bright and fully flaming soul between his antlers. "Forever and always, just yours."

Also by Opal Reyne

DUSKWALKER BRIDES
A Soul to Keep
A Soul to Heal
A Soul to Touch
A Soul to Guide
A Soul to Revive *(TBA 2023)*
A Soul to Steal *(TBA 2024)*
(More titles coming soon)

WITCH BOUND
The WitchSlayer
The ShadowHunter
(More titles coming soon)

Completed Series

A PIRATE ROMANCE DUOLOGY
Sea of Roses
Storms of Paine

~~THE ADEUS CHRONICLES~~
This series has been **unpublished** as of
20th of June 2022

If you would like to keep up to date with all the novels I will be publishing in the future, please follow me on my social media platforms.

Website:
https://www.opalreyne.com
Facebook Page:
https://www.facebook.com/OpalReyne
Facebook Group:
https://www.facebook.com/groups/opals.nawty.book.realm
Instagram:
https://www.instagram.com/opalreyne
Twitter:
https://www.twitter.com/opalreyne
Patreon:
https://www.patreon.com/OpalReyne
Discord:
https://discord.gg/opalites
TikTok:
@OpalReyneAuthor

Printed in Great Britain
by Amazon